Breathe, My Shadow

A Wraeththu Mythos Novel

Dedication

To Louise Coquio

The seeress who helps me weave stories and glimpse amazing worlds, with insight, humour, and a keen ability to listen and interpret. Thank you for your friendship and your presence throughout the years, the many late nights of gin and chats about writing, both yours and mine. Thank you for helping to guide the Wraeththu stories from ideas into reality – especially this one, as it was a demanding child!

Acknowledgements

Thanks also to my wonderful wyrd sisters, Danielle Lainton, Katie Kesterton, Debbie Cartwright and Paula Wakefield, for their friendship and support, chats about the book, jaunts beyond the veil and occasional therapy sessions!

Wraeththu Mythos

Breathe, My Shadow

Storm Constantine

IMMANION
PRESS

Stafford England

Breathe, My Shadow
A Wraeththu Mythos novel by Storm Constantine
© 2019

www.stormconstantine.co.uk

ISBN 978-1-912815-06-7

IP0157

Cover art by Ruby
Cover design and interior layout by Storm Constantine
Edited by Louise Coquio and Wendy Darling

Set in Garamond

An Immanion Press Edition
www.immanion-press.com
info@immanion-press.com

The Wraeththu

A Brief Definition of Their Origin
For the Benefit of Readers New to the Mythos

Humanity is in decline, ravaged by insanity, natural disasters, conflict, disease and infertility. A mysterious new race has risen from the ghettos and ruins of the decaying, dying cities. The young are evolving into a new species, which is stronger, sharper and more beautiful than their forerunners. Androgynous beings, they transcend gender and race. They possess keen psychic abilities and the means, through a process called inception, to transform humans into creatures like themselves. But they are wild in their rebirth and must strive to overcome all that is human within them in order to create society anew. They are the Wraeththu...

This novel is set in the future, once Wraeththu have replaced humankind entirely. A glossary of terms, places and key characters is provided at the end of the book, as well as a list of the days and months of the Wraeththu calendar.

A Word on Pronouns

Within the Wraeththu Mythos, hara are referred to as 'he', since back in the early 1980s when I first started writing within the mythos, this pronoun seemed to me less gender specific than 'she'. A lot has changed in both culture and language since then, (which necessitates the inclusion of this clarification), but to glue a new pronoun over all the stories and novels would feel at best clunky and contrived. I ask readers to look beyond the loaded meaning of the male pronoun, and to read it as non-gender specific.

Storm Constantine

Margenya

The dehar Aruhani has many faces, some known more than others.

He is Life, the arbiter of pearls and their hatching, fecundity in all its forms, the raw power of nature.

He is the aruna that brings about the pearls and enriches the lives and hearts of hara.

But he is also Death. He may be merciful, the guardian of souls, but can also walk as the Destroyer, without compassion or pity. In this guise, he has other names: Gelatenebris, the Cold Shadow; Decaelo, He Who Comes from the Sky; Fluctusaevis, The Cruel Waves or Flamma Esuri, The Devouring Flame.

And there is also another, most secret aspect of the dehar, conjured and fashioned by hara in darkened chambers, amid the smoke of acrid incense, invoked by croaking whispers.

This is Vindictris, the essence of Vengeance.

It is difficult to tell which aspect of Aruhani might have visited Margenya on that day when the world went black. There was an explosion but no flames, sounding like a dozen thunderstorms roaring at once, in duet with the collapse of mountains. The site was flooded, but not by the sea. Water came up from the ground.

Perhaps the dehar had swept down from the sky or up through dark subterranean streams. Or maybe Vindictris stalked in his dark cloak, with hands like bundles of burned sticks, a single talon pointing, making death happen.

When the light came back to Margenya – and it was gone for less than a minute – hara hurried to the centre of destruction. Something had happened there, blown up, gone mad. They found the wreckage of the building that had burst outwards in a shower of stone and wood and flesh. They found the black and red pieces of those who had worked and lodged there daubed over the ruins. All that remained of the structure was the walls of the kitchen, and in the debris, amid the shattered limbs and torsos, stood a har. He was motionless, black from head to toe, stained by the carbon of his colleagues, his friends. He suffered wounds – burns, deep cuts – but they would quickly mend. Otherwise, he was unharmed.

A miracle, they said.

They led him out of the carnage, and he went with them meekly.

For some time, he was deaf, and could see only in blurs. He was so shocked he couldn't speak and, when he remembered how to, could recall nothing of what had happened. Eventually, he healed, and one day walked away from the therapy centre where he'd been tended.

The mystery of the explosion was never solved.

Breathe, my shadow...

Chapter One

The house itself was never the problem. Tucked into a mellow suburb of Ferelithia, *Inglefey*'s design was quirky, with its carved lintels and eaves painted palest red – certainly not pink, but cream with a hint of blood. When Seladris moved into it, as it was a perk of the job he'd taken, he thought the design must have been deliberate, only discovering later it was an old house and had been built during the Human Era. Seladris was a maestera baker and had come to work for *Confitteri*, the celebrated establishment whose sumptuous confections were sold even in Immanion. In keeping with this, but only coincidentally, *Inglefey* resembled an elaborate yet tastefully decorated cake.

Seladris arrived at his new home in the early afternoon of a summer's day. He had never imagined he'd occupy a house so big. Its three stories soared majestically over him. The season had fully bloomed, yet it seemed the aching vividness of spring still throbbed from the trees and flowers. The sky was a clear deep blue and the chimneys of the house stood tall and starkly white against it.

Inside, the house was peaceful; its air seemed to hum languidly. Light fell in mellow bars through the tall windows, which were curtained only with sweeping drapes of dove-grey muslin that hung quiet in the windless day. The floors were mostly bare, here and there mosaiced with rugs of deep auburn, purple and gold. The furniture was old, and while somewhat battered upon the legs or surfaces, possessed an ageless elegance without being fussy. Floral perfume, spiced with an herby undernote filled the air – Seladris could see through the open doors to rooms left and right that bowls of fresh-cut roses, jasmine and honeysuckle had been left for him, garnished with sprigs of thyme.

He felt at once welcomed, protected and comfortable. He put his travelling bag beside the table in the hall, where he found a note advising him the larder had been stocked for his use: this was complimentary, but thereafter he'd be responsible for providing his own supplies. He would be expected at *Confitteri* at 9 a.m. the following morning. The noted was signed by Veredis har Mith, the owner of the bakery, who Seladris already knew was something of a "character" and a celebrity of the town.

Seladris put down the note and stood for a moment with closed eyes, soaking up the sun that fell into the hall. He took several deep breaths of the aromatic air, then glanced at himself in the tall, narrow mirror above the table, unsure as always whether or not he liked the tall, narrow har who stared back at him haughtily. His pale hair hung loose over his chest, devoid of style, which might be abnormal in Ferelithia and have to be changed. The light in the hallway flattered him, as if the mirror sought to make him feel at home. *Here, you are somehar else…* It had been the right decision to take this job. At such an esteemed establishment, known for its unusual sweet delights, he could exercise his creativity with flavours and textures to the full. And in a place such as *Inglefey*, hurts of the past would fade, be rubbed out, replaced with kinder feelings.

Seladris always found work when he wanted it, as if a dehar guided needy employers to him. He'd been working at a bar further north up the coast, when an acquaintance told him of the position in Ferelithia. Feeling neither hope nor nervousness, Seladris simply wrote and applied for the job, sure – without emotion – he'd get it. He provided a list of references, all of which he knew would praise his abilities. He described his talents without boasting. He sent drawings of confections he'd made, one of them a model of the palace Phaonica in Immanion, all in sculpted cake and sugar paste, along with his cramped construction notes written all around it, the arcana of his art. He'd made nothing like that for some time. He'd taken only what he called "invisible jobs" – in small cafes, bars, nothing grand, cooking plain food or serving drinks, no art to it. He was in a period of his life where he needed to sink into the surroundings, become unseen. But then, the news of *Confitteri*. A vague sense of restlessness had been poking at him for time, as if there was something he'd forgotten to do. So he applied for the job. And knew it was time to show himself again.

A reply came within a week from Veredis Har Mith, inviting Seladris to an interview. Several dates were given, but none further than a week away. Seladris arranged to go as soon as possible.

When he arrived, it was not Veredis who interviewed him, but two other hara who told him they were senior managers of the establishment. They did not take him indoors – perhaps guarding the bakery's secrets until he was officially employed – but spoke to him in a garden where hara might sit to enjoy tea and cakes on warm, sybaritic days. When, Seladris wondered, somewhat mordantly, was Ferelithia *not* warm and sybaritic? The garden cafe was busy. The interview wasn't that private. The interviewers were not bakers, certainly not artists, but accountants. They hired him without any fuss and told him a house came with the job. The salary was no more and no less than what Seladris had expected. He thanked the hara and shook hands. Within a week, he'd walked out of his former job and moved south.

Lunilsday, 16 Ardourmoon

On his first morning at work, Seladris went to receive his orders from Veredis, who occupied a spacious office beyond the display galleries. The entire premises smelled of vanilla, ginger, anise and cinnamon, of lemon, and butter and sage. He walked through the viewing galleries, where remarkable edible sculptures rested upon plinths, spilling marmoreal limbs or swatches of hair, or falls of vine tendrils and blossoms, all fashioned from sugar and paste. Inevitably, he had to pass by various members of staff, which led him to realise his colleagues would take some winning over. They stared at him with suspicion and, in a couple of instances, open resentment. Perhaps they'd expected somehar else to be promoted, somehar they knew.

Veredis sat behind a large desk of the palest bleached ash but stood up when Seladris came into the room. His family must have derived from a multiplicity of human ethnic types. His skin was dark, his lips Olathian full, yet his eyes were orientally poised, and of a rich violet hue. His shock of artfully messed hair was dyed (presumably) deepest indigo. He was of moderate height and extremely thin but possessed the gracefulness to carry this off and not appear merely malnourished. The components of his being complemented each other well, and the results were, Seladris thought, quite arresting.

Seladris took the seat Veredis indicated. After the initial introductions and listening to a repetition of the extent of his duties, which he'd been informed about during his interview, Seladris felt he should mention the attitude of the staff. His impression was that Veredis would not object to this enquiry. *Would* there be a problem with colleagues?

Veredis sighed through his nose. 'Their insolence is because I had to fire Plerander, the previous maestera. He was popular among the staff, and I liked the har myself, but I discovered he'd abused my facilities, *and* stolen from my stocks, to fulfil private commissions.'

'Oh… I see.'

'The hara here are still rumbling about it, but they also know I had little choice. He stole from me and had to be punished. Precedents to the contrary cannot be set, for obvious reasons. His two closest friends were dismissed along with him.'

'And they… were *also* popular?' Seladris asked.

'Yes,' Veredis said darkly. 'Still, I must make it clear I'm particular about these things. You've seen *Inglefey*. Do you like it?'

'Yes… of course…'

'Then don't I provide sumptuous accommodation?' Veredis interrupted. 'And isn't the salary reasonable?'

There was a pause, during which Seladris realised he was expected to nod and say yes, which he did.

'I have very high standards,' Veredis said.

'Then I look forward to impressing you,' Seladris responded, smiling. He was, in fact, quite confident about the quality of his work.

Veredis called for his personal assistant to show Seladris around. This was a pale, small creature with watery blue streaks in his platinum hair, which was confined in a thick loose plait. His name was Kizzy. Seladris thought this youthful individual resembled a harling's drawing of a sprite, but he was affable enough. While Kizzy flitted at his side, Seladris mulled over his interview with Veredis. He thought the har's displeasure was valid, but he could also tell his new boss was finicky, with a tendency to pettifogging, a har who might take offence easily and be slow to forgive – if at all. However, Seladris was adept at handling difficult types; they did not bother him. He prided himself on his calm, serene nature, which had taken years to perfect after a tempestuous youth, when he'd learned the hard way that a hot temper and flaring emotions were not the best tools with which to fashion an easy life.

While taking the tour of *Confitter*'s buildings, Seladris took care to introduce himself to every har, making no mention of the previous maestera, ignoring any mulishness, and smiling pleasantly to all. He made sure to *waft* through the kitchens and storerooms, exuding an air of unflappability. He would give them no reason to carp or criticise. He undertook a stock-take to familiarise himself with the ingredients favoured here. He met the hara with whom he would work most closely and encouraged them to speak about their own techniques and accomplishments. He examined all the display confections and began thinking about how he might improve upon the designs. In another life, he mused, he might have been a sculptor rather than a baker.

He returned to Veredis's office for refreshments in the afternoon and reported his thoughts. Already, he had ideas for two confections but asked if he might first take on a commission – a cake already ordered – to demonstrate his prowess.

'Generally, I'd have you create from your own imagination first,' Veredis said, 'to see what you can do, but in this case, very well. Your eagerness and confidence intrigue me. Now, please go home early today. I expect you still have things to unpack and want to get a feel for your new home.'

In fact, Seladris had already arranged, cupboarded and drawered his meagre possessions within the house. The few larger items he cared about had been transported ahead of his arrival in the town. He'd not brought many clothes with him, since he'd decided to restock his wardrobe completely. In any case, the blood would not wash out entirely from certain items.

On his way home, Seladris explored the town, orienting himself to its landmarks. He went to the harbour and walked along the beach but didn't enjoy it. Perhaps there would be other places more to his liking, where there were fewer or no hara obscuring the landscape and making noises.

Once back home, Seladris made himself a mug of black tea and wandered out into the front garden. Shadey Lane was set high above and behind the town. While *Inglefey*, situated at the end of the road, had only a small yard at the back and not much more than a patch of lawn at the front, there was space around it. The houses across the street, to the south, were larger, set back, and with longer front gardens, but there was no obvious sign of occupation. To the east, there was a crossroads, so the nearest house was some way off. To the west was a wide empty space, (much larger than that occupied by *Inglefey* and its modest plot of land), where perhaps another house had once stood, or else, long ago, the land had been planned for a property that had never been built. Now the area was like a miniature wilderness. There was a rough lawn that appeared to have been kept cropped by deer or rabbits. Flowers and shrubs grew in profusion, unkempt and wild. There were tall and ancient trees, one of them a Cedar of Lebanon. To the north came down the old forest, its rumble of dark hills.

Seladris did not care for close relationships with neighbours so appreciated the relative privacy. He'd use the space next door as an extension to his garden. He noticed that a pair of long washing lines had been erected further up the nibbled lawn. Perhaps Plerander had put them up, since there wasn't much room in *Inglefey*'s walled back yard for that. He couldn't see that anyhar living nearby would object; Shadey Lane appeared so quiet. The nearest house to the west was a good two hundred yards away, down the gently sloping road and, from where he stood, he could perceive no activity in or around it. Since the Devastation, Ferelithia had been claimed and renamed by hara. Its population was significantly smaller than that of the throng of humans who had once burgeoned here. One day, all these beautiful old houses might be reclaimed, but for now it appeared many stood empty. Perhaps Ferelithians preferred to live near the centre, by the sea. At Shadey Lane, the northern countryside butted against the order of the town, and in some cases had clearly broken through it. The unused plot next to *Inglefey* sloped upwards to the north, where trees and shrubs grew thickly. He would explore there soon.

Seladris went inside and prepared a simple early dinner of cold chicken sandwiches and salad. He poured himself a glass of tart white wine. This house was such a luxury to him, he couldn't decide where to eat, eventually choosing the western sitting-room, where plump and faded old sofas stood around the unlit fireplace. The softly ripened light of the sinking day poured into the room. Again, Seladris perceived an almost inaudible hum, which at one time might have been associated with an electrical appliance buzzing away to itself somewhere in the house. But there was no electricity in *Inglefey*. While the service had been restored near the town centre, it was not yet available out here. The lamps were oil, and there were candles. The stove in the kitchen was a huge, antique range that once Seladris lit it, would undoubtedly have to be kept compliant with fuel and cosseting, like a domesticated dragon; it provided heating and hot water for the entire house. As a baker, Seladris knew it was essential to establish an almost spiritual relationship with your stove, because they could be capricious. He intended to honour that code and keep his beast sweet, since he expected to work at home in the evenings. But not, of course, for the purpose of trading behind Veredis's back.

He sat on – or rather in, as it seemed partially to swallow him with cushions – the sofa opposite the fireplace, the surround of which was wood, intricately carved with patterns of vines and birds. Above the mantlepiece a painting hung on the wall. It was a peculiar picture, Seladris decided, being of a blue leopard, which seemed to have been caught in the act of jumping and twisting – or perhaps it had been flung or was falling from a height. Its face was turned to the viewer, snarling, its claws outstretched from the paws of its flailing limbs. There was no background landscape to provide clues as to the circumstances of the leopard, merely a wash of colours – blues and greens, with the occasional crimson streak – perhaps to represent foliage and flowers. The painting did not look that old – perhaps it had belonged to the sacked maestera, but why would he leave it behind? Unless, of course, he simply didn't like it. Seladris wasn't that keen on the picture. It made him feel curiously uneasy. The leopard was long and thin and strangely elastic. It bent in places it should not bend. It was a mottled, deep-turquoise blue, but its gaping mouth was scarlet, the long teeth yellowy-brown. He had a feeling it wasn't a leopard at all but a symbol of something else. At the weekend, he'd remove it, perhaps swap it with another painting in the house, as he'd noticed there were quite a few to choose from.

That night, Seladris went to his bed and for nearly an hour lay awake listening to the murmur of the house. Outside an owl crooned its ghost song to the darkness.

The bed was comfortable and yet, in the background of Seladris's senses, there was a smell to it. If he concentrated upon it, tried to identify it, it vanished.

Chapter Two

Meladriel lived in a sprawling, low house named *Eko Melosa* right next to the sea, on the northern fringe of Ferelithia. Here, the coastal road out of town was always gritty with sand. At high tide, water lapped over the end of Meladriel's long, sloping garden where it merged with the shore. In summertime, pale little crabs sidled through the flowers. A jetty poked out of the beach beyond the garden, and here a small, green rowing-boat was moored, which either rode the incoming tide, or during the ebb lay on its side in the sand. Long yellow seagrass rustled on the reaching dunes. At low tide the sea went far out, leaving the beach mosaiced with rock pools that were sometimes glorious with the jewels of anemones and vivid green weed that looked like hair, writhing with tiny transparent eels. Meladriel made dioramas to mimic the sea pools and sold them in Ferelithia's harbour market. He also painted pictures of storms, in which misshapen, slick creatures teemed through the corybantic waves and the drenched rocks looked like tormented faces. He had other professions too, which earned him more. Hara came to him with problems that were difficult to solve.

Meladriel was 68 years old, not counting his human years before inception. He possessed a sinewy beauty and appeared youthful, if rather solemn. In harish terms, of course, he was young. His skin was the colour of an acorn and his eyes were a golden orange. His hair was of many shades, but not dyed, simply streaked by the weathers of the seasons. He wore it in serpentine braids looped around one another, trailing feathery tails like the weed in the sea pools. In Ferelithia he had a reputation for surliness. Hara often wanted compassion and empathy from those they approached for help with *delicate* situations. Meladriel would not give that. He did his work – to most hara's satisfaction – but had never advertised his services as a nurse for the emotions. He was not a hienama and didn't intend to add that practice to his repertoire. Hara must take him as he was or look elsewhere for aid.

It was Pelf'sday and the sea air was restless. Meladriel was in his garden, round the side of the house, where half a dozen beehives stood. His bees knew where best to sup and the honey they manufactured was magical, a confection conjured from the nectar of dune flowers and the tough little heathers that swarmed over the rough land and rocks across the coast road. Meladriel, wearing no protective gauze, hummed as he worked, removing the combs from his hives.

The lives of the bees intrigued him; theirs was, he thought, a brutal existence. The workers drudged themselves to death, exhausted within weeks, replaced by others born of the queen. Thousands upon thousands of workers whose sole purpose was to labour until death. The drones, while leading what appeared to be a leisurely existence, were created only to mate with the queen. And just one of them won that privilege. The rest, once the act was consummated, were worthless, helplessly lingering around the hive, where the workers were no longer inclined to feed them, for they had no purpose in the community. They were left to perish because they could not feed themselves. And the queen? This paragon of bees was fit only to breed and breed, until her beauty was quite worn away. Once she'd used all the seed the victorious drone had placed in her during their aerial coitus, her doom was written. The workers began to nourish up a new queen, and there were no laments for she who had passed. Her function had expired.

So cruel the bees, Meladriel thought, and yet how ordered. The community ran like a machine and from this heartless industry magic was distilled: the honey of the seashore. The name of his home meant 'House of the Bee Goddess', adapted from ancient words. He wasn't arrogant enough to imagine himself a deity of the bees, but he knew they had one. Sometimes, during his devotions to the land and sea, he talked with her.

Meladriel could understand the language of the bees, the music of their wings. Now they told him they must go into their hives. He must leave them, for the Whirling Brightness was rising.

Meladriel felt a shock go through him. Why was the unstorm coming?

He carefully replaced the roof of the hive he'd been working on, took up the leaf-lined pannier of combs and walked swiftly back to his house. The unstorm could take an hour to manifest or be upon you instantly. He had no wish to be caught in its eye, nor even the foul penumbra of its extremities – the grume.

The back door of Meladriel's house, which was actually on the side of the building, was painted green, dulled by rain and the salty wind. It was hung with glass witch balls, dried swathes of the seaweed named Neptune grass, and old netting, tied together with specific knots of rough rope. The bones of swordfish and large bream were threaded through the net. These items created a threshold ward, across which few fel influences would or could venture. The door led onto a long, low-ceilinged kitchen, which had only one small, badly situated front window that looked out over the garden. The light was insufficient for a room so large, which meant the back part of it was always gloomy in the day. At night, Meladriel would light the dark with lanterns.

From his cupboard, he now took a flagon of honey wine and took a long draught from it, standing before the window. He could perceive the inexorable green-grey darkness over the sea drawing closer. He did not know what conditions provoked an unstorm's creation. Perhaps these events simply roamed the oceans and coastlines of the earth without cease, phenomena of terror. Not everyhar could see them. For some, those with the most acute senses, an unstorm brought depression, anxiety, often so fleeting as barely to be noticed. Others might be more seriously affected and suffer mood changes for several days. A few, like Meladriel, could see them clearly *and* what rode in them. These hara might be less affected physically by the phenomenon but were haunted by what they saw.

The oppressive grume undulated over Meladriel's garden, crushing sunshine in its path. There was no light to an unstorm, no flashes of brilliance, no thrilling roar of thunder. The phenomenon was silent and dull – until its eye was upon you. He could sense it; that throbbing, blinding madness within the heart of the gloom. It inflicted headaches; his skull began to pulse with pain.

'Get on with it and be done,' he muttered beneath his breath.

Dank, clotted air fingered round his house, as if seeking ingress, but it could not pass through his wards. The landscape was still, any living thing within the event unable to breathe or blink. It was a living death.

Meladriel perceived a flicker within the grume like myriad fireflies, splinters of light. The pain in his head rose up and roared.

The eye came on, enveloping the house, and within it was the fury of a natural storm condensed. No darkness now but cruel radiance: a light within which no untruth may survive. The eye whirled round, shattered and reformed, blasting the senses of its sole observer. Motes of life flew within it, and those of death. Voices were captured in its frantic motion: a shout, a whisper of love, a curse.

And then, within this vibrating chaos, a shape manifested: he who came from the sea. A hollow har. Little more than a harling in appearance, his skin was bleached and greened by the ocean, with dripping weed for hair and anemone eyes. His body was hung with ripped fishing nets, encrusted with sea urchins and barnacles. He held one finger to his lips, hanging above the ground, amid the warped carnival of light beyond Meladriel's window. The messenger.

Speak! Meladriel commanded in his mind.

The apparition did not, or could not, obey. Instead, its skin changed, as if rotting swiftly, colours of decay kaleidoscoping over its surface, until it was blue, mottled with darker shades, almost black in places. Rosettes of rot. Within the maelstrom now were cries – of both victory and pain. There was rough chanting, the hammer of drums, of feet against hard earth.

And then, singing through Meladriel's brain, the old music. And in his vision of primal dancing, of leaping flame, he saw the Pard Witch, beautiful, proud, demanding. Smiling.

No! Meladriel thought angrily, fragmenting the image in his mind. *I deny you. I banish you.* He turned his back to the window.

For some moments, the unstorm remained, as if it would never leave, then, suddenly, it was no longer there, had never been.

Meladriel drew in a shuddering breath, took a deep swig of the honey wine. His headache receded slowly, like the turning tide. He could hear his own blood seething like waves in his left ear.

He'd known this time would come, despite all the precautions that had been taken years before. That grim history could only be squashed down for so long; no force was strong enough to hold it forever. A deferred consequence, and now its moment was here. The past was coming back, and the dead would walk again.

Chapter Three

Olivian Grove was a residential area to the east of the town, lazing over the slopes of the sweeping hills. The villas here, once the homes of wealthy human families, were immense and scrupulously restored. High above the shore, their pale marble glittered in the brightness of summer afternoons. Exotic trees from far countries surrounded them, and the entire estate was bordered by olive groves. Ancient shrines were hidden in the hills beyond, where the spirits of the land now frolicked in greater freedom than they'd known for millennia. By night the houses glowed against the hills, soaking up starlight, becoming more beautiful.

In one of these grand old houses, transformed from the lavish residence of a long dead human dynasty into a thriving centre of commerce for a harish family and their vast staff, a harling named Ulien woke up crying. It took some minutes for his prime carehar, Ihrec, to come to his room to see what the matter was.

'Sssh, Uli,' said Ihrec, sitting down on the edge of the bed. 'Did you have a bad dream?'

'No! Ulien insisted. 'Somehar was in the room. They were made of buzzing.'

Ihrec smiled and stroked the harling's hair with a slender dark hand, whose nails were pale like pearl. 'We can see strange things in the shadows when we wake up from dreams,' he said. 'I'll sing a warding song so no bad memories can linger.'

And so he did, his low soft voice reaching out into the room, touching everything within it, driving fear away.

Ulien felt the peculiar sense of dread that had gripped him begin to dissipate, even though he could remember it at full strength very clearly. It *hadn't* been a dream, but he knew the folly of trying to convince Ihrec of this. His home was as free from horror as it's possible for a house to get. Even its shadows were tinged with gold.

As his carehar sang, Ulien glanced around the room. Everything seemed in its place. His toys were still. The looking glass was clear.

And yet…

Hadn't there been a mist over the glass, which had made it look old and broken? Hadn't there been a face behind the mist, looking out?

He remembered a long pale leg stepping out of the glass, and that strange buzzing sound.

Ihrec stroked his face and hair until Ulien began to feel drowsy. Nohar could banish fear like Ihrec. He was very strong.

'Honey dreams,' murmured Ihrec, rising so softly from the bed Ulien could not feel his weight lifting from the mattress.

The harling turned onto his side. Any vestige of the disturbing images was fading, because Ihrec had cast them out. As he slipped once more into sleep, Ulien saw Ihrec glide around the room, his long black braids swinging gently as he walked. He made gestures with his narrow hands, sang harder words than before. It made Ulien think of doors being closed and locked, the keys being taken away.

Ulien har Shadolis was seven years old, and little of childhood was left to him. He lived in *Velvets*, a huge old manse made of golden stone, with his hostling Thazri and his father Kazharn, neither of whom he was particularly close to. In spite of this, his relationship with his parents was warm and cordial. The family of har Shadolis held a high position within Ferelithia, because Ulien's father was the High Municiphar. It was said that after Kazharn had held his position for seven years, the Municipallion of the town had half-heartedly discussed whether the highest office should be subject to regular election, with different hara taking on the role. But since Kazharn did the job so well, and was respected by all hara in Ferelithia, as well as neighbouring phyles, it seemed a needless bother to replace him. Kazharn was not autocratic and would no doubt have agreed to step down had others wanted him to. But this never happened.

Kazharn was cinnamon-skinned, and his long umber eyes were shaped like almonds, for his human forebears had come from a hot jungled continent of the east. Ulien thought his father was as beautiful as a tiger and equally capable of deadly force. But he had no need to demonstrate his prowess, since being able to fight like a tiger wasn't needed in Ferelithia now and hadn't been for a very long time. Shedding his youth, and the hot blood of history,

Kazharn had settled down comfortably, like a cat before a fire. He had sheathed his claws and let down his hair, which flowed in waves of black silk down his back. If his purrs sounded occasionally like growls, it was only slightly.

Ulien shared his father's colouring, but with a faintly lighter shade to his skin. By contrast, his hostling was gilded, like the stone of the house. His hair was the colour of antique gold, very thick and slippery, always escaping any attempt to confine it, but in a deliberately artful way. Thazri enhanced the dwelling of the Municiphar and any function he attended with his chesnari. He was slender and of medium height, favouring the soume side of his nature, yet nevertheless Ulien had always known his hostling was far more dangerous than a tiger. Those who crossed him were banished immediately. There was no forgiving. In a town like Ferelithia, social reputation meant a lot. The withdrawal of Thazri's favour could feel like exile.

Ulien did not attend a school but was tutored at home by learned hara hired to fill his mind with knowledge. While other harlings were available as companions in Olivian Grove, Ulien was by nature a solitary creature. He played with others when his father decided too long a period had passed since his son had mixed with others his own age, but for Ulien such interaction was a chore rather than a pleasure. It wasn't that he disliked those designated to be his friends. He simply didn't enjoy doing things with other harlings. If he had to socialise, it was preferable to do so with his hostling and the mass of sycophants that always surrounded him. Thazri was more sympathetic to Ulien's desires and contrived to keep his son busy with adults so that Kazharn couldn't impose social obligations Ulien didn't like. His favourite times, though, was when he could be alone, out in the grounds of *Velvets*, where the old hill forests of Almagabra were held in check, existing only in little copses of ancient, forbidding trees. Ulien knew all the trees personally and had named them. He knew their spirits too, even though they were shy and wouldn't show themselves to his eyes. He knew them in his heart.

Lunilsday, 16 Ardourmoon

On the morning after the strange experience in his bedroom, Ulien had time alone. There was a lesson to be endured after breakfast, but then a glorious stretch of freedom. Later that day, he would go into town with his hostling for lunch but before that lay a few sweet hours in the garden. At breakfast, Ihrec had asked him if he'd slept well after having woken afraid, and Ulien said that he had, although he suspected he'd had some unnerving dreams of which he couldn't remember the details.

After Ulien's lesson, Ihrec made sure he was ready to go out later on and told him he mustn't spoil his clothes in the garden. 'Don't go wandering off,' he said, even though there wasn't that far to wander until Ulien fetched up against the walled boundaries of his parents' domain. 'And no delving in soil. I'll call you when it's time to leave.'

As *Velvets* had been built on a hillside, most of the gardens were sloping but for areas that had been deliberately terraced. As well as the tamed copses of forest trees, there was a yew thicket and a spiky grove of junipers that shivered with presence, ropy grey roots coiling over the ground around them. Old, sacred trees populated natural, open-air temples where they stood in contemplative dignity: terebinth, myrtle, plane and of course olive. *Velvets* had its farming groves for these species – all of them useful in one way or another – further up the hill behind the house, but the trees in the garden were fugitives. Ulien preferred them to the domesticated creatures higher up.

As was his habit, Ulien patrolled his territory, touching the trees with light, reverent fingers, stooping down to smell the flowers that grew between them. At festival times, the family and their staff would gather in various parts of the garden for seasonal rites. In summertime, the myrtle ruled, being the sacred tree of Kelosanya, dehar of Ferelithia and the patron of frenzied desire. This deity had been created by early settlers, once Ferelithia became a functioning town, because the area was renowned for its restorative properties that touched the soul. In Ferelithia, it was said, nohar could be sad or depressed. The area excited a natural instinct to be possessed by desire, to fall madly in love, if only for a season. Kelosanya, named for *kelos*, the recklessness inspired by fevered passion, embodied these attributes. The dehar had attendant spirits named *kelosi*, who sought to reach into the bodies of hara and pinch their hearts with fateful fingers, so they'd fall intractably in love with whoever they next laid their eyes on. Or so the legends went.

Even Ulien knew all the stories were made up and part of the tourist trade of the area, because Thazri had told him that. Still, nohar could deny Ferelithia was a joyous, healing area. Its spirits, while strong and sometimes mischievous, were benign.

Emerging from the yew thicket onto a sloping lawn, Ulien saw a har ahead of him. They were dancing, or at least... making movements that resembled a dance. In the bright light, the figure appeared to shimmer, sometimes to the extent where Ulien wondered if it was really there. He approached the figure slowly, not feeling afraid but slightly apprehensive. Was this a *kelos* spirit cavorting in the summer haze, waiting to strike? As he drew closer, he became aware of a buzzing sound, and this reminded him of what he thought he'd heard in his room the night before. *This isn't a natural kind of buzzing*, he thought, and was on the point of running away, when the figure stopped moving. It stood completely still, its arms by its sides, and stared at him. Then, its upper body leaned forward a little as if to examine him more closely. They were still at least twenty feet away from one another. Thoughts tumbled through Ulien's mind. This could be some kind of entertainer Thazri had employed for a forthcoming event. It could be a dryadhar, those hara particularly empathic with trees, hired to invigorate the occupants of the grounds. Or... it could be something else entirely.

'Who are you?' Ulien asked, quite loudly.

The har laughed. 'What a pretty little thing you are,' he said. 'Whose blood tumbles through your veins, little one?' He said this in the tone of a creature who might want to find out by tasting the blood.

'Are you working here?' Ulien said.

The har came closer and Ulien could see him properly now. Yet his colouring – from his long fair, dusty hair and his olive skin to his somewhat ragged and stained shirt and trousers – seemed strangely faded, like an old painting. There was no denying he was real, however. No spirit could look so solid, surely? The har put his head to one side. 'Yes. I'm working here.' He blew a kiss to Ulien. 'And here *you* are. I expect we shall meet again, don't you?'

With these words he turned and ran away, astonishingly swiftly, across the lawn and through a hedge on the far side. For a moment, Ulien could only stand breathless, as if he'd been running himself. He wasn't sure what had just happened.

After a minute or so, he heard Ihrec calling him impatiently, and headed back towards the house. Why was Ihrec yelling for him now? He met his carehar at the paved fountain area, quite some distance from the back terrace.

'Where have you been?' Ihrec demanded. 'I've been calling you for ages. Thazri is now cross as he's waiting to leave. And as we both know a cross Thazri is not a creature to enjoy.'

As far as Ulien was concerned, he still had plenty of time before lunch. He wasn't – and couldn't be – late. 'Are we going early?' he asked.

Ihrec blinked. 'What? No. Have you lost all sense of time, Uli? We should have left ten minutes ago.'

At these words, Ulien threw himself against Ihrec and hugged him. 'I'm sorry,' he said. That was all he could make himself say.

Ulien said nothing to Ihrec about what – or who – he'd seen in the garden. He allowed himself to be led by the hand, almost dragged, to the front of the house. Thazri was preparing to emerge from the front door, surrounded by his personal staff and the closest friends who accompanied him at almost every waking moment. They had serious business to attend to, the first of which would be taking lunch at the most elegant of restaurants in order to view and talk about the other diners. This would be followed by visiting the exclusive shops that catered to the rich of the town, perhaps dropping into a gallery where one of Thazri's friends had work on display. The group would then pass on to a seafront hostelry where bands would play and Thazri could display himself to what he considered to be lesser elements of the town. Then, with the day folded up and done, the carriage would take them all back to *Velvets*, where presently dinner would be served.

Such days out, which occurred at least once a week for Ulien, but never more than twice, were relentless in their repetitive nature. Ulien was able to drift into an almost dreamy state, lost in his own thoughts, while Thazri and his court conducted their affairs about the town. At various points, Ulien would be given treats to eat or drink. He looked forward to these moments.

This excursion began like any other. Thazri smiled at Ulien and kissed him, then everyhar went out into the sunlight. After a couple of minutes, Thazri's carriage came sweeping down on them from the stable block. Ulien loved the golden ponies that drew it. They seemed like kinder versions of Thazri. His hostling's friends always took care to fuss over him, forever glancing at Thazri to see whether he noticed. They needn't worry, Ulien thought. Thazri noticed everything. He climbed into the wide carriage, which seated ten hara, squashed next to his hostling.

The carriage driver expelled an ululating whistle and the ponies began to trot down the drive. Ulien especially liked this part of a day out: the ponies lifting their heads, tossing their glorious manes, and their speed picking up as they proceeded to the gates. By the time they passed beneath the arch, it was as if they were flying. Thazri liked to travel fast down the hill.

Once they were only a few yards from leaving the estate, Ulien noticed somehar talking to the house guards at the gates. An overwhelming sweet aroma washed over him. At first he couldn't identify it, then realised it was the familiar scent of honey. Bees were flying all around the guards and crawled through the hair of the har who was talking to them. Or it seemed that way

'Who's that?' Ulien asked Ihrec, pulling on his carehar's sleeve. He pointed at the guard house.

'That's Lurei and Fenice,' Ihrec said. 'You know that.'

'No, not them,' Ulien insisted, although by the now the carriage had passed by the guard house. 'The har with them, with bees in his hair.'

Ihrec laughed. 'Sweetling, there was nohar with them.'

'There *was*.'

'Well, I couldn't see anyhar.'

Ulien knew it would be pointless to ask the others about this apparition, since they were all focused on Thazri, who was relating an unflattering story about somehar they all knew. Whatever Ihrec said, Ulien knew he *had* seen somehar with the guards. The carriage had simply driven past too fast for Ihrec to notice.

Experiencing three strange events within the space of a day was disorientating. Ulien, knowing three to be a magical number, hoped there would not be more of them waiting to happen. Somehow, the experiences blighted the simple pleasures of the day. He couldn't wait to get home, because he needed to speak to the guards.

Ferelithia was and always had been a party town. Only for a few months of the year was it devoid of tourists seeking a hedonistic retreat. The local inhabitants tended either to be entertainers of some sort, merchants, innkeepers, spiritual teachers or the individuals who worked for such hara.

The town, that day, felt shivery. Not cold, because the air was as warm as it always was at this time of year, but jittery, unsure. Ulien felt light-headed as he walked beside his hostling towards the market. The light became harsh near the harbour, making shadows darker, spikier. Sometimes, he was sure he saw shadows that didn't appear to belong to anyhar or anything. Sunlight on the restless water glittered starkly. Small boats rocked on the high tide like nervous beasts, bumping into each other, then shying away.

Ulien knew these perceptions must be linked to the other peculiar experiences he'd had. He wished, perhaps for the first time in his life, there was somehar he could talk to about it. Thazri was out of the question, and Ihrec would only soothe him, say it was simply part of growing up. This was annoying, because Ulien knew Ihrec believed in spirits and sought always to appease them. He wore charms of mother of pearl and silver about his left wrist and burned scented oil before bizarre little sculptures in his bedroom. He never spoke of these things to Ulien and only laughed when Ulien tried to ask about them.

As for Kazharn, Ulien knew the only response, should he try to speak with his father, would be a tiger stare, then a change of subject, followed by something mildly threatening, such as the suggestion Ulien spent too little time with other harlings.

So now, Ulien studied the splintering dance of the sea around the boats, and the dismembered shadows that slunk along the narrow lanes leading off from the harbour. He must remember these things.

There was time before dinner to visit the guardhara at the gates. As he approached, Ulien considered that Fenice and Lurei had a very boring job. All they had to do was allow people to come in and go out of the estate. Soon, they would be relieved of duty as the night guard took over.

Lurei noticed the harling approaching and waved. On his patrols, Ulien often passed by the gate and spoke to the guards. Sometimes, they gave him sweets, if they had any. Lurei was Ulien's favourite of the two since Fenice was often ill-tempered.

'There was a strange har here earlier,' Ulien said, even before he reached the guards. 'Just before lunch. Who was he?'

'What?' Lurei said.

'He was a har who smelled of honey,' Ulien replied. 'He had bees in his hair.'

Lurei laughed and Fenice made a scoffing sound. 'I think I'd remember a har like that,' Lurei said.

'I saw him as we drove away,' Ulien said. 'He was talking to you. Who was he?'

'There was nohar,' Fenice said. 'The only har who's passed this gate since lunchtime was the posthar. And he certainly had no bees in his hair.'

Lurei laughed.

Ulien contemplated the two for a moment, thinking they were lying, or playing a trick, but saw they spoke the truth as they knew it. He nodded vaguely and ran off, even though Lurei called after him. There was no point in continuing the conversation.

Ulien ran to the myrtle grove. A rising sense of disquiet within him was hardening into fear. There were too many coincidences now to deny something strange was going on. He wondered again who he could talk to about it, and found his head was empty in that respect. The thought of trying to describe his experiences was too tiring. Nohar would believe him because they hadn't seen anything. And if there was something odd to sense, an adult would be able to do so.

Perhaps the rule of three was done with him. He would have to wait and see.

Chapter Four

Seladris was relieved that the rest of his first week at *Confitteri* passed
without any dramatic incidents. The staff became more amenable,
once they discovered there was little about him to dislike. He was
fair-minded, easy-going and if criticism must be given, he delivered
it graciously. However, he was careful to keep his distance. He
didn't want the hara he worked with to dislike him, but neither did
he want them to like him too much.

He rose early in the morning and was among the first to arrive
at work. Throughout the day, he worked hard and stayed late into
the evening. The project he'd been given was to create a cake for a
young har's feybraiha celebration. The parents had asked for a
paste-sculpture of the dehar Aruhani, and a representation of their
harling standing before the dehar, dressed in the robes and flowers
of the ceremony. They had provided drawings of their offspring.
Seladris began by sketching the scene. He decided upon a single-
tiered, square cake, representing a dais within a temple, although
the scene would be set outdoors. There would be a half-tumbled
shrine of white, moss-stained stone behind the dehar, and low but
spreading oak trees along the back edge, turning into flowering
shrubs on two sides, leaving the steps that ascended to the dais bare
of vegetation, but for a few strewn rose petals. After spending most
of the first day drawing different versions of this scene, he chose
one in the late afternoon and resolved to begin work on it in the
morning. Generally, his assistants would see to baking the base for
him, but he had a special recipe he liked to use – the ultimate in
buttery sweetness with a hint of salt and a trace of fragrant lavender
– and would bake it himself tomorrow. The work on the sugar-ice
sculpture could begin independent of the base.

For the rest of the day, Seladris assisted others in the bakery with
menial tasks – the undertaking of large orders requiring no
particular aspect of his art – where an extra pair of hands was always
useful. This was not simply to make a good impression but because

he wanted to immerse himself in the bakery's atmosphere, become part of it.

His creation grew over the week. Colleagues came to watch him work, to which he didn't object.

'It looks real,' Kizzy said, on Agavesday. He had brought Seladris a generous lunch of thick sandwiches and a pot of tea. 'I wouldn't be surprised if Aruhani moved.' He leaned closer. 'And the leaves on the trees and shrubs… incredible. You're so patient.'

'And that is why I'm a maestera and you're a personal assistant,' Seladris said lightly, adding another flower to a shrub.

'Oh, I don't know about that,' Kizzy said, grinning. 'You have to be pretty patient to work for Veredis.'

They both laughed.

'Merely a different kind of patient,' Seladris said.

'Yes, merely that,' Kizzy concluded wryly, raising an eyebrow.

Veredis did not come himself until the afternoon of Aru'sday, when the cake was finished. Seladris was surprised to find he felt nervous about the inspection, even though he knew the work was faultless. Veredis walked around the table where the cake stood, occasionally sniffing. His face was expressionless. Eventually, he said, 'Well done,' smiled brightly and left the room.

Seladris felt dazed. He supposed his boss approved.

At five o'clock, hara came in from the delivery yard to carry the cake to the covered cart that would bear it to its destination. It was secured upon a wooden base and covered with a wire dome swathed with protective netting. Seladris walked with it to the vehicle, like the parent of a harling watching his offspring leave home. He felt no real emotional connection to his creations but walked with them out of respect. They were alive, in a way.

There was a minor difficulty near the end of the day, when a few of Seladris's colleagues asked him to join them for a meal the following night. On this occasion, he was able to insist he had too much to do at home – there'd been so little time during the week to get anything properly sorted out – items and furniture moved to where he wanted them. This was true. Every evening, he'd merely cooked dinner and then collapsed on the sofa in the sitting-room to drink wine until bedtime. Still, this was not the reason he refused the invitation. He promised his colleagues he'd join them another time, and knew this event might have to be faced, since excuses can only go so far, and he was meticulous in preventing opportunities for hostility to creep in. Still, he knew how to be a dull companion, which discouraged hara from asking him out more than once or – at worst – twice.

Inglefey had already become a secure refuge, and there was little he didn't approve of. The sheets on the wide bed, however, still smelled unpleasantly musty and marshy, even though they looked clean. Perhaps they'd been taken from storage after Plerander had left. He decided he could stand the faint aroma for a few days and would wash all the linen over the weekend.

Wind came up from the sea on Pelf'sday. Seladris did his washing and then crammed it into a wicker pannier he'd found in the small laundry to the back of the kitchen. This he carried out to the empty plot beside the house. The air smelled of salt, and gulls hung in it, uttering complaints. Seladris had once heard a tale that the voices of those drowned at sea spoke through gulls. A few birds lumbered down onto the roof of *Inglefey* and watched him.

The sheets made crisp, cracking sounds as he pegged them to the line. He had to fight the wind for them, as the heavy wet fabric seemed to cling to him, as if in terror of being carried away to sea.

As he pinned the last in place, he discovered he wasn't alone. Through the flapping linen, he could see another har, also hanging out washing; his shadow stretched long on the ground. Seladris was instantly annoyed. Clearly, this plot was used by others to dry their laundry, most likely by more than a few, since this other har hadn't commented on Seladris being there. He picked up the empty basket and for a few moments stared at the long, slender shape as it danced up and down behind the sheet, almost like a shadow puppet. Then, sighing, Seladris walked back to his house.

At the threshold, he turned once and was surprised to see that there was no washing other than his own hanging on the lines next door. There was no other har, not even a shadow.

Once in the kitchen, he concluded it must've been his own silhouette he'd seen, or the shadows of sheets mixed with the wings of gulls that were circling around. Some mundane explanation, anyway. He'd felt no rising of psychic senses, no unease, not even a prickle to his skin.

Upstairs, he found other sheets folded in a linen cupboard on the landing outside his bedroom but was reluctant to make his bed with them. Like those he had just washed, they smelled distinctly... *off*. Fortunately, he hadn't damped the fire beneath the washing tub and could throw the whole lot in there. He went to smell the quilt on the bed. It too would benefit from being hung on the washing line to air in the fresh breeze. He didn't relish the thought of laundering it, since it was stuffed with feathers, which would clump and mat and thus ruin its comfortable plumpness.

He struggled downstairs with the enveloping quilt and dragged it over to the empty plot. There were no inexplicable shadows. He hoisted the quilt over the spare line and pulled it into place.

Billowy summer clouds moved fast across the sky; sunlight beamed and dimmed. Seladris squinted up at the rising land beyond the washing lines. There were tall conifers and what appeared to be spurs of natural rock rather than a constructed rockery, no doubt because Shadey Lane had once been part of the hill forest. Undulating patches of sunlight and darkness between the tall trunks were somehow inviting, but Seladris did not respond to this call. He went back inside to finish his laundry.

Once this task had been attended to, and he'd hung out to dry as much as he could in the available space, Seladris returned to his bedroom. He'd finish the drying tomorrow. Now, he'd turn the mattress, since as he'd removed the sheets he'd noticed a faint yellow greasiness on its surface. He was concerned this might be sweat left by a previous occupant – and not necessarily one as recent as a har. Wraeththu were magpies; they scavenged where they could and used what they found. It was likely most of the furniture in this house derived from before the Devastation. He felt slightly queasy that he'd slept in this bed all week and it hadn't been as clean as he preferred his sleeping place to be. The mattress, apart from the slight staining, appeared to be relatively fresh, but when he turned it, Seladris jumped back and uttered an involuntary cry. There was a hideous mass of greenish-black mildew on the underside, roughly in the shape of a body sleeping on its side. One arm was raised above the head, as if curled beneath a pillow.

'No!' Seladris said aloud. 'Absolutely *no!*'

He didn't want to dwell on the cause of the stain, mainly because it was quite possible a human had once died in this bed, and their corpse had perhaps lain there for some time. The turning had also released a stench of mould and rot, which was clearly what had been polluting the sheets. Plerander must have been a slob to sleep in this foul mess, Seladris thought. He shuddered and dragged the mattress out of the room. It was beyond cleaning. He must dispose of it.

Clawing and heaving the cumbersome article, while swearing beneath his breath, he managed to throw the mattress down the stairs. This was no easy task. It was heavy and awkward. It slithered reluctantly like an immense dead body, then caught on the bannisters and needed kicking and punching, seeming, on the whole, resentful of being removed. But eventually it was out on the lawn.

Hot and breathless, tingling with exertion and annoyance, Seladris went back inside.

There were beds in other upstairs rooms, which Seladris inspected carefully. While none were as wide as the one he'd slept in, he chose to replace it with furniture not sullied by mould or smells. He didn't need a large bed. He always slept alone. These other beds must have been used only for guests, as the mattresses looked new. He moved one into his room and hauled the discarded base into an empty chamber next to his own. He also appropriated a fresh quilt from one of the other rooms, after smelling them all meticulously.

After this, he went downstairs and opened a bottle of wine. He intended to drink for some hours.

That evening, Seladris went as usual into his sitting room. All week, he'd avoided glancing at the leopard painting above the hearth, still aiming to take it down at the weekend. Now, as he carried a dining-chair towards it, so he could climb up and remove the picture from the wall, he changed his mind. He put down the chair and folded his arms, stared at the gaudy image. Yes, the picture was strange and somewhat unsettling, but simultaneously also compelling. He wondered what its message was, what its artist had been thinking as he'd daubed the pigment on the canvas. Seladris drew closer. The paint was applied thickly, as if with a knife, yet the detail of the leopard was precise. He decided it could stay for now.

'Would you be sad to leave this room?' he asked. For a few moments he stood motionless – *listening* – in the humming silence of the room, not sure if he expected some kind of sign or not.

'You've won me over,' he said. 'Perhaps you've as much right to this house as I have.'

Talking to a painting! He thought. *So this is where you've ended up!*

He took his place on the sofa, lying down, staring at the ceiling. Now began the serious business of evening drinking, which was different from the way he drank in the afternoon. He'd perfected the art of using wine to empty his mind, passing the evenings in a kind of meditative state that bordered on unconsciousness. There was no particular pleasure to this, but certainly no discomfort; it soothed him.

I am an automaton, he thought, while thought was still possible. *Turned on during the day to work, to act like a living har, then… this.*

He closed his eyes, turned off.

Before midnight, his mind switched itself on again. He saw that two bottles of wine stood empty on the low table before the sofa. He could not remember drinking them. Now, sluggishly, he knew it was time to go upstairs, to sleep in the proper fashion.

The painting glowed in the moonlight, but he did not look at it.

That night, he dreamed, and the leopard spoke to him.

He was in a darkened place, outside, surrounded by densely packed pines. The throb of drums filled the night, and the smell of wood smoke. He walked through tall, ancient trees, coming at last to a hungry fire where hara were dancing. They cast flame shadows that leapt alongside them. These were proto-hara, Seladris thought. Memories of the first inceptions, the birth of Wraeththu.

The skin of one of the dancers was tattooed or painted in varying shades of blue. He wore the mask of a leopard and gloves adorned with long black claws. He noticed Seladris and shimmied towards him, playfully lashing out with his paws. This was not threatening, but more like flirting.

Then Seladris saw shadows beyond the reach of the flame-light; tall, motionless figures garbed in black with vague suggestions of pale faces. Were they watching or waiting? These Seladris feared greatly.

'Close the door,' said the leopard-har, his voice muffled through the mask.

Seladris woke abruptly, to the echo of a noise fading away through the quiet house. Had somehar knocked at the front door? He had not heard the sound exactly but felt the vibration of its passing. He glanced at the clock on the opposite wall, which told him the time was 4.30 a.m. Light was starting to bleed across the darkened sky beyond his window. The town held its breath. Even the gulls were silent.

Seladris lay blinking at the ceiling, breathing hard as if he'd been running. He put a hand over his chest, felt the panic of his heart. *A dream. They cannot find me here.*

Once he'd calmed down, he was wide awake, so got out of bed, put on a dressing-robe and went downstairs. He checked all the doors, which were closed and locked. He ate his breakfast of fruit and milk, standing up in the kitchen, gazing out of the window at the hurrying clouds. Perhaps he should move the leopard painting, after all. It must be poking old memories somehow and for this reason was bad for him. He might ask Veredis about it, see if it could be removed from the house.

After breakfast, Seladris finished drying his washing. He hung what was left on the lines, and there was no shadow to haunt him. He walked up into the pines at the back of the plot, and took a leisurely walk through them, gathering fallen cones and gull feathers. Why had this area remained empty? It was superior to its neighbours, having so much more land. If it was his, he'd build on it, raise a new, entirely harish house, full of light and air. He fantasised for some minutes about one day purchasing the land from the local Municipallion, or simply appropriating it. A lot of harish townships supported rights of occupation. If you found a place and liked it, and nohar was living in it or using it for trade or communal services, you had only to register that you were taking possession and it was yours. As long as you paid civic tithes to contribute to local facilities, you became an accepted member of the town's community. Seladris didn't know if Ferelithia had adopted this practice, seeing as it was such a thriving, popular centre. But then, if its properties were so much in demand, why was Shadey Lane virtually unoccupied? He must ask Veredis about this too.

In the early afternoon, Seladris went indoors and prepared a lunch of steamed smoked fish with aromatic lemon rice. He carried this meal into the sitting room and sat in his now usual place on the sofa. The leopard gazed over and through him, as if yearning for the outside. As he ate, he became aware of a strange smell, which grew gradually stronger. It was the reek of boiling greens, like the hideous stinking cabbage that was all he'd had to eat when... no, he mustn't think of that time. It was gone.

He put down his plate and went into the kitchen. The smell didn't appear to emanate from there, but it was everywhere – foul, rotten, thick and stomach-turning: to Seladris the very essence of insatiable hunger that could never be assuaged. Somehar else must be cooking nearby and the stench had drifted in. He went outside, sniffing the air, but the smell had gone. He couldn't imagine anyhar in Ferelithia dining on rotten vegetables, boiled or otherwise.

I will not be haunted by my own stupid imagination, he told himself firmly and returned to the sitting-room to resume his meal.

Once the washing was dry and taken indoors, Seladris built a fire in the back yard of the house, from sticks, broken branches and cones he'd gathered from the empty plot. Once he'd coaxed a sufficient blaze, he burned nearly all of his clothes, keeping only those he had on and others he'd bought recently to wear at work. There seemed fewer items than he'd thought there'd be. He must've disposed of some before he'd left his last job, even though he couldn't remember doing so. For just a few moments, he held onto a once much-loved amber-coloured shirt. Somehar he'd cared for had bought him that... hadn't they? Still, it was stained, ruined, even if the fabric was intact. Somehar had died in his arms once, had bled on him. Who? When? Time had devoured the memory. He threw the shirt onto the fire with all the other garments.

Seladris watched the flames devour the cloth. There were no words to say over this ritual pyre. He poked at it with a stick until everything was gone.

After this rite of cleansing, Seladris walked down to the town which, because it was the weekend, was thronged with hara from other places. Ferelithia, if not the jewel of Almagabra, (an epithet reserved for Immanion), was certainly the pearl, glowing bright against the glittering sea. Today, Seladris was more disposed to enjoy his walk among other hara. He was invisible to them, anyway. He went down to the harbour where colourful garments hanging on the clothing stalls fluttered skittishly in the balmy breeze. Beautiful fabrics in peacock colours and dramatic deep shades: voile, cotton, silk, lace, velvet and pleated crepe. He purchased several different outfits to suit varying moods and circumstances, which was an indulgence, since he didn't expect to attend many social occasions. With this in mind, he then bought some plain shirts and trousers to wear about the house. Even these functional garments were beautifully made, fashioned from the softest linen in shades of cream, sage and blue-grey. The Gelaming were sensualists, of course, as were other tribes of their country. They enjoyed luxury, even of the simplest kind – and perhaps that was the best sort.

Moving on to the food market, Seladris bought herbs and spices, newly cooked bread of two different kinds, and freshly caught shellfish. He acquired a small basket of dressed salad, then a net of lemons and tangerines, a jar of olives, and a crock of mixed fruit juices. From another stall he purchased a round of crusted, creamy cheese and a slab of bright yellow butter, stored in iced water. Heading back to Shadey Lane, he went into a vintner's and bought more wine, the most expensive he could afford.

Nearly all his money was gone for the week, but this didn't matter. Making such sumptuous purchases had banished the underlying discomfort he'd felt about the polluted bed, the blue leopard and the dream, the stink of rotten cabbage in the house, the destruction of his old clothes. He'd dealt with it all. Everything was good. Everything was smooth. Now, he felt very hungry and was eager to get home, eat everything he'd bought, while wearing supple bronze silk against his skin.

But still, he dreamed. He was walking through the streets of Ferelithia, but as a ghost. All around him, the bustle of the town was little more than a writhe of shadows. He couldn't make out the details of those around him. He wasn't afraid but felt strangely numb. Gradually, he became aware of swift flashes of movement, which he realised were spirits dashing this way and that through the crowds. They appeared slightly agitated, upset.

Then, as happens in dreams, he was suddenly in the market and a har was ahead of him, browsing the contents of a stall of curios. Seeing this har made Seladris's heart jump; he knew this one – but from where and when? The har turned to look at him, a smile of greeting on his face. 'Here you are at last,' he said. 'I thought you'd never come. Did you like my housewarming gifts?'

'Who...?' Seladris began.

'Never mind that,' said the har. 'It's good to see you.'

Seladris wasn't sure what this har actually looked like. He was slender, quite tall, his colouring fairly pale. His hair was abundant, fixed to the top of his head in spilling mounds, fixed with what looked like long narrow twigs and bones. The backs of his hands were tattooed in peculiar patterns that didn't seem... right.

'Wake up,' Seladris said to himself, sure and certain he must do so at once, before the strange har spoke again. His sleeping mind obeyed him without argument.

Chapter Five

On Lunilsday, as soon as Seladris reached *Confitteri*, he went to Veredis's office.

'I suppose you've come here for praise,' Veredis remarked tartly, but through a smile. He was watering the plants around the room from a silver jug with a long, ornate spout.

'Excuse me?'

Veredis stood on tiptoe to reach a high shelf. 'Your work. I'm very pleased with what you did last week. So are our clients.' He put down the watering jug.

'Oh, thank you. That isn't why I'm here.'

Veredis indicated Seladris should sit down and did so himself, clasping his hands on the desk. 'Is there something wrong?'

'Well, not wrong exactly. I simply wanted to ask you a few questions about the house.'

Veredis made an expansive gesture. 'Of course.'

'First, I've had to throw a mattress out and wondered if you could have it removed from the property. It was… full of mould and smelled bad.'

Veredis frowned. 'Oh, sorry about that. The har who conducted an inventory of the place after Plerander left didn't report it, which is odd. He's usually thorough. But yes, of course, I'll get somehar to see to it.'

'And…'

'Yes?'

'There's a painting in my sitting-room.' Seladris then realised he didn't want to continue because what he was about to say sounded ridiculous.

Veredis raised his eyebrows in enquiry.

'Oh, maybe I'll let that be,' Seladris said.

'No, what is it? You appear quite… *bothered.*'

'OK. Could that be removed too?'

Veredis grinned. 'Does it smell of mould?'

Seladris managed a smile. 'No, it's just not to my taste.'

'Then move it. There's a lumber room on the top floor, I believe.'

'I'd rather it was gone.' Seladris laughed tensely. 'This is going to sound stupid, but the picture's giving me nightmares. I hate the thing. And before you start thinking I'm deranged or paranoid, I'm not given to fancies of this type, which is why it's unnerved me.'

'I'll have to come and see this dreadful daub for myself,' Veredis said, still grinning. 'You've intrigued me!'

'You're welcome to come.' Seladris drew in his breath, then spoke quickly, before he could change his mind. 'I'll make you dinner as a thank you for my employment.'

'I'm happy to accept that offer,' Veredis said, 'assuming your culinary skills extend to full meals as well as baking.'

Seladris laughed affably, then paused a moment and said, 'Do you know anything about the empty plot next to *Inglefey*? It's such a beautiful area, you'd have thought it would have been used... in the old times. Was there ever a house there?'

Veredis stuck out his lower lip for a moment. 'I've no idea. I asked Kizzy to appropriate a dozen or so empty properties for the business a couple of years ago, and *Inglefey* was on his list. He chose the most whimsical places he could find, of course. That's his way. We claimed a couple of other houses in that street, further down from you.'

'I didn't know colleagues lived nearby.'

'They don't. I lease the properties out at present.'

'That's allowed? You can just... *collect* houses in this town?'

'Of course. If anything, long-term residents are encouraged to take over the buildings. Ferelithia has many visitors who often need accommodation for lengthy periods. Whoever claims the properties is required to renovate them and keep them in good order. My rents are fair and comply with local...' Veredis stopped speaking abruptly, his eyes narrow. 'Why am I telling you this?'

'I didn't mean to pry,' Seladris said, raising his hands in a placatory gesture. 'I just wondered what the system was, that's all.'

Veredis made a careless gesture with one hand. 'Fair enough. You might want your own place one day, of course.' He smiled. 'May I come over this evening, or is that too short notice? I really do want to see this picture.'

'Yes, come tonight. I only hope you think the leopard is as weird as it seems to me.'

'The leopard?' Veredis asked sharply.

'The painting is of a leopard.'

Veredis' face had taken on a peculiar expression. Was he concealing something? If so, why?

'You know of the picture, then?' Seladris said lightly.

Veredis smoothed his features. 'No. For a moment I thought you meant there was a big cat in the house!'

Seladris smiled politely. He always did, when he heard a lie.

With Veredis' permission, Seladris left work an hour early to prepare a meal. He had learned the art of making seafood risotto at one of his previous jobs, which the har who'd taught him had claimed required skills more like alchemy than cookery. To achieve the perfect texture and flavour required a kind of culinary magic. Seladris decided this dish was most likely to impress Veredis. He would lace it with saffron, bought from the sea-front market and *not* pilfered from Confitteri stock – tempting though it was to filch a few expensive strands. He'd had just enough money left to buy fish, mussels and prawns. Fortunately, the supplies that had been provided for him when he'd moved in had included staples, such as rice.

As he worked, he mulled over his decision to invite Veredis to his home. The offer had been rash, perhaps, but then Veredis didn't seem the type of har to encourage close friendships with employees. It should be safe.

An hour or so after he'd begun cooking, a pair of hara with a cart drawn by a skewbald pony arrived to remove the mattress from the front lawn. 'Looks like somehar died on it,' one of them said.

Seladris grimaced. 'I'm sure *something* did...'

'We'll take it to the burning yard,' said the har.

Veredis arrived at 7. A sleek carriage, drawn by a beautiful black horse, and driven by a beautiful black har, dropped him off and then departed. Once across the threshold, Veredis took a deep breath of the aromatic air. 'I was merely hungry, now I'm ravenous,' he declared.

'I can't leave the food for long,' Seladris said, 'but come into the sitting room. You can look at the picture while I finish off the meal.'

Following Seladris into the room, Veredis stood before the fireplace and folded his arms. 'It's unusual,' he said guardedly. 'But

41

frightening? I can't see that.'

'Unfortunately, I can't share my dreams with you,' Seladris said lightly.

'Hmm, I wonder why it bothers you so much.' Veredis's voice held a thread of what Seladris feared might evolve into suspicion.

He answered without hesitation, keeping his voice low, even slightly amused in tone. 'I think the painting might have a history. Perhaps the har who painted it *invested* feeling or memory into the work, even if unconsciously. *That* could be what disturbs me, rather than the actual image.'

Veredis pulled a face. 'OK. Maybe. I'll take it home with me tonight, see if it affects *me* in any way.'

Seladris doubted that was possible, because he suspected Veredis had a psychic skin so thick it was immune to subtle influences, but at least the thing would be out of the house. He turned to leave the room, but Veredis put a hand on his right arm.

'Wait a moment. There's something I didn't tell you.'

'What do you mean?'

'This house, or rather this area, *is* associated with a leopard. There's a story from the early times.'

'I must see to the food,' Seladris said. 'Will you tell me about it while we eat?'

'Yes, of course.'

Seladris was surprised – not because Veredis knew something but because he'd decided to share that information. In his experience, hara with secrets tended to keep them.

Veredis expressed lavish admiration for the risotto and drank a large quantity of Seladris's stock of wine while eating it.

'So... the leopard,' Seladris prompted after Veredis had put down his fork.

'Mmm, it's an odd tale. During the latter stages of the Devastation, what's now Ferelithia was the site of intense conflict – between different factions of humes, and later between human survivors and hara. There was a kind of Doomsday cult, a band of humes who wandered around uttering depressing prophecies and – if the tales are true – murdering anyone they believed their god might find pleasing as sacrifices. They too wanted Ferelithia, and sought to take it by force from other humans who were occupying it. But the cult members were among the first humes who ran into the Blue Leopard. They were eradicated before the rest.'

'Blue Leopard,' Seladris mused. 'A har, like in my dream?'

Veredis shook his head, took a sip of wine. 'The Leopard was rather more than a single har. It was an egregore, the projected personification of a tribe. When you speak of it, you're really speaking of a group of thirty or so hara who called themselves the Cerulopard – blue leopard…. Though the leopard was not merely *them* – it was an expression of their energy – their souls. But anyway, whether tribe or spirit, the Blue Leopard was called upon by the local phyle leaders to help dislodge the remaining human resistance in the area. There are different versions of the story, but this is the one I like most. The situation came to a head at midsummer around fifty years ago. There was fighting – naturally – some of it allegedly magical in nature. And no humes survived it. As for the Blue Leopard…' Veredis lowered his voice to a theatrical spooky tone. 'Nohar knows what happened to it. Its hara disappeared that night and were never seen again.' He laughed. 'Well, that's the story. Whatever happened, it left a scar on the psyche of the local phyles. They had come together to defeat a common foe, but there had been a high cost. They lost what I assume they regarded as a potent weapon that was *theirs* and yet it could be taken from them. I would imagine that the painting here is a symbol of the Leopard. But…' Veredis turned the stem of his wine glass in his hand.

'But what…?'

'The Blue Leopard is considered unlucky, that's all. A symbol of harish hubris. The Leopard thought itself superior to any human group but was somehow vanquished by the failing remains of a beaten community. The saying, "don't be blue" in Ferelithia doesn't mean "don't be sad". It means "don't be so bloody arrogant".'

'I see.' Seladris refilled Veredis's glass.

Veredis drank, wiped his mouth. 'Anyway, this is probably what you're picking up on. A pity you find the picture unbearable, though. It's clearly of historical interest and a relic of our collective past. I quite like it.'

'Did it belong to Plerander, do you think?'

'I doubt it. It was most likely here when we acquired the house. I'll have to check the inventory.'

'And hara lived here *before* you acquired it?'

'I assume so, as it had been cleaned up, renovated… There was no record of a claim, but that system only came in around twenty-five years ago. Took a long time for the remaining phyle leaders to settle down, wash off the war paint, and become a Municipallion.' He grinned. 'Anyway, I can't see a hume painting *that*.'

'Perhaps Plerander – or whoever else lived here before – found the painting somewhere, bought it from a market maybe? Just because the painting hangs here doesn't necessarily mean it was created here.'

'Well, yes…' Veredis began, then shook his head. 'Who knows? This hill and the forest beyond were known as Leopard's Shade – a term not used so much nowadays – but I guess it proves the Leopard *is* connected with it.'

Seladris pondered what he'd heard, while Veredis moved on from this subject but continued to talk volubly, regaling his new employee with anecdotes about *Confitteri*. As Veredis was a skilled storyteller, Seladris enjoyed hearing the gossip and appreciated not having to make conversation himself. He was able to listen and think at the same time. He was sure, however, that whatever the blue leopard's history might be, and however interesting, he wanted its image out of his house.

As time wore on and midnight approached, Seladris became slightly concerned he too might be considered part of the evening's menu. It wasn't that he thought his initial judgements about Veredis were incorrect, and he *was* disposed to friendship after all, but more that his employer might consider aruna simply as a second dessert. Rather than endure a difficult conversation, which might affect his working relationship with Veredis, Seladris changed his body language to appear forbidding. Fortunately, Veredis made no arunic overtures, either finding Seladris unappealing, correctly interpreting the off-putting signals, or else sensibly resolving to keep business and carnal pleasure at a distinct distance from each other.

Around 12.15, the carriage returned to take Veredis home. Before he left the house, he went with Seladris into the sitting room, where they carefully removed the leopard painting from the wall. It was extremely heavy and cumbersome, and now it was off the wall seemed far larger than it had appeared. Carrying it to the vehicle waiting outside wasn't easy.

'Are you sure about this?' Veredis asked, as they inched their way to the front door. 'It seems… well, it's part of the house.'

'I'd prefer it,' Seladris said, 'if you don't mind. Should we ask your driver to help us?'

'Sweet dehara, no!' Veredis exclaimed. 'He'd be most insulted. Tika's very particular about his hands. He's a musician.'

Seladris smothered a smile. He wondered if Veredis and Tika were related or perhaps chesnari.

Once the painting was stowed – a complicated manoeuvre regarded inscrutably by the beautiful Tika – Veredis thanked Seladris for the meal, hugged him stiffly, then leapt into the carriage with a farewell wave of his hand.

Once Veredis's vehicle had rolled off into the night, Seladris thought he might as well finish what was left of the wine. He felt strangely reluctant to go into the sitting room, with its bare, cleaner patch of wall above the fireplace. Was it odd that Veredis hadn't asked about the dreams he'd had? Seladris would have done so, in his employer's position. Veredis was, however, a little self-obsessed, so perhaps had no interest in knowing. If he *should* be affected by the painting, perhaps it was best he didn't know, anyway. They could compare notes on the experience afterwards.

Seladris sat at the kitchen table in candlelight, gazing at his reflection in the window. He could see little of outside.

Just as he was about to take a sip of his wine, a loud, cracking noise exploded through the house, and its walls and furniture shook violently. Crockery, pans and cutlery were thrown from the counter, dresser and table, and a series of crashes beyond the kitchen could be heard, as if every painting and mirror had smashed to the floor.

Seladris sprang to his feet, clinging onto the tabletop to keep upright. The shaking and groaning of the house seemed to last an eternity, but then ceased abruptly. In the following silence, Seladris heard what sounded like the occasional tinkle of falling smithers of glass.

An earthquake?

Cautiously, as his feet were bare, he picked his way through broken plates and edged into the hall. The mirror above the little table remained on the wall, but the glass in it had shattered; its pieces now lay glittering across the floor. All was still, but Seladris felt *Inglefey* held its breath; its atmosphere shivered, as if with fright.

'A quake, that's all,' Seladris told the house.

He went outside.

The night air was tranquil, not what you'd expect after an

earthquake, even in this quiet suburb. The town below lay peacefully, its myriad coloured lights hung like jewels around the neck of the sea. Seladris glanced up and down the road, but no neighbours were out, and most houses were in darkness. He had to admit to himself there had been no tremor.

That's when he saw them.

They came in a crowd down the hill, unnaturally tall, thin figures, dressed in what appeared to be black robes or cloaks, their heads hooded, framing indistinct white faces that glowed faintly in the dark. They seemed to rustle and bustle, stooping forward slightly, uttering no sound. There must have been around fifteen to twenty of them.

Seladris stared at this unbelievable sight for several seconds, which stretched into what seemed like long minutes. The bizarre group paid no attention to him, glided past him swiftly in the middle of the road, then veered off as one and made their way onto the empty plot beside *Inglefey*.

Seladris had focused so much upon these figures he'd failed to notice an even more peculiar phenomenon that had manifested behind him. Upon the empty plot, beyond the lawn where the washing lines stood, the windows of a house now blazed with radiance, as if a hundred lamps had been lit within each room. The light was yellow, bright as sunlight. If he should draw nearer, he'd see into every room, even though... there *were* no rooms. All that existed, painted on the night, were the lights from windows. There was no house to support them. These windows were ghosts.

The group of weird figures hurried towards what appeared to be an open front door and was absorbed swiftly by the glow shining from it.

Then all the lights went out at once, as if some mysterious being had turned off a switch.

The night was still and empty as before. All was silent but for the sudden mournful moan of a ship's horn from a vessel coming to harbour.

For several minutes, Seladris stared at the spot where the lights had shone, trying to process and understand what he'd seen. Those figures... no. Surely not hara. They'd been human, hadn't they, or *in*human? Phantoms, yet so solid to the eye. Something had happened here, something significant or bad. It remained. These things always remain.

Seladris felt light-headed, with several different aches crawling over his scalp. He found his way almost blindly to the door of *Inglefey*. Inside, he ignored the wine and went straight to the bottle of expensive Ferelithian yenayva he'd bought for "special occasions". Inexplicable manifestations must surely come into that category. He drank it straight from the bottle, winced pleasurably at its potency and the bitter yet aromatic flavour. This would calm his nerves.

When he went to bed, quite drunk, he slept undisturbed until the morning, and could remember no dreams.

Ferelithia

The town twitches in its sleep. Ferelithia is a place of lightness and freedom, of joy and pleasure. Its views of the sea are perfect. The hills and forests behind it might have been plucked from myth, when satyrs and nymphs had haunted the shadows, seducing the unwary. In Ferelithia, there is no place for uncertainty or for fear. Not now.

And yet, as a lone har, up in the area of Shadey Lane, experiences inexplicable sights and sounds, so the town, deeply dreaming, becomes aware of *something*. This is a feeling that doesn't belong, whispers that mustn't be heard. There is a flexing to the soil beneath streets still warm from the sun.

Night has come.

Memories open their eyes in the darkness, blink. Their bodies stir.

And something rises up, begins to creep through the streets of the town. It sniffs. It cranes its long neck to peer round corners. This is not the town it once knew. But then, such a nebulous cloud of energy has no real sense of knowing. It has only purpose, a programmed intent. The purpose is awake, yet unguided. There is no hand extended into the darkness, beckoning.

Not yet.

Chapter Six

Meladriel felt the tremor, knowing as he did so that most other hara would not. The earth was restless, turning.

In the past, they'd made an agreement. A time might come. Old faces must reappear behind the masks they wore. Was this the time?

He thought loudly: *Karn!* But there was only an impenetrable door in the ethers, as dense as if studded with metal spikes. It hurt to fetch up against it. Karn had closed it down long ago, that secret gate.

Pelker! Meladriel added, knowing it would not get through, would meet no other mind.

No matter, there were other ways to communicate.

In times gone by, when he'd been somehar else, Meladriel had worked with a band, originally known as Arcane Dance. He'd not been employed as a musician, but as somehar to carry the gear, to put up the posters and tell people about forthcoming gigs. He'd been healer, cosmetician and cook too, among other duties. The Dancers, as they'd been known, had travelled around together for well over a decade, until settling in Ferelithia. But that had not come easy.

None of the hara involved in the band were who they had been in those days. It was doubtful any of them would even refer to their former selves aloud.

Rue – well – everyhar knew what had become of Rue, once again *Caeru*, Tigrina of Immanion, a member of the ruling cabal of the Gelaming tribe. Rue the singer, flamboyant, crazy yet vulnerable, somewhat fey. Meladriel could remember the time when Rue had said to him, 'Don't *ever* call me Caeru. I'm Rue. Remember? Rue!' Then a toss of his wheat-golden halo of hair to emphasise his words. Caeru had to be an inception name: must've had bad memories connected to it. But apparently not anymore. Now he was Caeru har Aralis, one of the most esteemed hara of the Gelaming.

Amorel, the leader of the band and the most serious-minded of them, had moved across the ocean to Megalithica and, as far as

Meladriel knew, was still a musician and a very successful one – not simply a bass player but a maestro of many instruments. He performed in Immanion occasionally, and news travelled down to Ferelithia about him. Pharis, the drummer, had returned to his homeland of Alba Sulh to become a hienama, or whatever counted as one in that misty, mystical isle. And Karn the guitarist, desired by all, the one who audiences had bayed for…. Karn was now Kazharn har Shadolis, Prime Municiphar of the Municipallion of Ferelithia. Nohar, if they had any sense or care for their future, would refer to Karn the feckless musician in the Municiphar's company. To Kazharn, Meladriel no longer existed. But Karn must not be allowed to forget.

On Cala'sday morning, Meladriel loaded his hand-cart with items he wished to sell to the small shops on the harbour front: fragile candlesticks made of driftwood, as well as jewellery fashioned from fish bones, slivers of shell, and beautiful old glass found sea-polished on the shore. From the harvest of coast and surf, he'd concocted lotions and potions to soothe and calm, to bring sweet dreams. There were also jars of honey, some dark as tar, others golden transparent like the captured light of heaven; one of these he would keep aside. He packaged it very carefully.

The town was busy, as it always was. Few, if any, had felt the tremor. You had to be a certain kind of har to feel it, and even the most accomplished magus, if recently born, would be immune to its vibrations. It was more akin to memory than something tangible, *experienceable*.

The Municipallion, the town's omphalos, stood in the centre of Ferelithia: a beautiful, light-filled building as far removed as it was possible to get from the fusty old governmental edifices of the Human Era. This was a place of access, of communication and community – for most hara. The Nayati Kelosanya was attached to it, dedicated to the patron deity of the town.

After making his deliveries, Meladriel presented himself in the reception area of the municipal building – an acre of light and air, misted with the green scent of foliage plants. There were small groups of hara scattered about, talking softly. They were dressed in robes of matte silk in muted colours; every official in this town dressed that way. Those who wore their hair long allowed it to flow loose, because they never did anything it might get in the way of. A few sat conversing at low tables, which were surrounded by elegant ferns. Meladriel crossed the space of air to a wide reception desk set against the left-hand wall and asked for an audience with the Prime Municiphar.

'Might I ask your business, Tiahaar?' enquired the receptionist, a brown-skinned elfin creature with metallic viridian hair and eyes.

'It's personal,' Meladriel replied. 'We know each other.'

'Oh…' The receptionist appeared unconvinced.

'Would you ask for me?' Meladriel enquired. 'It's important I speak to him.'

'Name?'

'Meladriel.'

'Excuse me, Tiahaar.' The receptionist rose and passed sinuously through a door behind the desk.

Meladriel waited for over ten minutes, which felt interminable, but was perhaps marginally less insulting than an instant refusal. He doubted Karn's office was nearby. Most likely the receptionist had gone to communicate in private via mind-touch with other minions. There might be a forest of them to get through before he'd reach Karn. He must find another way to get to the har. It had been folly to imagine it'd be as easy as walking in here and making a simple request.

Just as he turned to leave, the receptionist slunk back through the door, a smile fixed to his face.

'I'm sorry, Tiahaar, I can't arrange that for you. Would you like to leave a message?' Disguised behind his gentle tone and sweet expression was the plea for Meladriel to read between the lines and not attempt to persist with his request, which would be embarrassing for both of them.

Meladriel stared hard at the har, who stared back bravely. It wasn't his fault. Meladriel ducked his head. 'No. Thank you.'

He left the building, a jar of sunlight still held in one hand.

Outside, Meladriel stood in the sunshine for some moments, thinking. He'd had no contact with Karn for decades, partly because he despised the way the har now presented himself as a grand creature of influence and respectability. But he was the only one who remained of the original hara with the appropriate experience and knowledge. There were others, yes – the former phylarchs, for example. But where were they now? Before the Ferelith had established a tenuous trading relationship with the Gelaming, its leaders had fled, perhaps because they had good reason to fear the Gelaming examining them too closely. Many of them had originally come to Almagabra from Megalithica, 'spreading the word' of Wraeththu, incepting any eligible humans they found as they swarmed over the land in their inexorable crusade, infecting and indoctrinating before moving on. No doubt the majority of the prime movers were now hiding in Jaddayoth, presiding over tribes that were more like cults.

'And you, my pretty-pretty,' Meladriel murmured, beneath his breath, 'what of you? Any har who thought you'd stay buried for ever was – and is – a fool.'

This land still hummed with memories, beneath the scorching light, the laughter, the merriment and revelry. Ferelithia had once been a place of shadows, and they still lay beneath.

Sighing, Meladriel placed the one jar of honey – wrapped so meticulously in straw and linen with a green silk ribbon – into his empty cart, which he'd left outside. He dragged it back home and there made some adjustments to his appearance. He'd not get past the first guards of the area he intended to visit if he didn't look smarter than he usually did. He felt he had no choice but to go to Olivian Grove, face Kazharn har Shadolis in his sumptuous lair.

Before attempting this confrontation, which he now truly dreaded, Meladriel went to visit his only close friend, Tika, who was a musician but not from the early times. Among his various occupations, Tika owned an elegant carriage that tourists would hire, and a glossy black horse to draw it.

Tika lived in the house of a har Meladriel didn't particularly like – Veredis har Mith. Veredis was too spiky in temperament for Meladriel's taste, and overly inquisitive about other hara's business. Meladriel rarely visited when Veredis was likely to be home.

The house was situated in a moderately affluent area on a clifftop overlooking the sea. It was furnished in a bare yet comfortable style. Its frontage was a wall of windows. Veredis didn't like clutter. Tika's two rooms were by contrast an absolute but homely mess. Meladriel knew Tika and Veredis had been friends since harlinghood but failed to see what kept them close now. They were so different.

He found Tika sitting in the sun, on the wide terrace behind the house, where trees grew in enormous pots and the glittering threads of narrow streams ran into a pond, from a water feature constructed of piled bluish stones. Tika was apparently writing a song. He had a guitar by his bare feet and copious pages of music spilled over his lap, being scattered by the mild breeze.

'Can I borrow Rhea?' Meladriel asked, even before he passed through the terrace gate.

Tika looked up, his skin velvety matte in the raging heat, which dewed most other hara with sweat. Tika laughed. 'What for? Ah… You want to impress, of course.'

Meladriel sat beside Tika on the stone flags that were almost too hot to sit upon. 'Yes, as a matter of fact.'

Tika wrinkled his nose at Meladriel's appearance: the rarely worn pleated tunic and long kilt of fine, slate cambric, the high boots of muted grey leather, carved out to look like sandals. His hair; bound up and back. The costume of a subordinate of the rich. 'You look weird,' Tika said. 'It doesn't work. Just be you.'

Meladriel grimaced. 'Impossible. I need to go to Olivian Grove.'

Tika uttered a hiss of contempt. 'Is there any danger I'll lose my Rhea?'

'No. It won't take long.'

'OK, then,' Tika said, 'but now you owe me.'

'A condition you prefer,' Meladriel said. He stood up. 'OK to get her myself?'

'Go ahead.'

Meladriel began to walk away but Tika gestured for him to stop. 'Hold on. I was going to call on you today to ask you a favour, so you've saved me some time.'

Meladriel walked back. 'What is it?'

Tika squinted up at him. 'Would you talk to one of Ved's hara? He has a situation, and it's your sort of thing.'

Meladriel frowned. He didn't relish meeting any confederate of Veredis's. '*My* sort of thing?'

'You owe me,' Tika reminded him. 'Also, you can charge him what you like.'

'OK, I suppose so. When?'

'I'll let you know. Ved has to speak to the har today.'

'What's it all about?'

'I won't tell you anything in advance, even though Ved has involved himself – stupidly. It might be nothing. Silly hara working themselves up into a tizzy for little reason and imagining things.' He shrugged. 'Not sure myself... Anyway, look at it with a clear mind. Better that way with weirdness, isn't it?'

Meladriel shrugged. 'If you insist.'

'Thanks. Remember, no sneaking off once you've brought Rhea home. You're going to tell me what you're up to.'

Meladriel laughed. 'Nothing, really. Just want to see an old friend and there are guard dogs in the way.'

Tika raised his brows. 'You *have* old friends?'

'See you later,' Meladriel said, and went round the side of the house to the stables.

'In *Olivian Grove*...?' Tika called after him, laughing.

The stables were situated in a shady part of the garden. In one stall reposed Rhea. In the other stood Tika's prized carriage. Meladriel shivered as he passed from the sunlight into relative gloom. The atmosphere felt strained, watchful. He went to Rhea, who was at the front of her stall. He petted the mare, scratched beneath her chin. She stamped and shook her mane, uttering a deep huff. Meladriel felt a prickle across his shoulders. Somehar was here... He glanced around, saw nothing, and the horse didn't appear discomforted in any way. Despite this, he couldn't dispel the feeling that somehar – or something – was hiding within the stables observing them.

He had to pass the carriage to reach the small room where Rhea's harness and riding tackle were kept. Was somehar crouching in the vehicle? Meladriel paused and gazed into the shadows. Nothing moved; there were no suspicious sounds. He shook his head. He was becoming spooked like a harling by a mere patch of darkness. He took Rhea's tack from its brackets on the wall.

Rhea knew Meladriel well, so she was compliant for him; she could be quite obstreperous if the mood took her. She looked glorious in the bright light, her mane as soft and luxuriant as a har's hair, her pelt gleaming as if polished. He walked her slowly through the town and out to Olivian Grove, determined to make the most of the pleasurable experience of riding her. He'd brought with him the jar of celestial honey.

The guards on the tall gates were very young, and clearly in love with themselves. They were pretty creatures – naturally – but with the mean streak required in all hara of their profession. Their duty was to stall and obstruct. To them the word 'no' was more stimulating than a sigh of love. One looked surlier than the other.

Meladriel, awkward in his smart attire, told them: 'I have a delivery for Tiahaar Kazharn har Shadolis.'

'You can leave it with us,' said the surly gatekeeper.

'It's a personal gift. I was asked to deliver it to the house.'

'What is it?'

'It's not my business to unwrap it and see. I'm a courier.'

'It's *our* business to keep the residents safe. Dismount and we'll open it.'

The guards allowed Meladriel to enter the estate and closed the gates behind him. This could be interpreted as accommodating or menacing. He handed them the wooden box that contained the carefully wrapped jar. Surely there could never be any threat to residents of Olivian Grove? In the past maybe, but now? This was Almagabra, for Aru's sake, not the wilderness of Jaddayoth.

Pelkers, Meladriel thought mildly, as he watched the guards tear into his gift.

'What's this?' the surly one demanded.

'What it looks like, I suppose,' Meladriel replied. 'A jar of honey.'

'And this requires personal delivery?'

Meladriel shrugged. 'It's not for me to judge, but I'd like to fulfil the desires of my client.'

'And who is your client?'

'Confidential.'

'Reveal the name of your client and this item might reach its destination. Otherwise, you can take it back to them.'

'Meladriel har Seagrass.'

They hadn't heard of such a har, not least because the latter part of the name had just been made up.

The guards went into a brief discussion. The quieter one, who Meladriel suspected might've taken a fancy to him, seemed to be arguing his case, if in a lacklustre fashion. The other simply liked obstructing hara and saying no.

Behind them, quite near to the boundary of the estate, reared the mansion now belonging to Kazharn har Shadolis. Its walls were as golden as the celestial honey. As Meladriel watched, a slender har came out of the house. Not Karn but Thazri, the creature he'd taken in blood bond and with whom he'd created – mandatory for one in his position – a perfect harling. To Meladriel, Thazri was far from perfect. His face was spiteful, all cheekbones and wide lips, with the eyes of a cobra. He was, in fact, Meladriel decided, an insect of a har, who now happened to be chesnari of the High Municiphar of Ferelithia, rather than a torturer for some gang in Jaddayoth. Meladriel couldn't discern fine details at this distance, but nevertheless knew them, as he'd seen the creature sometimes around the town. Behind him trailed attendants and companions, one of whom held the hand of a harling. A subdued child, Meladriel thought. He experienced, for the briefest moment, a twang in his heart, like the plucking of a guitar string that had gone out of tune. He told himself it was not envy, or even regret, but even so, he couldn't help imagining that honey house melting, pouring down in waves of molten gold, streaming round the knees of the privileged hara who didn't even notice.

His will faltered.

'Deliver the gift to Tiahaar Shadolis,' he said to the more amenable of the two guards. 'But give me a receipt at least.'

The guard nodded. 'Sure.' He smiled, confident of how beautiful that made him.

Meladriel didn't smile back.

The guard went into the gate lodge and spent some minutes dealing with this request. The surly one stood staring at Meladriel in a discomforting way. Meanwhile, a wide, low carriage painted cream and gold swept from behind the mansion, drawn by four palomino ponies. The insect climbed into this, followed by his entourage. Presently the carriage flowed through the gates, right past Meladriel, leaving a trail of exotic scent and laughter. The occupants didn't glance at him once, except, after the vehicle had passed, the face of the harling could be seen, looking back.

Meladriel clenched his fists, waiting.

Eventually, the receipt had been written and handed to him, so he could remount Rhea and leave this abominable place. He turned the mare back down the hill. He imagined the guards would give the honey to the insect's staff. Perhaps it would even be shown to Thazri himself. He wouldn't know what it meant, but it was doubtful he'd pass it on to Karn.

Once he'd taken Rhea home, evading as much as possible Tika's curiosity, Meladriel walked back to his house by the sea. He was annoyed that his heart felt like a boulder in his chest. He had to accept that the Karn he'd once known was effectively dead. He wouldn't be interested in anything Meladriel had to tell him.

The sun went down in the fire-sugar sky and painted the sleeping ocean with strokes of scarlet and orange. The tide seethed in. Meladriel sat on his jetty, his feet in the water. He leaned back on straight arms, tilted back his head. He'd replaced his uncomfortable, tidy clothes with soft shirt and trousers, and had let down his hair, thrown the cramped leather boots across his bedroom. He hated himself a little for going to Olivian Grove.

Close your mind to it, he thought. *It's nothing to do with you anymore. Not every story you read on a newssheet concerns you, and what you pull from the ethers is just like that. Somehar else's story.*

The night bloomed, bringing forth the singing creatures of the darkness. Listening to their song, Meladriel was lulled almost to sleep. He didn't hear the har approach, down the soft sandy path of his garden.

'Meladriel.'

The sound of his name jarred him. He turned quickly, saw the looming silhouette behind him. He didn't recognise the clipped voice; it took some moments to realise who it was.

He stood up, said nothing.

'What was the meaning of it?' Kazharn har Shadolis asked. 'The gift of honey?'

'You must know, because here you are,' Meladriel said, somehow managing to pull coherent words from his shock. 'I'm surprised you know where I live.' He got to his feet.

'You're not that hard to find. So?'

'It was nothing. I was mistaken.'

'That's not true. You've simply changed your mind since earlier today. You wouldn't come to me with nothing, Meladriel, of that I'm quite sure. You wouldn't have wanted to contact me at all.'

'Do you really want to know?'

Kazharn sighed. 'Of course not, because it'll be connected with something I'd rather forget. But... even so, what did you want?'

'An unstorm came, and with it a messenger. The land shook last night, and it wasn't simply an earthquake. Did you not feel it?'

Kazharn grimaced. 'No, go on.'

'It could be time. But...' Meladriel shook his head. 'We should ignore it. It's just wisps of smoke and memory, nothing solid. I realise now it means nothing to anyhar but me.'

Kazharn stood motionless for some moments, then said, 'Perhaps we could go into your house. It's dark out here.'

'I don't want you in my house.'

'Don't be petty, Mela. Let's go in.'

'Don't call me that. It's a name for friends to use.'

Kazharn made a somewhat exasperated gesture with both arms.

Meladriel uttered a sound of annoyance, then indicated that Kazharn should follow him up the path. He noticed that above, on the coast road, a carriage stood waiting. A golden lamp gleamed beside the driver.

In the kitchen, Meladriel lit candles. The buttery light revealed that Kazharn was dressed in a pine-green robe of limpid, layered muslin that left his arms bare. The cosmetics applied artfully to his face rendered him flawless. His sepia-coloured skin seemed dusted with pearl. Gold gleamed around his throat, among the folds of his abundant black hair and at his wrists. He smelled of lilies and looked as if he'd just called in on his way to a social event.

Still the same arrogant splendour, Meladriel thought, *but a clever har to be careful of.*

'You must tell me what you've experienced in detail,' Kazharn said. 'I can't make any decisions until I know.'

'I think perhaps we need only to be alert,' Meladriel answered. 'I experienced little.'

'That's not enough. What do you *think* will happen?'

Meladriel shrugged. 'I've no idea, only that something is shifting. What is buried doesn't necessarily die.'

'If there's any possibility what you suspect might be true, such energies can't be loosed in modern Ferelithia.'

'That's your problem, *Karn*, not mine. I don't care what happens to tourists from Immanion.'

Kazharn glared at Meladriel with disdain. 'Don't be an idiot. It'd touch everyhar. The fact is, we can't even guess what would happen, what the effects would be, but they certainly won't be pleasant.'

'Then contact Immanion. Let them deal with it.'

Kazharn choked out a laugh. 'I don't know why I'm laughing. That joke isn't remotely funny. It's a Ferelith mess, not theirs, and we don't want Gelaming poking around in it.'

Meladriel realised at this point that the words coming from his body did not reflect his true thoughts. He'd tried to contact this erstwhile friend because he knew they were perhaps the only hara left in Ferelithia who'd know how to deal with the situation – *if* there was one. Yet now he was being spiky and difficult, like a truculent harling, for reasons he didn't want to admit.

'I wish this hadn't happened,' he said abruptly, 'but I came to you today because I believe we're the only ones left in this town who understand what might come. Unless…'

'What?'

'You can find the others.'

Kazharn grimaced and laughed sourly. 'Get the band back together? Your wit astounds me.' He shook his head. 'No. We must make do with what we can find here and now.'

Meladriel uttered a caustic laugh. 'Of course. You don't want anyhar in Immanion to know your part in it, do you? That must be a constant worry for you.'

Kazharn sighed. 'Your attitude is obstructive. I ask you to put it aside and be objective. And, as you mentioned it, no, I don't particularly want my friends and colleagues to know certain aspects of my past, but that applies to just about any incepted har, yourself included.'

'And the Tigrina? It's not like he's half a world away.'

'I won't involve Caeru in this. He's not the kind of har to be useful in this situation anyway.'

'If you could even get to him. I imagine trying to meet with him would be as difficult as it was for me today trying to get to you.'

Kazharn blinked at Meladriel in a hard, meaningful way.

Meladriel held up his hands. 'Sorry. Let there be peace betwixt us. Tell me your thoughts on what we should do.'

Half of Kazharn's mouth lifted in a tight smile. He'd recognised the offering of armistice, because inescapably his memory had just slipped back to long ago gatherings around tribal campfires, and the ritual phrase of accord hara would utter before every act of magic. He nodded vaguely. 'As you will. First, please comply with my request. Tell me everything, in as much detail as possible.'

Meladriel did so. At the end of it, Kazharn was silent for some moments, then said, 'You're right. We should monitor the situation. This might only be a… shiver… nothing more. You must keep me informed.'

'How, exactly?'

'I'll have a pass sent to you, which you may present at the Municipallion. This will allow you to make appointments with me.'

'Won't hara wonder about it?'

'No, I have agents undertaking several different tasks. You'll simply be another of them.' He paused. 'Will you want paying?'

There was a pause.

'You can go now,' Meladriel said in a flat tone.

Kazharn inclined his head. 'I had no wish to offend. I thought you might find payment useful.' He glanced, perhaps unconsciously, around the humble kitchen.

'I'm happy with my life, Karn, as you are no doubt happy with yours. We each made our choices.'

Kazharn regarded him steadily. 'Thank you for the honey. Despite your defences, I understood its message, and I know you had courage to do that. But…'

The silence was uncomfortable.

'I guess you had to attract my attention somehow.'

Meladriel opened the kitchen door. 'Goodbye, Karn.'

'Goodbye, Mela.'

Meladriel sat for some moments at the kitchen table, his mind empty. It felt as if Kazharn har Shadolis had wiped him blank somehow. Then he got to his feet.

He went out into the garden, down to where the land met the shore. Here, he built a small pyre of dried wrack and driftwood broken into sticks. He lit the fire and scattered sea salt over the flames, which roared momentarily blue. He cut his arm with a thorn and let a few drops of his blood fall onto the embers.

Kazharn was not enough for the task ahead, and in one thing he'd been right – their old friends had broken all ties to Ferelithia. The hienamas who must surely have known *exactly* what had occurred all those decades ago had gone, melted into other lands, other lives. They'd left no instructions and no records of their procedures. Those who were left to deal with the situation now needed help of a different kind.

'Send somehar – *something* – to me,' Meladriel murmured. His hands made stroking gestures above the flames. He breathed in the smoke.

'From future or past, from the land or sea, from body or soul, send forth.'

For a moment, he fancied he saw within the flames the strange har he'd glimpsed during the unstorm.

Already with you, a voice lisped in his head. *You'll know…*

Chapter Seven

When Ulien saw the beehar at the gate again, this time well in advance of passing by, he gripped Ihrec's arm. 'There! There!' he hissed.

Ihrec glanced to the side. 'That har with the parcel?' he said.

'Bees,' Ulien managed to say.

Ihrec frowned at him in a vaguely worried way. 'Where?'

The smell of honey was so strong it was almost nauseating. The har with the guards was looking at Ulien with eyes of molten gold. Then it was over, and the carriage was careering down the hill.

'You saw him,' Ulien said. 'Don't say you didn't.'

Ihrec smiled, stroked his hair. 'It was nohar special,' he said. 'It looked like a delivery, that's all.'

'What's the matter?' Thazri asked sharply.

'Nothing,' Ulien replied.

The town that day was calmer. The little boats in the harbour dreamed upon the water and gulls hung lazily above them. Thazri paraded himself, and everyhar turned to look at him. He rewarded market traders with his custom. For example: 'These lemons, I've heard, are as good as *ours*.' And he would hold the fruit to his perfect nose, inhale deeply, smile. 'We'll take two dozen.'

The stallholders favoured with Thazri's attention would incline their heads gratefully, knowing that today they'd be packing up few of their wares to take home.

Ulien found himself thinking, *what is my life to be? A creature of leisure like Thazri or a har of rank and power, like Kazharn. Is there something else I could be? A stall holder in a market? A gull upon the air?*

They dined on the upstairs terrace of a restaurant, shaded by miniature lemon trees growing in huge terra cotta pots. Thazri glowed – his skin, his hair, his eyes. He flirted with the staff and gave the prettiest of them a golden ring from one of his own fingers. Ulien knew this meant something but shrank from considering what.

He wandered downstairs as he needed the bathroom, passing into the shadowy interior, where the light was sepia, and the air smelled of lemon, thyme and garlic. He went into the corridor that led to the toilet facilities. A door was open at the end of this narrow passage, a bright rectangle of light. There was a yard beyond, not used by customers, but perhaps where the staff would sit to eat their lunch, and deliveries would be unloaded. Ulien saw a har pass over the light, become a narrow silhouette at the threshold like a shadowy spectre. He turned quickly into the bathroom.

The air here smelled of sandalwood and roses; the facilities were spotlessly clean. Ulien could hear hara talking in the yard, a sound that faded away.

Leaving the room, he glanced into the sunlit yard, saw a har sitting on a barrel across the way from him. His hair was dusty, his clothes old, yet he was striking in appearance. Other barrels were piled around him, one had fallen onto its side and on this he rested his bare feet. The har raised a hand to Ulien, who was unable to resist venturing outside.

'Hello again, little one,' said the har.

It was he who'd Ulien had seen in the garden a few days before. 'Hello,' he said politely. There was nothing supernatural about this har, even if he seemed a little weird.

Now he brushed back his pale, darker-streaked hair with one hand and said, 'You are Karn's son.'

Ulien had not heard this name before. If Thazri should shorten his father's name, it was to call him Kaz or, on very rare occasions, Kazzi. He shook his head. 'No, my hostling is Thazri, my father Kazharn.'

'I see.' The har laughed. 'New skins for a new era, of course.' He smiled warmly and reached out with one hand, beckoning Ulien to him with an open palm.

Ulien saw a strange, stylised pattern on the har's inner forearm, which represented an animal of some kind, in turquoise and gold. He wasn't sure whether it was a tattoo or painted on.

'Don't be afraid,' said the har.

Just these words made Ulien think that perhaps he *should* be afraid. 'Who are you?' he asked, trying to conjure some of Thazri's haughtiness into his voice. 'You work for my family?'

'I'm no enemy of yours,' the har said, 'despite what you're thinking now.' He winked. 'Your hostling is an idiot.'

Ulien couldn't prevent the spurt of laughter that came out of him. He loved Thazri but had always secretly thought him rather foolish without knowing why.

The har laughed too, a conspiracy of humour.

'How is he an idiot?' Ulien asked.

'He's an expensive statue that can speak, an ornament that can roon. His head, if you were to open it, would have very little brain. He is a symbol to Karn – your father – of his own success. He always wanted that success.'

'You know my father.'

'Yes – or I did, long ago.'

Ulien wondered if this could possibly be the beehar he'd seen at the gates of *Velvets*. He couldn't recall what that har had looked like – only the scent of honey and the hum of bees. 'Were you at *Velvets* earlier?' he asked.

'I might have been.'

'Did you have… bees?' Ulien screwed up his eyes. 'I mean…'

'No, I didn't have bees,' said the har. 'But I will meet with one who has.'

'You *will* meet…?'

The har laughed. 'I can see what is to come.'

Ulien felt this was the truth, no matter how odd or perhaps self-important it sounded. 'Was *this har* at our house?'

'It seems likely, from what you said.' The har got to his feet. 'Thank you, little one. Go finish your lunch. But do not speak of me.'

Ulien snapped, 'Why?'

'Because nohar will believe you.' He grinned. 'Isn't that the way?'

Ulien paused for a moment, then said uncertainly, sure he'd get no sensible reply, 'What's happening?'

The har grinned. 'Strange and wondrous things. You must not fear what is to come.'

'But what…?'

The har jumped to his feet, bowed to Ulien stiffly from the waist, put a finger to his lips. 'Be patient, little one. Soon, there will be learning to enjoy.' And then he sauntered into the dimness of the restaurant.

Ulien stood still for a moment, breathless again, as he'd been when he'd encountered this har in the garden.

When he returned home in the late afternoon, Ulien fully intended to speak with the houseguards as soon as possible, but then found he had no need to, since one of them came to up the house minutes after Thazri's party had alighted from his carriage.

The group were still in the hallway, some hara already dispersing to whatever tasks they had to attend to before dinner. Thazri stood in front of the long, antique mirror, glowering at himself. It seemed there was something in the reflection he didn't like. Then a househar came through from the domestic areas. He held a box in his hands.

'Tiahaar,' he said to Thazri. 'There has been a delivery for Tiahaar Kazharn. Lurei just brought it up from the gate.'

Thazri turned from the mirror and raised his brows. 'Then give it to me.' He held out a hand.

The househar barely hesitated. He placed the parcel into Thazri's waiting palm. Ulien saw the object was heavier than Thazri had expected. He nearly dropped it. Eyeing it with some distaste, Thazri went into the dining room off the main hall. Here, he put the parcel on the glossy walnut table.

Ulien followed. 'What is it?' he asked.

'It's been opened already,' Thazri said.

'Yes, Tiahaar,' murmured the househar, who had followed them. 'Lurei and Fenice thought it best to check the contents since the delivery har was unknown to them.'

'Of course.'

Thazri delved into the fragrant straw packed around the contents. He drew out the jar of honey. At once this seized the light and glowed, making Thazri appear even more golden than he usually was. His arms were bathed in the light. 'Honey...' he said.

Bees, thought Ulien. Again, he felt unaccountably breathless.

Ihrec had also now come into the dining-room.

'Look at this,' Thazri said. 'Dare you taste it, Iri?'

Ihrec lifted the jar, untied the string around its top, removed the lid of waxed paper. He sniffed the contents.

'Is it... safe?' Thazri asked. If there were poison, Ihrec would know.

The carehar raised an eyebrow, then dipped a finger into the honey. Thoughtfully, he then sucked the finger. 'Very good,' he pronounced. 'Almost... too good.' He passed the jar to Thazri, who glared at it.

'Can I taste?' asked Ulien, desperate.

'I don't think...'

'It's safe,' Ihrec said. 'He'll like it.'

Thazri scrutinised Ulien for a few moments, then handed him the jar.

Ulien dipped a finger into it. The honey felt warm, somehow tingly. It held onto him. He heard the hum of bees in the room. Slowly, almost with difficulty, he lifted the finger to his mouth, let the golden liquid drop onto his tongue. The taste made him shudder, twisted his emotions into a plait both wondrous and disorientating. He experienced a painful yet delicious twist within his chest that made him want to run outside. He thought of a har with bees in his hair. He thought of a strange figure dancing in the garden, manifesting in the yard of a restaurant.

'You clearly like it,' Thazri said, smiling now.

'It's for my father,' Ulien said, putting down the jar.

The jar simmered upon the table, toying with the late afternoon sunlight.

'An odd gift,' Thazri said, 'and there's no card, no indication who sent it.'

'The guard gave a name,' said the househar. 'He told me it was Meladriel har Seagrass.'

'Never heard of them,' said Thazri.

'Nor I,' added Ihrec.

'Won't you taste it?' asked Ulien.

Thazri drew in his breath. 'No. I don't care for overly sweet things.'

'It's magical,' Ulien said.

Ihrec laughed. 'Made by a master, there's no doubt,' he said.

'Bees made it,' Thazri stated flatly. He turned away and made for the stairs.

Ulien and Ihrec exchanged a glance. Ihrec dipped a finger once more in the honey, sucked it greedily, then replaced the paper cap on the jar.

'Get changed,' Ihrec said. 'Then you can go outside.'

Ulien knew it was vital he witnessed his father's reaction to the gift of honey. This object was connected with everything else that was happening, he was sure.

Kazharn came home early that day. Ulien, who'd been loitering near the house, hardly paying any attention to his garden territory, sped inside once he heard the hooves of Gull, Kazharn's magnificent bay gelding, trot up the driveway. Gull's steps always sounded crisp and precise, perfect rhythms, as if somehar was playing an instrument; there was no other horse like him on the estate. The stable hara called him Dancer.

Kazharn rode round to the stable yard, giving Ulien time to run through the house to the yard door, which was close to the kitchens. This domestic domain was full of noise – the clatter of pans, the gush of water, the whistle of a kettle, the pad of swift feet across the tiles, many voices, and the louder, curt orders of the cook. Dinner was under way, a lavish affair as guests would be present.

Kazharn came into the house. He was dressed informally, so clearly hadn't been at the Municipallion that day, wearing a long dark linen coat over shirt and trousers of indigo cotton. His hair was confined at the nape of his neck in a silver clasp the shape of a nest of snakes. Perhaps this ornament was a charm to curb the resentment of hair that wanted to be wild but was rarely allowed to be.

The cook came out of the kitchen almost at once and handed Kazharn a large mug of coffee. At this point, Ulien made his presence felt.

'There's a parcel for you,' he said.

Kazharn appeared surprised to find his son in this place. 'Really?' He sipped the coffee. 'Perfect, as always,' he said to the cook, who couldn't help but simper as he went back to his domain.

'It's honey. A jar of honey. Come and look. It's... special.'

Kazharn raised his brows. 'Honey? Who'd send that?' He took another taste of his drink.

Was he hesitating? Ulien wondered. 'There was no card but the houseguards were given a name.'

'What was it?'

Ulien found he couldn't remember, which was strange. 'It had the word grass in the second part, I think,' he said at last.

Kazharn grimaced. 'Can't think who that might be. Let's investigate.' He put down the half-finished coffee on the shelf that ran along the corridor and placed a hand on Ulien's shoulder. Together they went to the dining-room.

The honey still held court on the table, spinning webs of golden light. Ulien could see now there were bubbles in it, like globules of molten gold or sparks of captured sunlight. The air smelled thickly of honey and, strangely, of the sea. A muted sound like distant waves seemed to emanate from it. This was clearly no ordinary gift, and no ordinary honey. It still sat in a nest of scattered straw, ribbons and string, and its presence filled the air with a sense of imminence, which must have been growing stronger while it had been left on its own.

Kazharn halted at the door. 'Well...' he said.

At this point, Thazri manifested, clearly also having been waiting for Kazharn to arrive. He looked irritated. 'You're home early,' he said, as if this was a crime.

'Yes... What's all this about?' Kazharn indicated the object on the table.

'I've been waiting to ask you that,' Thazri said.

Ulien thought his hostling was being rather too dramatic about the situation.

'Who left it?' Kazharn asked.

'Meladriel har Seagrass,' Thazri said. 'Who is that?'

Ulien saw the reaction, and Thazri must also have done so, even though Kazharn smothered it swiftly: shock. 'I know the name,' he said without hesitation. 'It's a har who occasionally worked for me.'

'What does this gift mean?' Thazri demanded. 'It means *something*, that's clear.'

It's a jar of honey, Ulien thought, *even if it's a special kind of honey. Why is he so angry?*

'I really don't know,' Kazharn said. 'I'll talk to the houseguards, make enquiries if necessary.'

'Do you have an admirer?' Thazri said spitefully, then rolled his eyes theatrically. 'Oh, stupid me, you have hundreds, of course. I expect you've lost count.'

Kazharn sighed discreetly. He picked up the jar. Would he taste it?

No. He put the jar back on the table, but rubbed the fingers of his hand together, as if they'd been scalded.

At this moment, Ulien felt strongly compelled to tell his father everything that had happened over the past few days, and probably would have done so if Thazri hadn't been there. The moment passed.

'Get ready,' Thazri said. 'Remember we have guests tonight.' Having made his displeasure clear, he now chose to thaw. He touched Kazharn's face with a gilded hand, kissed him on the mouth, an act to establish ownership.

Kazharn smiled uncertainly. He seemed a little disorientated. 'How could I forget? It's why I'm early.'

The guests were the har Alikas, a family from a town further up the coast, who were business colleagues of har Shadolis. They had a son, Hai, a couple of years older than Ulien, who Ulien found tolerable. They shared an interest in nature and could talk about it. Kazharn and Thazri acted as the perfect hosts, a role they had practiced for years. Ihrec sat with the younger hara to keep them entertained and in check – not that Ulien or his companion were the type to cause disruption. Ulien noticed his father seemed preoccupied throughout the meal, although he hid it well. Only a son would be able to tell – or a chesnari. Thazri betrayed no misgivings, nor delivered any speculative glances. He charmed his guests, as always.

After the dessert had been consumed, Kazharn got to his feet. 'Will you excuse me for a while?' he said. 'There's a small task I need to attend to.'

Thazri's smile froze, but only slightly. 'Do be quick, Kaz,' he said. 'I've hired musicians for later, and there will be fireworks in the garden.'

Clearly, the guests needed to be charmed more than usual.

'It won't take long,' Kazharn said.

Within minutes, horses' hooves sounded on the driveway. Ulien had to go to the window to look. This wasn't Gull. In fact, the horse standing outside was harnessed to Kazharn's second best carriage, its roof down. He must've ordered it to be made ready before the meal.

Wondering, Ulien watched his father being carried off swiftly into the night. He wore no coat, no outdoor clothes. Only the robe he'd put on for the occasion, his arms bare.

The evening continued smoothly. Once conversation over the table was concluded – a moment decided by Thazri, who simply rose to his feet – everyhar went outside onto the terrace. Here a wooden table had been placed, surrounded by comfortable wicker chairs. A wheeled serving table stood nearby, laden with wines and spirits produced on the estate. Lanterns of filigree had been hung in the nearby trees, throwing out patterns of light. The musicians had gathered, but Thazri told them they must wait to begin their performance. They had to wait for an hour. But fortunately, the har Alikas were good friends and there was plenty to talk about.

Kazharn eventually came out onto the terrace. He seemed to Ulien to be smouldering, but he smelled of the sea. He brought it with him. Where had he been?

Thazri laughed and said, 'Our guests must think you very rude, Kaz. You've been gone an hour.'

'I apologise,' Kazharn said.

'Not trouble, I hope?' said Navri har Alika.

Kazharn laughed. 'No, a small matter. It's resolved now.'

Thazri narrowed his eyes.

Ihrec of course wanted Ulien to go to bed almost immediately after the guests had left, but Ulien knew he had to overhear what might transpire between his parents once they were alone. He went along with Ihrec's commands, but lingered near the main sitting room, where the party had drunk its final liqueur of the evening, distilled from *Velvets'* own oranges and allspice. Thazri and Kazharn came in from outside, having walked with their friends across the lawns to their carriage.

'Kaz,' Thazri began, 'where did you go earlier? It was to do with the honey, wasn't it?'

Ulien, behind the partly open door couldn't see his father's response, but there was a small silence. Then Kazharn said, 'Yes. It's connected with an old business, Thaz. Nothing to worry about.'

'But what did the gift mean?'

'It was a... signal... a code, that's all.'

'Oh, this Meladriel is one of your secret agents, then.'

Kazharn uttered a short laugh. 'If you like.'

'Strange I've not heard of him before, but of course you keep so many secrets.'

'I've not had dealings with him for years. There's no mystery about it.'

Thazri uttered a sound of disdain. 'So, he can't just come to the house – or even your office in town. He leaves a gift that mystifies everyhar, so it becomes not very secret at all, in fact painfully obvious, then you leave our important guests and go charging off into the night to see him. Is that really nothing to worry about?'

'Meladriel... is somewhat *dramatic*,' Kazharn said. 'The honey is a code for something from the past. He's concerned a troublesome individual might be returning to Ferelithia.'

'Who could cause trouble for you... for us? What kind of trouble?'

'Nothing serious. It would be embarrassing, more than anything.'

'An old lover? A disreputable one?'

'A disreputable old acquaintance,' Kazharn said. 'Don't worry. It's being dealt with.'

'Is he an assassin, your secret agent?'

Again, Kazharn laughed, rather unconvincingly. 'You think my job's much more exciting than it is, Thaz.'

'So, whoever it is will be paid off? Why? Tell me what danger they present?'

'Really, nothing. Please don't think about it. I've seen to the matter.'

'And the honey?'

'Eat it,' Kazharn said. 'It'll be the best.'

At this point, Ihrec appeared and took hold of Ulien by the arm. 'What are you doing?' he hissed in a low voice.

'Listening,' Ulien answered.

Ihrec sighed. 'It's rude to do that.'

Ulien didn't say anything. He let himself be pulled upstairs.

The honey was moved to the kitchen, where it sat upon a shelf. Ulien went every day to taste it and noticed that many others must be doing so too, because the contents of the jar didn't last very long. The staff in the kitchen somehow seemed brighter, more beautiful. They laughed more.

The honey never appeared on the family breakfast table, and as far as Ulien knew neither his father nor his hostling ever tasted it. By the end of the week, the jar was empty.

Chapter Eight

The studio was made of glass, set above the sea, surrounded by dune grasses and palm trees. The sand was perfect, the beach stretching for eternity in a gentle curve. The sea was perfect, glinting in the sunset. The sky – perfect – was a glorious picture of fiery colours, fading to purple and indigo high above, where the first stars began to blaze. No hara walked along the shore of fine white sand. The spot was lonely, yet tranquil, an archetype of beaches. A subtle breeze blew.

A har walked barefoot out of the building of glass onto the wooden deck that surrounded it. He was dressed in a loose white robe that revealed his tanned chest, where a single medallion hung. This ornament too was made of glass and resembled a staring dark-blue eye. Some said he never took it off. His tawny hair was tied into a loose bun at the back of his head. He held a large heavy glass of transparent wine, from which he now drank, thoughtfully.

He was here alone, Amorel har Nohar har Nowhere, and his creativity had been disturbed.

He could only work when isolated from other noisy minds and busy souls. He needed silence, stillness, for his muse to stir itself and sing to him. During these periods of intense creativity, he stoked his inner strengths. At the end of it, he burst like an exploding star into the live performances of his music – in chaotic cities and towns, the night churning with heat and noise. During this time, he endured the presence of others en masse, because it was his life's work to do so. He knew he had no choice. The price of being able to create such wondrous music was to share it.

In the past, he'd written most of the lyrics and music for his band in Ferelithia. He'd played various instruments and had since mastered more. Now, rather than writing of the birth of his kind and their particular obsessions, he wrote in abstracts – colours of the soul, lamenting cries into the universe, but also litanies of hope. Despite the rarefied nature of his work, it was very popular, because he'd always been able to craft a good tune. He knew also how to make hara dance; they were allowed this during certain parts of his performances. As a counterpoise, during other moments of the concerts, his purpose was to make the audience think, to still them, inside and out, render them too stultified even to weep. Then he would lift them again, in soaring, rising chords, and they'd hold up their arms to him.

He was loved. Hara dreamed of touching him. They imagined him as a teacher, a guru, and could also visualise clearly what it would be like to lie naked against his lithe body, caressed by the fall of his hair. He, of course, held himself aloof. And that functioned only to make them love him more.

Precisely three weeks before the annual live tour, his musicians would come to him, like followers to a hienama, and they would learn their parts. He had a week left to be ready for them.

Amorel had great power, most of which he chose not to make use of. He had great riches but was disinterested in acquiring *things*. He enjoyed good food and was particular about his wines. His musical equipment, of course, was the best. His clothes were of the finest fabrics yet without ostentation. But he was not a har to fill his abode with expensive objects. He liked clear space. He didn't even own a horse, never mind a carriage, but had certain supplies delivered to him once a month from the nearest town. He also had an arrangement with a farming family two miles inland, who delivered fresh produce to him once a week – milk, eggs, cheese and various meats and vegetables. A young har who was a son of the farm came to clean his home at the same time, not that Amorel made much mess. He barely impacted upon his living space. Sometimes he took aruna with this son of the farm, who was dark-skinned and dark-eyed and gentle. Afterwards, Amorel might weep – a reaction he carefully concealed.

There was a chesnari, who'd been acquired like a fine instrument fifteen years before. He lived in a grand house two days' travel up the coast. During the concert tours, he and Amorel would meet, undertake the required socialising as a celebrity pair, taste each other again, then part until next year without resentment or yearning. Amorel also had an adult son he rarely saw, who restored old buildings. This son had once sent Amorel the skull of a human child he'd found at a site, in the rubble of a bedroom. The skull had been flawless, polished by time. It held no stories, but Amorel still kept it on a shelf in the living space of his studio. It reminded him how time can exact prices, how nothing is permanent or sacred. Even the innocent can be prey.

Amorel had been innocent once and – he thought – indescribably stupid. He despised the har he'd once been, had no patience or pity for the idiocies of youth. In his opinion, there was no excuse for it at all, just a selective blindness concerning lessons of the past, a supreme arrogance and a misguided sense of self-importance. These commonly held traits among the young allowed atrocities to happen. He knew. He had witnessed them. And part of him, in his isolated castle of glass, surrounded by the understated fruits of his talent and persistence, could not and would not forgive or forget.

When he'd left Ferelithia he intended not only never to return but also to forget about it completely. That song was over, done with. He'd forgotten the words, the music. He knew this because as soon as he'd reached the fair west coast of Megalithica, where he'd willed his new life to start, he'd sung the memories of Ferelithia into a small, ornately carved wooden box, which he'd wrapped in silk and buried among the dunes of another beach, very deep. Singing the past away had been like spiritually vomiting – a purge of sorts. His life was ordered now – neat, arid, *clean*. There was no space in it for unclean dreams and last night he'd been trapped in one.

He'd been back in Ferelithia, young again, full of heat and urges: anger, joy, mania, laughter, growls and lust. He'd been rooning Leupardra, in a dank rotten house, saying, 'Karn mustn't know about this,' and Leupardra laughing, his long fingers tangled in Amorel's hair, his legs wound so tightly around Amorel's back one sudden, strong twist of muscle and bone would break his spine. Leupardra had tasted of blood, of waxen white lilies with their poisonous pollen. He was a primal goddess, his lips bruised and succulent, his soume-lam like boiling honey.

It was just a dream. It hadn't happened. It *had* happened.

'I won't ever let you go,' Leupardra had breathed, while Amorel cried out in ecstasy that felt like pain.

'You will,' he'd said at last, panting upon the body beneath him, which was now cool as the late summer twilight. 'You have too many to keep.'

'Never too many!' Leupardra had laughed then, put his fingers into Amorel's gasping mouth. 'You're mine,' he said, 'all of you.'

Amorel jerked his head away. 'You're a bitch, a witch.'

'Yes, and like all good witch-bitches I'll reward you, you'll see. But that makes you mine.'

Amorel had awoken then, his body still throbbing in the aftershock of aruna, the kind that's like a beating, but a violence he'd craved.

Throughout the day, the vile images stayed with him, an indecent haunting. He felt violated, tainted. Even the sea hadn't been able to purify him. He'd showered, swum, meditated, chanted but all the time felt unsafe, shaken, like at the beginning of illness. He'd not been ill since he'd been har.

'Sweet Aruhani, grant me your blessing,' he prayed into the balmy evening air. 'Take from me this unclean memory. Haven't I worked to escape the past? Haven't I atoned?'

Aruhani did not speak or make his presence felt in any other way.

Amorel drained his wine in a series of long gulps that made his eyes water. He dropped the glass, which didn't shatter but rolled across the wooden decking, coming to rest against the white railings, where it rocked for a moment or two.

You accomplished all this by yourself. You made it. You worked for it.

Of course he did. Of course.

Chapter Nine

On Cala'sday, Seladris went to Veredis's office the moment he arrived at work, curious to discover whether Veredis had experienced uncanny disturbances the night before.

Without preamble, Seladris asked, 'Did you dream anything last night?'

Veredis – to his considerable satisfaction – appeared troubled. 'No. There were no dreams, but... something else happened.'

'What?'

Veredis gestured for Seladris to take a seat. 'Well, I left the painting in the carriage as I didn't want to ask Tika to help me with it...' He sighed. 'No, that's a lie. By the time I got home I simply didn't want it under my roof. I'd had to sit opposite the thing all the way home and didn't like the way it had stared at me.' He laughed. 'See... you influenced me! Anyway, Tika's my oldest friend, more like a brother. We share the house. When we got home, he looked at the painting for some moments, then said, "Are you mad, bringing that in here?"'

'Why did he say that?' Seladris demanded. 'What does he know about it?'

Veredis pulled a face. 'I wondered the same and asked him. All he said was that he felt it was... *unpredictable*. Had bad energy attached to it.'

'Did you tell him what I think about it?'

Veredis wrinkled his nose. 'Not at first. Just said you didn't like it. Admitted *I* didn't like it. And I really didn't by then. So we left it in the carriage and went to our separate beds. I decided I should sell the painting. Somehar might want it.

'Now, a little scene-setting... I like a bare space to sleep in, so there isn't much furniture in my bedroom. A beautiful old floor, though. I have a large mirror in the room. After I got into bed, I was lying awake, thinking about the evening and your... situation. Then, a smell came into the room.' He grimaced. 'It was a smell like rotten flowers and bad breath. Disgusting.'

'How vile,' Seladris encouraged.

'Gets worse. I saw movement in the mirror,' Veredis continued. 'A shape, sort of undulating like smoke, but there was nothing in the room. It was only inside the mirror – hardly more than a shadow, but I felt it was looking at me, and it wasn't friendly at all. Then it was gone. It doesn't sound much, I know, but it really shocked me. It was so real.'

'And you've had nothing... like that... happen before in your house?' Seladris enquired carefully.

'No, never.' Veredis grimaced.' I didn't sleep well after that. Kept waking up and hearing things, but that might have been my imagination. I was spooked.'

Seladris pulled a sour face. 'Maybe. Let me tell you what happened to *me* after you left last night.' He related his own experience.

Afterwards, Veredis shook his head slowly. 'It's like you've prodded a nest of... something,' he said. 'I don't mean to suggest it's *all* down to you but... I told Tika everything at breakfast and he said nothing's happened up at Shadey Lane for years.'

Seladris blinked, spoke more sharply than he generally allowed. 'What does *that* mean exactly?'

'Meaning hara had reported witnessing phenomena up there at one time, but the activity faded away. Until you came. Plerander never experienced anything and, believe me, we'd all have known about it if he had.'

'Could Tika offer any further insight into my situation?' Seladris asked, unable to keep a thin blade of ice from his voice.

Veredis appeared not to notice the tone. 'Well, first he advised we return the painting to its original place, rather than simply get rid of it, and second we should consult one of the early harish settlers, who'll know far more of the history and can perhaps give us more specific advice. I agreed with his suggestions.'

Seladris was silent for a moment, then said, 'Well, thank you, I suppose... for taking this seriously.'

Veredis laughed. 'I could hardly fail to, since I took some of the haunting home with me last night.'

'There's more to it,' Seladris said abruptly. 'I've experienced... other phenomena in the house.'

'Will you tell me about it?'

'OK.' Seladris related all that had occurred since he'd moved in, Veredis expressing surprise and interest as he spoke. At the end of the story, Seladris said thoughtfully, 'It began simply when I washed the sheets. *Are* these phenomena all down to me? I don't know. I'm not scared easily, but it feels as if whatever force is responsible is getting stronger, perhaps heading towards some kind of peak. Then who knows what might happen? I want all this to end before we find out.'

'Understandably,' Veredis said. 'Tika's busy for the next couple of evenings, but I'll keep the painting in our stables until he's free and...'

'I don't want it back in my home,' Seladris said abruptly.

'I understand that,' Veredis said smoothly, 'but Tika thinks it should be returned so we can find out what's going on.' He paused. 'I'll compensate you for your trouble.'

'That's not necessary,' Seladris said stiffly. 'What concerns me is this situation might be dangerous.'

Veredis grimaced. 'Well... what can I say? Nothing's hurt you so far, but...' He shrugged. 'I'll talk to Tika tonight about finding somehar to help you... *us*. I'll make sure we talk to them before the painting goes back. If they think it's dangerous, we'll put it somewhere else.'

Seladris nodded uncertainly. 'OK.' He paused. 'This must be kept... private. I don't want to appear ungrateful, but I'm uncomfortable with involving others.'

'Don't worry,' Veredis said airily. His tone held a note of dismissal.

Seladris left the office.

As he walked to his workroom, Seladris tried to squash the feeling that Veredis was trying to take over the situation and might make him do things he didn't want to do. This whole *haunting*, if that was what it was, could be intensely personal. Seladris didn't want to let anyhar into his life who might cause disruption. It could only do more harm than good.

Seladris found a list of commissions on his desk. It seemed news had spread fast about his prowess. He was relieved he'd be able to immerse himself in work.

That night, Seladris suffered no disturbances in the house. Was whatever had troubled the tranquillity of his home already passing? Had he been over imaginative, too worried? However, he did have a significant dream, albeit not as disturbing as others he'd experienced in the house. He found himself sitting crossed legged before a canvas which was propped against a tree – perhaps a palm tree? – somewhere outside. The location and its details were indistinct. The only clear image was a series of holes in the ground in front of him, which appeared to be full of brightly coloured pigments – sun yellow, sea turquoise, livid green, scarlet red. He plunged his hands into the paints, which were thick and viscous and stuck to his hands like clay. These he smeared over the canvas before him, creating a mess of clashing colours. The action was somehow cathartic. He felt that if he slapped pigment onto the canvas for long enough a picture would emerge and it would tell him something. In the meantime, he would enjoy the simple physical pleasure of applying the paint.

When he awoke, that was all he could remember of the dream.

Aloytsday, 25 Ardourmoon

The following day, Seladris worked until late and drank as usual before going to bed. As he was undressing in his bedroom, he experienced a prickle in his skin and turned round quickly. He saw what at first he thought was somehar lying on the floor in front of his dressing mirror. There was a long, dark *mass*. He was wary of approaching it. Was this real? Drawing in his breath, he drew closer to the shape, and saw it was only a length of fabric bunched up; flimsy dark material, like a veil. The way it lay on the floor had made it appear uncannily like a body. It must be part of one of the costumes he'd bought the other day. A couple of them had included shawls and this one must've fallen from its hanger. He picked it up, let it hang from his hand, wondering how it had found its way across the room from the wardrobe. The material felt *sticky*, rather like a cobweb.

Seladris was filled suddenly with a sense of revulsion. He felt compelled to tear the fabric in two, but it resisted his efforts. So he let it go, and it fell back down exactly into the long shape that looked like a body. It had been so light in his hands, and yet it fell… *heavily*. He knew then this *thing* wasn't right… didn't *belong* in this world. He must get rid of it.

Fighting a wave of nausea, he bent to pick up the fabric. But as he did so it drifted away from him, bunching up like some kind of… *insect*. He was forced to *chase* it round the room. Then, as if tired of the game, it billowed up and threw itself out of the open window. Seladris was right behind it and leaned out to see where it went, but there was nothing outside. Not a wisp of it.

Aruhanisday, 26 Ardourmoon

Two days later, Veredis came to Seladris's workroom mid-morning. 'How busy are you today?' he asked. 'Could you finish early again?'

'Yes.'

'Then we can begin our investigations. Tika's spoken to a friend of his – somehar who might help us – and he can see us today.'

Seladris experienced a slumping sensation within. 'Who is it?'

'A har called Meladriel,' Veredis said. 'He was one of the first settlers here.' He pulled a face. 'Honestly, he's not a favourite har of mine, but… Tika likes unusual hara. Meladriel's an eerie creature but knows his way around the weird.'

'Oh…' Seladris had no idea how to respond to these disclosures, but they did not fill him with hope.

'I'll come and find you when I'm ready to go,' Veredis said. 'Around 3, maybe?'

'OK, thanks… and the painting?'

'Tika will help us replace it after we've seen Meladriel – *if* the har thinks it's safe to do so. We don't need to put it back into your living-room. It can be put in a room you don't use.'

Seladris nodded. 'I appreciate your help.'

Veredis waved a hand at him. 'No problem… Oh, I did check *Inglefey*'s inventory, by the way. I don't know what it means, but there's no mention of that painting. I guess Plerander must've bought it and left it behind. Strange my har didn't make a note of it when he checked the house, though.'

'Have you asked him?'

'Not yet. He's away. I *will* check when he returns. I'm sure he just forgot or else thought as it wasn't my property it wasn't worth mentioning.'

'You really think so?'

Veredis shrugged. 'We'll find out.'

Seladris's mood improved during the ride in Tika's carriage. The roof was furled back, and the seats were comfortable, strewn with thick fleeces. He was relieved to discover he wouldn't have to travel with the blue leopard close to him. The painting had been removed from the carriage. On the horizon, out to sea, lurked the suggestion of rain clouds, but for now the day was warm and dry. As the perfectly sprung vehicle flowed along the road with barely a jolt, Veredis talked the entire time, about work and colleagues, words that Seladris allowed to drift over him without spoiling the pleasure of the journey. It was possible to believe he was merely out for a sociable drive with friends, and not on his way to meet a potential moonwit, who would no doubt be keen to invest his situation with dire meaning and prophecies of doom. Still, it was possible the meeting might be useful.

Around a quarter of a mile out of town, Tika turned the carriage onto a coast road that ran along a low cliff top. Below, in the dunes of the bay, a few sprawling, single-storey houses were set apart from one another, with long gardens that rolled quite steeply down to the beach. Tika turned onto a lane that led to one of these dwellings and once they arrived pulled his horse to a halt.

Seladris followed Veredis out of the carriage. A har with loose, wild hair was walking up the garden to meet them. This individual didn't look conspicuously crazed – as first-generation eccentrics often did – but he appeared wary, perhaps resentful. His clothes were simple, his feet bare. He'd have been classically beautiful, but for his forbidding manner, which soured his expression, pinched his mouth. He stared at Seladris the entire time while Tika made somewhat awkward introductions. The coolness between Meladriel and Veredis was striking, like a curtain of cold rain falling inexplicably from a clear sky.

'Did Tika explain everything?' Veredis demanded.

Meladriel inclined his head slightly. 'He's told me enough, which isn't much. I prefer to listen to your case with an unbiased ear.'

'Believe me, there'll be plenty for you to ponder.' Veredis smiled brightly, and Seladris caught Meladriel exchanging a glance with Tika.

This meeting could not possibly go well. Whatever Seladris said, clearly Meladriel *was* biased against him from the start. The dour har stared once more at him for long, uncomfortable seconds, then nodded curtly and said, 'Come inside. We'll talk.' He gestured at the green side door of the house, which Seladris saw was hung with sea junk: knotted netting, glass balls and the bones of large fish. Typical adornments of the dwellings of the shamanically-inclined.

In a dark, low-ceilinged kitchen, where the single window seemed ridiculously small, Meladriel bade his guests be seated at the table. He took some minutes to make a hot drink, which had a tart herbal flavour, yet was undeniably black tea. He also offered home-made biscuits tasting strongly of lemon yet smoothly sweet, kissed with oil of rose and a hint of salt. As a baker, Seladris could not help but admire their taste, texture and scent.

Meladriel sat down at the head of the table and said to Seladris, 'I don't yet need to hear your story, Tiahaar. I need your first question.'

Seladris knew this was important but had no idea what the best question would be. Rather lamely, he said, 'Do you think phenomena I've experienced in Shadey Lane relate to something that happened there in the past?'

Meladriel poured himself more tea. 'What do you think?'

Seladris replied coolly. 'How can I possibly tell? I'm a newcomer here. What do you know about that place and what might be haunting it?'

'I'll tell you what I know,' Meladriel said. 'But first, you must learn how Ferelith was created.'

'Veredis gave me the history,' Seladris said.

'I'm sure,' Meladriel responded, refilling cups from an enormous earthenware teapot. 'Please, enjoy your tea, eat more biscuits.' He put down the pot. 'This is the tale.' He laced his fingers on the tabletop, leaned forward. 'In the days of the Devastation, the town you know as Ferelithia was coveted by a number of small tribes. They don't exist anymore but eventually came together to create the Ferelith. The early days weren't easy. As you've no doubt heard, the human occupants of the town defended it fiercely. They'd erected fortifications. They had weapons. The local phyle leaders had already formed a coalition in order to secure the town. It was always regarded as a significant and beautiful site and had a special allure to them. Its own magic.' Meladriel paused. 'Do you find the place beautiful, Tiahaar?'

Seladris drew in his breath.

'Do you not think so?' Meladriel murmured.

Seladris shrugged awkwardly. 'Yes, it's a beautiful spot, but that's not really what I'm here to discuss.'

Meladriel was silent for a moment, his eyes hooded. Seladris perceived a gleam within those eyes that made him uneasy.

'You've only just arrived here, yet you're impatient to be gone.' Meladriel laughed somewhat coldly, and Seladris had the impression the har wasn't just speaking about the visit to his home. 'The history is important, Tiahaar. It's what makes a place. Energy is laid down in layers – memory, events, influences. Ferelithia's combination of layers has made it what it is. It empowered the humans who fought to keep hold of it, and the hara who sought to take possession. You must know the history in order to understand the present. Are we in accord over this?'

Seladris found the question quaint. He shrugged again. 'I apologise. Please, say what you must.'

Meladriel gestured languidly with both hands. 'Accord is important here, because discord has a loud voice. Who knows what may hear it?'

Seladris squirmed on his seat, wishing he hadn't come here. This har was performing for an audience and enjoying every minute. How could this absurd display possibly help him? The kindest thing he could think was that Meladriel's routine was designed to ensure his customers got their money's worth. 'Please, continue,' he said.

Meladriel raised his hands gracefully, mimed an action of opposing forces. 'If you can imagine one side of a conflict calling upon powers of the land, then the other side doing the same, you can imagine that the land in effect fights itself. This causes deformities in the inherent energy of a site, and in the expressions of that energy. It may concentrate in certain areas, working with natural formations in the landscape to create vortexes and power spots. This, I believe, is partly behind what you've experienced. Now, if I haven't *bored* you too much, I would like you to tell me, in as much detail as possible, everything that has happened to you in that house.'

Seladris blinked at the shaman, uttered an uncertain laugh. 'I'm here voluntarily, Tiahaar. And I'm uneasy, not bored. Forgive me if I seemed otherwise.' He began to tell his tale, which Meladriel listened to without interrupting. Veredis, however, felt compelled to add detail when he must've considered Seladris's descriptions were lacking. Nohar told him to shut up. Perhaps the extra information, which wasn't incorrect, was helpful. At the end of the story, there was a brief silence.

Then Meladriel said. 'Now you may ask me more questions.'

Without pause, Seladris said, 'How exactly is the Blue Leopard

I've heard about connected with Shadey Lane and the empty plot there?'

'That plot has been uncanny since long before our time,' Meladriel answered. 'Many tried to build on it. Strong energy lurks there, and some humans had the sense to know it, but no house would stand for long. Only a vision of a house, to be inhabited by an individual who could drink the essence of the land. A har named Leupardra considered himself to be this, wanted to be.'

'Who is that?'

For a moment, Meladriel faltered, as if listening to an inner voice. Then he took a breath and continued. 'He was the Pard Witch of the Cerulopard, who danced to summon flame, life – and sometimes death. He tried to live there, and he found the hidden gates to the cellars, the only part of a house ever begun in that place. They had been fastened shut and buried for a reason.'

'I think I dreamed of him,' Seladris said.

'Yes, you did. Called him, didn't you?'

'I'm not aware of calling him, or *anything*. Can you explain to me what you mean?'

Meladriel glanced briefly at Seladris's companions, then fixed him with a stare. 'Do you want me to?'

Seladris felt he was trapped, balanced on a wire above a gulf. He could fall now, so easily, for he guessed that this strange, shamanic har *knew* him, and would say what he knew, connect it to the present and the past. And then Veredis would know, and Tika. Dare he ask them to leave him alone with Meladriel now? But perhaps there was a price for knowing the truth and one of them was candour. Seladris couldn't decide if he wanted to pay that price.

The seconds expanded. Tika shifted uneasily on his seat. Veredis stared at his hands far too intently.

Seladris was tempted to try and communicate in mind-touch with Meladriel but was aware this presumption would not be taken well. He knew this type. They revered clarity. They exposed secrets and expected the costs of fate to be met.

'I did not call upon anything knowingly,' Seladris said carefully. 'But there have been incidents – periods – in my life, which perhaps resonate with the history of Shadey Lane. If you know of these things, I request you honour their privacy and respect my position.'

Meladriel nodded once, his expression stern.

'I'm not first generation,' Seladris continued, 'but I was born to a small phyle that consisted mainly of incepted hara. We lived in an area that was... unsafe, and we paid for the risk we took. My hara were killed but for the three harlings they had, of which I was one.'

'Seladris,' Veredis cut in, 'you don't have to tell us any of this...'

Seladris held Meladriel's gaze. 'I believe I do,' he said, thinking *or he will tell you more.* 'I was the only harling to survive to adulthood. Those who took us were... brutal, cruel. They had no respect for life or for the gifts inception had given them. I was tough, though. Eventually, I escaped, but I had to kill to manage it – become like *them*, I suppose. The legacy of that time has... lingered.'

'You are... what? Forty years old or so?' Meladriel asked.

'Thirty-four.'

'A long time not to clean away the dirt of the past.'

'I don't consider myself dirty.'

'You are,' Meladriel said in an eerily serene voice. 'You carry the dirt with you. You stain others with it.'

'*Please...*' Seladris said, very softly, with the palest flicker of outrage in his breath.

Meladriel closed his eyes for a few seconds. 'Very well. I'll tell you this: you can use this opportunity to heal your hurts or you can simply run away, as you always do. Ghosts have smelled you out, put a hook in you, but it's more than it seems. If you want to end this, you must clean the dirt away.'

'I see. Will you tell me how?'

'Will you pay me?'

'Yes. If that is what it takes.'

Meladriel laughed. 'Oh, far more than that. Shed a skin. *That* will hurt.'

Seladris could tell that both Veredis and Tika were growing increasingly uncomfortable with this conversation, which had ventured into territory none of them had expected. No doubt they wished to leave the house but weren't sure how to escape without interrupting or giving offence. Leaving without words would be worse.

A brief stroke of mind-touch feathered Seladris's thoughts. Of course, it was permitted for Meladriel to take this liberty; he was higher in spiritual rank: *You have blood on you, fairly fresh.*

I did not spill it, Seladris replied.

Bad things happen wherever you go.

Yes. But isn't it also possible that's just the way of the world, coincidence?

Telling yourself that is one way to live with it. Can you wander the world forever?

I'm prepared to face it now, if you can help me understand what it is I'm facing.
You must find that out for yourself.

Aloud, Seladris said, 'What must I do? Am I in danger?'

Meladriel narrowed his eyes and Seladris could not suppress a shiver. 'You're *har*. You can protect yourself – can't you?'

'That's not why I'm here, Tiahaar. I was told *you'd* help me.'

Meladriel got to his feet. He took down from a rough shelf a small earthenware jar, stoppered with aged cork and bound with dried seaweed, which he handed to Seladris. 'This is sea salt,' he said. 'I've spoken over it and commixed it with warding herbs. Use it at your thresholds.'

Seladris turned the jar in his hands. 'Doors and windows? What about the hearths?'

'All places of ingress,' Meladriel said.

'Then what? Should the painting be put back in place as Tika suggested?'

Meladriel glanced at Tika and did not speak for some seconds. 'Replace it, yes. In the exact spot it hung before. You must do this. Be vigilant and keep a record of all that happens.'

'Can't you come to the house?' Veredis asked. 'Surely you'd have more idea of what's going on if you did so?'

'Not yet,' Meladriel replied, keeping his attention on Seladris. 'If the Pale Ones appear at night, don't go outside. Don't let them become aware of you. If they do, they'll be harder to shift than anything else out there. And that's not something I'd want to help you with.'

'What are they?' Seladris asked.

'Very old entities, bodiless energy moulded into a shape.'

'Human?'

'This phenomenon is older than humankind.'

'What has this to do with the blue leopard?'

'Energy is drawn to energy of similar nature. Disregard the Pale Ones for now. Focus upon your own purification. Put the salt in the water when you bathe, no more than a pinch. Place wreaths of blackberry bramble on your doors, front and back. Burn an incense of benzoin, anise and basil and carry this through all the rooms so the smoke may linger there. Put betony beneath your pillow to seal your dreams...'

'Can you supply these materials?' Seladris asked.

Meladriel shook his head. 'They are easy to purchase elsewhere.'

'Don't worry about that,' Veredis said, placing a hand briefly on Seladris's shoulder.

'The salt will cost you a week's wage, Tiahaar,' Meladriel said. 'I assure you of its potency.'

Seladris blinked wordlessly at the cost.

'*I'll* pay it,' Veredis said.

'No,' Meladriel said, without moving his gaze from Seladris. '*He* will.'

Seladris nodded. 'As you say.'

'For three days, you must take the precautions I've described. Then return to me and report. I must have the payment at this time too.'

'The week's wage will cover the second consultation too?' Seladris asked stiffly.

'Yes,' Meladriel said. He stood up, bowed his head. 'That is all for today, Tiahaara.'

Rather awkwardly, Veredis and Seladris got to their feet and went to the door. 'Thank you,' Seladris said.

Tika was last to rise. Standing at the threshold, looking back, Seladris saw Tika clasp Meladriel's shoulder before he came outside. Meladriel remained standing, his back to them, the door left open.

'Did that go well or not?' Veredis asked dryly as they reached the carriage.

'Just get in,' Tika said. He sounded tired. 'Let's go.'

'Head to the market,' Veredis said, climbing into the carriage. 'We need to get Seladris's special provisions.'

Meladriel kept his back turned until he was sure his visitors had left his property. He felt light-headed, almost dizzy, which he'd managed to conceal from them. That har, Seladris… Was it possible he'd initiated the return? He was a vortex himself.

Meladriel sat at the kitchen table and munched on what remained of the biscuits, barely tasting them. When Tika had told him earlier a little of what to expect, without revealing the details, he'd imagined Seladris would be a sensitive har who'd somehow picked up on memories of the past that had been stirred up. The unstorm could have been the cause rather than the effect. Meladriel hadn't considered the house, *Inglefey*, to be significant, and hadn't known about the painting that hung there. Did anyhar? As far as he knew the Cerulopard had dwelled in the forest beyond the town, not in houses. He was aware of the empty plot, of course, as the Cerulopard had considered it a sacred site. Leupardra had worked dark magic there, but it had since been sealed, rendered inactive.

The fact iron skinned Veredis had also experienced something, perhaps only because he'd taken the painting home, was remarkable, but also unsettling.

These events confirmed what Meladriel had suspected. He would have to report to Kazharn. The thought of that sent a sizzling twinge up his spine. This was not wholly unpleasant. Meladriel chastised himself and straightened his thoughts. Was Seladris the assistance that the spirit he'd conjured in the sea-fire had alluded to? That couldn't be so – the har was a mess. Too scattered to be of use, not in command of his abilities, or aware of their extent.

Still, Meladriel could not ignore a sign, so he'd help the har sort himself out. In his current state, Seladris was too weak to be of use, but perhaps he could be an asset once his demons were purged. Meladriel would not yet visit the house, nor view the painting. His presence might open wider the crack between the past and present. Seladris was ignorant of history's truths and that might be helpful. His observations would be unbiased, even if his own history deadened his soul. It hadn't damped his inner sight, so that could still be used.

What he'd heard that day explained the peculiar feelings he'd experienced in the stables at Veredis's house. The painting had been watching him.

Gripped by what felt like a twisted knot of reluctance and anticipation, Meladriel walked into town. The hour wasn't late, so he might be able to pass a message to Kazharn at the Municipallion; it would still be open.

Ferelithia, in its bright summer gown, its heart full of joy, now seemed tasselled with shadows. There was blood beneath the streets and heartless presences in the darkest corners. Flickering across the scene around him, Meladriel saw Leupardra with his tribe, parading through the streets, clad in the finery of their flesh, adorned with the jewels of hair and eyes and lips like hungering, carnivorous flowers. Leupardra, the har without limits or restraint. He'd believed himself immortal, that he could act as he pleased without consequence, sure in the knowledge that those with the most power were enthralled by him, by what he could do.

Shadows lay long across the central plaza of the town. An ache stirred behind Meladriel's eyes. He felt momentarily dizzy. The shimmering outline of the Municipallion seemed to lean to one side precariously.

Within the building, cool dimness soothed his senses. Voices murmured in a low insect hum. The har on duty at the desk was the same one as the last time Meladriel had been here. Recognition was instant; a moment of alarm smothered by a welcoming smile. 'May I help you, Tiahaar?'

Wordlessly, Meladriel held out the wafer Kazharn had sent to him, which the receptionist inspected. Containing his reaction, the receptionist sweetened his smile and rose to his feet. 'One moment please, Tiahaar.' As before, he passed through a door behind the desk.

Meladriel exhaled through his nose, only then aware he'd been holding his breath. The very idea of Kazharn, or rather his current position and power, made Meladriel feel awkward. He knew this was a sense of inadequacy, a feeling he scorned, because it was unwarranted. Old scars, apparently, still throbbed. He should work on that.

After only a few minutes, the receptionist reappeared. He inclined his head slightly. 'Would you come with me, Tiahaar?'

Meladriel nodded, forcefully suppressing a vein of anger that was expanding within.

He followed the receptionist across the hall and into a corridor. From here, it seemed he was guided through a mythological maze, up stairs and along passages, at the centre of which would be a sacred entity, perhaps benign, perhaps deadly. Ultimately, he was disgorged into an antechamber of the Municiphar's office. Here a high-ranking minion held court, a faintly green-skinned Colurastean, his hair bound up in coils. The main hall receptionist delivered his cargo to this imperious har and departed. The Colurastean scanned Meladriel with an excoriating gaze for some moments, then lisped, 'Follow me, please.'

Meladriel was conducted through tall, narrow double doors to the inner sanctum of Kazharn's temple.

This was no dark chamber, seething with incense smoke and the dull glow of coals, but a wide, airy room, overlooking the harbour. Here, Kazharn har Shadolis stood beside his desk.

'Thank you, Urmeen,' he said to his assistant, 'please bring us refreshment.'

The Colurastean slithered out.

'So…?' Kazharn indicated Meladriel take a seat beside a fireplace across the room, where a display of dune grasses and wildflowers burst from the summer-cold grate. He sat opposite his visitor. A low table stood between them, empty and polished.

'I met with the har,' Meladriel said. 'I'll tell you all he said.' He kept the tale brief and to the point.

Kazharn listened patiently, then put one hand against his mouth in thought.

Meladriel waited. During this time, Kazharn's assistant returned with a tray containing a jug of purple cordial diluted with sparkling spring water, two glasses and a plate of pastries. When he departed, Kazharn poured two portions of the cordial, set one before Meladriel on the table between them.

'In your opinion,' he said, 'is this har you've met connecting with historical energies?'

'My opinion is biased, as yours will be too,' Meladriel replied. He took up the glass, tasted the drink: damson and allspice, piquantly blended. 'My fear is that he is, but that might only be fear. He's a damaged har, vulnerable, his energetic defences inadequate. Lingering echoes in the vicinity might have affected him, even adhered to him. Whether this heralds a greater threat I don't yet know. But…' He paused, reluctant to reveal what his small ritual had revealed.

'But?' Kazharn asked silkily.

Meladriel looked at him directly. 'What are we afraid of exactly? Leupardra's return, in some form or another? The rise of old, unhealthy forces? Tainted echoes? What? If any of this is real, how will it affect Ferelithia, its inhabitants, if at all? Perhaps only you and I, and maybe a few others, can even sense these forces. Our concerns are nebulous to say the least.'

'We never knew what the legacy would be,' Kazharn said stiffly, 'only that there might be one. We took this town by force, unnatural force. All of us that day – in whatever capacity we lent our strength – were asked to remain vigilant as long as we remained in this town.'

'Yes, and all the others who took part have gone. Nohar else is left but you and me. Isn't that in itself unnatural?'

Kazharn laughed harshly. 'Perhaps we are the unnatural ones in staying here.'

'I disagree.'

Kazharn sighed wearily. 'I didn't really mean that. It's not something either of us want, but on that day, we made a pledge. We didn't know what we might one day have to defend against, but we were prepared to meet it, if necessary. Others didn't honour it, of course. They left the town, but we remained. We can only assume we were meant to. Now, Ferelithia has developed into a highly attractive yet somewhat naïve town. Its egregore would be susceptible to stronger influences, which could cause all kinds of trouble.' His voice became firmer. 'We've become complacent. We should have trained hara up to share our duty, kept them vigilant.'

'*We*?' Meladriel snapped. 'You were privileged to know more than me.'

'*I* should have, then,' Kazharn responded. 'Or perhaps... our estrangement was unwise. We are this town's – this tribe's – guardians, whatever has passed between us. Is that too late to mend?'

'Yes,' Meladriel said, 'but that doesn't mean we can't work together to deal with a common problem.'

Kazharn nodded, somewhat vaguely, his thoughts clearly partly elsewhere. He drew in a breath. 'I suggest you visit the site, Mela. Send me word if you think it's necessary I do so as well.'

'I *will* view the site, but I want to see what happens with our unwitting volunteer first. Allow a few days. I'll monitor him closely, but he won't be aware of that.'

Kazharn raised his brows. 'You're sure he's not in danger?'

'No,' Meladriel answered bluntly, 'but such things never bothered us in the past.'

'That is hardly a recommendation to repeat the process,' Kazharn said dryly.

'It's what we always did, isn't it? Fan the flames, observe. It was our education, Karn.'

Kazharn nodded, his expression thoughtful. 'Indeed. Well... I hope our fears are groundless, but at the very least you'll have to contain this har. If he's agitating an old nest, he needs curbing.' He pulled a wry face. 'Which might be no more complicated than persuading Veredis har Mith to move the har somewhere else.'

'That would be the best outcome,' Meladriel said. 'Let's hope it's realistic.'

Chapter Ten

Seladris sat in the carriage with the jar on his lap. Tika had erected the roof of the vehicle, because rain had come in from the sea, but perhaps also to give his passengers privacy. For some minutes there was silence in the dim, enclosed atmosphere; the sounds of the horse's hooves outside seemed to come from another world.

Veredis stared at his companion, fidgeting like an excitable puppy, at last unable to stop himself saying, 'Please talk about it, Seladris.'

'No.' Seladris softened the refusal with a smile. 'You heard everything back there. I'd rather my past was kept private. It's not who I am now.'

'But maybe it would help…'

'Really… no.'

'I'll come over again tonight. We'll face this together.'

'No…' Seladris frowned. 'Or rather… *why*? Is this entertainment for you?'

Veredis exhaled impatiently through his nose. 'I guess I'm supposed to be insulted by that and say "pelk you!" or something. Throw you out onto the road. Won't work. I'm coming over. No argument. Show me a har who's a saint and I'll show you a har who's probably got something wrong with them. For Aru's sake, Seladris, let's get this done, get to the bottom of it. It's my property, remember, and I'd rather find out what's going on. I promise to keep in confidence anything I learn about you.'

Seladris raised his brows. 'Like all the hara you gossiped about when you came to dinner with me?'

Veredis rolled his eyes. 'That was different. You think I can't tell the difference? I know I'd pay for it if I betrayed your confidence over this. I'm a superstitious har at heart and believe in consequences. Also, Meladriel terrifies me. I'd never want to invoke *his* disapproval.'

'All right, then,' Seladris said. He sighed. 'All right.'

After a brief visit to the market in town, where Veredis purchased the items Meladriel had listed, Tika drove home so they could pick up the painting of the blue leopard, which was then ferried to *Inglefey*. Seladris was far from happy about this but had to trust Meladriel knew what he was doing. On the journey from Veredis's house, the painting was propped against a seat, its face hidden. Once they reached *Inglefey*, all three of them carried the blue leopard back into the sitting-room. Regardless of danger to his hands, Tika assisted to place the picture back on the wall. He seemed to be a har of few words, but Seladris found his presence soothing, reassuring. He was like a muscle of strong energy. 'Will you stay?' he asked.

Tika glanced briefly at Veredis, then said, 'This is *your* business, Seladris.'

'If Tika stays, it'll be too easy,' Veredis said in an airy tone. 'Also, I wonder if the apparitions would even dare to appear.' He patted Tika's shoulder. 'Go home. I'll stay to offer support. If I need you, I'll send a shriek into the ethers, I promise.'

Tika made no further comment and left the house.

Seladris and Veredis stood before the picture in silence for some moments. In the afternoon light, it appeared innocent enough. The house was quiet, calm, filled with honeyed light and the scent of flowers.

Seladris said, 'I hope you're right to let Tika leave. I'm not sure about this. Meladriel's instructions were vague to say the least.'

'Time to trust your instincts,' Veredis said. 'You know, those super-honed ones we're supposed to have?'

Seladris smiled grimly. 'I don't think either of us are super-hara, Veredis.'

Veredis linked arms with him. 'Ved,' he said. 'It's what my friends call me.'

'And to my friends, I am Dris,' Seladris said.

Before anything else, Seladris attended to the instructions Meladriel had given him, using the items Veredis had purchased. Veredis waited for him in the western sitting-room, beneath the gaze of the leopard.

His task complete, Seladris then prepared a tray of food they could pick at, which also held a large stoppered jug of wine.

'We mustn't get drunk,' Veredis said, pouring them both a glass.

'Slight drunkenness might help,' Seladris replied.

They clinked glasses, sitting side by side on the sofa, staring at the leopard.

The sun lowered itself into the sea until it hung like a half-shut eye, leaking crimson tears of light.

'We take so much for granted,' Veredis murmured into a comfortable silence between them. The wine jug now was empty. 'Like you, I'm second generation, and I can't really imagine what it was like in the beginning, the violence of it all, the catharsis. No wonder there are ghosts left behind.'

Seladris paused before answering. 'I don't have to imagine it,' he said. 'I *know* it. But maybe it was inevitable, the bloodiest of births, struggling out of darkness.'

Veredis nodded. 'Perhaps.' He was sitting sideways on the sofa now, leaning against the arm, his brown narrow feet up on the cushions, his wine glass cupped in both hands. He extended a foot and nudged Seladris's arm. 'You can trust me, you know. I'm not quite the idiot I choose to appear.'

Seladris laughed softly. 'I can see that, and quite early on in our friendship too! I imagine that's an honour.' He squeezed Veredis's foot. 'We all have our armour, Ved.'

'So?'

'So, what?'

'What happened to make you come to Ferelithia?'

Seladris stared at Veredis for some moments. 'You're quite relentless, aren't you?'

'I'm thinking that maybe we should begin to invoke… whatever it is in this place. Connect with it. And I believe the past is our best invocation.'

Seladris sighed through his nose, closed his eyes briefly. 'OK. I came here because it was time to… re-emerge, and whenever I have to do that, the opportunity is there for me. *Confitteri* was my opportunity.'

'Re-emerge from what?' Veredis asked carefully.

'Calamity,' Seladris replied. 'Bad things tend to happen around me regularly and for a time I have to gather my strengths again, hide, I suppose. Margenya – the last big town I worked in – was the worst, though.'

'Why?'

There was a silence for some moments, then Seladris said. 'The hara I lived and worked with there all died. They died around me.'

'How?' Veredis's voice was now a whisper.

'I was the chef in an expensive and popular inn. There was an explosion. My world went black and when I could see again, I was surrounded by the pieces of everyhar I knew.'

'An *explosion*? How did it happen?'

Seladris sighed deeply. 'Nohar knew. There was talk of an oven malfunctioning, of gas underground, an unexploded device from the old wars, a deliberate attack… Nothing was ever proved. Not even the psychic investigations turned much up. To everyhar in the immediate area, the world went black. None standing close to me survived and whatever caused it didn't leave a trace. But…' He glanced at Veredis. '*I* knew. Whatever follows me will never let me rest or be content. It's old, and it's resentful.'

'Were you hurt at all?'

'Cuts, some quite deep, a few burns, a ringing brain… Disorientation.' Seladris frowned. 'It was weird. My clothes weren't burned at all… just…' He screwed up his face, shook his head. 'Took a month to recover but, considering where I'd been standing, I should be dead.'

'Hmm,' Veredis murmured. 'Am I risking my life by even knowing you?'

Seladris grimaced, took a swig of wine.

'So everyhar you befriend dies?' Veredis persisted.

Seladris shook his head. 'No, no… I don't mean it to sound like that. Bad things just tend to happen around me – disruption, accidents, conflicts and so on. Sometimes it's more serious and hara have been hurt.'

'That's… bad,' Veredis said awkwardly.

Seladris nodded. 'That's one way of putting it. I've learned how to control the phenomenon to a degree, by keeping my distance from hara. For years, things had been fine. But what happened in Margenya simply proved to me I'm ultimately powerless.'

Veredis wrinkled his nose. 'You know, it *could* just have been coincidence – all of it. Everyhar has bad experiences, or bad luck.'

Seladris grimaced. 'I wish I could believe that. Meladriel said otherwise – in mind touch.'

Veredis rolled his eyes. 'Well, he's Tiahaar Doom, isn't he? Likes to make pronouncements of horror. I don't think we should simply believe you're a walking curse. Colluding in that belief merely helps make it real.'

Seladris stared at the har he now realised was becoming a friend. Was this dangerous? Would everything be taken from him again? Dare he believe that at last he could be cleansed of this curse and live like a normal har? He held onto Veredis's foot, felt the prick of tears in his eyes.

Then the house shivered.

Veredis jumped to his feet, while Seladris put his glass down slowly on the table before them.

A series of shuddering creaks sounded, like those made by expanding wood, yet coming from a distance, as if through a gate between the worlds.

Seladris stood up, took Veredis's arm and led him to the window. The sun was merely a sulky nimbus on the horizon, but the stars and a half moon were bright. Seladris wrapped them both in one of the diaphanous curtains, not sure why he did so.

Out in the hall, the front door opened slowly with a screeching whine, then banged against the wall with a crash. There was silence for a moment.

Then, a faint sound of shuffling, and a hum like bees, or almost like bees, as if a multitude of voices whispered together, heard from a long way away.

Veredis and Seladris clung to each other, their backs pressed against the window. Seladris held his breath, afraid even of making the slightest noise.

Shadows spilled through the open doorway of the room, stretched long across the floor.

Seladris knew the shadows must not touch them.

Following these insubstantial inky blots, the figures came. In the confines of the house, they seemed to pour into the room for ever, but Seladris could tell there were no more than he'd seen in the road the previous night. They rustled and buzzed, mimicking the sounds heard in dark woodlands at dusk. They clicked, like tiny bones breaking. Close to, they were freakishly tall, with small heads, their faces almost devoid of features, the eyes mere black holes, the mouths black slits. They didn't appear to be aware of the living hara in the room, simply groped in front of themselves as if blind, feeling their way. Their hands were grotesquely long and spindly, like sea-bleached sticks. They moved towards the fireplace, filling the room, bringing with them a smell, not of death or rot, but dampened fires, old wood, shuttered rooms.

In front of the painting, they reached out eagerly, touched it with their spiky fingers. Then, they *pushed*. The painting sank into the wall, plaster folding over it as if wet. And the figures followed after.

For some moments, Veredis and Seladris did not move. Veredis had buried his face in Seladris's hair, the curve of his neck. He was panting, as if he'd been running. Then he whispered, 'Is it over?'

'Well, they've gone,' Seladris murmured.

'What happened? I couldn't look.'

'They went into the wall.' Seladris let go of Veredis and approached the hearth. The painting hung as before, untouched.

Veredis followed cautiously, rubbing his arms. 'Are we meant to try and follow? Is that what Meladriel meant by them leading us?'

Seladris shook his head. 'No, I don't think it's that. Remember what else he said. The cellars of a house. Last night, those things went into a light that was like a door. That's where we'll look.' He paused. 'You can wait here if you'd prefer.'

Veredis grimaced. 'No. I'll see this through. If I back out now, it'd break the spell.' He rubbed his fingers over his face, took in a deep breath. 'I mean the *luck*, the timing… everything happening in order.'

They went out to the plot next door. The night was undisturbed as it had been the day before, but a thin, chill wind came down from the hills, smelling of earth, eclipsing the aromas of the sea. Seladris had fetched a lantern from the kitchen. Its saffron beams spilled over the empty plot, revealing nothing but scattering shadows.

Seladris found a long stick and handed the lantern to Veredis. 'Light the ground for me,' he said, and began to beat at the longer grasses and weeds beyond the cropped lawn.

'The lights appeared about here,' he said. 'I'm sure of it.'

Veredis held the lantern high. 'There,' he said. 'A stone. Where you were clearing a moment ago.'

There was no cairn, no great slab, merely a single rock, maybe five inches high, standing up from the earth.

'Hara would have seen this when they searched for the Cerulopard,' Seladris said. 'Surely?'

Veredis shrugged. 'Dig around it. Let's see.'

Seladris put down the stick and clawed at the soil and roots at the base of the stone. He tugged at it. 'Goes deep,' he said.

Veredis squatted beside him and put down the lantern. Together they tore at the earth. After some moments, Seladris rested his hands on his knees. 'We need more than our fingers to clear this. Would you go to the kitchen, Ved, and bring gardening tools? There are some in the cupboard near the back door.' He smiled. 'I don't want to leave you out here on your own.'

Veredis rolled his eyes. 'Thoughtful of you.'

Left alone, Seladris crouched beside the stone. From what he could see there were no markings upon it, and yet it appeared to have been planted deliberately. When he touched it, he felt nothing, but perhaps a dozen old hexes masked its purpose, sealed its magic.

Veredis returned with a garden fork and a spade. He'd also had the foresight to bring another lantern.

They dug for over an hour, until Seladris's spade hit stone or metal. The buried rock was revealed to be a carved pole, and they'd still not reached its root. But they had found *something*.

The hole they'd excavated was six feet deep, like a grave but far wider, and hadn't been that difficult to dig with the appropriate tools. Beneath their feet, still partially buried, was what appeared to be a pair of horizontal doors, like those of a storm cellar, but fashioned of pocked iron not wood. The handles were bound with chains and a huge padlock, wound with strings of bones and leather, and plaits of disintegrating fabric. The stone pole pierced the metal above the handles, as if – impossibly – it had been shot into it. *Something* had certainly been bound in this spot.

'Must we open it?' Veredis asked.

It was a rhetorical question, voiced merely, Seladris thought, to indicate that Veredis really didn't want to see what lay behind the iron.

'I think it might be unwise,' he said. 'Something was clearly imprisoned here, whatever it was. Your friend Meladriel should be told of this.'

'Not *my* friend,' Veredis said. 'Think you're right, though. This place has been sealed for a reason.'

'Yes, let's not risk releasing whatever might be in there.' Seladris managed to smile. 'I think we should cover it again.'

'Agree.'

Silently they replaced the earth.

'I think you should come back to my place tonight,' Veredis said as they stood over the closed hole.

'OK,' Seladris said simply. He could find no reason to argue.

Ferelithia

Ferelithia writhes and whines.

As hara sleep, they find strange dreams waiting in the darkness. They wake up, panting in their beds, not even remembering what dire images shook them to wakefulness.

They might climb from their nests of quilts, go to their windows, stare out over the town. Everything looks the same. The air is warm, perfumed with night-blooming flowers. The sea glistens, shifting only gently in its own deep sleep.

What is wrong?

And there is something wrong, isn't there?

In the distance some hear what sounds like a crack of thunder, but is it perhaps instead the sound of something breaking, the groan of a giant bone under such pressure it eventually snaps?

Some hara are more sensitive than others. Only a few hear the unaccountable noises that echo over the sleeping town. What are these sounds? Voices? Are they chanting or singing? Laughter or the cackle of carrion eaters? Or are they not voices at all?

Then, undeniably, a single voice rings out in the darkness. It seems to come from high up, the forests behind the town. It is ineffably beautiful, and the throat from which it pours must belong to a creature too lovely to behold. The song holds within it every emotion known to harakind. Anyhar who hears it must weep, even though the song is a summons to war.

Chapter Eleven

There was a place in the garden of *Velvets* where few ever went; a small, dark grotto, where a spring of fresh water issued from the rock. To Ulien, it was one of the most beautiful spots on the estate – but even he didn't go there every day. It was a place of significance, accessible only in times of meaning. He did not fear it but respected it.

Ulien had been told, when he'd asked his tutors about it, that long ago, in the Human Era, the grotto had most likely had a religious function. Water springing from rock; two elements combined. There were aspects that suggested that, while the grotto hadn't been entirely fabricated, some of it had certainly been embellished and shaped over the millennia. A small, open-roofed cave, which had a natural ceiling of spreading ferns and shrubs growing abundantly from the lip of the rock, the grotto was cut into the lower slope of a hillside, approached by shallow winding steps between thickets of juniper. Above, at the top of the hill, a council of stately cedars stood in a misshapen ring.

Within the grotto, where the walls were damp and greened with moss and ferns, water ran down in several places into a stone trough that circled the chamber. Opposite the entrance, a crude lion's head cut from the rock dribbled into a semi-circular pool. From here, the water sank underground once more, to emerge as an ocean-bound stream near the town. There was no doubt in Ulien's mind that this place was so sacred you could not go there all the time or just when you felt like it. Today, he climbed the hill.

He took an offering of flowers to whatever might be present in the shrine, even though he felt the site had no permanent guardian. Entities visited it, perhaps, or could be called there. The raw elements themselves guarded and protected the site.

As he entered the cave, he was aware at once the atmosphere felt different. This put him on edge. He knew he was not alone, and whatever was in there with him wasn't a spirit entity.

First came a cough, and a faint rustle of movement. The shadows were deep that day; Ulien could see nothing in the light that slanted in from outside.

'Who's there?' he demanded.

He saw a brief glint of sharp light, heard a shuddering sigh.

'Little one,' said a voice.

Ulien knew immediately this voice belonged to the strange har who he'd come across twice before. He had no choice now but to accept he was being stalked, watched. This har was mad, perhaps dangerous. He had a purpose. *Run!* a sensible part of Ulien's mind insisted. But he didn't.

'What are you doing here?' he said haughtily, in the voice of his hostling.

Something moved sinuously out of the shadows, like a snake on its belly. Ulien stepped back, then took another step, reversing towards the light.

'Don't be afraid. I'm recovering, that's all. Wait. Let me show you.'

The shape on the floor unfolded, stood up, and yes, there stood the har Ulien had met before. 'They came here, you know,' he said, 'to pray to the old gods and goddesses, hoping they could be saved. But *we* were about to happen to them, and the gods turned away their eyes.'

Ulien said nothing. He could just turn round and walk away, tell Ihrec about this, and then it would be ended. He should have spoken about it after the first meeting in the garden. *Why didn't you?*

'You think ill of me because I speak the truth?' said the har.

'I don't know your truth,' Ulien said, 'you shouldn't be here. You must go. Leave me alone.'

The har laughed. 'Ah, the most ineffective words in language: "leave me alone." How many, do you think, who say those words, really *do* get left alone?'

A small but potent hot flame coursed through Ulien's veins. 'All right!' he snapped. 'What is it you want with me?'

'Just for you to know the truth,' the har answered, 'because one day the town will honour you as they honour your father. Don't you want to know?'

'What truth?'

'The past. What else?' The har sighed, walked languidly around the grotto, running his fingers over the damp walls. 'When Kazharn was Karn and put his hands into the fire.'

'I'll tell him about this.'

100

The har laughed. 'Oh, please do!'

'Then give me your name.'

'It won't mean anything.'

'I think it will. Seagrass, is it?'

Again, a hard laugh. 'That? No. It isn't even real. I am not him.'

'I order you to go. You're trespassing here. You're not to come back.'

The har snickered meanly. 'Ah, the little cub of the great tiger bristles his whiskers, wrinkles his cute little nose in a snarl. It's not me who should go, but you.'

'Me? This property belongs to my family. *You* are the intruder.'

'This property is stolen goods, but that's beside the point. What I meant was you need to go outside your sanctuary into the world.'

'I *do*, not that it's any of your business.'

'With your friends, who you play with every day? On your way to school in the town?'

Ulien could not immediately think of a reply to this.

The har put a finger to his lips, gazed upwards as if in thought. 'Ah yes, of course, you're actually a prisoner here, aren't you? A prisoner kept in ignorance of his own heritage.'

Ulien took a breath. 'Why do you care that I should know *the truth*, as you call it. This isn't for my benefit, my family's or this town's. It's for you. Tell me the *truth* of that.'

'They will never tell you if they can help it,' the har said. 'And only very few remember it now. I think you should know, because some things shouldn't remain buried. And if you're aware of it, you'll be the first honest and aware leader this town ever had.'

'There is no leader, only the Municipallion.'

'Of course,' said the har in a sardonic tone. He smiled.

'And why do you care about all this? Who *are* you?'

The har shrugged, smiled privately. 'Do you want to go outside, Ulien? Into the town without your hostling? Into the countryside where even the air tells tales. I can take you there.'

A shiver trickled through Ulien's flesh, a frisson of excitement. He tried to shout it down. 'Are you mad? You've given me no reason to trust you.'

'And yet you haven't run off. You're still here, talking to me.'

Ulien uttered a sound of annoyance and turned to walk away. *I must make him see he does not control me!* He took a step towards the light, but a hand closed on his left shoulder. 'Oh… not yet.'

Ulien swung round, ready to strike out, but the har was some distance away from him, near the pool. Had he just stretched out his arm unnaturally, or moved extremely swiftly, or not touched him at all?

'You may call me Tuli,' said the har, pressing one hand to his breast. 'I'm not your enemy, Ulien har Shadolis. If I am anything to you, now or in the future, it is as a teacher.' The har drew closer, taking strange limping steps. He put his hands upon Ulien's shoulders, gazed into his eyes. His own eyes were lambent, and it was difficult to discern their colour. Blue, green, grey? He exhaled over Ulien's face and his breath was soothing, perhaps intoxicating, yet it smelled of empty rooms, dried ancient flowers. 'Let me show you,' he said. 'I promise that nohar will realise you've slipped out. You'll be back before you know it, but this time with knowledge.'

'Where will you take me?'

'It's a surprise.'

They walked out through the gates of the estate, and the guards never even looked in their direction. Ulien felt strange in his skin, as if he was fading away. Being invisible in the world wasn't wholly pleasant, even if it was intriguing.

'Look at them,' Tuli murmured, 'a squandering of potential. As guards, they should be able to sense us, *see* us. They are useless for their purpose.'

Ulien couldn't dispute this opinion.

Time seemed inconstant. It should have taken about twenty minutes to walk to the outskirts of the town, but they arrived within minutes, or in no time at all. This was like being in a dream, but awake. Ulien wondered whether he was in fact safe yet couldn't find fear within himself. It seemed almost preordained that he should survey the town in this way. What he saw was its shivering.

Ferelithia cowered. If it had eyes, they would be darting this way and that, alert for threat. The buildings appeared weirdly pinched, as if they'd drawn up their limbs like a spider feigning death. If they were very quiet, very still, what was out there might not notice them. And what did stalk the town, circling its perimeter? This was only a thought, but Tuli answered it aloud: 'What makes you think it's outside the town?'

'What is it?'

'A combination of elements. A return. A memory.'

'That means nothing to me. Speak plainly.'

'Like I said, I will show you, but not all at once. That would be too much. Come...' Tuli took hold of one of Ulien's hands.

At once, the air flexed and shimmered, and then Ulien was staggering into a new scene. He was on a hill road, with large houses to either side. His attention was drawn to one particular house, which had a large empty space next to it, as if another house should be there but was not. The white and blood pink house standing beside it flared in the morning light. It was very much alive and looked like a dwelling from a fairy-tale; a confection. Its chimneys were spirals of candy, its walls slabs of marzipan and sugar icing, its windows a glaze of sugar. It seemed to ooze a smell of vanilla and butter. In this way, it looked like a trap for the unwary.

Tuli stood upright in the road, his arms crossed. 'Go into that house,' he said.

Ulien's head was still swimming from the shift. 'There might be hara in it.'

'You'll be quite safe,' Tuli said. He gestured with one hand abruptly 'Believe me, there's nohar home. The back door is open. Go look around.'

'You're not coming?'

Tuli shook his head. 'Look on this as... an educational exercise. Go in there, then tell me what you felt. If you find my heart, bring it to me.'

'What?!'

'Just go.'

Ulien went around the back of the house and as Tuli had predicted the door there was unlocked.

He stole inside and was aware the house turned its attention towards him, as if it were sniffing him. It did not, however, feel hostile or threatening. This was a powerful house. It knew things. Ulien went through the laundry room and into the kitchen. Here, in the stillness, he was compelled to bow and say, 'I ask for your permission to walk your rooms.'

There was no obvious response, but after a moment Ulien became aware of a soft sound, like purring. He assumed it was acceptable for him to continue. He went into the hallway, where there was an empty frame upon the wall above a table. He felt a mirror had once hung there but had been broken. Flickering shadows moved round him, and eventually he understood they were images of the same individual, perhaps somehar who lived in the house. Even though Ulien remained standing in the hallway, he sensed this figure shimmering throughout the building. The occupant, who was clearly not at home in person, walked from room to room, engaged in the activities of life: cooking, eating, cleaning, sitting down to read, lying in bed with open eyes. Ulien received no clear image of this har, as his outline was blurry and indistinct, but he felt strangely familiar. *Why are you important?* Ulien wondered. As he thought this, the house shuddered as if shaken by an earthquake. He was no longer welcome. He ran for the back door.

Outside, he found Tuli sitting on the lawn, his head thrown back so his face could soak the sun.

'That house is haunted,' Ulien said. 'Is that what you wanted to know?'

'I already knew. What did you find?'

'Nothing. I saw a har moving around the house, then the earth shook, and I had to leave.'

'Hmmm.' Tuli pondered these words for a few moments then jumped to his feet. He smiled. 'This house is named *Inglefey*. If you think its name, and visualise it very clearly, you can come whenever you wish. You may also make yourself visible to any you find here, if you feel you should.'

'Why would I come here again?'

'To meet its occupant.'

'Why?'

'The first rule of investigating mysteries is that you should work things out for yourself. Use your mind, your imagination. Pay attention to your dreams. In this way, information flows to you. Explore with your new skill, little one.'

'Can I... can I go to other places?'

Tuli laughed. 'Ah, you like it, don't you, this freedom?'

'Yes,' Ulien answered. What else could he say?

'There, you see. I'm not a threat to you. I bring gifts. You're a very sensitive young har, Ulien, with great potential. Soon, it will flower, especially with my help. No mind will be closed to you, no doorway or gate.' He reached out to clasp Ulien's arm. 'And, of course, you can go to other places. It's really very easy when you know how.'

'Then how do I do it...?'

Tuli grinned widely. 'You hardly need me to tell you. When you are in your garden, you can simply think yourself out. I've awoken this ability in you with my breath. Didn't you feel it?'

Ulien was confused, unsure of what he'd felt. 'I… I don't know. But… if I can do that, how do I get back?'

'You can do it now. You can take us both back.'

'How?'

Tuli rolled his eyes. 'Oh, do use your imagination, harling! How do you think? How did we get here?'

Ulien thought for a moment, then said, 'Give me your hands.'

Smirking, Tuli did so.

Taking hold of them, Ulien closed his eyes and imagined the grotto at *Velvets*. *Go home!* He thought, putting all his concentration into it. Nothing happened. He opened his eyes. 'I can't.'

'Trying too hard to see,' Tuli said. 'Believe you are already there, rather than trying to force something to happen. It's that simple. Try again.'

Ulien did try – eight times in all. He thought he was incapable, but while Tuli was sarcastic and annoying, he was also patient. 'Don't think,' he said, 'Believe.'

And then, on the ninth attempt, when Ulien thought he might as well give up, the ground shuddered, and the air convulsed around him. He opened his eyes and found himself on the hill above the grotto, in the grove of cedars. He laughed. 'I did it!'

Tuli clapped his hands. 'So you did.'

Ulien frowned. 'But it was supposed to be in the grotto. The place isn't quite right. What if we'd come back *inside* the rock?'

'That wouldn't have happened, trust me.' Tuli leaned forward in the way that was unsettling, bending in half from the waist like his spine was hinged. He took Ulien's face in his hands, kissed his brow. 'Well done, little one,' he said. 'You learn quickly. Have fun.'

And was gone.

'But…' Ulien's voice was blown from him. He gulped air. *Can I go only into the town, and to that house?* He wondered. *Or can I go anywhere I can imagine?*

Chapter Twelve

Veredis insisted that Seladris should stay for the weekend. 'We'll look after you for a day or two,' he said. 'Let things settle at *Inglefey*.'

Seladris felt so drained and exhausted, he didn't argue.

On Pelf'sday morning, Seladris slept late. Veredis didn't wake him, since both of them had had little sleep and, anyway, there was no work that day. They'd sat up for most of the night, drinking and talking about what had happened at *Inglefey*.

Seladris didn't want to be driven out of his home by this weird activity, but also thought a time of relaxation would help him. He had warmed to Veredis, not least because the har appeared genuinely to want to help. Neither did he feel uncomfortable in Tika's company (although Tika appeared to keep himself busy elsewhere most of the time) and found he could sleep well in this airy house on the high coast road.

But on Aghamasday, Seladris found a strange restlessness creeping over him. He couldn't stop thinking about the events at *Inglefey* and had a strong urge to speak to Meladriel about them, even though he suspected his reappearance so soon at the cottage by the shore might not be welcome.

Veredis laid out lunch on a table in the garden. Tika had gone out, so Seladris felt able to speak a little more freely. He was conscious Tika was a friend of Meladriel's and there was curious, awkward dynamic between Veredis and the shaman.

About halfway through the meal, Seladris said, in the most casual tone he could muster, 'I think I'll visit Meladriel again today.'

Veredis raised an eyebrow. 'Perhaps not a bad idea. I've a feeling he'll be more forthcoming if you go alone.'

'Do you mind me asking what the problem is between you?'

Veredis shrugged. 'No, it's trivial really. Just a clash of personalities. I find him dull and oppressive; he finds me flighty and meaningless. If it wasn't for Tika, our paths would never have collided.' He paused. 'I can ask Tika to give you a lift there later, if you like. He won't be long.'

Seladris shook his head. 'No… I'll walk. I need to think carefully about my script for the occasion.'

When Seladris knocked upon the green door to *Eko Melosa*, Meladriel appeared – as Seladris had predicted – unhappy to see him again so quickly. 'I didn't expect you back yet,' he said stonily.

'Didn't you,' Seladris replied in a tone indicating this wasn't a question but a suspicion of the contrary. 'Well here I am. I want to tell you what happened last night.'

'Come in.'

Seladris passed into the murk of the kitchen.

'Tea?' Meladriel asked.

'Thank you.' Seladris sat at the table, while Meladriel poured him a drink from a cloth-covered pot.

'I think you know more than you revealed yesterday,' Seladris said. 'Am I in danger?'

'Perhaps you'd better tell me why you think you might be,' Meladriel answered. He placed a mug of dark brew on the table and then leaned against the sink, arms folded, his expression closed.

Seladris related the events of the previous evening. 'They came into my house,' he said. 'I can't live with that, Meladriel.'

'Then move out. That might solve everything.'

Seladris laughed coldly. 'I'm not stupid. Don't treat me as if I am. I'm fully aware that my… history might be catalysing events at Shadey Lane. This hasn't happened to anyhar else who's lived in that house, as far as Veredis knows. It's part of *me*. But it's also part of this town, this… landscape. And the phenomenon isn't random. I think you know *exactly* what it is. If you can help me, then do so. Don't play with me.'

Meladriel drew in his breath through his nose. 'The anger you're expressing is food to some forms of energy,' he said at last.

Seladris expelled a snort. 'This isn't show time,' he said. 'Speak to me honestly.'

Meladriel straightened up. 'All right,' he said. 'Drink that and come outside.' He left the cottage.

Seladris sat rigid at the table for some moments, then took a minute to finish the tea. After this, he followed Meladriel into the garden.

The har was already some distance away on the beach, building a fire near the water's edge, within a ring of smooth slate-blue rocks and a handful of pitted white stones the size of a har's fist. Seladris approached, but Meladriel did not look up. His hands wove meaningfully on the air above the arrangement of stones. Occasionally, he leaned forward to cast gnarled, blanched fingers of driftwood onto the nascent flames. Once Seladris stood before him, he said simply, 'Sit.' His eyes remained on the fire.

Seladris sat down on the opposite side of the circle of stones. The remains of old burnings could still be seen beneath the new. Meladriel sprinkled fragrant grains of cedar resin onto the flames. Seladris remembered the stately ancient tree that grew on the empty plot. Meladriel hunkered down, murmuring words Seladris could not make out. He saw that at least half a dozen bees were crawling through Meladriel's hair. This observation was followed by a strong scent of honey, which he considered might not be real.

'Take in the smoke,' Meladriel said.

Seladris leaned forward, breathed deeply.

'Consent to show me your bygones,' Meladriel said, 'Reveal to me your mysteries.'

Seladris shivered. The har's words sounded like an invocation to a deity.

'I consent,' he said.

Meladriel closed his eyes and slowly raised his face to the sky, intoning:

'Spirit of land, spirit of sea,
spirit of air, spirit of thee,
come forth in the breath where air and fire pleat
on the threshold of water, where elements meet.'

He sees me as fire, Seladris thought.

He does, came back a cool, perhaps amused response. *Now, relax, let your mind wander free. Think of nothing. Your thoughts are merely waves upon the infinite ocean. You need do nothing. Just be.*

In his mind's eye, Seladris visualised himself floating above the surface of this nameless sea. It was dark as cobalt, heaving slowly, but with no great waves. The horizon stretched away into infinity. This was a plane of water, limitless. For a while he drifted, half dozing, lulled by the motion beneath him. Then he was jerked to full awareness by a short, sharp tug, deep within him. He gasped and opened his eyes.

For a moment, reality roared at him, a mass of smoke and fire thundering in. Then Meladriel's hand was upon his shoulder and there was only the landscape of the shore and the thin fumes of burning driftwood.

'You didn't want to come back,' Meladriel said, his mouth curving into what approximated a smile.

'It was peaceful there. I'm sorry. Nothing happened.'

Meladriel laughed. 'Did it not? How long were you in there, Tiahaar?'

'Five minutes, ten...?'

'More like forty-five,' Meladriel said. 'Take care when you stand up. In this reality, you suffered wrenchings you didn't feel in that place.'

'What?' Seladris got to his feet, and his head reeled with dizziness. His legs were stiff, his back and ankles aching.

Meladriel supported him. 'You see? Come back inside. Your ghosts are prowling out here, wondering what I'm up to.'

'What?' Seladris murmured again, glancing round. He felt cold.

'Come.' Meladriel put an arm around his shoulder, guided him to the path that led to the cottage.

Once inside, Seladris groped his way to the table. He could barely see in the dim light. 'What did you do to me?' he asked. 'How long will... *this* last?'

'More tea,' Meladriel said, 'the most potent nepenthe for a harish frame.' He began to make a new brew, and there was silence between them as this was done. Seladris felt he wanted to sleep; his head and eyes ached mildly.

'There is one thing you must understand about the incepted, first generation hara,' Meladriel said, sitting down. 'New abilities, new faculties opened within them, which were completely alien to them. It wasn't long before they realised they could affect reality dramatically. They were like unruly children playing with faulty weapons. There were unspeakable accidents. Tribes that will be forever warped grew from the great inception. You know this first-hand, of course.'

Seladris nodded, incapable of commenting.

'Other tribes,' Meladriel continued, 'like the Gelaming, sought to eradicate such abnormalities, re-educate the surviving hara of the deviant tribes. Wild lands like Jaddayoth harbour some of those who escaped Gelaming *concern*. What hara found in Ferelith was like a weapon. The Devastation had released it. The Cerulopard were part of that. Leupardra believed he was a force for the future. He believed in himself. Fell for his own glamour. He was… misguided. What he invoked was too powerful for him to contain, and harish energy acted only as a conduit and an amplifier for this force. It's a natural phenomenon, and under normal circumstances the sentient species of this world would never become aware of it. Humans only caught a whiff of its scent. Hara could and *can*… see it. Like you can.'

Seladris blinked, took a sip of the tea Meladriel offered to him. 'So you believe my history, and the memories I've stored, have reacted with what exists here naturally?'

'Essentially, yes,' Meladriel said. 'This might not be a bad thing… for either of us.'

Seladris stared at his companion for some moments, then said softly, 'You're a guardian, aren't you?'

Meladriel nodded once. 'Of a kind. You could say I'm a watchtower.'

Seladris grimaced. 'Guardians generally want to drive me out of town as soon as possible.' He laughed coldly, fell silent abruptly, fixed Meladriel with a stare. 'What did you see in me?'

Meladriel leaned forward, his hands clasped on the table. 'I think you know what I saw since you've never forgotten it.'

'Tell me. How do I know if I recall it correctly?'

Meladriel drew in his breath and was quiet for some moments. Then he began to speak, his gaze remaining steady on Seladris's face. 'As a harling, once you were taken, you were never cowed, never beaten. You hid your anger, let it simmer like a cauldron brew. Even so young, you were determined to escape your fate, whatever the cost. You knew you needed to fight, and you fashioned a weapon for yourself. When the pelki they called feybraiha occurred, you learned how to call fire from the air, the same fire that energises any living form. You shaped the lightning, and with this you burned. Some you attacked took a while to die. Some might even still live but disfigured beyond recognition as a har. All your hatred you poured into the energies feybraiha awoke within you. Aruhani can be a ferocious force and your coming of age led you to him. Dehara of aruna, life – and death. He is the essence of harish power for good or ill. Once your act of liberation was done, you simply walked away. You had no intention of using such power ever again, because it hurt you to do so. You were too young to control it properly. But sometimes it came regardless, unprompted. You never blamed yourself entirely for this, because you believed the darkness that followed you had been awoken and shaped by your gift. You believed it was comprised of the remnants of those you'd destroyed. You considered it your nemesis; afraid it would burn your life forever.'

There were several moments of profound silence.

Then Seladris said faintly, 'Well… it seems I'm more obvious than I thought.'

'No, I'm simply more adept than you thought.'

Seladris huffed out a short laugh. 'So, what now?'

'I will come home with you.'

Seladris raised his brows. 'I see… Will you open up the cellar in the empty plot?'

'I can't tell you that yet. But first, you must sleep, regain your strengths.'

'What… here?'

'I have work to do. You'll be perfectly safe alone. Nothing can get in.'

Seladris didn't sleep easily at any time. He couldn't imagine being able to drift off in Meladriel's home. 'I can try,' he said.

'You won't need to.'

Seladris glanced briefly at the mug he was holding, wondered. Staring at Meladriel in a faintly challenging manner, he drank from it again.

Once Meladriel had shown Seladris to the bedroom, his first instinct was to go down to the shore, stand in the surf and weep. This was nothing to do with his own feelings but rather what he'd absorbed from Seladris while the har had been in trance. Meladriel knew many stories of the Devastation and Seladris's wasn't the worst, but what did that matter to Seladris?

Horror to be dragged from the side of your parents' bodies, which were still warm, and which you hoped – just hoped – were still alive. Horror to be thrown into a cell with other hara who, for whatever reason, your captors wanted to keep, like you. You heard the key turn and they did not come to feed you for some days. It is difficult to kill a har, but not difficult to torture him. Horror not to know what your fate would be, when escape was almost impossible.

Too many of them beyond the locked door, and they were too alert.

Seladris had had only one choice: build walls within himself or crumble entirely. His walls were strong, and he hid within them, until the day came that fate had given him a way out.

Meladriel had experienced the younger har's fury and pain. He did not think Seladris had killed with pleasure but with grim bitterness. And yet there were unanswered questions, feelings, hunches that Meladriel couldn't yet process. He'd give them time. More subtle impressions had been eclipsed by Seladris's memory of wanting to remove the evil of his captors from the world. *Let them all be gone.* That had included those who'd once been captured, like himself, but who'd eventually become part of the tribe, forgetting their origins or how they came to be what they were. In his fury, Seladris had had no pity for them. But his actions had affected him deeply. The chinks in his armour were tiny, but enough to let the enemy in: guilt and its sibling, shame. He'd been followed by the confusion of the dead and had accepted it as his burden, because part of him knew he'd done wrong that day. He'd not escaped his captors, he'd *become* them. But Meladriel was aware now that Seladris had not analysed his condition correctly; there was more to it.

Meladriel accepted he must now go to Shadey Lane, because he saw in Seladris the echoes of Leupardra, another young har who'd acted in anger and had done wrong. Leupardra, though, had been proud and vain and full of himself. Seladris was retiring, defensive and tired to his bones. But, to Leupardra, the vehicle might seem fitting. Meladriel's skin prickled. Even thinking such a thing was dangerous.

He returned to the dying fire and scattered sand on the embers, once more murmuring words to the spirits of the shore. *Contain and protect.* Performing rites at the shoreline was like working in the twilight at dawn or dusk – those brief but infinite moments, when the light turned, of being in a no place, beyond time. The shoreline was a weaker reflection of this but served its purpose.

Meladriel maintained beehives in several locations around his home. This was so his bees could produce honeys created from the nectar of a variety of flowers. Each comb was like incense, in that it contained properties of the plants from which it derived and could be used for a range of purposes.

Meladriel now began his rounds, which would take him several hours. This was not a harvest day, but a time of devotion, when he spoke to the bees and listened to the song in their wings. Those nearest home were mildly agitated, but nothing to worry about. Those further up the dunes and around the cattle paddocks closest to the sea flew dreamily from hive to flower and back, unperturbed.

Finally, as the sun moved landwards, Meladriel reached the hives that stood at the treeline of a pine forest that curved up and around to the east, eventually meeting with the older deciduous woodland above Shadey Lane. The honey from these hives was darker and with a hint of bitterness, enfolding the tang of colophony, the resin of the pine. As he approached the hives, Meladriel noticed a grist of bees flying, some ten feet up in the air, in a dense formation resembling a helix. A stillness came over the land. Meladriel stood motionless several yards from the hives. He was aware of a hum within the earth, a slight ripple beneath his feet. Something stirred or had been disturbed. He sat down and composed himself to smooth the ruffled energy of the site. Had an entity of some kind come slinking through the forest? He couldn't perceive anything overt.

Then – a burst of laughter. This wasn't sinister, but simply the sound of hara without cares, enjoying themselves on a dazzling late spring afternoon. He opened his eyes and saw them ambling out of the trees, into the sunlight. A dark har and a har of honey. The dark one, slightly taller, pulled his companion to a halt, bent to kiss him.

Uncomfortable heat sizzled up Meladriel's spine. This wasn't a vision. He was seeing the past. It was a memory of when his tribe had first been considering how to take Ferelithia and had often explored its extremities. What Meladriel witnessed now was the time when he and Karn had gone to the forest alone and had taken aruna together there. That time of limitless, delicious possibilities, even in the midst of conflict and uncertainty. They'd been innocent then. Dark issues hadn't been their concern; they'd trusted their phyle leaders would make everything right. How soon that innocence had been violated. They'd not even suspected that before the year went cold, they would no longer be together.

Hara at that time had been taught by their spiritual leaders, the early hienamas, to scorn the attachments humankind had set so much store by. Love was a dark force of undoing. Hara were above that. They were told 'never say "I love you" to anyhar, because it gives them a weapon that can be turned upon you.'

Karn and Meladriel knew that. They knew it very well. When they came out of the forest, still smelling of each other's bodies, they spoke in mind touch.

Love me?

Yes. Love me too?

Always.

Meladriel closed his eyes, uttered a sound of despair. He willed himself to blank out the memory, to seek instead the temporal incongruence that allowed the past to leak into the present. He identified it as a sliver in reality – tiny and easily sealed. But its presence was a bad omen, a warning perhaps. Forget. Forget. Forget. Keep it buried.

Back at his cottage, Meladriel found Seladris was awake, drinking tea at the kitchen table. He appeared hollow-eyed and vulnerable. Meladriel shuddered. He perceived echoes of his own younger self, during the few times when emotional wounds had weakened him.

You are har, get over it...

The past or the present?

The afternoon was sinking into the sea; the air felt drowsy.

'Feeling better?' Meladriel asked.

Seladris shrugged. 'I didn't sleep for long. Your drug didn't work that well.'

'Hardly a drug, merely a comfort. We must eat before we go to Shadey Lane. A good meal.'

Seladris didn't look like a har who ate heartily. No doubt a picker, frugal and mean, because he could have control over food, unlike other aspects of his life.

Meladriel prepared a meal of three varieties of bread, smoked fish, strong yellow cheese, a slab of white, salted butter and dark red apples with creamy flesh, accompanied by honeyed wine. The beverage was a ritual brew, steeped in a variety of puissant herbs: it brought fortitude and opened the doors of the mind a crack, without compromising their function to protect.

Meladriel set all this upon the table, Seladris watching him as if his mind was empty.

'Eat,' Meladriel said.

Seladris filled his plate and Meladriel was surprised to see him eat hungrily. 'You enjoy food,' he said.

Seladris appeared surprised. 'Who doesn't?'

Meladriel shrugged. 'You struck me as an ascetic type.'

Seladris pulled a face. 'Fuelling the body is a ritual of life. It should be fulfilled with awareness.' He continued to eat, apparently with relish.

Meladriel wondered who had told him those words. *Have you ever had mentors in the past, Seladris – perhaps individuals who sought to mend you? Did you believe they could? Were you always disappointed?* He kept the thoughts locked; Seladris did not hear them.

After they'd eaten, Meladriel took Seladris to the shore. He conducted no ritual, merely sat upon the sand and stared at the sea. He told Seladris to do the same. 'Clear the mind. Digest your meal.'

Seladris sighed. He sat with his legs stuck out straight, like a harling.

Meladriel was aware of a slight attraction to this har; it had stolen upon him stealthily. It wasn't physical exactly, more like a gradually emerging empathy. He admired Seladris's strength, the perfection of his masks. His arms and hands were strong, yet slender. He had killed with them.

They sat for an hour without speaking, then Meladriel announced it was time to leave.

Chapter Thirteen

They walked for some time in relaxed silence, then Seladris asked, 'Have you been to Shadey Lane before, Meladriel?'

'A couple of times,' he replied, 'but it wasn't a place open to us.'

'What does that mean?'

'It was the territory of the Cerulopard, and the phyle leaders allowed them privacy. Hara like me could come only when invited and then never into their inner sanctum.'

Seladris frowned. 'Were the Cerulopard bad hara?'

Meladriel shrugged. 'They were simply a part of that time. We're in no position to judge them now.'

Seladris glanced at his companion sharply. 'Surely *you* are. You were there.'

Meladriel uttered a soft, bitter laugh.

They ascended the hill to *Inglefey*, which glowed like a temple dedicated to the sunset.

'I love that house,' Seladris said. 'I want to live in it. I feel as if it's meant for me.'

'Then make clearing it your priority,' Meladriel said.

'I thought clearing *me* was the priority.'

Meladriel eyed him slantwise, his expression unreadable.

They reached the empty plot, which for some moments Meladriel observed without speaking. He was like stone; no thoughts or feelings leaked from him. The disturbed ground where Seladris and Veredis had dug looked like a fresh mass grave.

'You want to see the stone we found?' Seladris asked.

Meladriel shook his head. 'The house first,' he said. 'Show me around.'

Inglefey drowsed in the mellow light. Meladriel stepped into the hall and drew in a deep breath. Seladris began to move towards the sitting-room, where the painting hung, but Meladriel had already walked into the dining-room opposite, which Seladris had not yet used. It was a dark room, lit by sunlight only briefly early in the day, owing to the tall trees and rambling outbuildings that cast a shadow.

Seladris felt it had a dank subterranean quality to it.

'This room has never been used that much,' Meladriel said. 'It's empty.'

Seladris didn't reply but allowed the har to walk past him back to the hall.

Meladriel investigated all the other downstairs rooms, offering no opinions, his expression bland. Seladris waited by the sitting-room door. He did not glance into it. The wine must've affected him. He felt restfully numb.

Eventually, Meladriel walked past him into the sitting room. For a moment Seladris felt he'd become invisible, *removed*. He could simply float... 'Did Leupardra live here?' he asked harshly, re-establishing reality.

Meladriel shook his head. 'I doubt it.'

'Why?'

Meladriel stood in front of the painting. He reached out to it with one hand but did not touch it. 'They didn't live in houses.'

'What about the picture? Does it come from that time?'

Meladriel shrugged. 'Hard to say. If it didn't, it was certainly inspired by it.'

'Is it *him*? The leopard?'

Meladriel didn't answer. 'Fetch tools to open the ground again,' he said. 'And, if you have one, a hammer to break the seal.'

'What? Are you serious?'

'Yes. It's important I see what's beneath.'

Seladris had not expected Meladriel to act so swiftly. 'Maybe there should be more of us. It seems...'

'We need to know,' Meladriel said sharply. 'You'll understand why.'

'I'll show you all the tools I have,' Seladris said. 'There are lanterns too.'

Meladriel dug faster than Veredis had, and because the ground had been loosened this also hastened the work. Meladriel dug precisely, making the hole no larger than it needed to be. Within half an hour, the metal doors were revealed, the stone pole rising from them. Seladris felt oddly repulsed by the sight, as if the doors, and the shaft that pierced them, didn't belong in this world. The act of sealing, and its method, felt ancient and forbidding.

Meladriel squatted down inside the excavation and laid his hands flat against the metal plates. He shook his head.

'Touch them too,' he said to Seladris.

Seladris laid one hand against one of the doors, found it inert. No energy pulsed into his fingers. 'I don't feel anything.'

Meladriel nodded but made no comment.

Seladris offered him the long-handled sledgehammer they'd taken from the tool cupboard. Meladriel stared it for a moment, then took it in both hands.

'Is it strange or merely fortunate these tools are available to us so readily?' Seladris said.

Meladriel swung at the metal, which resounded loudly, echoing through the evening. In the trees further up the plot, roosting rooks lifted up in a clatter of wings and hoarse cries of alarm.

'I mean,' Seladris said, 'perhaps whoever buried this... cellar... lived in my house. These could be *their* tools.'

Meladriel continued to hammer the lock. Below, or within, the resounding clunk of the strikes, there was another sound, like the deep tolling of a bell. Seladris wasn't sure if this sound was real or in his head. He was aware his breathing had become fast and shallow.

Eventually, the lock splintered apart, as if made of glass. Shards flew off it, and Seladris protected his face, yet nothing hit him. When he lowered his hands, he saw Meladriel was also unmarked. The remains of the lock had melted into a shapeless lump.

For some moments, Meladriel simply stared at the doors, then threw away the hammer and pulled at the metal handles with both hands. With a crack like thunder, the stone pole snapped in two and the doors burst wide. Meladriel staggered backwards, panting.

Seladris raised the lantern, peered into the darkness beyond. 'There are steps,' he said, then glanced back at Meladriel. 'I expected it to smell like a grave, but it doesn't. Were *you* expecting a grave?'

Meladriel lifted the second lantern. 'Follow me.'

In the fluctuating light of the lanterns, Seladris saw a stone staircase of about a dozen steps, which led to a large, low-ceilinged chamber. Dusty strands of cobwebs and earth hung down at the entrance. The glow of the lanterns didn't penetrate very far, but from what he could see, the cellar was empty. Cautiously, he followed Meladriel down into it. Both of them had to stoop to avoid knocking their heads against the ceiling. Here, the light revealed images upon the wall: paintings of leopards and hara that resembled cave pictures of prehistoric times. Seladris went closer to examine the images nearest the door and realised the cellar was in fact a natural cave; the walls were solid rock, plastered over sporadically, so that lumps and spurs poked out of it in places. The place smelled of dry, rotten brick, earth and, strangely, of musty flowers.

Meladriel ventured ahead, diminishing into the darkness, haloed by the feeble radiance of the lantern, as if its light was weakened by the room. After a minute or so, he halted, froze.

Seladris went to him, raised his lantern. 'Sweet Aru… is this… is this *them*…?' he murmured.

In the far corner, bodies were piled: spreading out across the floor. They reached almost to the ceiling which sloped to become low at that point. Little more than mummified skeletons, still draped with ragged clothes. Seladris saw the wink of jewels in the light. There was no smell of death here, only a rather sickening, lingering aroma of old blooms and – bizarrely – face powder left too long in a drawer.

'Who did this?' Seladris asked, not expecting a reply.

Meladriel had hunkered down at the edge of the heap of corpses, holding the lantern over them.

Seladris didn't feel afraid, or even particularly nauseated. These husks were empty. Disposed of. Hidden. Did Meladriel know who these corpses were? Why would he not speak? Was this part of some kind of ritual? 'If you know who did this,' Seladris said evenly, projecting all of his will into the words, 'then tell me.'

Meladriel drew in his breath, stood up as straight as he was able. He looked Seladris in the eye, shook his head briefly, as if to intimate he could not yet answer questions. Stooped over, he began to examine the walls.

Seladris followed him, also forced to stoop. If this har was to speak at all, he would do so in his own time. Displaying impatience and irritation would accomplish nothing.

By holding his lantern close to the wall, Seladris could make out scenes of ceremony, and what looked like some kind of initiation or bestowing of rank. The figures were depicted as both hara and leopards, and also as were-leopards, shapeshifters. They were in a primitive style, yet beautifully rendered. He felt these pictures should be in a museum somewhere, relics of Wraeththu's early history. 'As you won't talk, I'll take a guess about this place,' he said. 'I think it must have been claimed by the Cerulopard. Their headquarters, lair… whatever you want to call it. I think they made these pictures.'

Surprisingly, Meladriel spoke, although his voice was strange – tight. 'You're right. The Cerulopard did create these images.'

'And was this their lair?'

'No.'

'Some kind of ritual site, then. Not a comfortable one, unless they sat down. The ceiling is so low.'

Meladriel offered no further remarks.

Seladris sighed, moved further up the wall. He drew in his breath sharply. 'Sweet Aru,' he breathed. 'My dream.' He held the lantern high, illuminating a further section of wall.

There was Leupardra, the Pard Witch, adorned in his leopard skin, with its dangling paws, the snarling mask over the top half of his face. He danced before a raging bonfire; his hands curled into claws. His tribe mates were merely blurred shadows around him, caught in poses of leaping and striking. And beyond them, the Pale Ones, tall, motionless, blank-faced and dire, against a backdrop of soaring bleak pines.

And to the side of this image the words daubed in flaking white paint: *Remember my command. This is your blood debt to the Blue Leopard. Remember.*

Seladris moved further along the wall, and there was Leupardra, depicted in skilled detail, lithe and beautiful. A different artist had created this. His left arm was held out stiffly, his index finger pointing. And the Pale Ones clustered behind him, their spiky hands curled at their chests, their pose that of *listening*.

'He *sent* them, didn't he?' Seladris said, in a tone of awe and also grudging respect. 'He summoned and sent them. By all dehara, what *were* they?'

'What lived here,' Meladriel said, still in that strange, strangled tone. 'Ancient things.'

'And this was how Leupardra dealt with the human problem in the area?' Seladris swung the lantern over to what lay in the corner. 'And that, presumably, is the price he paid.' He paused. 'This is the link between him and me, isn't it? *I* dealt with a problem once, and although I didn't call upon etheric entities to aid me, I did leave a pile of bodies.' He waited, but Meladriel did not speak. 'I wish you'd talk to me now. Can't you give me even a shred of an answer?'

Meladriel glanced at him, swallowed with difficulty, as if

something was stuck in his throat. 'I think you've identified the link... at least partly.'

'So, what do we do now... with this lot?' Seladris gestured at the floor. 'Do we have to report it to somehar?'

'This place is dead,' Meladriel said.

'But...'

'Do you have left any of the salt I sold you?'

'Yes, of course I have. Shall I fetch it?'

Meladriel paused a moment, then said. 'No, tell me where it is.'

'On a shelf in the kitchen, by the stove.'

'Do you have oil for burning?'

'Yes, there's a canister in the larder.'

Meladriel began to head towards the cellar entrance.

'You want me to stay here?' Seladris asked, his voice high.

Meladriel paused, turned. 'Yes. I want to know if you think it's dead too.'

'So... it's safe?'

'Do you feel threatened?'

'No.'

Meladriel disappeared into the open air.

For a while, Seladris stood motionless, staring at what he believed was the remains of the Cerulopard. Such hubris. Had Leupardra's conjured servitors turned on them? How had this happened? The answer, of course, could not be painted on the walls. Who had sealed this tomb? He was sure Meladriel knew the answers.

A compulsion came over him. Without thinking, he placed the lantern on the floor and began tearing at the bodies, scattering bones. 'Where are you?' he muttered. 'Where *are* you?'

He was looking for Leupardra, sure he'd know when he'd found the har, even if only a shard of bone remained. He only stopped clawing at the remains, when Meladriel called his name: a looming shape at the entrance.

'What are you doing?'

Seladris ignored him, until Meladriel marched over and took hold of his arms from behind. 'Stop it,' he said.

Seladris dropped back limply against him. 'We *have* to find him,' he said. 'We *must*.'

'Find who?'

'Leupardra, of course.'

Meladriel turned Seladris to face him, shook him slightly. 'You're making assumptions, not thinking – or feeling – clearly.'

Seladris tried to wriggle free. 'I know what I have to do. *This* is what I feel. I'll spread the bones out, sort them. You don't have to help, but you can't stop me.'

Meladriel let him go. 'This will accomplish nothing.'

'Maybe I wouldn't need to do it if you told me what you know,' Seladris said, pointing at the bones. 'These hara were murdered. And you know more about it than you want me to think.'

Meladriel stepped away. 'I won't stop you.'

Seladris released a cry that was part growl, part groan of frustration. 'Will you at least hold a lantern up for me?'

Meladriel did so.

Seladris laid out the bones in a calmer manner. It didn't take as long to untangle them as he'd thought, since they were mostly still attached to one another. He worked in silence, until the job was complete, and a crooked row of skeletons lay on the floor before him. 'This can't be all of them,' he said. 'There isn't anywhere near thirty bodies here. Did some escape?'

Meladriel said nothing.

Seladris stood up. 'He's not here.' He stared at the bones, the pathetic remains of vibrant lives. A cold worm burrowed through him. 'Did Leupardra do this, Meladriel? Will you at least answer that?'

'What do you think?' Meladriel asked. 'Tell me.'

Seladris shook his head. 'I think there are around fifteen of those weird pale creatures, from what I've seen. Same number as the bodies here... maybe? I wonder now whether Leupardra didn't simply summon those entities, but *made* them, provided them with... vessels.' He glanced at Meladriel. 'Am I anywhere near right?'

'Just speak,' Meladriel said.

'Perhaps,' Seladris continued, 'Whatever Leupardra did...' He gestured at the bones. '*This* was the result. These hara might have given themselves willingly, but if this is the truth of whatever happened here, ultimately they were sacrifices.' He exhaled slowly. 'You still don't speak. Does this mean I'm right or wrong?'

'It's important for now I don't influence you.'

Seladris grimaced. 'I don't want to believe this story, because I rather like the idea of the Pard Witch, but it makes sense to me. I *feel* it's right. He might not have understood the risks. What must we do now? Report this to somehar? You didn't answer my question about that before.'

Meladriel pulled a sour face. 'Not publicly, no. We seal the chamber again, but before that we cleanse it.'

'A ritual of some kind?'

'Of a sort.'

Seladris glanced at the canister of oil, said dryly. 'You intend to burn the evidence.'

Meladriel nodded. 'This will begin the cleansing, might even be the end of it.'

'It doesn't feel right to do that. Somehar should be told. What about the paintings on the wall? I don't feel they should just be destroyed. They record history from a time when hara had abandoned the means or the inclination to keep such records. And, surely, the decent thing to do would be to bury these victims properly?'

Meladriel sighed impatiently. 'You're speaking like an upstanding citizen, Seladris, but in this case we cannot be like ordinary hara, resolving matters in an ordinary, sensible way. We burn the bodies. We seal the tomb. The records remain hidden. You have to trust me. I will explain what I can, but not here.'

Seladris stared at Meladriel. *Can he be trusted?* 'I don't like this, and in the event of all this coming to light I want it on record I don't approve.'

Meladriel exhaled irritably through his nose. 'Noted,' he said coldly.

'Before anything else, there's something I want to do.'

'What is it?'

'My own ritual.'

Meladriel stared at him for a moment, then shrugged. 'Very well.'

Seladris turned his back on Meladriel and began to walk between the bones carefully, on tiptoe. This felt to him like a ritual dance. Would the burning end the disturbances in Shadey Lane? Were his imaginings even the truth? Perhaps Leupardra's remains were here after all. Perhaps the Blue Leopard had never been more than the hara who lay dead around him.

I have made a story, Seladris thought. *I've imagined an explanation. Perhaps it's up to me to make it real. Speak to me in dreams, dear bones, if that's the only tongue you have...*

He bowed to the bones and retreated. 'Do what you must, Meladriel.'

Silently, Meladriel dribbled oil over the remains and scattered the salt. Then, he motioned for Seladris to retreat to the door. He lit the oil and joined Seladris at the entrance.

'We should say something,' Seladris said.

'Words mean nothing.'

Seladris ignored this and held out his arms. 'We give you freedom, hara of the Cerulopard. Be purified by this untainted salt. Take flight to the realms beyond on the smoke of these cleansing flames. We release you and bless you, in the name of the Aghama, he who is first of all, the star and our master.'

For a while they stood watching the growing flames, which once they took hold seemed to devour the bones with increasing hunger. Then Seladris led the way outside, where Meladriel pulled the doors shut. There was no lock now, but perhaps this wasn't needed. Meladriel had kept back a little salt and oil, which he now applied to the doors and rubbed into them.

'Let nothing disturb the peace of this land,' Seladris murmured. 'May seen and unseen walk in harmony, each in their proper realm, and there be amity between us.'

'Stay in the past,' Meladriel said abruptly. 'That's all I command.'

Seladris stood up, took a step back.

There was a moment of utter stillness, as if the world paused in its rotation.

Then the earth shook.

At once, Meladriel grabbed Seladris by one arm and yanked him out of the excavation. To Seladris, the land seemed to scream, and the soil itself writhed underfoot. Stumbling, he attempted to run across the grass, but it was difficult to remain upright, even held in Meladriel's ruthless grip.

Before they reached *Inglefey*, there was a mighty crash, and a hollow moan. They were thrown to the ground. Seladris curled into a ball to shield his face from flying earth and sticks and stones. He felt Meladriel covering his body with his own. A storm of earth raged around them, seeming to last an eternity. Until the world shifted and there was only calm and silence.

As one, they raised their heads, scrambled uncertainly to their feet.

The ground had collapsed, bringing half the slope of the empty plot down with it. All that remained in the bright moonlight was a huge ragged wound in the earth, as if a meteor had struck it. A few uprooted trees lay across it, their branches twisted and broken.

'There's no doubt the Cerulopard are truly buried now,' Seladris said.

He began to laugh. Relief, release, the precious hope their work was done.

Seladris followed Meladriel back to the cottage by the sea. The night was calm, the horns of ships calling low from the water, like mournful sea beasts. Meladriel was silent, as ever, and seemed dazed, almost unwell. Ever since they'd left the cottage earlier, his mood and mien had become darker, almost fearful. This was unnerving, because Seladris wanted the har to make him feel safe, and it seemed what they'd found in the cellar had affected Meladriel profoundly, even harmfully. But for the moment Seladris was not inclined to speak either. He found it tiring, trying to communicate with a wall of a har who didn't respond. Stultifying. Perhaps only patience and guile would tease the shaman's secrets from him.

Seladris was aware all hara carried their own scars and bitter memories, the experiences that made them what they were. He *had* looked for teachers in the past, and some of them had been wise, but now he couldn't always put the right face to the words he recalled. One of them had said, 'It was essential we were born in darkness and rose from that darkness. We are the result of the human experiment. We are what must be. But this can't come easy.'

Meladriel was perhaps the ideal teacher Seladris had once dreamed of finding: strong, mysterious, full of secret knowledge. Now, the reality merely tired him. He could no longer muster the enthusiasm to win this har over, unlock his reserve. His behaviour now, and the unsettling energy oozing from him, bordered on madness. Seladris wondered if he should be afraid.

Inside the cottage, Meladriel placed a kettle of water on the stove, then clearly changed his mind and brought out liquor from his store. This wasn't wine, something stronger: a fierce yenayva, which he said had been conjured in the copper belly of a still named Nefertara, owned by a friend. The drink was flavoured with the tart essences of dune grasses and flowers.

Meladriel held out a small clay cup of this elixir to Seladris as if

125

offering a dose of poison. Seladris stared at the cup for some seconds before accepting it.

'A strong liquor helps,' Meladriel said. He drank quickly, standing before the window, gazing at the shore. Presently, he refilled his cup, drank that quickly too.

Seladris sat down at the table, put the tip of his tongue in the cup. The spirit burned him, but he liked the taste, took a sip.

Meladriel's body shifted, as if he awoke. He put down his empty cup and stretched his arms and shoulders, shook his hair. It was as if some heavy burden had fallen from him, or perhaps had been wrestled with and vanquished. 'Clarity has come to me,' Meladriel said. 'Your problem is not as severe as it seems.'

'Oh? How did you come to that conclusion? Was it the deep conversation we had?'

Meladriel turned. He looked very tired but somehow more *present*. 'You're strong. You carry a kind of... parasite, but this is perhaps more of a symbiotic relationship than a drain on you.'

Seladris choked out a laugh. 'You're suggesting I find pleasure in hurting others? For that is what my *problem*, as you call it, boils down to.'

Meladriel drew a hand through his hair. 'No, I'm suggesting your situation can be put right. You named the demon a long time ago, and perhaps sought means to banish it. This was the correct course, but so far you've been denied. All you lack is the means.'

'What do you suggest?'

'For a start: Rest.'

'What?' Seladris grimaced. 'Is that the best you can come up with?'

'Yes.' Meladriel closed his eyes for a heartbeat. 'You're tired, always tired. Sleep does not refresh you as it should. You deny yourself rest, because it's part of your self-punishment. If you weren't so tired, you'd be in a better place to deal with the problem.'

'I don't, and can't, believe it's that simple.'

Meladriel shrugged. 'I can't force you to accept it. You *would* be of more use to me if you attended to your troubles, but that's your choice.'

'Use to you?' Again, Seladris laughed without humour. 'I don't give a shit about what you want.'

'Really? I thought traditionally the shaman and client had a kind of contract.'

'You're not my healer, Meladriel. I don't know what the pelk you are to me.'

Meladriel took a seat opposite Seladris. He rubbed his hands slowly, forcefully over his face, sighed deeply. 'Very well. You get your wish. Talk. Ask.'

Seladris narrowed his eyes, wondering what trick this might turn out to be. 'First, do you promise to answer me truthfully?'

Meladriel shrugged. 'I won't lie to you. That must suffice.'

Seladris closed his eyes briefly. 'Better than nothing, I suppose. OK, do you think the images and ideas that came to me tonight are correct? Did Leupardra summon etheric entities into some of his hara and use them as weapons against the humans in the town?'

Meladriel did not reply for some moments. He stared at Seladris. 'You are making one big assumption,' he said.

'Which is?'

'That the bodies we found are, in fact, members of the Cerulopard.'

'Are they not?'

Meladriel gestured gracefully with both hands. 'I'm simply offering my opinion, as you asked. It's not for me to say who those bodies belonged to. I'm merely suggesting you can't be sure either.'

'I thought you were there... that you know the answers.'

'I was there, yes, on the outside. I was among a small group of hara who were summoned by the phylarchs to add our will to a... particular rite. I didn't see what Leupardra and the hienamas did beneath the earth – or what *to*.'

Seladris wasn't sure he believed this but pressed on without challenging Meladriel's words. 'So you think Leupardra might've sacrificed hara of *other* phyles?'

'Are you sure they're hara?'

'Well... some of them wore jewellery.'

Meladriel raised his brows.

Seladris sighed. 'No, I'm not sure. So, you think they were human?'

'I'm not saying that.'

'So... They could equally have been the bodies of Leupardra and his elite. Except... I get the impression you don't think that.'

'You accept my word, my perceptions? How can you be certain I wasn't deceived myself? You are har, psychically aware, yet the information you've picked up has been muddled, perhaps a riddle, a trick, a blind. Let's assume the local phyle leaders ordered the bodies to be concealed and sealed within that mass grave, but as to why, and who died there…' He pulled a face. 'The history is dark. No record was left to us.'

Seladris sighed deeply. 'So, you're saying we'll never know. Any of the explanations could be true.' He paused. 'But we were talking of *my* suppositions. Now, let's hear yours, and also the truth that you *do* know, but have so far chosen not to reveal.'

Meladriel drew in a breath through his nose. 'Yes, I was there on the night when the ground was sealed, but as I said we… I… didn't go into the cellar itself. I saw Leupardra enter it, but I didn't see him walk out. I was sent away from the site after a hienama emerged from the cellar. He told those of us waiting outside to go into the town at once. There was… trouble to deal with.'

'What did you *do* there, while they were inside?' Seladris asked.

Meladriel shrugged. 'All I'd been told was that the creatures you call the Pale Ones must be contained in that place. Those of us outside stood guard to prevent interruption and to add our energy to that of the hara beneath the ground, like a power source.'

'Didn't you hear anything?'

Meladriel paused, clearly trying to remember. 'I don't recall anything.' He shrugged. 'Honestly, I don't think Leupardra was in that pile of bones we found. If he was, then it involved a brilliant sleight of hand I never noticed.'

'To say that, you must've seen him after that night, then?'

Meladriel looked away, but not before Seladris saw the pain in his eyes. 'Others saw him. I… wasn't around for a while after that night.'

'Meladriel,' Seladris breathed, his eyes wide. 'Tell me… *tell* me what happened.'

Meladriel shook his head. 'Their way was not my way. That's all you need so know.'

'Was that why you were so quick to burn the remains tonight?'

'No, that wasn't the reason. A bad influence lingered. It needed purging.'

'But surely, we should have tried to find out who those bones belonged to? Their identity might have bearing on what's happening now.'

'No!' Meladriel snapped. 'Even if it has, it was important the site was cleansed and resealed.

'How can you be so sure?'

'Because once I saw what was inside, I knew it had to be secured again quickly. It's clearly attracting interest from the entities Leupardra summoned, or beings similar to them. There was no way the place could have been left open.'

'Why? What can they do with old bones? Make them walk?'

'It's not that, but the potential for portals.'

'Meaning?'

'We don't want more of them, or a nexus point forming for such energy. Leupardra was playing with a fire he couldn't understand. The Gelaming understand it more, moving between realities, through the ethers. You can use this phenomenon to travel distances, to visit other realms, or you can let *things* in. Local energy was long ago warped by forces smoking through from another realm. This is what created the Pale Ones. It was an energy Leupardra believed he could tap into and control.' Meladriel refilled his glass. His hands did not appear to be entirely steady.

'How well did you know him, Meladriel?' Seladris asked.

The shaman was silent for a moment. 'Well enough.'

'You asked me to trust you, but you don't trust me at all.'

'Again, an assumption. Perhaps I'm simply concerned for your safety.'

Seladris was aware of a feeling stealing over him like a dark, heavy fog. 'Meladriel, this question you must answer the most honestly of all: have *I* brought the Pale Ones back to Ferelithia? Have I reawakened the past?'

Meladriel stared at him, and Seladris felt bizarrely that it was like waiting for another kind of answer, he wasn't sure what. 'This is all I can tell you…' Meladriel said. 'You are not unconnected, and perhaps your presence in *Inglefey* has somehow acted as a catalyst or a fuse that's starting to fizz, but you're not responsible. The hara who sealed that cellar are. You must not worry about that, Seladris.'

'Dris,' Seladris said abruptly. 'My friends call me Dris.'

'Am I that?' Meladriel managed a bleak smile.

'I think it's important… like being a united front. I don't know why I feel that, but I do – despite your… well… you know what I mean. You're not a hara har, are you?' He smiled encouragingly.

'You could say that.' Meladriel touched his chest with the fingers of one hand. 'I am Mela. Let us be in accord.'

Seladris inclined his head, then said, 'What are your plans for me now?'

'We must perform more cleansing rites, visions of release. I'll do my best to clear you. You should attend to this yourself too.'

'Tell me what to do.'

'Like I said, you must rest, and I can help you with that. It's important you accept that you can't run from the past or your actions there. Neither can you continue to blame yourself in the present.' Meladriel gestured with both hands. 'What's done is done. All you can do is live your life now to the best of your ability. If you feel you have to atone, find a way to do so that isn't self-indulgent, dangerous or extreme. There are many who need help – and help may manifest in the smallest of gestures.' He paused. 'You must learn to accept the part of yourself who is the ghost. This will sound unlike me, even to one of short acquaintance, but… perhaps you should learn to love it.'

Seladris expelled a snort of laughter, incapable of commenting.

Meladriel's expression remained unamused. 'Think hard, Dris, of what this really is. It is a bane to you for now, but it could be an asset.'

Seladris shook his head. 'It's not controllable. It hates me.'

'It's part of you,' Meladriel said.

'It's not *just* me,' Seladris snapped. 'See if you can summon it. Find out for yourself. You won't love it, I assure you.'

Meladriel smiled. 'It might come to that, but not yet. And you are wrong to think it's comprised of anything but your own essence and energy – and memories too. We must build your resources, give you the means to control this aspect of yourself. It's had free rein for far too long and will resist. We must be ready for that.'

'Sounds fun,' Seladris said dryly. 'Can I have more of your dangerous and uncontrollable yenayva?'

Meladriel refilled the cup.

'I want to draw the paintings we found on the walls. Is that OK?'

Meladriel considered for a moment. 'I wouldn't. At least, not yet.'

'Portals?'

'Maybe. Why risk it?'

'I think you know why. I feel strongly they should be preserved in some form. It's Wraeththu history, even if a dubious part of it.'

'How well can you remember them?'

Seladris closed his eyes. 'As if I'm still there.'

'All right,' Meladriel said.

'All right, what?'

'Draw them.'

'Is this a "light the fuse" occasion for me?'

Meladriel laughed softly. 'Perhaps so.'

'Then I must stay close to you.'

Meladriel was silent, and Seladris wondered if his remark had been interpreted as a clumsy pass. 'I mean...'

Meladriel made a dismissive gesture. 'No, it's all right. I just wonder if that will help. You might *need* to be alone. I think you should carry on your life as normal, if you can. Rest well, eat well. Go to work. Socialise...'

Seladris's laughter interrupted him. 'There's one thing we have in common,' he said. 'I don't really socialise. It can sometimes end with my friends in pieces. We're not that far into my rehabilitation yet.'

'I see. Well, just continue to work as normal and live in the house.'

'And the painting? I'm not convinced what we did will prevent grotesque entities wandering through the door. Would you have the leopard here?'

'No,' Meladriel said. 'There's somehar else who can take it.'

'Who?'

'I can't say for now. Please don't press me about it. The har concerned is well known in the community.'

'I doubt I will have heard of him.'

'Doesn't matter.' Meladriel paused. 'Stay here tonight. I'll ensure you good sleep. If you want to, return to work tomorrow. If necessary, I'll ask Tika to help move the painting, once I'm sure there's somewhere we can take it.' He stood up. 'I'll make us supper. It's late.'

'Where will I sleep?'

There was a brief tense silence. 'Have my bed. I'll sleep outside. I do that often.'

'Thanks.' Seladris knew he was disappointed. He couldn't help it. But what else could he expect from a har like Meladriel?

Chapter Fourteen

Once supper had been consumed, and Seladris, duly sedated, had gone to bed, Meladriel went out to the shore to think about – relive – the events of the evening. It had taken all his strength to conceal his turmoil.

Before he and Seladris had set out for *Inglefey*, as they'd sat upon the shore, Meladriel had seen the ghost of an unstorm in the distance, hanging above the waves. It didn't approach the land but wavered this way and that. He had heard a strange refrain on the air, like the ululation of a ritual song, but so faint he could barely hear it, and if he strained to listen, it fell silent.

He had felt as if the past was an unstorm in itself, hanging over him, threatening to unleash its ferocity. It was as if he was to be judged, but for what? His part in the past was insignificant really, his only importance being in that he survived it, was still here and could remember. Karn had known more, of course, but had chosen not to tell. He'd been ambitious, even then.

Meladriel had glanced at Seladris sitting beside him on the sand, wondering whether he was the cause of what was happening, a catalyst, or merely a coincidental creature caught up in the vanguard of a storm. Can a har ever truly be free of his past, when the past is soaked in blood?

On the walk to *Inglefey*, the landscape squeezed in. Meladriel could not speak, aware of the rising irritation in his companion, but incapable of changing the situation. Nothing seemed permanent, reality was shifting, undulating. Songs came from the hills and the sharp cruel bark of laughter. He glanced once sideways at Seladris and saw Leupardra walking beside him. A blink, a clearing of the eye, was enough to exorcise that illusion.

Karn had once said: 'You complete me', but there was another, more beautiful still, who did more than complete; they enhanced a har, made them more than they were. Leupardra.

Meladriel unclenched his jaw. He mustn't give in to weakness or foolishness.

At the house, he heard humming in the air, but could not find the source. It came from the walls perhaps, or from the ground beneath. He heard somehar speak his name, but it wasn't Seladris, who stood stiff and angry by the sitting-room door, his arms crossed defensively.

Meladriel could smell dirt. He didn't want to look upstairs. This house, so close to the place of power – maybe Karn and Leupardra had come here together. It seemed likely, but the house would have been abandoned then, forlorn and dusty, its human occupants perhaps recently fled or slaughtered. Hara would have yet to bring light back to it. And there *was* light here, struggling to become dominant. Darkness and memories slithered about it like eels, breaking it up, but not strong enough to dispel it. The healthy energy was robust enough not to be dissipated. Good intention had spawned it here. Surely, the flibbertigibbet Veredis was not responsible for that.

Eventually, Meladriel had to view the painting. He felt he had to squeeze past Seladris, even though there was plenty of space. Auras had grown larger as the sun fell.

The picture glowed in ruddy light. It seemed freshly painted, bright with colour and life. But there was a vicious streak in it. Who had been the artist? From Seladris's report, it appeared the Pale Ones were drawn to this picture, had even used it as a portal and yet... Meladriel took a couple of steps closer to the hearth... it didn't look old.

It was time to move outside.

Seladris was little more than a phantom during the first stages of the procedure. Meladriel could barely perceive him. Every other component of the environment was far stronger, demanding attention. Seladris followed. He did as he was told but he wasn't comfortable. He wanted to talk to ease his tension. He wanted questions to be answered.

But the truth is, Meladriel thought, privately, *I probably know little more than you. I was the one kept out, once. I was faced with the fortress of silence, its impenetrable walls, the faces in the high windows looking down. They who knew all.*

He and Seladris took tools from the small room that was hardly more than a cupboard in the kitchen. Seladris carried the lanterns.

Tension rose like steam. Meladriel could not fill his lungs as they crossed the empty plot. His hearing was diminished by a screaming hum in his ears. Snatches of song rose and fell, waves of sound.

He saw the ghost house ahead of them, its windows burning with tangerine light, as if the sunset was caught within. This was the building Seladris had described. It didn't exist. To the side of it was a patch of turned earth, but as Meladriel stared at it, the image wavered, and he saw the doors to a storm cellar. The house itself was peculiar, formed of natural rock rather than built. Sometimes it appeared as an immense monolith scored with veins of light. Perhaps different edifices had been constructed or raised here over the millennia. Offerings had been made. Life.

Meladriel accepted the vision and chose to ignore it, because he thought it was designed to distract.

They began to dig at the earth, but all the time Meladriel could barely see the soil. He saw only the doors, waiting, and the pole that pierced them, which was bound with hexes and seals.

What right had they to breach those seals? Wasn't it the most absurd folly? And yet, Meladriel had to know what lay beneath.

His leaders had told him. *The Pale Ones still walk. Leupardra orders we must seal this ritual chamber with the evil locked within. They must be contained. Add your energy to the group, Meladriel. It is your duty.*

But that had been the end of the story, not its start. Leupardra's initial conjuration had taken place at the same site, days before. His rite had awoken the first unstorm Meladriel had experienced, which had pulsed across the land, dragging its heart of deadly chaos, the grume all around, covering the town with its weird stagnant energy of unlife. Leupardra, perhaps, had not even sensed it, but it was there. Deities of death had walked in the hem of the grume, with veils for faces and the wounds of the world upon their bodies. Meladriel had hardly been able to bear it. Breathing had felt like inhaling thick mud, thinking like nails driven into the soft tissue of his brain. His senses had been heightened to the point of pain; his awareness stretched.

Had the unstorm aided Leupardra's conjuration or simply been attracted by it? But whatever the answer, Leupardra had succeeded. His summoning hadn't been a cleansing so much as an obliteration. Nothing could stand in its way; it was the devourer, perhaps an aspect of Aruhani that existed before Aruhani was even shaped in the minds of hara.

The energy of the landscape, twisted and shaped by Leupardra, had taken on the form of tall, unnatural shapes that moved without being seen, a numbing undoing. Humans had simply stopped as the Pale Ones passed over and through them. They extinguished life force, without violence, without pain, a simple ceasing. And Meladriel recalled it *had* been only humans who were affected. The flowers had still sung of summer, animals had been undisturbed, but for the occasional pricked ears, quivering noses, eventually walking away from the nothingness left of their former masters. There had been a smell of dust, and a slightly corrupt sweetness, little more. Occasionally, a peculiar clicking had been heard. Then, mostly, silence.

Death walking.

And all this… it had come from here.

Meladriel struck at the metal doors and the world itself rang and shook to his blows. He felt like a titan, striking the anvil that conjured wars and ruin. The reverberations banged through him, rattling his cells. He was coming undone… And then… then…

He pulled the doors and the pole cracked in two, like a scene from myth. Only a puff of wan air came out of the darkness beyond.

'Did you expect a grave, Meladriel?'

Poor child. It is *a grave. Can't you see that?*

It was far too difficult to speak, make sound. His body was still ringing. His ears were deaf. It was as if his eyes were bound with translucent silk that allowed only a misty view of the world.

The mist of death in warriors' eyes.

Into the Underworld, then.

As soon as he reached the bottom of the steps, Meladriel knew the Pale Ones were not contained in this spot, even if they were still drawn to it. Leupardra, in his pride, had made the fundamental mistake of the novice magician. He had conjured his force but had not thought too deeply about how to dismiss it.

Where had it gone?

The centre of power had been here, in this underground chamber, but not the results of that power. The Pale Ones had vanished, yes, into the landscape, but gone? Hara had believed this was possible, if the proper precautions were taken, the correct seals fixed.

What *had* they sealed in here?

The paintings on the walls resembled records from a tomb, and so they were, in a sense.

The place was otherwise empty. Even when Meladriel saw the remains heaped carelessly on the floor, he felt no rising of power, no echo of it. These were husks.

The discovery of the bodies released him somewhat. He became more aware of Seladris beside him, the trembling urges within the har's body and mind. He was straining now for answers. He believed he saw the corpses of the Cerulopard dismantled around them, but was he correct in that assumption?

Meladriel couldn't tell. But if that idea was correct, how had these hara got here? Had they been deposited after the site had been sealed? How? Lies. Deceit. Tricks. There was a kind of ringing static around the bones, preventing clear identification, certainly of a psychic kind. But he knew they must be destroyed. They were, in a way, an anchor, for something.

But if we should release it by burning, what then?

Do it anyway. You know you have to.

He must permit Seladris, who might've been led to him deliberately, to play his part. He must not dismiss this har's conclusions. He had to trust they had a purpose.

He could barely hear Seladris's voice. Only snatches.

'Should we report this?'

Tell Karn... Let him decide.

No.

Anger banished weakness, re-established clarity.

Are we in accord?

No. We never were.

'We must burn it.' Had he said that aloud?

He found himself in the kitchen of *Inglefey*, searching for a canister of oil. He was standing at the door, watching himself. Then he was outside, at the entrance to the cellar again.

The ghost house stood over him, that was really an immense statue or a circle of densely packed standing stones.

He heard movement.

He was inside the cellar.

There was Seladris, tearing at the bones.

'We must find him!'

I don't think he's here, Seladris. He was far too clever for that. If anyhar or thing wished him ill, he hid himself, but somewhere very safe. Not here, in the death space. Somewhere else.

Meladriel either said those words aloud or thought them loudly, but he could tell Seladris couldn't hear them.

'We should say something...'

Just stay dead.

The flames, so beautiful, like a ballet of colour and light.

The night was coming back, the real night, the sounds of darkness, of rustlings in the trees outside, the mournful hoot of an owl, the choir of insects.

Seladris's heartfelt words. His goodness. His feelings, and the words he spoke within: *I killed you and now I'm sorry. I feel love for you. I want you to be free and without pain. I want you to fly.*

And Meladriel's own hard thoughts: *Stay dead.*

For a moment, it was again Leupardra standing beside him, but this was impossible. Leupardra would never apologise, or even care. Such sentiments were weakness, and in the world following the Devastation the weak were subjugated or ceased to be.

Get out of him, you shit.

Seladris turned his head and Leupardra looked out of those tired eyes. *Who are you to utter commands, honey har?*

But then there was only Seladris, lit by flames.

Meladriel closed the iron doors upon it all. He re-established a slew of lesser seals, because he was too dazed to form anything stronger. He couldn't remember what had happened. *When* was this?

The ground shook.

Meladriel's first thought was that whatever lurked here intended to claim Seladris as the cost for the evening's events. That mustn't happen.

Somehow, they were out and running, while the world turned into a maelstrom.

The anger of the dead.

The mischief of the landscape.

The weakness of a har – himself or his companion.

Bad old feelings: jealousy, misery, grief.

Meladriel wanted Leupardra to be broken bones in the ground, consumed by fire, but doubted his wish was granted.

There would be more to come.

Chapter Fifteen

Miyacalasday, 24 Ardourmoon, Central Alba Sulh

Two brown-skinned harlings came running from the lake, up the wild grass lawn to the lodge, shrieking and pushing each other around. A har dressed in loose black trousers and shirt, with mist-pale skin and long, straight black hair, plaited loosely over one shoulder, came out of the wooden building. He carried a shallow wicker pannier of herbs, one edge of it resting against his hip, the other held in an outstretched arm. 'Hey!' he called. 'Shut the noise, you terrible brats! You'll wake the sleepers in the woods.'

The harlings paused, looked at one another, giggled conspiratorially in the way harlings do in the presence of adults they might've offended, then came running to the har, hugged him. He put down the basket and placed a hand upon each of their heads. 'Inside, bratlings,' he said. 'I've made you biscuits of butter and lavender, of spider webs and otters' dreams and the whispered secrets of owls.'

A thunder of feet into the kitchen.

The har, who was Pharis har Sulh, gazed out for a few moments over the serene and placid lake and into the dark forests beyond. The land undulated away into wild hills, hazy with distance. The sun poured down in liquid light, fermenting myriad scents from plants and trees. Insects hung, shimmering, in the fizzing air. Pharis breathed deep, murmured within his mind a prayer of thanks to the world.

Pharis wasn't rich. He could have been, but riches didn't interest him. He had status, which was an inevitable by-product of what he did, but this hadn't inflated his sense of self-worth. Most of what he earned went back into his community, the small settlement of healers living deep in the revived forest landscape of central Alba Sulh. This had once been the hunting grounds of kings, and ghosts of the distant past remained, but these were faint visions, neither benign nor malign, no more than nebulous moving pictures between the trees at twilight.

Pharis hadn't abandoned his interest in music, but now it was part of his spirituality. He knew the magic of rhythm and taught it to others. He was the master of the dance on nights of ritual and initiation. He conjured spirits with the beat of the heart, fingers upon taut, tanned animal skins, the rattle of seeds in a dried gourd.

Hara came to Herne's Chase Retreat to be healed, or if they didn't need healing to be made better in other ways – to know themselves as the dehara knew them.

The area had once been named King's Chase, referring to its original function, but the hara who'd created the community wanted to change that. They didn't believe the past had be eradicated completely, but it sat better with their sensibilities to rename the landscape after an ancient indigenous god rather than ancient men. In the Human Era, much of the Chase had been cleared – scoured – at first to provide arable land, but later as the centuries advanced to accommodate the ever-spreading towns and their industry; the land was porous with old mines. Now all signs of human depredation had vanished, or at least were only ruins.

One of the specialities of Herne's Chase Retreat was the Sleep of Reclamation. This was a state induced by herbal narcotics, chanting and fasting, during which the sleeper ventured into the dreamscape of his kind. Here, the most vital lessons could be learned – the histories of all the ages: before Wraeththu, before humankind even, spreading out in a limitless vista of endless information, experienced as images, sounds, smells and feelings.

Deep within the forest, in an area known as Hart's Bothy, was a long single-storied lodge, which contained dormitories of comfortable beds, where the sleepers laid their heads and ventured into the realm of dreams. The area was surrounded perpetually by a faint, restful humming, like that of insect wings, but this was the vibration of the dreamstate, a dome of energy that enclosed the site.

Under the care of the sleep-watchers, no client risked madness, not that the word was ever mentioned in preliminary consultations. But there it was, the looming spectre, held at bay by those who knew the territory.

Pharis didn't enter the dreamscape himself – that task was for others, among them his chesnari Aedisa, a sleep-watcher of great experience. He and Pharis had been chesna for many years, but only in the last few had decided to raise a family. They were sure now the world was a safe place into which to bring new lives. The land had settled, remembered itself. Hara too were at peace with themselves, apart from in a few areas far to north and south, but nohar went in there, nohar came out.

Pharis and Aedisa wanted to be with pearl together, which had required considerable spiritual discipline and weeks of physical preparation. Aedisa's pearl had dropped first, followed only two days later by Pharis's. The pearls had hatched on the same day. From the moment the harlings within them had opened their eyes upon the world, they had been raised in the spirit of the community, trained to be self-aware, mindful, to care for and respect others and the land. They knew also how to protect themselves. Pharis taught them how to heal and how to make healing sound; Aedisa taught them how to dream.

Pharis did not deny his past, but neither did he fear it or feel guilty about it. He was prone to saying to clients worried about themselves, 'Show me a har who claims to be without blemish, and I'll show you a liar.'

The important thing, he would say, is to live your life well *now*, not dwell on the past, or feel obliged to apologise eternally for it.

He relieved hara of existential burdens.

Externally, Pharis appeared serene, rather a dreamer, with his long dark eyes, fey-pale skin and cloud of black hair, but inside he was still somewhat fierce, although in a different way to how he'd been before. He had become a warrior-guardian, prepared to fight if needed. While he'd worked hard to expunge demons of his early Wraeththu life, and to an impressive degree had succeeded, like Amorel he too found certain things difficult to forget or forgive, but he *had* accepted them. He had laid his uneasy memories into a secure place in his heart, where they slept peacefully. As far as he was concerned, that meant he'd won. If clients came to him haunted by spectres, he smote the hauntings out. Ancient ghosts, in whatever form, held no threat to him, because he *knew* them and their origin.

On that day of mellow sunlight and boisterous harlings eager for sweet treats, Pharis had no presentiment of danger. He fed his sons lunch, and then threw grain to the family's chickens. He began to think about what to prepare for dinner, since Aedisa was working that day and it was Pharis's turn to cook. He was expecting a client later, who was visiting only to pick up a remedy Pharis had made for him, but otherwise his day was free. He decided he'd fish for trout and serve this with cold potato salad and a mix of leaves. The harlings could go with him, despite the fact they tended to frighten the fish. Aedisa had made a large bowl of custard the day before, which needed finishing, because not even the cold store would keep it fresh for long in this heat. They could gather wild strawberries to go with it and that would be dessert. Thus decided, Pharis called to his sons to fetch their rods so they could all go to the river.

While some argument ensued over the whereabouts of one of the rods, Pharis waited on the porch. He saw a swiftly moving shadow in the light, and for a moment a chill skittered over his skin. Then he realised it was only a har running along the lakeside towards him. His first thought was that there had been an accident. He put down his fishing rod and the basket he'd placed over a shoulder and headed down to meet the approaching har. It was Caraki, who worked at the Dream Lodge.

'Caraki, what is it?' he demanded as the har drew close.

'Go to the Lodge,' Caraki said in a croak, before leaning down, hands upon knees, to catch his breath. His dark red hair was damp and tangled. He must've pushed himself hard to get here quickly, because he was a strong runner.

Now, foreboding placed a dank hand on Pharis. 'OK,' he said in a measured voice. 'Will you watch my harlings for a while? We were going fishing.'

Caraki coughed, straightened up. He wiped sweat from his eyes. 'Sure, Pharis, of course.'

Pharis opened his mouth to speak, paused, then again spoke calmly. 'Is Aedi all right?'

Caraki grimaced, shook his head, then said, 'Just go. Something happened.'

'Sweet Lunil, is he...?'

'No. Something attacked him. He needs you.'

Without further words, Pharis ran off, imagining as he did so that he was loping on all fours like a wolf. This gave him greater speed.

When Pharis hurtled into the reception area of the lodge, hara at the desk regarded him with horrifyingly concerned expressions. The High Hienama of the establishment, a stately black har named Fallami, with intricately neat narrow dreadlocks that fell to his thighs, drifted forward to take his hands. He was dressed in a simple belted robe of dove grey that left one shoulder bare.

'What's happened?' Pharis demanded. 'Where is he?'

'I'll take you, but I want you to know the facts beforehand.'

'Then tell me!'

'He was in the dreamscape, all as normal. It wasn't a difficult case, just a har seeking advancement. Then, one of the watchers noticed Aedisa's body shaking, which became increasingly violent. He was making sounds of distress. The watcher tried to rouse him, to no avail. I was called. I could see the situation was serious, but I managed to pull him out of it. However, there have been... effects.'

'OK,' Pharis said, calmly, although he was far from calm within. 'Take me to him.'

Aedisa had been moved to a private room. He lay on a bed, covered only with a thin, patterned blanket, staring out of the window. One of Fallami's staff sat beside the bed, keeping watch.

Pharis hurried to his chesnari's side, dragged an oak stool from beside the wall, sat down. 'Aedi,' he murmured. 'I'm here.'

Aedisa turned his head. His dark skin looked weirdly grey and dusty. There was blood in his beautiful eyes.

Pharis took his chesnari's hand, raised it to his lips. 'What happened?' he said.

Aedisa opened his mouth, but the only sound that came out was a croak. Inside, his mouth was bloody too. He must've bitten his tongue badly.

'Ssh,' Pharis said. 'It's all right. Don't try to speak yet.' He glanced over his shoulder at Fallami, who was looming over him. 'What other effects?'

'Disorientation, vomiting. That has diminished. We've yet to determine for sure if there are any internal injuries. Preliminary scans indicate not.'

'What happened in there?' Pharis demanded. 'What attacked him?'

'Fortunately, we were able to speak to the client,' Fallami said. 'He told us what he saw. In the middle of a guided inner journey, while Aedisa and his client were sharing images, something burst into their vision. The client could do nothing; the thing was too powerful. As far as I'm concerned that har isn't responsible for what happened. Whatever it was went for Aedisa, it ignored the other.'

'And what was it, this thing?'

'Well, it's odd, and certainly symbolic. It resembled a gigantic blue leopard.'

'A what?!'

'A blue leopard. The client was emphatic about the colour.'

'Fuck!' Pharis exclaimed, an archaic curse that wasn't generally heard in the environs of Herne's Chase Retreat. He appeared frozen in shock.

'Does this symbol have meaning for Aedisa?' Fallami enquired delicately. 'An ancestral motif, perhaps?'

Pharis expelled a sigh, slumped a little. 'No, I'm sure it has no meaning for him,' he replied, 'but it does for me. Fuck!' He shook his head, spoke as if conversing only with himself. 'Maybe something leaked out during aruna, and Aedi picked up on it without either of us realising, but I've never felt memories of that time near me when we're intimate. How could he know?'

On the bed, Aedisa shook his head, uttered an urgent sound, as of denial.

Pharis took his chesnari's hands in his. 'Oh Aedi, if I've brought this on you, I'll... I'll find it, get rid of it. I swear!'

'You think it's still around?' Fallami asked, alarm in his voice. 'I thought it was only a dreamscape anomaly.'

'I think it might be, yes. But I don't know why. This isn't just a random image, Fallami. I wish it was.'

'Hmm... Well, you *did* make the pearls together in quick succession,' Fallami said, in an infuriatingly patronising tone, 'which if you recall, I did advise against at the time. I warned it could leave both of you open to... influences.'

Pharis chose not to respond to that remark, because all he could think of to say was: *well that was nearly five years ago, so it's taken its fucking time to manifest!* Instead, he returned his attention to his chesnari. 'Aedi – the blue leopard. I'm sure I know what it is. It's connected with the Devastation, with my tribe in Almagabra as it was then. It was... a dangerous entity, but our leaders contained it. I have to tell you now that there was always a suspicion that it might return in the future. I never told you of this because I didn't believe it could affect me here. I'd forgotten it. But, by Aru, the moment I heard those words the past came back.'

'Perhaps I can help,' Fallami said, in a conciliatory tone.

Pharis glanced over his shoulder again. 'Have strong wards put around him,' he said.

'I've already attended to that, naturally.'

Pharis nodded. 'Thank you. I'll give Aedi healing now, so he can speak. I need to know all that happened. Will you join with me?'

'Of course.' Fallami glided to the other side of the bed, sat down on a seat a member of his staff had moved there for him swiftly.

Pharis stroked Aedisa's face. 'As we send healing, Aedi, try to let us see what happened in the dream walk. OK?'

Aedisa nodded slightly, closed his eyes.

Pharis and Fallami each took hold of one of Aedisa's hands. They linked their free hands above him.

It seemed Aedisa retained little information of what had happened to him. Pharis picked up images of the blue leopard but they were indistinct, like a moving pattern of blurs. He thought that if the idea of the leopard hadn't already been suggested to him, he wouldn't even recognise this shape in Aedisa's memory as a big cat. Also, once he and Fallami had inspected Aedisa etherically, they found he wasn't as damaged as he appeared. The shock of the attack, the sudden violence of it, had traumatised him, yet there were no physical or mental injuries – apart from the strange hue to his skin and burst blood vessels in the eyes. His skin was already returning to its normal shade. The event was past.

Once this information had been absorbed, Pharis and Fallami gave Aedisa half an hour of agmara healing. This sent him to sleep. He breathed without difficulty. His slumber appeared calm.

Fallami withdrew his hands, as did Pharis. They stared at one another.

'Have you any idea now what this might mean?' Fallami asked.

'No… it's puzzling. It was the appearance of an attack, yet without true harm. A threat? A warning? I'm not sure. May I ask your opinion?'

Fallami grimaced. 'Perhaps a warning…' He shook his head. 'It's as if whatever Aedi saw has taken the trouble to remove any evidence we might track. Or… maybe it was nothing more than a shared buried memory surfacing.'

Pharis reached out and stroked Aedisa's hair gently. 'Perhaps. I'm not convinced, though. The only time Aedi might've had access to my past was during aruna, and that has always been sweet between us, no shadows of the past. Surely, I'd have known if he'd stumbled over that vile old stuff. But neither do I have any other explanation for this.'

'Then all we can do is remain alert. If anything else happens, anything at all, however slight, let me know.'

'I'll certainly do that.'

Fallami stood up, walked around the bed. He leaned down and hugged Pharis to him. 'There's no immediate danger and no lasting injury. Of that I'm sure.'

Pharis returned the embrace. 'Thank you. Knowing you think that is a relief.'

Fallami straightened and turned to leave, then paused, turned back. 'May we talk again later, Pharis? I'd like to know more about the history you think might be behind this attack.'

'It's not something I enjoy telling others...'

'I appreciate that, but I have to know. I'm concerned for the safety of all my watchers and clients. Surely you understand?'

Pharis nodded. 'Of course. Shall I come to your cottage later?'

'Yes, after dinner. Let's open a bottle or two and talk into the night.'

'Usually I relish the prospect of that,' Pharis said, 'but this time?' He sighed. 'Ugly old wounds.'

Fallami put a hand upon his shoulder. 'Just scars, Pharis, just scars. I'll see you later.'

Chapter Sixteen

On the morning following the events beneath the ground next to *Inglefey*, Seladris wanted a day to himself before returning to work. He was eager to draw what he remembered of the wall paintings before the memory faded.

Rising early, he found Meladriel was in the kitchen, dressed in a loose shirt of thin linen through which – against the light – could be discerned the outline of his body. Seladris wondered what Meladriel had been like in the early days, before bitterness had taken root in him. 'I'm going to ask for a day off,' he said.

Meladriel turned briefly from the stove, nodded. 'Hungry?'

'Of course. Can I help?'

'It's done. I made enough for two. Was going to wake you.'

Seladris then found himself wishing – briefly – that this had happened, that he'd been roused by Meladriel's hand. He sat at the table. 'I need to get the drawings done, before the images fade from my mind.'

'Makes sense.'

Meladriel was distant, apparently preoccupied with serving the scrambled eggs and pancakes he had made.

'I'm going to see Veredis, but...may I come back here? I'm not ready to return to *Inglefey* just yet.'

'If you want to.' Meladriel paused. 'You don't have to go back there at all, you know. We can still work together on the situation without you being in its centre. Veredis could find you somewhere else to live.'

'No, *Inglefey* is *my* house,' Seladris said. 'Whatever's there is an invader. We must get rid of it.'

'Can only do my best.' Meladriel placed plates of breakfast on the table. 'Enjoy,' he said.

'That painting has to go,' Seladris said. 'We should never have put it back.'

Meladriel sat down, loaded his eggs with salt and pepper. 'Tika just wanted it out the way.'

'I don't blame him, but it must still go.'

'I'll see to that today.'

Seladris walked to *Confitteri*, hoping to find Veredis at work early. He also hoped asking for leave wouldn't be inconvenient. However much Veredis might sympathise with his problems, he was still the boss, and commissions needed to be fulfilled.

There were few hara in the building, and those who were greeted Seladris without questions in their eyes. It seemed Veredis had kept his promise of silence.

On Seladris's desk, three orders were waiting for him. He felt guilty then, asking for time off, but at least he could begin work while he waited for Veredis. He went to Kizzy's office and asked to be informed when Veredis arrived. He had to wait an hour. During this time, he made sketches for his commissions and wrote notes for his assistants, so they could prepare the unadorned cake-slabs upon which he'd craft his sculptures. None of them were too complicated. In between these tasks, he scribbled one Cerulopard picture from memory: Leupardra standing tall and lean, dressed in the leopard skin, one arm stretched out, commanding the unthinkable. Looking at it, Seladris shivered and turned the paper on its face.

Rather than Kizzy coming to call him, Veredis himself came into the workroom. 'How are you?' he asked, without preamble.

'Somewhat battered,' Seladris replied. 'I stayed at Meladriel's place last night.'

'Really?' Veredis's eyebrows arched dramatically.

'Not in *that* way, Ved,' Seladris said impatiently. 'We've been working on the situation. Meladriel came to *Inglefey* with me.'

Veredis sat down on a stool by the worktable. 'Something happened.'

Seladris uttered a short laugh. 'You could say that. Want to hear it?'

Veredis rolled his eyes. 'Don't be absurd! Speak!'

Seladris related the story.

'Amazing!' Veredis said, shaking his head. 'Although that's an inadequate description. I wonder what really happened in the past. Who did those skeletons belong to? It reeks of some atrocity being committed.'

Seladris nodded. 'I think the phyle leaders were responsible. Leupardra acted for them.'

'Perhaps they killed him to try and get rid of those pale horrors.'

'That's something I've not considered,' Seladris said.

'And by doing so, they created a monster,' Veredis continued with apparent relish. 'Leupardra was transformed by death into something abominable.'

Seladris laughed. 'You're being carried off by your own grisly ideas.'

Veredis grinned. 'Perhaps. I do like a good drama, and what a fine one this would make. I can see it now, being performed for tourists at seasonal festivals.'

'Well, let's find out what the end is before you write and sell the idea.'

'There's a chance we'll never know, unless Meladriel is lying and really *does* know exactly what happened.' Veredis frowned. 'I wonder who this other har he spoke of is.'

'Would Tika know, do you think?'

Veredis made a dismissive gesture. 'I've no idea. His relationship with Meladriel is a locked room. I don't know if they confide in one another.' He shrugged. 'Anyway, there's a more important thing to discuss – how do *you* feel? Is Meladriel's direct involvement helping you?'

Seladris grimaced. 'Too early to say. He wants me to believe I can control the phenomena that happen around me. I'm not sure he's right about that.'

'It won't hurt to believe it,' Veredis said. 'I'm a firm believer in belief!'

Seladris smiled wanly. 'That might not be enough.'

'Whether it is or not,' Veredis said, 'his ideas do make sense.'

'He says I don't get enough rest.'

Veredis narrowed his eyes. 'Mmm.'

'What that's supposed to mean?'

'Is that the only thing you don't get enough of?' He raised his hands to fend off Seladris's glare. 'I mean, if you hold hara at arm's length all the time, you can hardly be intimate with them.'

'You don't need to be intimate with a har to see to physical needs,' Seladris snapped coldly.

'That sounds like fun.'

'I don't want to talk about this.'

'Fine.' Veredis got to his feet. 'So what happens next?'

'I was going to ask for a day off, but then saw these orders had come in and... well I want to work. At least for some hours. After that, I'd like some time to begin the drawings of the Cerulopard.'

'Take as much time off as you need,' Veredis said. 'I own *Inglefey*, so feel partly responsible for your... troubles. If the current commissions need to be handed out to others, then so be it. I *do* have other good bakers, Dris!'

Seladris laughed, then said, 'I know, but I don't want to put you out. I'll finish as much as I can today. Whatever's not completed, I'll delegate. I promise there won't be delays in the orders.'

'I have no doubt of that.' Veredis turned over the paper on the desk that Seladris had drawn on, stared at the drawing for a few moments. He didn't comment, but put it back as before. 'Follow your instincts. Are you staying at Meladriel's tonight as well?'

'Not sure.'

'You're welcome to come to us for dinner and stay the night again, if you wish.'

'Thanks...' Seladris picked up the drawing of Leupardra, stared at it. 'I can't avoid returning to *Inglefey* forever. I really want to go back. Perhaps Meladriel's mysterious friend will take the painting away and I can return tonight.'

'Well, the offer's there.' Veredis hugged Seladris briefly. 'Just promise to keep telling me everything.'

'I will.'

'Oh, I'll get that payment for you, so you can give it to Meladriel for the salt. Don't argue.'

'OK... thanks. But I must pay it back – you know that.'

Veredis grinned. 'Shut up. It's a loan.'

Chapter Seventeen

Lunilsday, 29 Ardourmoon

At first Ulien had hardly dared to experiment with his new ability. He wanted to desperately but was worried it wouldn't work, that it had all been some kind of dream or hallucination that Tuli had made happen. Or else it would work far too well – he wouldn't be able to control it and would find himself far away, lost.

So, for a few days he'd thought about it, but only imagined his journeys. He'd even tried to summon Tuli but the har didn't appear. Frustrated and anxious, Ulien had felt he couldn't just ignore this unbelievable thing that had happened to him. He must do *something*, but it was almost too great to contemplate – at least alone. He wished Tuli hadn't left him to deal with it on his own.

Then, on Cala'sday morning, after his lessons, he decided that perhaps it would not hurt to try and move from one side of the estate to the other. He didn't *have* to go outside after all. It would be a small move and surely safe. This he attempted and initially nothing happened. And then, just as he was about to give up, (partly relieved, partly disappointed), he shifted, immediately and completely. The world gulped him up then spat him out in a formal garden on the other side of the house. Fortunately, nohar else was near. Ulien's body fizzed pleasantly. For a moment he could hardly breathe, swaying on his feet. Then he laughed aloud, held out his arms and spun round in a circle. Never had he felt so free.

Before trying anything else, Ulien moved himself back to where he started. This was by a tree at the bottom of the hill that led to the grotto. He decided this must be his anchor spot, the place to where he must always return. Tuli had not told him this, but he felt it was important.

I can do it, he thought. *I really can. I can travel like a ghost, without moving.*

He was sure his father couldn't do this, nor his hostling. Ihrec? Maybe... One thing Ulien was certain about: he was no longer the har he'd been only a few days before. And nohar else knew.

Ulien went into the house for lunch. Ihrec remarked that he seemed excited. Ulien attempted to sober himself. He behaved meekly; eyes downcast. Ihrec continued to study him carefully, suspiciously.

There would be no visit to the town that day, and only one other lesson after lunch. Ulien waited impatiently to get through this tedious delay to further experimentation. He repressed, with great effort, the urge to fidget and sigh as his tutor droned about... what? Ulien could barely hear the words. They were gibberish to him.

Once released, he walked slowly through the house into the garden, savouring each moment. He sought to make himself invisible as Tuli had done when they'd walked past the guards that day. He couldn't tell if this was successful or not since he didn't pass anyhar.

By his designated anchor tree, he breathed deeply, tasting all the scents of the air: the sap of trees, the ichor of flowers, the skeins of smoke from a bonfire higher up the estate. Birds reported on the state of their affairs, passing information to one another. A snake sunned itself on a flat stone, dreaming of the time it had been a god. To the world and its creatures, its plants and trees, harakind were hardly more than a noise most of the time, only identified as threats when appropriate. Humans had been the same before them. Very few were noticed as beings of importance by creatures of nature. But Ulien knew that now he was one of the few.

Take me to a place where I will learn, Ulien thought. He wasn't sure who or what he was addressing but he felt subtle attention turn upon him.

The scene around him melted, like water splashed onto a painting. The colours ran down. Birds flew around him in a spiral, lifting him in the cradle of their wings. He went into the sliding colours; his eyes open wide. He stepped out into a new location.

To the southeast of Olivian Grove, tall cliffs overlooked the town. There were no houses here because the ground was too steep and spiky. Ulien found himself on a natural platform high on the cliffs; it was not entirely level but sloped in places, creating tiers. This was the realm of birds, for gulls nested here and patrolled their territory, uttering shrill cries. The air was clear and tart, almost sparkling. There was a structure ahead of him – what looked like an ancient ruined shrine – with a down-sloping pathway of cracked marble slabs leading to it. Aged junipers, with leaves so dark they were almost blue, clustered beside the path and plants with tiny pink flowers swarmed over the ground between them. This place felt melancholy. How had any har or human ever reached it? Ulien presumed humans must have built the shrine, but he could see no path or steps leading down the cliff. You could only fly here – surely? – or travel as he had done, like a ghost. The shrine was a circular building with a domed roof, which was partly intact. He walked down the path towards it. There was no door, only an open entrance. Within, there was a table or altar, drifted with dead leaves and twigs. A dilapidated stone stairway to the left of the chamber led to another floor, but it didn't look safe to climb.

Ulien's flesh prickled and he became aware he was no longer alone. He could not see another being but felt them. Presently, he saw a shadow behind the altar. He could perceive no details of this figure but could feel its excitement, as if it had sought this place for a long time, perhaps wondering if it even existed. The figure brushed a hand over the altar, as if to clear it of debris. Beams of sunlight fell into the room and when the hand passed through this light it became real, briefly. Now the figure ran past Ulien, so quickly Ulien staggered back, even though whoever it was had no true physical presence.

He followed this vision up the marble pathway, around a corner shrouded by trees, rising up a gently sloping hill. There was another structure here, similar to the shrine below, this one in better condition. Juniper trees embraced it protectively and its entrance was in shadow. The figure, in sunlight, before he stepped into the shade, looked more like a har than a ghost, a little like Tuli perhaps. It was hard to tell, because his appearance vacillated from moment to moment. As he was about to disappear into the shadows of the second building, Ulien called out, 'Wait!'

The har paused but did not turn.

'What did you find here?' Ulien demanded, his voice hard, because he knew he had very little time to get answers here, at least from this manifestation.

'They're not temples of love,' the har said in a bitter voice. 'Stop thinking that they are. She is darker. Haven't you seen enough to believe me now?'

The har clearly saw someone other than Ulien. This didn't matter. 'What are they, then?' he asked.

'A waking place,' said the har. 'Be careful.'

Then the figure was gone.

Ulien stood upon the path, staring into the shadows ahead of him. *A waking place?* What could this mean?

'Tuli!' he said aloud, but no har answered, even though Ulien stood motionless for several minutes waiting. *'Please,* come.'

Nothing.

A cloud passed across the sun, dimmed the day.

She is darker... What had the figure meant by referring to a female? A human? Or... perhaps a human goddess from ancient times? This was a sacred place, after all. But a goddess of what?

Ulien heard a faint song on the breeze, a single lovely voice, vacillating, barely audible. The sun stepped from his veil of cloud, threw brilliant light onto the path. Ulien saw it sparkling. He leaned down and discovered seashells had been set into the marble. Also, there were long, narrow prints, leading away from him, as if from wet feet. Ulien caught glimpses of a wavering figure ahead – hair like clouds, a golden gauze, a robe of floating stuff. He experienced an overpowering feeling he couldn't describe. It was like anticipation but also hunger. He heard laughter, that echoed around the cliffs. Who was this entity? *What* was it?

There are many faces of love...

The air closed in, watchful.

You must go now.

There was something here Ulien didn't understand. It might be dangerous. He closed his eyes, wished for home, terrified he wouldn't be able to escape. But then the air enfolded him, took him away.

By the anchor tree, Ulien collapsed to the grass and curled up, his hands over his head. He felt strangely crushed, as if he'd narrowly escaped a terrible event and had been bruised by flying wreckage. He had to tell somehar what was happening, but who? He shrank from confiding in his parents, or even Ihrec, not even sure himself why he should feel that way. Hara were innately magical, weren't they? Wasn't this what his tutors had taught him? But if so, why didn't they use their magic, *live* it? Claiming "we are better than any who came before" meant nothing if it wasn't put into practice, surely? But there was a whole world beyond Ferelithia. Perhaps hara were different there.

Ulien mulled over everything Tuli had said to him. He remembered the blood-pink and white house. Somehar lived there. Perhaps they were the one he should speak to. But not yet. He couldn't travel anywhere else just yet. He needed real life, real hara, real events.

Back in the house, Ulien went to his bedroom, and was able to lie down on his bed in peace for a few minutes before Ihrec came looking for him. Ihrec stood in the doorway, assessing Ulien with a cool expression. 'You look sallow,' he said, and came further into the room. 'Are you feeling all right?'

Ulien sat up, nodded, but slowly as if it pained him a little. 'Yes. I fell from a tree, that's all. Hit my head.'

'What?' Ihrec pulled Ulien to him, began to feel his face and scalp.

'It's nothing,' Ulien said, squirming a little. 'Really. Just feel a bit shocked. The wind was knocked out of me.'

Ihrec rested his hands on Ulien's head and closed his eyes. 'Be still now. Let me check.'

Ulien enjoyed the comforting warmth flowing from Ihrec's hands. He felt better almost at once, more real. When Ihrec removed his hands, Ulien hugged him instinctively.

'Well, no damage I can see,' Ihrec said. 'But you seem to have taken quite a knock.'

'I know. I was careless. It won't happen again.'

Ihrec narrowed his eyes. 'Was it *only* a fall, Ulien har Shadolis?'

Ulien widened his eyes, adopted the posture of contrite harling. 'Yes, honestly it was.'

'Hmm.' Ihrec folded his arms. 'Anyway, there's an event at the Orangery today. Much delicious food to eat, and entertainers to watch. Would you like to go? We'd be a bit late, but there's time.'

Ulien thought that was exactly what he needed. 'Yes!' he said.

'Good. Get changed. Be quick.'

Chapter Eighteen

At the Municipallion, Meladriel was informed that Tiahaar har Shadolis was engaged elsewhere that day but had left instructions that should his new agent wish to see him, then Meladriel must be brought to him.

'And where is that?' Meladriel demanded.

'The Orangery on his estate,' replied the receptionist, a different har this time to the one he had met before. 'Tiahaar Shadolis is entertaining visitors from Alba Sulh.'

'I'll try again tomorrow.'

'No Tiahaar, the Municiphar was most emphatic you should see him today if you presented yourself here.' The receptionist paused and closed his eyes briefly, clearly in mind touch with another. After a moment, he said, 'Somehar will come for you. Please take a seat while you wait.'

Meladriel stood at the windows, staring out at the day. He didn't want to go to Olivian Grove, see Kazharn's life there. Was the har playing with him? He must know Meladriel would shrink from visiting that place.

A low sleek carrier drew up outside, drawn by dappled grey horses with black manes and tails. Beautiful show horses, for the purpose of impressing visitors, no doubt.

The receptionist came over to Meladriel, touched his arm. 'Your transport, Tiahaar,' he murmured softly.

Meladriel went outside.

The Orangery was a sprawling, elaborate complex high on the hills of Olivian Grove: tiers of greenhouses, an estate office that looked like a mansion and a warehouse of turrets and windows. Within the greenhouses, Kazharn's staff grew a variety of citrus fruits, which were mostly exported to Immanion.

Behind stretched the hill groves, where trees were grown for their fruits and saps and leaves – harvested to make medicines, perfumes, condiments, and the superior juniper-infused yenayva liquor for which Ferelithia was famous.

Meladriel's transport came to a halt at the steps of the estate office. Strains of rhythmic Ferelithian tribal music and the hum of conversation emanated from open windows on the first floor. The flag of the Ferelith rolled lazily around its pole atop this building. The design was a sunburst, cupped by a stylised, curving lemon tree on the right and a juniper on the left. A wide-winged gull, symbolically rendered, hovered protectively above. Meladriel grimaced. No sign of a blue leopard. None at all. Yet it was there, unseen, he thought, crawling around the juniper tree, ready to pounce up and grab the bird from the air.

Meladriel realised he'd have to get out of the carriage. The vehicle sped off the moment his feet made contact with the ground. He stood staring at the steps ahead of him. What was Kazharn up to? What was he trying to prove? Meladriel was not dressed for this occasion and would be mercilessly visible in whatever crowd Kazharn had herded within.

Eventually, Meladriel forced himself to climb the steps and walk into the reception area. An event host swooped down on him at once, no doubt thinking a new gardener had come in here by mistake.

'Tiahaar?' this individual demanded.

Wordlessly, Meladriel held out his pass.

'This way.'

Meladriel followed the har down a short passageway and into a shady office. The bright scene beyond the window looked like a painting, stylised flowers and trees, too perfect.

'Please take a seat. I'll have refreshment brought to you.'

Meladriel couldn't be bothered to refuse this offer.

The room felt cut off from the rest of the building. He could still hear faint sounds but a low vibration in the room was more dominant. This was the purr of an indoor space at rest in the warmth of a summer's day.

Presently, the door opened and Kazharn came in, dressed in official robes fashioned from a sumptuous and elaborately embroidered fabric of purple, deep teal and gold. He was enfolded in a cloud of sandalwood perfume and followed by a har bearing a tray.

'I'm sorry you had to come here,' Kazharn said, without preamble, 'but if you had something to tell me, I didn't want to wait to hear it. Please, take a seat.'

Meladriel did so. The room was no longer restful. Sounds outside had become louder.

Kazharn gestured at his minion, who set down the tray and glided out. Kazharn poured out the tea. 'Well?' he said.

'I went to *Inglefey*.' Meladriel replied, then recited an edited version of events.

Kazharn remained standing, sipping his drink. Meladriel knew the tea too would have been grown on these hills. His own cup remained untouched

'You were in that cellar on the day it was sealed,' Meladriel said bluntly at the end of his narrative. 'Who died there?'

'I wasn't told.'

'Is Leupardra among those corpses?'

Kazharn uttered a short, cold laugh. 'No.'

'*Did* he die, Karn?'

For a moment they stared at one another, then Kazharn averted his gaze, walked to the window. 'Whatever happened to him, it wasn't good, and only death or madness could have been the result. But I'm almost certain he wasn't in that cellar when it was sealed.'

'Almost…'

Kazharn shrugged, wouldn't meet Meladriel's eyes. 'Short of actually inspecting the bodies, yes.'

'You're lying.'

'Why would I? We're working on this together.'

Meladriel uttered a cry of pure exasperation. 'You knew what was in that cellar yet chose not to tell me. Yes, we're supposed to be working together on this, so *why* not share the information?'

'It was a simple disposal. A precaution – as far as I know.'

'Who *were* they, Karn?'

'I can't tell you.'

'Oh, you have an idea, I'm sure.'

Kazharn turned away. 'Casualties of Leupardra's actions probably. Infected with whatever energies he conjured… maybe. I can't say. I was told to keep my mouth shut as was everyhar else who was there.'

'For Aru's sake, Karn!' Meladriel snapped. 'There was no reason not to tell me that. You could simply have said, "there's some embarrassing and perhaps hazardous evidence left in a hole in the ground. Cleanse it." Would that have been so hard? You're ridiculous. Pelk this!' Meladriel stood up. 'I'm done with you.' He stamped to the door.

'Mela, wait!' Kazharn said in a commanding tone.

Meladriel obeyed but kept his back turned

'You know as well as I do,' Kazharn said in an infuriatingly reasonable tone, 'that with any investigation of this type, the less prior information investigators have the better. Your results are uncontaminated by expectations. Wouldn't you have done the same? Did you tell this Seladris all *you* knew?'

Meladriel turned round, suppressing his body's desire to shake. 'I have done so now.'

Kazharn smiled. 'Sit down again – please.'

Meladriel did so, furious that being around Kazharn made him feel and behave like an angry harling. It was despicable, demeaning, yet impossible to alter.

'Now... I'm sorry if you feel I've misled you, but I felt it was essential you examine the evidence without prejudice. I trust your capabilities, Mela. I always did.'

Meladriel drew in his breath. He wouldn't comment on those remarks. 'Seladris wants the leopard painting removed from the house. He hopes this will calm the situation down. *You* must take the picture. I'm sure you have some vault full of treasures somewhere you could put it in.'

Kazharn considered this idea for a moment, then shook his head. 'No, as the painting appears to act as a focus, it should stay in situ for now. We need to know whether there's still anything out there for it to attract.'

Meladriel shook his head firmly and slowly. 'No, Karn. It must be *moved.* Seladris doesn't want to leave the house permanently but neither does he want to live in it while possibly dangerous entities are wandering through it. If they're drawn to the picture, it should be secured somewhere safe, where it can be observed.'

'I think it's the location that's the focus, not the painting,' Karn said coldly.

Meladriel uttered a sound that was almost a growl. '*Clearly*, the location is important – I'm not stupid – but if the painting is removed from the house perhaps discarnate entities will no longer cluster there. At the very least, we need to see whether that's the case.' He paused. 'Also, since the ground has been... purged... it's possible the phenomena will cease altogether, as Seladris suggests. We have to wait and see about that. But the painting should be removed. If you won't come and fetch it, I'll… I'll throw it in the sea.'

Kazharn couldn't repress a laugh. 'Really, Mela?' He pulled a sour face. 'I would dearly love to think burning the bodies and closing the site is an end to the phenomena, but we still need to be alert and cautious. But…' He sighed through his nose. 'I understand your reasoning and will fulfil your request.'

'Thank you.'

'I'll send somehar over the house later to pick up the painting. Will Seladris be there to let them in?'

'Tell me what time and I'll ensure he is. Let's say around 5. He's at work at the moment but will be going back to my place later this afternoon. In fact, send us transport there.'

'As you like.'

Meladriel fixed Kazharn with a stare. 'OK, our business is done, but for one thing. Before I leave, if you know anything else – anything at all – you must tell me.'

Kazharn paused, then gestured with both arms. 'I can tell you no more. Like you said, we can only wait and observe.'

Meladriel shook his head. 'I don't believe you, Karn. You were one of Leupardra's helpless roon-slaves. You *must* know more.'

Kazharn blinked in affront but didn't otherwise react to the remark. 'You said it – I was *one* of them. Privileges didn't extend to information.'

Meladriel laughed coldly. 'How much of your current success is down to those privileges?'

'You're wrong.'

'Whatever. Seladris can go back to his house and we'll see if anything else occurs. I'll continue to work with him to help him clear his past. You take the painting into custody and observe it. If anything happens, you tell me. Is that plan acceptable to you?'

Kazharn nodded. 'Of course.' He paused. 'I wish you weren't so hostile, Mela. It doesn't help. Is it that you resent what I've become?'

'That you think so highly of yourself? That you can even ask me that question?' Meladriel's mouth stretched into a sneer. 'I don't care what you are, Karn. It's not my world.' Again, he stood up. 'I take it you won't be present tonight.'

'It wouldn't be appropriate.'

'Of course not.' Meladriel began to walk to the door.

Kazharn caught hold of his arm. 'If you would allow it, I'd prefer to leave first. Wait here for a few minutes. Finish your drink.'

Meladriel said nothing, closed his eyes. He felt Kazharn walk past him. *Just let it happen,* he thought. *Whatever it is, let it happen. Don't put yourself through this.* He put his hands against his face, breathed deeply. He must calm himself.

Then the air filled once more with the presence of another har. Meladriel lowered his hands and opened his eyes. He expected to see that Kazharn had returned, but the har standing at the threshold was Thazri. How long had he been lurking, trying to listen behind a closed door? They stared at one another for several uncomfortable moments, then Thazri said, 'Who *are* you?'

Instinctively, Meladriel held out the pass Kazharn had given him, but Thazri only uttered a sound of irritation and brushed it away. 'You are *him*, the one who brought the honey, aren't you?'

'I work for the Municiphar,' Meladriel said. Thazri was an enemy in his path, unmoving, hostile. Meladriel couldn't get past him to reach the door.

'Really?' Thazri drawled, then put his head to one side and frowned, adopting an insincere pose of concern. 'Has my chesnari just *upset* you, Tiahaar? You seem quite... distressed.'

Meladriel kept his expression bland. 'Excuse me, Tiahaar. I must attend to my work.'

'Work,' said Thazri flatly, clearly unprepared to move. 'Tell me what this is.'

'You must ask the Municiphar as it's confidential information,' Meladriel said, realising quite suddenly he was beginning to enjoy this confrontation.

'Well, I'm asking *you*. You know who I am, of course?'

Meladriel smiled, couldn't help expelling a short burst of laughter.

'That amuses you?' Thazri said. 'No har is indispensable, Tiahaar. Remember that.'

'Indeed not,' Meladriel said, holding Thazri's gaze.

Thazri took a step towards him. 'All right. You force me to ask this question that will no doubt be embarrassing for both of us. Is there something between you and Kaz? Something that has bearing on the present, on my family? I know there's more to this than either of you say.'

So, he must've questioned Kazharn and received no satisfactory reply. The honey had done its job well. 'No,' Meladriel said, 'I assure you our relationship is professional. I work for the Municipallion.'

'Then what did he just ask you to do? You look unhappy about it, but believe me, you'll look even more unhappy if you don't enlighten me.'

'I'm a historian,' Meladriel said.

'Just answer me.'

'That *was* an answer.'

Thazri's eyes were narrow with suspicion and suppressed anger. 'Why does Kaz need a historian? What or who from the past is coming back?'

'Let's hope nothing,' Meladriel said.

'He's asked you to do something dangerous, hasn't he?'

'I can't discuss this.'

'Does he have a hold over you or something?'

Meladriel rolled his eyes. 'Ask the Municiphar if you want to know more. It's not my place to tell you.' He bowed mockingly. 'I must go for I have urgent business. I hope you enjoyed my gift. The honey came from my own bees.'

'You will not...' Thazri began but was interrupted by the shock of Meladriel taking hold of his upper arms. For a moment, Thazri spluttered incoherently as Meladriel moved him aside. He was clearly too surprised to resist.

'Good day, Tiahaar,' Meladriel said. He walked out of the room, and then slowly and purposefully towards the sunlight outside. He imagined that at the very least an argument would later take place in Karn's household. Thazri was jealous, insecure. That was a delight in itself.

Meladriel walked along the pathway running beside the event hall that led to the main road from the estate. There was no transport waiting to take him home, but this didn't matter. Part of him despised the sliver of satisfaction he felt inside. *Petty. Like them. The stupid ones. It's beneath you.* Still, he wished he'd added 'Ask him about Leupardra' to his repertoire of putdowns.

Chapter Nineteen

Ulien was standing at the window in the events hall when he saw the beehar walking from the building. His skin seemed to squeeze his bones for a moment in a jolt of recognition. What was that har doing here? For a moment, a scent of honey filled Ulien's nose. Of course. The har had come here to see his father.

Before he fully realised what he was doing, Ulien walked quickly out of the hall, hoping not to attract any unwelcome attention from hara who might ask where he was going. For a moment, in his haste and excitement, he'd forgotten Tuli had taught him how to be *unnoticeable.*

He passed through the shady reception hall, and out into the sunlight. The beehar walked quickly too, but he wasn't out of sight. Ulien ran onto the lawn rather than following the har down the path. Ulien could catch up with him by a grove of ancient yews near the gates to the domestic grounds of the estate.

What are you doing? a cautious part of his mind demanded.

Seeking answers? Ulien told this prim, prudent aspect, which he despised. *Is that all right with you?* The cautious part of him withdrew, silent. He didn't feel afraid or even shy. He knew that of all the hara in Ferelithia, this was the one he was meant to speak to. Perhaps he was the har who lived in the blood-pink house.

As he drew nearer to the beehar, Ulien called out 'Tiahaar!' The har didn't stop walking, though, or even look around. Ulien increased his pace and yelled, more loudly, 'Beehar! Wait!'

At this, the other har did stop and turn to see who'd called to him. Ulien saw the har's expression become oddly still. His face was quite bony, the nose long and slim, his mouth perfectly sculpted. Ulien felt this har achieved quite effortlessly what some other hara – especially among Thazri's minions – might use considerable cosmetics to attain. He found this lack of artifice or grooming arresting, like coming upon a place of natural beauty he'd never discovered before. *A hidden temple on a high cliff.* 'Please excuse me, Tiahaar,' Ulien said breathlessly, 'but may I speak with you?'

The har laughed a little but didn't appear comfortable. 'You too?

I take it you are the spawn of Karn.'

So, he used the old name for his father, like Tuli did. 'I'm Ulien,' he said, touching his chest with one hand. 'Yes, Kazharn is my father.'

The beehar sighed through his nose. 'And you want to know who I am and what business I have with him.'

'Well... not just that. I'm hoping you can... help me.'

'In what possible way?'

'You brought the honey. I know there's a secret. They would never tell me, but I know.' Ulien drew closer, aware he must not babble, but keep his words slow. 'I have secrets too that not even my parents know about.' Ulien had no idea what inspired those particular words. He hadn't planned them.

The beehar grinned, rather insultingly. 'I see. You think I might be interested in your secrets?'

'Well, you work for my father on secret things, and...' Ulien took a deep breath. 'Something is happening. I've... seen things... *done* things. I can't tell anyhar, but I *have* to. If you work for him, as an agent, can't you work for me too?'

The beehar laughed more freely. Perhaps he considered Ulien's suggestion absurd.

'I'll find a way to pay you!' Ulien said desperately. 'I need to know if what's happening is connected with my father's secrets. I don't know anyhar else who can help me.'

'You understand about the nature of secrets?' the beehar said, still smiling. 'They need to be kept.'

'Not always,' Ulien insisted. He closed his eyes for a moment, debating whether to talk about Tuli. Now, his experiences seemed unlikely, something a harling might make up to get attention. Oh well, what was the worst that could happen? This har might tell his father, then there would be questions, perhaps punishment because he'd approached a stranger with a ridiculous notion. The outcome might not be good, but still the words came from Ulien's mouth. He couldn't stop them. 'I've... met somehar,' he said. 'Somehar very strange. The first time I saw him he stepped out of a mirror.'

The beehar became still once more, stared at Ulien, his eyes half closed. Then his gaze flicked back towards the Orangery. A pause. Clearly, he came to a decision. 'They wouldn't want you talking to me. You do know that, don't you?'

'Yes,' Ulien said, 'but I saw you and... I felt I had to. Please,

Tiahaar. Listen to what I want to tell you.' He paused. 'Maybe it will even help with... your work.'

'This is too dangerous. Karn would be furious and your hostling... well.' He shook his head.

'I can take you somewhere,' Ulien said impulsively. 'We can go there without moving.'

'What?'

'The har I met taught me how to. I found a place. A secret place. We can go there.' Ulien wasn't sure whether he had the strength or experience to transport another har with him who wasn't Tuli. His sensible side was shrieking that if he was successful his absence from the event at the Orangery would be noticed. There'd be trouble. Impulsively, he reached out and grabbed hold of one of the beehar's hands, who at once tried to pull away, but Ulien held on hard. 'Please,' he said. 'Let me show you. It won't take long. At least... I have to try. Please. Will you relax and let me take you somewhere?'

The beehar uttered a sound partway between a snort, a growl and a choke of laughter. 'All right, little adept. Show me what you can do.' Clearly, he believed this would be nothing.

For the dehara's sake, work! Ulien thought. He closed his eyes, conscious of the long, sinewy hand in his own. A hand that held within it decades of life and experience, belonging to a har who knew real magic. Ulien could tell all this in an instant. His plan could never succeed: it was ludicrous!

No! he told himself. *Concentrate.*

'Whatever you're trying to do, you'd better hurry,' the beehar said in a low, amused voice, 'because a har is marching towards us with rather a grim expression on his face.'

Ulien sensed this was Ihrec. *Now or never.* He banished mundane reality from his thoughts, concentrated on the ruins he'd found on the cliff, conjured the scent of the air, the mew of gulls, the wind in his hair. He uttered a cry and then...

The beehar fell against him briefly, then staggered back, waving his free arm to find his balance. They were at the ruins.

'Aru's lim... what?!' the beehar exclaimed. He pulled free of Ulien's hand as if the contact burned him.

'This is the place,' Ulien said triumphantly. 'You can't reach it except by... flying.'

The beehar rubbed his hands over his face and through his hair.

164

He looked around himself. 'Who taught you this?' he snapped.

'He's called Tuli,' Ulien said. 'He came out of a mirror and says he's my teacher.'

The beehar stared at Ulien for long, uncomfortable seconds. He glanced around himself once more, then said, 'OK. I am Meladriel, and I think we need to start again. I'll listen to what you want to tell me.'

There was a curved stone bench beside the path, littered with twigs and dried leaves. Ulien cleared this and sat upon it. Meladriel sat cross-legged on the unkempt grass, looking up at him.

Ulien began the story, which of course included seeing Meladriel at the gate some time before he actually visited the estate. Meladriel did not react to this revelation. He listened with full attention the whole time Ulien spoke.

At the end of his tale, Ulien said, 'Do you know Tuli, do you think?'

Meladriel grimaced, paused for a heartbeat, then said, 'I hope not.'

'You think you might, then?'

Meladriel stared at the harling in a discomforting manner. 'I will be honest with you. I'm not sure how much I should tell you. Knowing about something might make you vulnerable to it.'

'Even if it's contacted me already?' Ulien said dryly.

Meladriel twitched a smile. 'OK... I expect you know that Ferelithia had rather a troubled start as a Wraeththu settlement?' He paused for the answer.

'Everywhere was troubled, or so my tutors say.'

Meladriel nodded. 'True... mostly. But Ferelithia was particularly troubled because of the way hara took the town. They used... *questionable* magic. Some died for it.'

'But some survived,' Ulien interrupted in excitement. 'Tuli must be one of them.'

'Many survived,' Meladriel said. 'Such as me... and your father. That's not the point.' Again, a pause. 'This Tuli... in my estimation is somehar from the past, or else somehar who has an interest in the past. He clearly has an interest in your family.' He drew in a long breath. 'You won't like this, Ulien, but my advice to you is to tell your father all you just told me. I don't think it's something you should deal with alone – or with *me*, for that matter. There might be dangers. Your father has a right to know, so he can take action to protect you. I really can't help you behind his back.'

'You're a good friend to him,' Ulien said, unable to hide his disappointment.

Meladriel laughed coldly. 'No, not a friend. I work for him.'

'And what work is it? I know it's connected with the past, because I... heard him say so. Surely Tuli is part of it in some way? It's too much of a coincidence otherwise.'

'You might be right, but it's your father's place to deal with it, not mine. It's also your father's place to tell you about the work I do. I'm not family, Ulien. I'm not his friend. But I *am* concerned about you. It's clear you need help, but there's a limit to how much I can do... because of my position.'

'Meaning you could help me absolutely if you had the freedom to do so. What is the first thing you'd do... in that situation?'

Meladriel rolled his eyes but didn't appear offended or inclined to keep silent. 'Well, given this Tuli has the ability to enable an untrained harling like yourself to access the ethers and travel through them, I'm assuming he's very powerful indeed. He might be planning for you to make contact with me in the future – in which case you pre-empted him – or he could already be watching us, observing our interaction.'

Ulien glanced around himself, suddenly spooked. 'You think so?'

'Ulien, hara have to train for years, under extremely skilled hienamas, to master travelling the Otherlanes – if that was even how we got here. I can't do that. I don't know of anyhar who can, outside of Immanion. So yes, Tuli is a powerful, well-trained har. He hasn't revealed any purpose to you other than that he – allegedly – wishes you to know the truth about the past. But why? You have to ask yourself what he seeks to gain from this.'

Ulien thought for a moment. 'My mind says only one thing to me: revenge... Or... perhaps he wants justice for something in the past?' Ulien shook his head. 'I can't think of anything else, but I don't believe it's simply about teaching me to be a leader of hara.'

'You are wise,' Meladriel said. 'But also – and this is only supposition – this Tuli might seek to get to your father through you. Think about it. To hurt Karn, a bitter har might consider hurting those closest to him.'

Ulien frowned. 'I don't get that feeling from him. I don't fear him. Surely I would, if he wished me harm?'

Meladriel shrugged. 'Depends how adept he is at manipulation, doesn't it?'

Ulien's mind was a jumble of thoughts. He tried to calm himself, sift through them. 'Why would he want you and I to meet?'

'Because of… history,' Meladriel said. 'The original harish settlers here were complicit in the removal of the existing human inhabitants. It got nasty. Your father and I were involved – not to a great extent, but on the edges of it. At least, Karn claims not to know more than me. I do wonder about that.'

Ulien detected an interesting situation. 'How close were you to my father?'

Meladriel stared at him silently for a moment, then said, 'Pretty close – for a while. Things didn't work out.'

'Oh…' Ulien experienced a shudder of embarrassment, simultaneously wondering why he should react that way.

'It was very long ago, and I probably shouldn't have told you that.'

'Why? You wanted to.'

'Because it might be playing into Tuli's hands – reviving old… conflicts.'

'Perhaps he has a purpose for you too. If you won't help me, you should still meet him – for your own sake.'

Meladriel grimaced, then grinned. 'I've a feeling I'll only meet this peculiar har if he wants me to.' His smile dropped. 'But you're right, I should confront him, if only to establish who he is. My dearest wish is that he's second or third generation at least.'

'Wouldn't that mean he might be trying to avenge an ancestor?' Ulien asked.

Meladriel grimaced. 'In those early days, few hara knew how to breed, but stories carry down the years, I suppose. So maybe.'

There was a silence between them for some moments, which were not uncomfortable. Then Ulien asked tentatively, 'Will you tell my father we met? That is… if *I* don't?'

Meladriel fixed him with a stare. His eyes could be weapons from which a har might flinch away. 'I'd have to. Not to do so would look very bad if our meeting was discovered. This kind of secret could be used to harm. You must surely appreciate that.'

'I suppose. But…' Ulien sighed deeply. 'If I tell him, I'll be punished, I'm sure. Punished for being honest. Is that fair?'

Meladriel shook his head, smiling gently. 'You see, just by saying that, you know you're doing wrong, right at this very moment. Be *honest* before things get worse. In my opinion, it's your best defence. Tuli is counting on you to keep quiet.'

'Unless he knows that is exactly what you'd say to me.'

'Supposition is a wonderful thing,' Meladriel said. 'It's like clay. We can shape it whichever way we want.' He stood up. 'You must go home. Go to your father.'

'Come with me!' Ulien said impulsively.

'No, that won't happen,' Meladriel said.

'I want to talk to you again.'

'It's best not.'

Ulien got to his feet. 'I'll find you,' he said decisively. 'You'll see.'

Meladriel shook his head. 'I want to state for the record I am absolutely not encouraging you to do that. Bear in mind that punishments may be flung about in several directions.'

'He won't find out. I promise.'

Meladriel held out his hands, as if to ward Ulien off. 'Talk to him about what's happened to you. I insist.'

'But don't tell him about talking with you, I suppose.'

'Tell him that too. I don't care. Nothing can repair our friendship, so it doesn't matter. Just be honest.'

'As you are? You want to talk with me, Meladriel. I can tell. You know what's happened to me is connected with what you're doing for my father.'

'And you have too much of your conniving hostling in you, little minx!' Meladriel shook his head once more, but he didn't look angry. Quite the opposite, Ulien thought. 'Go home.'

'I could leave you here. What, then?'

Meladriel laughed. 'Don't be an idiot. There'll be a way down the cliff through one of the temples. Early hara couldn't fly, Ulien, and neither could early humans, who clearly once built this place.'

'Don't you want to explore?'

'I shall. When you've gone.'

'But I want to…'

'Go!' Meladriel insisted. 'Don't be a brat.' He paused, softened. 'We'll probably meet again.'

'Oh, we will,' Ulien snapped, in what he hoped sounded like an ominous tone. He focused his mind and prepared to leave, wishing he didn't have to, wishing adults weren't so difficult and obstructive. *I will never be like that,* he thought, and then he was home, staggering against his anchor tree in the garden.

The explanation Meladriel feared most was that the har who'd contacted Ulien har Shadolis was Leupardra. It wasn't impossible because nohar knew what had happened to the Pard Witch all those decades ago. Or they *claimed* not to know.

He was aware he was secretly pleased that Karn's son had wanted to speak to him. And – he knew he must admit this to himself too – he was also warmed by the idea of Karn being told about it. He'd be furious, of course. As for the insect... He'd buzz about like an angry wasp, stinging everything except what he really wanted to sting. Marvellous! Meladriel only regretted he couldn't witness the row. All this simply showed what a bad parent Karn was, because Ulien didn't feel he could confide in his own father. As for the hostling – well, what har in their right mind would try to talk to *him* about anything other than what could be bought in a shop or eaten in a restaurant? The fact Ulien had sought Meladriel out felt like a petty victory to him, but pleasurable, nonetheless.

If that was my son, Meladriel thought, *I'd have been able to tell something was troubling him. He'd have wanted my help, not thought twice about confiding in me. We'd be investigating this matter together. And I'd protect him with my life.*

He knew that in the very near future he'd inevitably be talking about this with Karn.

It had felt weird, being with Karn's son face to face, seeing his father in him, because Meladriel had made a decision long ago. He'd resolved never to have a harling, because there had only ever been one har he'd have wanted to do that with. Now he had met Ulien, who he found he liked and who had, in some bizarre interpretation of reality, been taken from him. *The harling I never had.* But best not to think too much about that. It would lead only to pain.

For now, he must focus upon what Ulien had found. The place clearly had relevance and perhaps had been important to Leupardra. Had it been one of his places of power? At the area's uppermost point, the building was in a good state of repair. Meladriel decided to investigate that first. But for a few moments he stood looking down on the town. Its white stone sparkled in sunlight. The sea beyond it was like turquoise crystal. Who would ever guess this idyllic area had once been a place of carnage and horror? The old voices, which had pleaded in vain, had been utterly silenced.

Meladriel set about exploring the site. The upper building was circular – a large lower chamber from which a spiral stone staircase climbed to the first floor. The walls were inset thickly with seashells, indicating it might once have been sacred to Aphrodite, an ancient human goddess, associated with the sea and also very strongly with the madness of love and erotic desire. Not so different to Kelosanya, now that he thought about it. The stairs appeared sound so Meladriel walked up them. The upper room was smaller and the only item within it was a pedestal, which looked as if it had been designed to hold something. Whatever that was, it was no longer there, perhaps a cult statue of the goddess. Meladriel stretched out his hand to hover above the pedestal. He fancied he could feel very faint vibrations of energy still emanating from it, merely a tingle in his fingertips.

He went back downstairs and investigated the lower chamber more thoroughly. The floor was cracked, and grasses and shrubs grew through it in abundance. He found a sturdy stick and searched through the foliage. But nothing remained to provide any clue as to what might have happened there in the past. Dropping the stick, Meladriel closed his eyes and focused upon picking up historical information psychically. But no images came to him. It was as if the place had been scoured deliberately, leaving no evidence behind.

He walked out into the sunlight; the heat hit him in a blast. For a moment, he was dazzled, but then he saw before him on the gently sloping path a har standing very still, looking at him. Instinctively, Meladriel constructed a shield of protection about himself. 'I come in accord,' he said to this figure, not sure how real it was. He bowed politely. He couldn't discern much detail of the har because his shape shimmered, and perhaps not just because of the heat. *But if this is Leupardra, in some form*, Meladriel thought, *I'd have known straight away, wouldn't I?* Which meant it wasn't the Pard Witch. Perhaps it wasn't even the har Ulien had met. 'Tuli,' Meladriel said softly.

There was nohar standing on the path, but he heard the faint echo of laughter. A soft breeze lifted dried litter from the ground for a few moments, then all fell still.

Caught you unawares, Meladriel thought.

He went down to the lower building, which had suffered heavy damage. But among the unruly foliage and debris Meladriel found something Ulien had missed – a stairway down through the floor.

This had once been covered by a wooden hatch that had rotted and splintered away. The top stairs were blocked by rubbish, which Meladriel began to remove. These steps must lead down inside the cliff. It would be interesting to discover where he emerged at the bottom – if that was, in fact, possible. He hoped now he hadn't been ridiculously overconfident in making Ulien leave without him. If this exit was blocked, he could be trapped.

Fortunately, once the initial debris had been removed the steps appeared mostly clear, other than for a few broken stones. After he'd descended for a minute or so, Meladriel found there were corridors leading off from the stairwell; the few he investigated gave access to chambers carved from the rock. All the rooms were bare, but he would need more time and proper equipment to investigate thoroughly. He'd need light, for a start. As he descended, so the light from above grew progressively dimmer. He knew it would be dangerous to proceed in utter darkness and realised this was another aspect he should have considered before he'd sent Ulien home. Would he be stuck here now? Any thoroughfare through dense rock would inevitably be unlit. He was aware of an increasing sense of pressure upon him, like the force of a malevolent will. That, along with the oppressive darkness, began to sap his strength. This was not a good place.

Much as he knew it would be a further drain on his energy, Meladriel conjured in his right hand a faint petal of werelight to illumine his path. He hadn't conjured this light for a long time, having had no need for it, but knew he'd have to keep it shallow so as not to weaken himself further. He hoped his energy reserves wouldn't be depleted entirely before he reached bottom of the path – and hopefully an exit from the cliff. He didn't relish the idea of having to rest and recharge his inner resources in the heavy pitch blackness. Now, within the feeble nimbus of wan light he progressed as swiftly as he dared. The stairs twisted and turned, occasionally transforming into a level path for quite a distance. Eventually, symptoms of psychic exhaustion began to manifest. He felt increasingly dizzy and weak. Soon he must extinguish the light and rest. But then, just as he doused the glow, he perceived a faint pale glimmer below. It appeared to be daylight. Assessing it would be safe to pause for a few minutes to gather his strengths, Meladriel crouched on the stairs. He breathed deeply, willing himself to relax. There were no sounds, and he didn't sense any other presence nearby, but still the place felt uncanny. He was eager to reach the outside.

Once he felt restored enough, he continued his descent and eventually reached a narrow crevice in the rock. This wasn't a doorway granting easy ingress, but a hidden entrance. He squeezed through it sideways with some difficulty, grazing a hip quite painfully in the process. For a few terrifying moments he thought he was stuck and panicked, struggling to escape. Then, he felt what seemed to be a hand or paw of some kind fastening onto the back of his neck. He uttered a defensive roar, threw out pulses of protective energy in blasts – which was difficult as he was already running at low ebb. But finally, with a cry of fury and effort, he fell through into a passageway of natural rock. Rays of sunlight slanted along it, not brightly but sufficient to show the way. Meladriel rolled away from the passageway, his body curled up. When he came to rest, he could only lie on the sandy floor, hugging himself, barely able to move. He ached all over and breathing was difficult – as if the rock had squeezed him through a jagged birth canal. His body trembled spasmodically; exhaustion prickled every fibre of his being. *Shows what an easy life does to you,* he thought bitterly, *I'm magically unfit. Must get that fitness back.*

After resting only for five minutes or so, he got slowly to his feet. He was in a long, narrow cave, where the black rock walls leaned in towards each other, creating a roughly triangular chamber. He glanced back at the jagged slit of blackness through which he'd emerged. *Had* something grabbed at him during his struggle to escape? Now, he wasn't sure. That passageway was weird, though. It seemed to be a symbol of birthing, as he realised it would be far more difficult – if not impossible – to get back into it than it had been to be expelled. Perhaps, in ancient history, it had represented the vulva of the goddess, and this cave was a place of initiation into her mysteries. But if that was the case, how *had* people climbed up to the temples on the cliff? A mystery that could not be solved immediately. He needed to get home.

Fumbling forward, Meladriel came eventually to the opening of the cave, which was small and obscured from casual observers outside by thick vegetation. Squeezing through, this time without the difficulty of what he now termed "birth by solid rock", he emerged onto the lower slopes of a hillside forest, a mile or so from the town.

Once he was free and standing amid the trees, he realised he faced quite a walk to get home. The sea wasn't far off, maybe only a quarter of a mile or so. He must use this journey as an opportunity to replenish his energy reserves with sunlight and sea water. Fear had made him reckless; he'd used too much of his own strength to light his way within the cliffs.

Once he'd made his way to the beach, Meladriel took off his boots and walked along the tideline. The tide was nearly high and presently wavelets washed refreshingly over his bare feet. He decided that Karn would have to be told about what had been discovered, whether Ulien confided in his father or not. It was clear to Meladriel that the temples – or whatever the buildings on the cliff were – had been involved in Wraeththu's conquest of Ferelithia's original human inhabitants. Had Leupardra unspeakably contaminated an ancient sacred site? That would not have been beyond him. He'd respected nothing of earlier eras. Did the mysterious Tuli want him to know about the place? Or was this har simply stupid and short-sighted, not accounting for Ulien telling somehar else his secrets.

Meladriel mulled over all Ulien had told him. The pieces of the puzzle were spread all around him, but he couldn't yet perceive the picture within them. The unstorm; *Inglefey*; the empty plot; Leupardra; the painting; Ulien; Tuli… how did all these pieces tie together? He remembered something Ulien had mentioned in his narrative – Tuli asking him to find his "heart" in *Inglefey* and bring it to him. What did that mean? Was that an artefact of some kind? He wondered also whether Tuli would appear to him in person now. He was fairly sure the image he'd glimpsed by the temple had been him. So, if Tuli hadn't known Ulien had spoken to Meladriel, he certainly did now. This could provoke antagonistic behaviour, communication, or further concealment, which depended entirely on Tuli's motives. Meladriel couldn't imagine they were benign.

He was so deep in thought, it came as a shock rather than a slow realisation that his pace had become sluggish, that his body now ached more than it had before. It was almost as if something heavy crouched upon his upper back, weighing him down. Meladriel blinked – his sight was cloudy. He was still some distance from home, and now he knew it was vital he reached it quickly.

Chapter Twenty

It was inevitable that when Ihrec witnessed his charge disappear into thin air, in the company of a har he didn't know, there was going to be trouble. As Ulien walked from the garden to the house, he was aware of a ringing tension in the atmosphere. He was tempted to 'travel' again to escape the consequences, which he could visualise quite painfully.

Even before he reached the terrace, Ihrec emerged from the living-room window doors, swooping down on him like an enormous angry crow, his black braids a great tattered wing. 'Ulien!' he screeched, clearly in a state of panic. 'Where did you go? We've had hara searching for you everywhere. What...?'

Before Ulien was forced to make up a convincing response, Kazharn came out of the house, followed by Thazri. Neither looked pleased to see the return of their son.

'Ulien!' Kazharn roared. 'Get in here at once!'

This seemed a ridiculous command since Ulien was heading in that direction anyway, with Ihrec's right hand clamped to his shoulder.

His parents stood in stiff, arms-crossed postures as he slunk past them into the shade of the sitting-room. Of the two, Thazri appeared the least agitated, but Ulien was not surprised by that. Kazharn came into the room last and closed the windows. Immediately, the atmosphere felt stuffy.

'Now,' Kazharn said. 'Explain yourself.'

Ihrec relinquished his claw-like grip of Ulien's shoulder. Ulien rotated his arm for a moment to dispel the ache. Now he was in the theatre of confrontation, he didn't know how to begin. The right words were essential. They would open everything else.

'Well?' Kazharn demanded. 'We're waiting.'

'Somehar you used to know has been... stalking me,' Ulien said.

Thazri began to utter some words, but Kazharn silenced him with a ferocious gesture.

'Meladriel?' Kazharn spat, even as Ulien opened his mouth to continue.

'*No*! Somehar else. We... we don't know who it is.'

'We?'

'I talked with Meladriel, because I... know he works for you, doing... secret stuff.'

'You don't know *that*,' Kazharn said. 'You were wrong to approach him, very wrong. But never mind that. How exactly did you vanish before Ihrec's eyes? Did Meladriel spirit you away from here?'

'No. I spirited *him*. It was... something... Tuli taught me, the har who's been following me.'

'Kaz...?' Thazri said softly, but Kazharn only shook his head, again made a gesture for quiet. He blinked slowly, staring at his son.

Both Ihrec and Thazri remained silent, Thazri biting the skin alongside a fingernail. He looked very uncomfortable, which was such an unusual sight it was disorientating.

Ulien swallowed. His throat felt sore.

'You had better tell me everything,' Kazharn said.

Ulien nodded. 'I know. Meladriel told me I should. He can't help me because of *you*.'

'Ulien, that's a terrible thing to say!' Ihrec couldn't help crying.

Thazri uttered a weird hissing sound. 'Kaz!' he said, louder this time. 'What does this mean?'

Kazharn would not even look at him, raised once more a commanding hand. In a dark and chilling voice that sounded deceptively mild, he said, 'In your no doubt fascinating narrative, you must also include everything that Meladriel said to you. Everything, Ulien. I mean it. I'll know if you lie or prevaricate. So, begin.' He sat down on one of the sofas and indicated Thazri and Ihrec should do likewise.

On trial, Ulien stood before the adults and told his tale. At one point, when Ulien disclosed what Tuli had said about his hostling, Thazri cried, 'This is shit, Kaz! Shit! Who is this creature? Another of your historical admirers? For Aru's sake!'

Kazharn once more made a signal for quiet and Thazri said, 'Don't you try to silence me again with your *regal* gestures, Kaz! You're not in the Municipallion now. Whatever the pelk it is you're involved in, it's involving us all now. Get it sorted! You're the all-powerful one, aren't you?'

'Let the harling continue,' Kazharn said. 'We might then have more idea of what we're dealing with.'

Thazri gestured curtly with one hand. 'Your fault,' was all he could manage to say.

Because he felt his parents were acting like idiots, Ulien spared no detail in all that Tuli and Meladriel had said to him, smugly pleased at the discomfort these words invoked in the adults before him. One thing he didn't disclose, however, was that Meladriel had revealed his former relationship to Kazharn. Ulien sensed this would be going too far and the consequences could be horribly messy. At the end of his story, he said, 'That's everything.'

Kazharn appeared to have taken control of his feelings. 'Thank you for your honesty, Ulien. We're not angry at you for what you've done, as you were clearly coerced, but only because we feared you were in danger – abducted or worse. Disappearing like that was a foolish thing to do. You must surely understand that.'

Ulien glanced at his hostling, who for some reason shook his head briefly. Ulien wasn't sure of the message in that but kept speaking. 'I'm sorry for making you worry,' he said, 'but I had to do it. I knew you wouldn't have let me talk to Meladriel. I had no choice.'

'You should have spoken to us,' Kazharn said reasonably.

'I didn't know how to.' Ulien glanced at Ihrec, who of course had mostly disregarded the first fears Ulien had expressed about this situation, but he didn't want to get his carehar in trouble, so said nothing about that. 'It's easier to talk to a stranger about something so… unlikely. Meladriel doesn't know me, and he works for you, so I thought he must be trustworthy.' Ulien was proud of these words because he thought they sounded mature and sensible.

'It was still a stupid and reckless thing to do,' Kazharn said coldly, unimpressed. 'And as for complying with what this *Tuli* suggested, that was clearly insane. Didn't you consider for just one moment how unwise that was? He could have done anything to you.'

'I didn't feel in danger,' Ulien said. 'Everyhar tells me to trust my instincts and I did.'

'Well, because you're so young, you lack the experience to make informed decisions,' Kazharn said. 'Did you consider that?'

At this point, Thazri stood up, strode across the room and took Ulien roughly in his arms. At first, Ulien thought this was an aggressive move, then realised that Thazri was only hugging him, but so fiercely it was uncomfortable. 'Oh, leave him alone, Kaz!'

Thazri snapped. 'You can't blame Ulien for this. Who are you *really* shouting at?' He took a step back and held Ulien's face in his hands. 'I'm sorry,' he said. 'I know I'm not the best of hostlings, and it's pitiful you feel you can't talk to us. That will change, I promise. You can tell me anything in future and I'll listen.'

Ulien realised, almost as a shock, there was genuine emotion in Thazri's eyes. A fire of protectiveness. He'd always considered his hostling wasn't that interested in him. Thazri was never mean or cruel to his son, but hardly affectionate or nurturing either. He employed Ihrec to attend to that side of being a hostling. Now this.

Thazri kissed Ulien on the forehead. 'Now, enough of this *cheerful* chatter! How about some late afternoon tea? Come along, Ihrec. We'll go to the kitchens and forage.' He turned to his chesnari. 'Except for you, of course. And what are *you* going to do?'

Kazharn shrugged arrogantly. To Ulien he looked terrifying, an inadequately capped volcano, with smoke leaking from him.

'Right. I'll tell you,' Thazri said. 'You're going to go and find your... *whatever he is*... and speak to him. You will tell him not to communicate with our son again. You will then, between you, sort out whatever mess it is you're keeping from us. Are you capable of that?'

Again, Kazharn gestured coldly. 'I will speak to Meladriel, yes. We will take whatever action we can.'

Thazri stroked Ulien's hair, 'And you, little pearl, are *not* to go wafting off into the Otherlanes, unless you take one of us with you. You must promise this and swear to it. I'm not trying to stop your fun, but to protect you. We don't know what's going on and there are many potential dangers. Do you understand?'

Ulien nodded. 'Yes.' He realised then that Thazri understood "fun" and how important it was in life – far more than Kazharn ever could. The revelations today were intriguing.

'We must talk further, Ulien,' Kazharn said. 'The implications of what you've learned are huge. We can't pretend it didn't happen.'

'I don't want to do that,' Ulien said. 'Quite the opposite. I want to know all about it – get better at it.'

'Well...' Kazharn began.

'You will,' Thazri interrupted, 'but enough for now. We can talk again later.'

As Ulien walked to the kitchens with Thazri and Ihrec, he said, 'Maybe I need different tutors – ones who understand what Tuli showed me.'

Thazri uttered a wordless sound. 'I think you do,' he said.

By the time Meladriel reached his home, he felt strangely squeezed. The sea and sunlight had done much to restore him, but what had started as a suspicion within now felt like an undeniable fact: something dank had clung to him and was still there. He must rid himself of it at once.

Seladris was in the garden reading a book on beekeeping, the sea creeping away from him into the late afternoon sun.

For a moment, despite his debility, Meladriel studied the har. He looked vulnerable, fragile and yet not. What was the truth of Seladris?

He leapt up when he saw Meladriel approaching and cried, 'By Aru, what's wrong? You look dreadful.'

Meladriel sat down heavily on the sandy grass. There was a buzzing in his ears, but nothing like bees. He was panting now, wilting beneath the weight of a burden that couldn't be seen. 'There's ointment... green jar... kitchen,' he said, gasping; with every passing moment it was becoming more difficult to breathe. 'Back shelf, labelled... Balsam of Oragan. Bring it.'

'But what...?'

'Now!' Meladriel urged.

Seladris ran up the path and presently returned with the jar.

Meladriel took off his shirt.

'Oh!' Seladris said.

'What? Tell me.'

'There are marks on you... small circles.'

'Help me. Salve on my back.' Meladriel scooped up a handful of the greasy balm and began applying it to his chest and arms.

'What is it?' Seladris took the jar, sniffed its contents, grimaced a little, but then began hesitantly to cover Meladriel's back with salve.

'Something hitched a ride,' Meladriel said. 'It's on me.'

'What is?' Seladris drew back his hand.

'Won't hurt you. Parasite, possibly from the ethers. Can't attach itself to anyhar else in our reality.'

'But how...?'

'Just help me! Explain later. Need to act quick, or else we'll need a hienama.'

'OK... What about the rest of you?' Seladris made a fluttering gesture at Meladriel's lower body.

Meladriel gave him a bleak glance. He sighed, then took off the remainder of his clothes but for his underwear.

'Your skin colour is... weird,' Seladris said. 'Should I go and fetch somehar?'

'No. Just help.'

Once he was more or less covered in the ointment, Meladriel walked slowly down to the shoreline and waded into the retreating tide. It was difficult to proceed in a straight line.

Seladris followed behind. 'Is there anything else I can do?'

'Make tea.'

'Tea? Just that?'

'Yes...'

'It's your remedy for everything! But all right.'

Once Seladris had returned to the house, Meladriel lay down in the water, let it wash over him completely – the wavelets were subtle elemental fingers massaging his body. It was important to use the outgoing tide as a conduit – its quality was to wash away, take impurities with it far from land, where they would dissipate into the deeps. The salve he'd applied was both a warding and exorcising unguent. He hadn't had cause to use it for years. The substance was old, and he wasn't sure it would have retained its protective properties for so long. Despite what he'd said to Seladris – he had no real idea what had assailed him, only an instinct of it. An odour, a sound too faint to be heard. Its attachment hadn't been accidental, he was sure. But neither was the parasite deadly. Perhaps a warning or a show of strength. *See what I can do.*

It must be him, Meladriel thought. *Who else would do these things?*

He had to trust that the power of the tide would do its work. He closed his eyes. Frills of water splashed over his face. An image assailed him: he and Karn in the sea, resting in the power of the tides, those great muscles of water. Becoming one in them. Making promises that were only hopes, and never to be kept.

No! Meladriel thought, banishing the image. He thought instead of Seladris – the compelling mix of contradictions. A har who had once killed to survive, yet now smelled only of warm bread, of lemon and honey.

This image soothed Meladriel as the diminishing waters cleansed his body and spirit. After only a few minutes in the water he could feel relief stealing through him. The tide, along with the salve, had dissolved and dislodged whatever etheric matter had fastened itself to him.

As the last of the discomforting sensations left him, Meladriel again thought he heard the faintest echo of laughter – not cruel or even spiteful, quite joyous. Perhaps insane.

By the time Seladris came down the garden carrying mugs of tea, Meladriel felt more or less restored. He sat up and rubbed away the vestiges of the salve.

'The marks are gone,' Seladris said, handing him a mug.

'Yes...'

'Will you tell me what happened?'

Meladriel nodded. 'OK. It concerns the har I've been reporting to about all this. His son.'

He began by explaining who Kazharn was and that Meladriel had arranged with him for the painting to be taken away. Then he began the stranger tale of Ulien. He didn't give all the details, just the bare facts of what had happened. Seladris didn't need to know about Meladriel's past involvement with Karn, for example. Tell one har, and eventually the whole town would know. Seladris would one day let it slip to Veredis, who would tell Tika... and then... What on earth had possessed him to tell Ulien about it? Did he secretly *want* hara to know? Best not to think about that now.

'The harling travelled through the ethers without a *sedu*?' Seladris interrupted at that point in the story. 'Mela, that could be...' He gestured widely. '... world-changing for all hara.'

'I know, but the ability might only be temporary. We'll have to see. Let me finish.'

'Of course. Sorry.'

Meladriel continued the story to the end.

'So, what will you do now?' Seladris asked.

Meladriel sighed. 'Well, we don't know what we're up against, really, so this Tuli character has to be found and confronted.' He shook his head. 'Easy to talk about, of course. I think it'll be difficult in reality, unless we can use Ulien to draw him out.'

'That seems... callous. He's just a harling.'

'I know how it sounds, but Tuli is clearly playing a complex game, knowing everything, pulling strings to make hara dance... He could even be watching us now. We have to interrupt his little scheme, find out what he wants.'

Seladris glanced about himself, grimaced. 'What do you think that is? How does it all connect?'

Meladriel shrugged, winced as tiny teeth of pain nipped his shoulder, then departed. *Just a weak remnant. Nothing to worry about.* 'He wants, I imagine, to cause disruption, to slash the frivolous, beautiful face of Ferelithia with a blade. Ruin it. Ruin us.'

'Isn't that rather a big assumption?'

Meladriel glanced at Seladris sharply, disapprovingly.

'Well… it has to be said, Mela. Why do you think that? Perhaps he just wants to get at certain hara, not the town itself.'

'Because if it involves Leupardra I can't help feeling he'll want to get back at us in the most catastrophic way he can. Remember, he saw himself as the leader of the Ferelith, despite the fact there were phylarchs. Whatever happened to him, he was taken out of the picture. And now Kazharn is the virtual archon of the tribe, rich and powerful, in the position Leupardra no doubt wanted for himself.'

Seladris nodded. 'Yes, of course. It's likely he'd be furious about that.'

'Oh, he certainly would! Leupardra was a vain and proud creature – confident of his own superiority. I'm quite sure he despised us all. He won't just want to take Kazharn down, but the whole tribe. We'll all be punished. I know him. I remember what he was like and how he operated. Part of his power came from merciless retaliation.' Meladriel grimaced. 'Alternatively, if it turns out we're dealing with a follower of Leupardra rather than the har himself, this individual is clearly acting with his idol in mind.'

'Somehar with an immense grudge, then,' Seladris said. He was silent for a moment. 'Perhaps you should use your intuition here. Could Tuli really be Leupardra in the flesh, meaning he didn't die? Or is it a haunting? Has he come back? Or is it somehar else. What do you *really* feel, Mela?'

Meladriel didn't answer for a moment, then said, 'I don't know – yet. To me the worst scenario is that it really is the Pard Witch, who for some reason has chosen this moment to return, or somehow link with you at Shadey Lane… I don't know. All I *am* sure about is that for the time being whoever's behind it all seeks to unsettle us, frighten us. We don't know where's it's leading – we can only fear the climax of it. He's enjoying himself at our expense.'

Seladris pulled a sour face. 'It all seems nonsensically elaborate,

181

though. All the weird experiences I had at *Inglefey*. What's the point of them?'

'They could have been a sort of by-product – perhaps something our enemy didn't account for. Maybe *you* hold the solution we need, Seladris. That could be to our advantage.'

Seladris laughed somewhat bitterly. 'Not mine, though. You and the illustrious Kazharn can use everyhar, of course. Ulien, me…'

Meladriel shot him a tired glance, snapped, 'Then go. Deal with it on your own.'

'Thanks!' Seladris snapped.

Meladriel sighed, shook his head. 'I'm sorry. Today has been… exhausting. Anyway, you *do* have to go back to *Inglefey*.'

'You're kicking me out of your house?'

Meladriel managed a bleak laugh. 'We're not inside it, so no, but anyway, I didn't mean that. Kazharn will have the painting removed this evening. You need to let his hara in.'

'What's he going to do with it?'

'See what happens when it's somewhere else – or so he says. I had to argue to get him to take it, by the way, but you're welcome.'

'I appreciate it.' Seladris pulled a scornful face. 'I can't wait to meet this har.'

'You won't. He'll send underlings to take us to Shadey Lane. He didn't specify exactly when somehar would come for the painting.'

'I see.'

'Kazharn's… *manner* is one of the reasons we're no longer friends.' Meladriel got to his feet, again winced as a remaining needle of pain went through his body.

Seladris looked up at him, head to one side. 'You're not right, are you? Do you need me to fetch a hienama?'

'No, it'll fade. The suckers went deep, that's all.'

'Suckers?!'

Meladriel laughed weakly. 'Metaphorically. Etherically.'

'Ah, well that's so much better, then!' Seladris shook his head, sighed like a hienama might to an exasperating patient. 'You should rest. I'll go to *Inglefey*. Sleep a while and I'll cook us a meal when I get back.'

Meladriel smiled, somewhat sourly. 'OK.' Seladris seemed to think he was now a fixture. Meladriel was uncomfortable with this – and yet not. 'You might be waiting a while, though. Kazharn won't be thinking of our convenience.

Seladris got to his feet. 'Oh well, we'll manage.' He brushed sand off his trousers, then paused, before saying, 'What do you think would happen if we just did nothing? I mean, simply let the painting go, try to carry on with our lives.'

Meladriel stared at him for some moments, several different futures flashing before his eyes, some of them – perhaps – desired. 'If we do nothing, if we seek to ignore it all, I can't help feeling that hara in Ferelithia would *change* – and not for the better. I can sense this sickening… influence. Perhaps the town would change – horribly. Perhaps disasters would fall upon it, apparently natural, but not. Unaccountable runs of bad luck, unfortunate coincidences. Those thoughts are what haunt me, more so after today.'

'Sounds similar to what's happened to me over the years.'

'Well, perhaps that's the connection you have with all this,' Meladriel said. 'The truth is, we don't know what happened to Leupardra – whether he lived or died.'

Seladris took Meladriel's arm and they walked back to the cottage. 'I still wonder about the motive,' Seladris said. 'Does our mysterious antagonist really wish us harm or are we merely tools to achieve a desired end?'

'Perhaps both,' Meladriel said, fighting the urge to tear his arm from Seladris's hold, mainly because it was pleasant. 'We're at a disadvantage because too much is hidden from us. I'll speak to the bees about it.'

Seladris laughed. 'Really?'

'Yes, tomorrow. My head's not in the right place to communicate with them now. And I need the bees fresh too, as they begin their day.'

'You're amazing.'

They went into the house, and Seladris began to make another drink, clearly very much at home. He knew where everything was now; when he filled the kettle with water at the sink it looked as if he'd been doing so for years. Meladriel sat at the table. He still wasn't sure what he thought or felt about this familiar behaviour, but it didn't feel entirely bad. Yet in one version of the immediate future, he was on his feet, yelling 'Get out!'

Seladris clearly hadn't picked up on this rather loud thought; he appeared blissfully unaware of it. 'So,' he said, having put the kettle on the stove. 'Ulien might *have* to be used as bait.'

'He's already involved, so it isn't using him,' Meladriel said. 'It's unlikely he can be shut away safely from this anyway. We simply need to work *with* him.'

Seladris rolled his eyes. 'His parents might feel differently.'

Meladriel uttered a short, cold laugh. 'Quite! Kazharn will attempt to keep me away. I can't speak for… the other.'

'Why won't you say his name? Is there history between you and this harling's hostling?'

Meladriel had to look away from Seladris' wide enquiring eyes. 'No, he just symbolises a kind of har I despise.'

'Like Veredis…'

'What? I don't despise Veredis… I just…'

'You do.'

Meladriel shrugged irritably. 'I detest shallow hara. It's a waste of what we are. It's like undoing a great tapestry into a mess of broken threads, so that the picture it showed so beautifully is ruined.'

'I see,' Seladris said, clearly suppressing amusement. 'Your position is clear.'

After he'd brought the tea to the table, he went to stand behind Meladriel, and put his hands on the har's shoulders.

Meladriel tensed, fought the urge to shrug Seladris off.

'Relax,' Seladris said. 'You're trying to help me, and I *do* feel better. Let me help you now. These are hands that can knead dough, remember, to produce a bread so perfect your wishes will be granted if you eat it.'

'Then make me some bread.'

'Be quiet.'

Meladriel closed his eyes, and like an unconvinced, nervous animal, only partially allowed the pleasurable sensations of being stroked and rubbed to soothe him.

'You really should relax,' Seladris said. 'Nothing bad will happen.'

Meladriel opened his eyes and gazed out of the window. Out there… the sea coiling lazily about itself in playful currents. He imagined a figure hanging over the sensual waters, a finger to its lips. A harling of the sea. Then another image flowed across his inner eye: a goddess riding to shore on an immense scalloped shell. Foam born. Aphrodite, goddess of desire, eternal, as powerful as she ever was. But what else was she now in this new era beyond the rule of humankind?

Meladriel put his hands into Seladris's hair and quite roughly dragged him forward. Seladris staggered round the chair, uttered a sound, partly surprise, partly… something else. Meladriel wanted to taste what was within. Was it a lie? A promise? A bed of pleasure? Something ancient and rotting? He pulled Seladris's face to his own, began to devour the other har's breath, *eating* it. Seladris allowed this for a time. His lips were soft, compliant. Then he bit Meladriel's tongue – not enough to hurt – and pulled away. 'You're hungry,' he said, putting his hair over his shoulders. His eyes were wide; he was shaking. 'Perhaps I *should* make bread.'

'I don't know why I did that.'

'I didn't think you did. Are you better? You made a meal of me; it felt like that.'

Meladriel laughed softly. 'The smell of you, perhaps, inviting like bread.'

'And how did I taste?'

'Of sugar and vanilla cake,' Meladriel said. 'The rest of you is locked behind a door.'

'You're very weird.' Seladris went to pour himself more tea, still unsteady. Holding the mug with both hands, he looked out of the window. 'There's an expensive vehicle coming down the path,' he said.

Chapter Twenty-One

After a spontaneous feast of cakes and sweet ginger milk, Thazri told Ulien he wanted to speak to him alone. They went up to Ulien's bedroom, and for some moments Thazri stood before the long mirror and stared into it – clearly not to examine himself but to inspect the glass itself. He reached out and touched its surface. How lovely he was – a har who couldn't be anything but famous and admired. Looking at his hostling, Ulien began to wonder if Tuli truly had Thazri's measure. At this moment, Thazri didn't appear remotely stupid or empty; he appeared thoughtful but resolute. This was an aspect of his hostling Ulien had never seen before.

Then, fixing a bright smile upon his face, Thazri turned away from the mirror to face his son, who was now sitting on the side of his bed, 'I haven't been in Ferelithia for that much longer than you have, Ulien,' he said.

Ulien wasn't sure how to respond to this disclosure. He shrugged awkwardly.

'I came here three years or so before you were made – that's all. I came for a holiday and during that time, because I was showing myself off so well, your father *saw* me. But, of course, that was what I was here for. I didn't have much money; my life was dull. I was after a chesnari – if the business arrangement I had in mind could be called chesna. My aim was a rich Ferelithian. Immanionites were beyond me, you see. So... next best option.' For a few moments, his gaze became unfocused, as if looking into the past. Then he shook himself and continued. 'Kaz saw what I could be and asked me to become this thing, this... *artefact* – the model consort of a high-ranking har. He was powerful, as wealthy as I could want – the deal was sweet. We didn't undertake a blood bond, because that would have been a lie for both of us, but a formal ceremony took place, officiated over by the nayati hienamas to make me his life partner, give me a formal role in the life of the town.'

Ulien squirmed in a mixture of disgust and embarrassment. He couldn't look at Thazri's face.

Thazri laughed, but there was regret within it. 'I can see you don't want to hear this, but I feel you should know. There's always more than one history.' He sat down beside his son. 'I wasn't part of this town's early days, Ulien, but even *I* knew the Ferelith had a reputation – a past they chose to cast off. That was part of what attracted me to Kaz. He seemed so glamorous – had once been in a band with the Tigrina, for Aru's sake! – and was now the highest-ranking har in Ferelithia, Immanion's younger sibling: The Pearl of Almagabra. Me?' He shrugged. 'I had no intriguing past, no delicious secrets. All I had was my looks and my ambition, a low-ranking, second generation har from a small town near Immanion. I was dazzled by what Kaz could offer me. But don't for one minute think I haven't tasted the darkness he hides.'

Physically cringing, Ulien drew in his breath to speak – anything to silence these words – but Thazri placed the fingers of one hand gently over his son's lips.

'Hush. Don't flinch from this,' he said. 'You've had lessons on life from your tutors, from Ihrec – you know what I mean. There are times when a har is naked in every single way. That's when I've seen things. Our partnership might not have been forged in the flames of *kelos*, but affection grew over the years. At least… for me.' He withdrew his fingers from Ulien's mouth and instead combed them through his son's hair. 'You have much of your father in you – it's so clear to see – but also much of me too. I didn't believe we could even make a pearl together, because… well, we had hienamas to help us.'

Ulien fought the urge to put his hands over his ears. *Please, don't tell me this…*

Perhaps picking up on this thought, Thazri continued. 'Well, maybe you don't need to hear more than that! Let's just say our qualities combined have made a har greater than either of us. Seeing you today, standing there before us, feisty and uncowering, made me realise that in you our strengths are heightened. You're not plagued by our weaknesses of arrogance and vanity – or secretiveness.'

Well, that's not entirely true, Ulien thought, but remained quiet.

'Therefore,' Thazri continued, 'I have something important to say to you. I will speak to you as a fellow har, not as to a harling or a son. Do you understand?'

Ulien nodded, dreading what might next be disclosed.

'Whoever this Tuli is, or whatever his motives might be, he will come to you again. I can't help feeling Kaz and I have no control over that. Even if we watched you all day and all night, I have no doubt he'd find a way to make us sleep or insensible. The same with whatever guards we set around you. Or else he'd simply spirit you away from beneath our gaze.'

Ulien nodded. 'Yes,' he said.

'So far, he hasn't shown any inclination to harm you, or anyhar else. You must remain vigilant, though, and be aware this situation might change. But while Tuli continues to be amiable, you must try and find out as much as you can about him and what he wants. Be compliant. Flatter him. Use *my* wiles on him – well, not all of them, obviously! – but also remain Kaz's son. Be alert, watchful, far from gullible. Manipulate him as he seeks to manipulate you.'

'He may be watching us now,' Ulien said.

'I don't think so. Not at this moment. Not here. Can you feel anything to suggest otherwise?'

Ulien paused, considered, then said, 'No. I don't.'

'Well, then, we are safe to talk for this short time. There is another thing I wish to say.'

'OK…'

'This Meladriel who works for your father. I believe he's an agent of the Municipallion, and perhaps had a similar function for the original leaders of the Ferelith. My instincts tell me he's dangerous but effective. Your father is secretive about him, but I feel that he'd be able to protect you far more effectively than we can. Bear this in mind.'

'I will.'

Thazri smiled sadly. 'Kaz would be furious if he knew I'd talked to you like this. He wants you kept out of everything, as do I, but I'm also realistic enough to accept that isn't possible. Tuli has shown himself to *you*, not us. I'm hoping he sees you as a naïve harling who may be deceived easily. Let him think this – act up to it. But remember all I've said to you.' Thazri sighed. 'At this point, the hostling – unexpectedly revealed as rather more than the harling thought – should offer some means of protection, perhaps an amulet or a way to call through the ethers. I can't do that. I wish I could.'

'Threc might,' Ulien said.

Thazri nodded. 'I'll speak to him and we can talk about it later. Is there anything you want to ask me?'

'No,' Ulien said. He felt almost dizzy with his hostling's untypical behaviour and wanted time alone to think about it. 'Later, perhaps,' he added, so as not to sound cold or unappreciative.

'OK.' Thazri kissed Ulien's forehead and stood up. 'We'll get to the bottom of what's going on and give this har what he wants. I suspect it's a grudge from the past, so maybe he can be appeased. I believe you can help with that.'

'I'll do what I can,' Ulien said.

'But do not take risks. Remember how I deal with hara and use that to your advantage.' Thazri smiled, blew a kiss to his son and left the room.

For some moments, Ulien had to lean down and press his face into his hands. He took deep breaths. Never had he heard Thazri speak like that. In the darkness, he mulled over the disclosures that Thazri's life was in fact a profession. His job was to be Kazharn's consort, and to fulfil his role and function properly. He did so to perfection, even down to being somewhat spiteful and shallow, apparently caring only about frivolous and inconsequential things. Ulien thought that Thazri confided in nohar, because he had no friends, only the tools of his trade. A lonely life perhaps, living behind a mask. The Ferelith believed him to be Kazharn's chesnari, but he was not. At best, they were business partners who'd grown fond of one another. This all seemed so clear now but only because Thazri had allowed Ulien to see – and, in addition, had revealed some important professional secrets.

Ulien lowered his hands, straightened up on the bed, and drew in a deep breath. *I have an ally*, he thought in wonderment, *somehar I would never have guessed would be one.*

And then the air grew hard.

Ulien leapt from the bed and stood tense in the middle of the room. He heard an echoing sigh. The air sparkled with black motes that held a brilliant speck within. A musty smell came, redolent of dead flowers and rancid perfume. Then Tuli stepped out of the mirror – first his head and torso in the weird stoop he adopted, followed by one leg, then the other. He used his hands, as if to push himself from the glass.

'What have you done?' he hissed. His eyes were very dark, almost completely black, but for sporadic motes of brilliance pulsing within them. His hair seemed full of dust.

'I don't know what you mean,' Ulien said, taking a couple of steps backward. Just a moment ago he had felt strong and protected. Now, he did not. Tuli was angry; it was clear to see. 'What's wrong?'

'You've told them *everything*,' Tuli said in a sing-song voice. He put his head to one side, rather too much so to appear natural. 'Didn't I tell you not to?'

'I... can't remember,' Ulien said. Neither he nor Thazri had felt Tuli near – he was undeniably more powerful than Thazri thought. Ulien's glance flicked towards the door. Dare he try to run away, call for help?

'Don't even think about it,' Tuli said softly. 'We need to have a little talk.'

'I'm sorry,' Ulien said. 'However I've upset you, I'm sorry.'

Tuli shook his head. 'You can't be trusted, can you?' he said. Then sighed in mock sadness. 'You've disappointed me, Ulien. You really have, and after I gave you so much. This makes me sad.' He leaned forward, his fists clenched by his sides, and his voice now was like hard splinters. 'And you're as stupid as that piece of nothing who spawned you. Don't you realise I could end you all with a snap of my fingers.' He demonstrated a snap, but fortunately nothing or nohar ended.

Ulien flinched. 'I... I was trying to help.'

'Help?' Tuli laughed, an indescribably sinister sound. He turned his back on Ulien and walked around the room. His feet were bare; Ulien saw that they were black, as if with coal dust. There was blood between the toes. 'How, exactly, was gabbling out everything going to help me?'

'You want... justice,' Ulien said. He was becoming increasingly dizzy, but knew he had to focus, try to remain calm. 'How can you get that if nohar knows about you? Something bad was done to you, I think, a long time ago.'

Tuli laughed, this time in a more natural tone and clapped his hands, which were also stained with sooty streaks. Ulien noticed that the fingernails were abnormally long and sharply ragged. He was sure they'd not been like that before. 'Oh, clever, clever harling.' Tuli stopped moving, folded his arms. 'Don't *ever* presume to take action of your own. Do you understand? You *will* help me, but only when and how I instruct you to. Is that so hard to grasp?'

'No, Tuli. I'm sorry.'

'This is a very delicate time, and you're behaving like a big clumsy dog, knocking things over, making a mess...'

Tuli reached out with his blackened claws and drew them lightly over Ulien's face. 'I want you to be a good little puppy.' His face hardened. 'But you have to take the consequences of being bad. It's the only way a good puppy learns.' His claws dug into Ulien's skin. He felt his flesh rip as Tuli scratched his cheek deeply. 'You don't have to be *pretty* to help me, and I can take all your prettiness away, bit by bit. Just a little now, though, so you understand. Perhaps you don't need both your eyes...' His other hand swooped up to cage Ulien's right eye. 'Oh, it doesn't have to be ripped out, simply made useless. I regret to say it won't look the same.' He didn't appear harish now, but like a dead thing, or a demon from some soulless realm – soot black, dead white, with creases of blood red.

At that moment, the core of Ulien's being became utterly still. He knew he was about to be harmed, horribly, and there was only one way out of it. He couldn't call out – nohar would come in time. He must leave. Now. And there was only one place he could think of where Tuli wouldn't go. He closed his eyes upon the terrifying vision in front of him and forced every ounce of will into one honed purpose. There was no margin for error. He must act quickly before Tuli realised his aim and stopped him. He focused his intention upon the blood-pink house.

At *Inglefey*, Seladris was tidying the house, waiting for Kazharn's hara to arrive. He'd been picked up from Meladriel's cottage by a single har in a light touring carriage, who could offer no information as to when the painting would be collected, other than that somehar would come for it sometime during the evening.

Now, idly cleaning surfaces that were already spotless, Seladris was thinking warmly of what had transpired with Meladriel, aware he felt aroused. He wanted this har, and because Meladriel was a strong shaman, he wouldn't be endangered; old curses would slide off him like butter from a hot blade. Seladris was sure that soon they would come together, and he didn't want to visualise what that might be like. When it happened, he wanted the experience to be entirely new. Instead, he replayed every second of the breath they had shared, the faint images that had passed between them. Meladriel had been cautious of course. Even in sharing breath he had protected his privacy. Seladris had respected this; he was the same. But still, those moments of being among the bees, of hearing songs in the beat of their wings. The scent of honey all around. These impressions had been Meladriel's gifts – all he'd been able to give for now.

Seladris knew the dangers of opening himself up on an emotional level. He knew that lust was a bane that disguised itself as love. Meladriel wasn't even his type. Seladris, when he occasionally took lovers who lasted for more than a night, opted for dark, lithe hara whose ouanic aspects slightly overshadowed the soume. He thought of them as wild animals, creatures who could not be tamed. It was safer that way. And yet, Meladriel... the har was balanced in his being. Anyhar could see that. But there was damage within, and that was intriguing. He was a wild animal of a different kind.

These thoughts consumed Seladris so completely, it was like being in trance. Time passed unnoticed.

So the dull, heavy thump that came from the hallway was a horrible intrusion. It jolted him back to reality, like waking from a deep sleep. He didn't want to think about what the sound might signify, because in his heightened state of awareness he knew that trouble had just landed in the house.

Wiping his hands on a dish towel, Seladris ventured out of the kitchen. He considered picking up a weapon – a knife, perhaps – but then thought this probably wouldn't help him. But he didn't feel threatened or afraid. Perhaps this was simply the aftereffects of thinking about Meladriel. A kind of protection.

In the hallway stood a dazed young har, his face blackened and dripping with blood, which had already spattered down onto his pale cream shirt and was now falling in splats onto the wooden floor.

'Who in Aru's name are you?' Seladris demanded. 'What are you doing here?'

The harling looked at him; he appeared wretched, terrified, 'Please help me,' he said. 'Please.'

'Tell me who you are!'

'Ulien....' The harling stammered. 'Ulien har Shadolis.' He put a hand to his face, saw the blood, made a sound of distress.

'Ulien!? Sweet dehara... did you come through the ethers? Why?'

Ulien didn't answer, continuing to dab a hand to his face, then look at the blood while moaning, repeatedly.

'Come, come,' Seladris said. He took hold of the harling's arm and dragged him into the kitchen. 'Sit!' He pushed Ulien into a chair and then set about finding domestic medical supplies. He recalled seeing some salve and linen cloths somewhere in a cupboard. These found, he swiftly located a ceramic bowl and filled it with water into which he added salt. This he carried to the table. 'Let me bathe that wound,' he said. 'Then we can see how bad it is.'

The young har was weeping now, his tears mingling with the blood. 'He was going to take an *eye*,' he said. 'I had to come here, because he can't come into this house. I'm sorry... I...'

'Hush,' Seladris said. He could see now the harling's face was badly gashed, as if by a ferocious animal, and the wounds were deep, looked like they needed stitching. If only Meladriel had come here with him, but of course Seladris had *told* him to stay behind. Typical!

Seladris cleaned Ulien's face as best he could and applied the salve, which helped with the bleeding. He made a wad of the linen cloths, which he soaked in the saltwater, and told Ulien to hold this tight to his face. 'Don't worry,' he said. 'Your father's hara will be here soon.'

'No! No!' Ulien cried. 'I need Meladriel. Do you know him? I need him. Nohar else can help.'

'He's.... he lives somewhere else, Ulien, quite a walk away. You're in no condition to go there.'

'I can if I know where it is... Or you could show me... in your mind... We could go... I can *move* us there.' Ulien began to weep again, helplessly, clearly in no state to do anything of the kind.

'Well, you're safe here for the moment,' Seladris said. 'I'll get the hara to take *me* to Meladriel and tell him. Bring him back with me.'

'I'll be all right. I'll be able to get there. But I need...' Ulien's eyes rolled in his head and Seladris thought the harling was about to faint.

'What you need is to lie down for a while. Tell me what happened, OK? Come with me.'

Ulien's entire body was trembling but Seladris managed to half carry him into one of the downstairs rooms, where there was a sofa – not the room containing the painting. He sensed that might be dangerous.

By the time Ulien was lying on a couch in a lesser salon, his skin felt cold. Seladris was concerned he might be poisoned. The scratches had been filled with black dirt, and although he'd managed to bathe most of it away, he wasn't a skilled healer. The dirt had been *odd*. Flaky, like scales, and yet also like soot. It was clear Ulien needed more care than he knew how to give. He laid a fringed blanket over the harling, which had hung over the back of the couch. Then he sat on the floor beside Ulien. 'I'm no healer,' he said, 'but let me put some agmara energy into you.'

'OK,' Ulien murmured.

Seladris put one hand on the harling's forehead, the other on his chest and concentrated for a moment to summon the healing current of agmara. He'd never trained to use it properly but was adept enough to make it flow through him. 'I'm Seladris,' he said softly, 'a friend of Meladriel's. I know you saw him earlier today and I already know some of your story. So tell me how you ended up in my house, bleeding onto my hall floor.'

Half of Ulien's face curved into a weak smile. 'You know about Tuli?'

'Yes. Did *he* do this to you?'

'He *did*. He said he'd take an eye too. That's why I had to escape, and I know he can't enter this house because...' He paused, looked furtive.

'Because you came here before.'

Ulien glanced away briefly. 'Yes. I'm sorry. He told me to come in here but... I don't think he could come himself. That's why I thought of coming here now.'

'That was the right thing to do,' Seladris said. 'Meladriel told me your story. It's all right. If you feel safe here, that's fine by me. You need some wards around you, clearly.'

'My father will be angry,' Ulien said. 'He told me not to shift again, but I had to!'

'He'll understand,' Seladris said softly, doubting that was true. 'Why did Tuli attack you?'

'Because I told hara about him. I told Meladriel and *he* said I must tell my family. I shouldn't have. Meladriel was wrong. It made Tuli furious and now he doesn't trust me. My hostling said I should fool him into trusting me, but it's all ruined now. He wants to hurt me.' Ulien half rose, glanced around the room. 'I don't know if I'm really safe here. He's so powerful. When I came in before, it might've been only a test.'

'Hush, you're safe,' Seladris murmured, again unsure of the

truth. He didn't attempt to apply more healing, hoping what he'd managed to channel would help. 'I've seen things in this house, but not the har you describe. Perhaps he fears the things I see. They *are* pretty horrible.'

'You don't know that!' Ulien snapped. 'We thought we were safe at home. Thazri said we were, but we weren't. He was watching us all the time.'

Seladris squeezed Ulien's shoulder. He couldn't think of anything to say. The harling might be right.

At that moment, he heard a vehicle coming to a halt outside, the stamp of horses. 'Your father's hara are here,' he said. 'I'll send word to your family, as discreetly as I can. I agree you must see Meladriel. I'll ask them to take me there.'

'I don't want my father to know,' Ulien said miserably. 'Can you... can you ask them to tell my hostling, Thazri?' He shook his head. 'No, they'd just tell my father anyway. Everyhar who works for him is like a dog, fawning over him, wagging their tails.'

'We have to tell them, Ulien. Your parents will be worried.'

'I know.' Ulien put a hand tentatively to his face. 'It's not my fault.'

'It isn't,' Seladris said. 'It's the fault of actions long ago.'

'My father's....'

'It would seem so, but not just him.'

Ulien uttered a bitter sound. 'I've started to hate him. I never felt that before.'

'Well, maybe that feeling isn't entirely down to you, eh?'

A knock sounded on the front door.

'Wait here,' Seladris said.

He went to the door and opened it upon two fine hara who looked him up and down appraisingly, before one of them said, 'Tiahaar Kazharn har Shadolis sent us.'

'The painting,' Seladris said dryly. He gestured for the hara to enter the house. 'I'll take you to it.' He directed them to the room where the painting hung. They made no comment on it, undoubtedly having no idea why they'd been asked to fetch it. The blue leopard appeared to resist being removed. They struggled with it, hurt themselves – a long splinter from the frame deep into a palm, the heavy frame sliding from their hands to bruise a foot. Seladris said nothing, simply watched, feeling a small but pleasurable amount of satisfaction.

Once they'd heaved and dragged it to their vehicle – and it scraped and chipped the immaculate paintwork as they manoeuvred it inside – Seladris said, 'Be so kind as to deliver a message to Tiahaar Thazri for me. It's vital he receives it immediately.'

The hara swapped glances, and one of them said, 'Yeah?'

Seladris paused, unnerved by their direct, condescending gazes. 'Tell him… Ulien paid me a visit.'

Again, an exchange of glances. 'What?'

'I think you heard. Tell Thazri all is well, but for now only the painting should be removed from this house. It's very important you remember this precisely.'

'We're not going to the *Velvets* estate until later,' one of the hara said. 'The painting's going somewhere else.'

'Well, I think you *should* go to the estate first,' Seladris replied. 'I can assure you your employer will be far from happy if you don't deliver my message.'

'Tiahaar Thazri isn't our employer,' insisted the other har, annoyingly. 'Tiahaar Kazharn wanted the painting removed. We're following his instructions.'

'What's this about?' said the first har suspiciously. 'Why are *you* trying to send messages to a har like Thazri? Ulien would never come here.'

A spurt of anger ignited in Seladris's heart. If he directed them to tell Kazharn instead he wondered whether Thazri would even get to hear the message. 'Just do as I ask,' he said, 'please.' He softened his expression, smiled hopefully. It was all he could do. 'It's a… personal matter. And it *is* connected with the painting.'

The hara exchanged a glance and no doubt private communication. Then one of them said, 'All right.'

Seladris considered for a moment asking these hara for a lift to *Eko Melosa*, but realised they'd simply refuse. Also, now he was in the moment, he was unsure he wanted them to know where he was going. No problem. He'd just have to walk there as quickly as he could.

Kazharn's hara jumped to the driving seat of their vehicle and soon it was clattering away up the path.

Seladris went back inside. Ulien was peering round the sitting room door; his hand still held the cloths to his face.

'They've gone,' Seladris said. 'There was no point asking them to take me to Meladriel. I'll hurry to him as quickly as possible by myself. If for any reason you feel threatened here…' He paused, really didn't know what to suggest.

'If that happens there's nothing I can do,' Ulien said miserably.

Seladris considered. 'OK… We have no choice, then. I'll make you a hot drink, and I think you should eat something too. I have cake – sugar will help, I'm sure.'

'For what?' Ulien's eyes were wide.

'For you to feel well enough to come with me,' Seladris said.

'I could…'

'No!' Seladris said. 'We walk. I'll not risk anything else.'

Ferelithia

The town shudders in the balmy heat of early evening. It feels twinges of discomfort within its being, as if it is assaulted by a horde of minute but invisible enemies.

A son of Ferelithia is in pain. He has released a sky-splitting scream, without realising who or what might hear it. He is maddened in his agony, writhing and screeching, tearing at his hair, his skin.

Ferelithia knows this individual is part of its own fabric, has helped shape it. He's been gone for a long time, wandering, hardly more than a wisp of memory. But something has brought him back.

He stands in the light now, revealed, where before there was only a shadow.

He cannot be healed.

He threatens others, seeking only to spread his pain.

When a har has nothing to lose he becomes an avatar of calamity, fit only to drag others down into his pit of despair.

Ferelithia's instinct is to cast flowers over an ugly wound so it cannot be seen. Surely the sweet scent alone will restore and repair? But this one is black inside, diseased to his core. Flowering the surface will achieve nothing.

And what of the other voice, a cry pure and radiant? An innocent, who is also a son of Ferelithia. Isn't it the town's duty to soothe this har too?

The more Ferelithia is poked and hurt, the more its being coalesces, finds reason.

Call to the sea. Call upon the ancient powers. Call upon the new powers. Weave the mesh, spin and seethe. The waves make it. The air makes it. Make one from many. Make it shine. Make it bigger than the sky.

But how?

Through hara. Through life. Through substance. Through belief.

Chapter Twenty-Two

The Tigrina of Immanion was attending a play in the city. During the afternoon, high summer had burned the graceful white buildings, the high towers that speared the evening, the painted domes of nayatis; those wombs of stone and crystal that nurtured dehara. Now, in the simmering evening, pennants on lofty poles above the Hegalion and the palace Phaonica hung listless or flapped like dying fish, parching on the land. Beyond the harbour, where swanlike ships drowsed, the sea lay quiet, exhausted. Yet the city did not sleep. Hara were languid and listless, yet drawn out inexorably into the night, to its delights.

The air within the vast theatre was highly scented with an aroma of roses and myrrh but was also too hot. It was packed to capacity because the lead actor was currently blazing like Sirius, the star that rose with the sun at this time of year. Everyhar wanted to stare at him then discuss breathlessly how his performance had been faultless. He was young, beautiful and brimming with pain at the horrors of history. Star of the Dog Days, baying into the indifferent reaches of space.

Caeru wasn't that interested in the performance but was unable to sneak out and go home because he was Tigrina, and to do so would be an unthinkable insult to the playwright and the cast of the production. The trouble was that the play wasn't *real*. It was hackneyed and sentimental, allegedly presenting the story of a first generation har struggling with his new condition. Much whining and sighing and handwringing. The star blazed too gaudily, in Caeru's opinion. And what the writer had failed drastically to capture was the fact that first generation hara hadn't thought much about their new condition at all; they'd simply revelled in it, thoughtlessly and carelessly, ignorant or uncaring of the consequences. If hands were ever wrung, it was generally to clean them of blood. The time for reflection and uncertainty had come far later, once the ashes of conflict had sifted down and greenery

199

had devoured the battlegrounds and the ruined cities. Only then could a har hold out his hands before him and stare at them in terror.

Idiots, Caeru thought without much energy. Every generation must rewrite the past, perhaps. Why should he care about it?

He'd always been somewhat cynical about harakind and his own tribe – the Gelaming – in particular. But he enjoyed being Tigrina and adored the luxuries of his life. He loved his family and his friends. He could ignore the rest.

Of all the members of Amorel's old band, Caeru was the least likely to suffer from the effects of bad memories. He accepted the past as simply history, no longer relevant. He wouldn't act like that now, so it didn't matter. Everyhar had behaved like a pelker back then. Not even his chesnari, the Tigron Pellaz, knew the truth of Caeru's distant past. He didn't conceal it out of shame or fear, but simply because it was too tedious to talk about. He felt he couldn't be blamed for something he'd had no control over, or full knowledge about. He'd been a stupid kid, one of the incepted. So had everyhar else. Just forget it. Which was why he hated certain modern young creatives who sought to rummage through the debris, unearthing ancient tombs, hoping for dramatic curses to come flying out, but releasing only dust. Just for a while, during such performances, Caeru *remembered.* He wasn't uncomfortable about that exactly, but simply wished it didn't happen.

Sometimes hara might say, 'Will you sing for us, Tiahaar? Sing one of your old songs?'

And he'd smile and answer politely, 'no.' The only time he sang now was when alone and usually only to the cats who lived with him. They seemed to like it. When harlings of the family had been young, he'd sung to them too, but it was doubtful they'd remember that.

Sometimes he'd amuse himself, thinking how, if he actually consented and performed one of his band's old songs when asked, the listener would recoil in horror. 'Yeah, we didn't worry about stuff back then,' Caeru would say, in this fond fantasy. 'Want more?'

But he was Tigrina, so he couldn't. He didn't mind. Success came with a price.

Eventually, the performance was over. Caeru had to endure a further half hour of boredom, being presented to the cast and crew. He smiled graciously, said the right things, ate and drank sparingly at the reception, while his attendants paid more attention to speaking to everyhar, bestowing the attention of Phaonica, the palace where the Tigrina lived with his consorts, the Tigrons, elevated above all.

When he'd had enough and it would not be considered impolite to leave, Caeru signalled to his staff and together they sailed out into the night where a carriage awaited them like a magical vehicle from an ancient fairy-tale. *You are the queen of this story,* Caeru thought wryly, *but are you a good or an evil one?* This made him laugh inside.

On this night, against his will, Caeru remembered himself. He recalled being on stage, a tangle-headed whip of a har, clad in black leather and ripped fabric, bangled to the elbow on both arms, his eye sockets made up to be black holes. His voice had soared, vibrating like the arcane vowels of an invocation. He remembered the hands reaching out to him from the audience, to his band mates – Amorel the leader, sombre on a bass guitar, Pharis invoking primordial gods on the drums and cool, snaky Karn, his black hair bleached and dyed lilac, taking aruna with his guitar, making it sing and scream. Caeru remembered also those who came to dance onstage among them, lissom as cats. The night the blue leopard danced...

Was he missing all that, after all this time? Had the price he'd paid to become Tigrina been worth it?

Pellaz believed Caeru's life had changed at their meeting. It had, but not for the first time.

As the carriage bore the Tigrina and his party home, and while his companions talked animatedly, mostly about the play and who they desired from among the actors, Caeru gazed out over the streets. The carriage roof was down. Security hara on glossy dapple-grey horses with polished hooves surrounded the vehicle, less a precaution nowadays, more of a public show. Entertainment. Immanion excelled at that. The city shivered feverishly with life in this quarter of theatres, festival halls and night clubs. Street performers cavorted in every square – musicians, poets, tumblers, small drama groups, fire dancers. The clientele of bars, cafés and restaurants filled the walkways, spilling out of the buildings, expelled by the heat. Caeru gazed upon them with a fond condescension.

Then he saw something that jerked him to full alertness.

The carriage and its escort were crossing a small plaza, where fewer hara were gathered. It seemed cooler there. A group of performers were enacting some kind of musical drama, by the light of living flame – torches of tar set upon blackened poles. The actors were dressed artfully in torn rags, their faces smeared with grey and brown panstick to mimic filth.

Sweet dehara, another fantasy of the past?

No, not that.

One har wore a leopard skin over his head, the paws knotted loosely over his bare chest. He writhed and twisted to the eerie clamour of bizarre instruments. Caeru blinked. No. This was coincidence. *Must be. How could these young hara know?*

He told one of his companions. 'Tell them to stop the carriage. Now.'

This command was obeyed.

Caeru looked back. The small audience was of course starting to stare, because the carriage bore the seal of the house of Aralis and was surrounded by sleek guards, the finest of hara. The performers had also ceased what they were doing. The har in the leopard skin skipped over to the carriage.

Caeru drew back instinctively. *That face.*

'Coins for us, fair Tigrina?' the performer said, holding up grubby paws. Dirt that was painted on. 'Coins for our song and dance?'

'Pay them!' Caeru commanded. He carried no coins himself, but one of his companions delved into a purse.

'How pretty you are,' said the performer, his head to one side, his fingers curled like claws over the side of the carriage. He bounced and grinned like a cheeky harling, but beneath was darkness; steel. 'Marvellous, *wondrous* Tigrina. You're a dehar come to life.'

Caeru's companion wanted to offer the money to his employer but the Tigrina indicated curtly this har must pay the performers himself.

The leopard-har enfolded the offered coins in a paw. 'How fair the night,' he said, 'how high the cliff where a voice rings out like a bird, like a prayer, like a curse.'

'Who are you?' Caeru asked.

The har laughed. 'You know very well.' With these words, he blew a kiss to the Tigrina. 'Lest you forget!' he said and pranced erratically away.

Caeru flopped back against the cushions behind him. He felt as if he'd been punched in the gut.

'What, by Aru, was that about?' one of his companions asked indignantly.

'Tell them to drive on,' Caeru said. 'I'm tired.'

Back home, Caeru divested himself of uncomfortable formal garments and put on a simple matte silk robe. He cleaned his face of cosmetics and brushed out his wheat-coloured hair. He knew that Pellaz was in his personal apartment, because he'd said earlier there were letters he'd wanted to write this evening and was anyway in need of time to himself, since he and Tigron Calanthe were going away to Megalithica very soon. Caeru went to his consort's apartment swiftly.

Pellaz was clearly surprised when Caeru swept into his study without knocking at the door. 'What's happened?' he demanded at once, because it was obvious to him that Caeru was *ruffled*.

'Pell, do you remember when we first met...?'

'Er...' Pellaz immediately looked furtive.

Caeru closed his eyes, shook his head. 'No. I mean... what I said to you then. I told you I'd come to Ferelithia only two years before. Do you remember?'

'Of course,' Pellaz replied cautiously, clearly not remembering at all.

'Well, it wasn't true,' Caeru said. 'I'd been there for a long time, since the start.'

'So...?'

'There are things I've never told you. I want to now. Because...' Again, Caeru shook his head in confusion, his expression twisted. He began to pace around the room. 'I don't know. I really don't know. But I feel... Pell, I *have* to tell you.'

Pellaz put down his pen, straightened in his chair. 'Rue, that was... well a very long time ago. What's upset you now, brought all this back?'

'I just saw a har who's *dead*,' Caeru said. 'At least, I thought he was dead. He's very dangerous. Mad. And that scares me because... I know about mad things violating my home, my body, and... Pell, he's *seen* me.'

Caeru collapsed into a chair, put his head into his hands.

Pellaz clearly came to the conclusion that something bad might be stirring rather than the Tigrina having a fit over something irrelevant, which was not uncommon. He left his desk and went to take Caeru in his arms. 'Nothing like that will happen again,' he said firmly. 'Phaonica's wards are so strong, not even the sun exploding could break them. What terrifies you so much?'

'Ferelithia was built on blood,' Caeru said. 'I have that blood upon me.' He dragged his hands through his hair. 'He demanded payment from me. Tonight. It means something. Sweet dehara! Pell, we must send agents to Ferelithia. It must be checked!'

'Well, I might see to that, if you just calm down and tell me what this is about.'

Caeru drew in his breath, closed his eyes. 'All right... It began with the blue leopard,' he said.

Pellaz listened to the story but it was painfully clear to the Tigrina that his consort thought he was over-reacting. Why would this piece of history come back to haunt him now? There was no reason for it.

While trying to sound sympathetic, Pellaz said there was no point upsetting the Ferelithians by sending agents to the town. If anything else occurred, then yes, Immanion must intervene, but what Caeru had experienced could simply be an isolated incident. And nothing much had happened anyway.

'But that har I saw tonight *knew* things,' Caeru said. 'How could he know?'

'You read too much into it,' Pellaz replied. 'It was a coincidence that awoke old ghosts. That's all. You'll feel differently in a few days, I'm sure.'

'I want you to be right but...'

'If anything happens while I'm away,' Pellaz said. 'Call Katarin to Immanion. Let her investigate for you. Send word to Cal and me, of course, if you need to.' He embraced Caeru briefly. 'I'm sure it's nothing to worry about.'

Caeru agreed to Pellaz's suggestions, but he didn't feel reassured. A sense of threat still hung over him, smelling of musty smoke.

Chapter Twenty-Three

Lunilsday, 29 Ardourmoon

After Seladris had departed *Eko Melosa* to wait for Kazharn's hara at *Inglefey*, Meladriel lay fully clothed on his bed. For the first time in decades he seriously doubted his abilities and his knowledge. Whatever hovered around him – and around Ulien and Seladris – was clever and powerful. This did not feel like a disembodied force, or coagulated memories from a distant past, or even energy that had soaked into the landscape leaking out to replay itself upon the screen of reality. This felt like it had a dynamic personality behind it – something living, something real. Could it be Leupardra?

Meladriel turned onto his side, sighing deeply. How to draw this *being* out? He needed to know what it was. Sweet dehara, he needed to be working more coherently with Karn. They should lure this thing to them – fool it and summon it. Leupardra had been a vain individual, and Meladriel detected vanity within the entity menacing them now; it liked to show off. Perhaps they could capitalise on that. But the ancient wall between him and Karn could not be broken down. *Be honest,* he told himself. *You envy his success, you hate the one he chose to be his chesnari, you still can't forgive him for not loving you enough. He did something enormous with his life, because even though Rue was the singer, Karn was always the front har. Still is. He's always known how to play a crowd.*

But even if he and Karn could plaster over the past, it was still likely that to be successful, they probably needed others who had once been intimate with the problem. But of course that couldn't happen.

Meladriel sat up on the bed, resolving to take action straight away, but his brain seemed to rock, unanchored, within the cradle of his skull. He must rest, restore himself completely. He must assess Seladris for the trials ahead. Tomorrow he'd take the har to the bees, let them meet him.

In the kitchen, Meladriel mixed himself some berry cordial with water and drank it, gazing out of the window. He must also consider other aspects of Seladris. Why had he felt compelled to share breath with the har earlier? It was asking for trouble. He didn't want commitments. In his experience they rarely led to a good place. His physical needs were met by friends who understood him, who didn't make demands. Veredis har Mith, for example, would no doubt be horrified if he knew how much Tika contributed to Meladriel's well-being. Perhaps it was time for that comfort again. He was loath, however, to confide in Tika about what was going on because, once he knew, he might be perceived as a threat and be in danger. Tika was young; second generation. It seemed inappropriate to drag him into this mess. So he must be kept in ignorance for now, for his own wellbeing. Meladriel was aware that at some point in the future, hara might be needed for the fight who were strong and fresh to it. If such a time should come, he wanted Tika by him, whole and healthy.

The tide was far from shore now, and the distant waves seemed to glow. If only it were possible to wash all unwanted things away in the retreating tide.

Meladriel became aware of the sound of an approaching horse. The hoofbeats were strange – almost like a musical rhythm, some unearthly thing. He peered out of the window, sucked in his breath abruptly and stepped back out of sight of the har who approached.

Kazharn har Shadolis drew his horse to a halt outside the house. Meladriel's first thought was to ignore the knock on the door that was inevitably going to echo through the rooms at any moment. He heard the unmistakeable sounds of Kazharn tying his horse's reins to the wooden rail beneath the window. He heard Kazharn speak affectionately to the animal, pat its neck. But he didn't knock. He came right in, like an uninvited ghost. He did, however, open the door to come through it, which Meladriel supposed was at least some mercy.

In the kitchen, Kazharn and Meladriel stared at one another for some moments.

Then Meladriel said, 'Why don't you come in?'

Kazharn made an exasperated gesture and said, 'What, by all the dehara, did you think to gain?'

'Other than an uncomfortable dinner time in your household?' Meladriel replied. 'Nothing.'

'You should have brought Ulien right to me,' Kazharn said. 'You know you should. He's my *son*! I've no idea how your stupid whim has worsened our situation, but I'm sure it has.'

Meladriel crossed his arms. 'Stupid whim?'

'Well, for Aru's sake...'

'Shut up!' Meladriel interrupted. 'All I saw was a harling in distress who, for reasons known only to yourself, could not turn to his parents for help. You think he *wanted* to come to me? As far as I see it, he thinks I'm the only help he can get.'

'You're making the grandest assumptions, as always...'

'As always?' At that moment, Meladriel felt a strong desire to punch Kazharn hard in the face. But there'd be no going back from that. Instead, he laughed bleakly. 'You're incredible. Can't you at least take some responsibility? I didn't ask for Ulien to seek me out, but I couldn't ignore him, Karn. He was too upset. And...' Meladriel softened his tone. 'He did take me somewhere I think might help us.'

Kazharn paused for a moment, appeared to take control of his temper, also altering his tone. He nodded. 'I knew of that place – even before Ulien told me what happened today.'

'You did? Thanks for providing the vital information!'

'The Sill of Shrines. It was Rue's station... that night.'

'What was it – originally?'

'A pagan site associated with an ancient mystery religion. That much is obvious.'

'How is it reached? The exit I found seemed... one way.'

'You have to come down to it from above. The path meanders for a couple of miles over the cliffs.'

'Interesting. I never thought to try and find a way that led *up* off the ledge.'

'It was always well hidden,' Kazharn said, 'and no doubt has become more so over time.'

'I take it nohar's been up there since...'

'No, nohar's been up – that I know of.'

'I think I saw Tuli there and...' Meladriel sighed. 'I suppose we need to be in accord again so I can bloody well tell you everything. Do you want tea?'

'No, something far stronger. You know I was never a tea har, no matter how much you believe in its magical properties.'

'Sit,' Meladriel said. 'I have wine with a kick like a *sedu*.'

Kazharn glanced at a shadowed doorway at the side of the kitchen. 'Do you never use your sitting-room?'

'Yes, but only for entertaining another kind of friend.' Meladriel fetched the wine, poured it into two goblets of thick, green glass. 'Here.'

Kazharn took the wine, tasted it, made a faintly agreeable sound.

'Good enough for you, *your grace*?' Meladriel asked.

'So, tell me,' Kazharn said, taking another drink.

Meladriel related his story, during which Kazharn refilled his own glass twice.

'The situation is changing, becoming more hostile,' Meladriel said at the end of his tale. 'Whatever attached itself to me certainly wasn't friendly.' He paused. 'What did Leupardra do to that site, Karn? I can't imagine it was associated with the Pale Ones or what comprises them. Did he desecrate the place?'

'He recognised it as a place of power,' Kazharn said guardedly. 'He placed Rue there that night because, of all of us, he was the har most in tune with the energy that resided there.'

'You mean… he called upon a goddess of love to vitalise beings of *death*?' Meladriel couldn't keep the disgust from his voice.

'Not exactly. There are many faces to the goddess, to all deities. Love, destruction, madness – all to be found beneath the fair face of Aphrodite.'

'Are you sure about that?'

Kazharn shrugged. 'I didn't study the subject, no, but Leupardra did. He wouldn't have called upon anything that might have hindered his aims.'

'And, of course, you believed whatever he said.'

'Let's not get into that, Mela.' Kazharn grimaced. 'Our focus now should be to protect Ulien, keep him out of whatever Leupardra's planning as much as possible.'

'I agree, up to a point.' Meladriel poured himself more wine. 'I don't think he should be closeted away, though, because that'll only encourage him to be secretive and by that easier prey for this Tuli creature. Treat him with respect and keep him informed. Your son is part of what's happening, whether you like it or not. There are some situations that won't go away simply by throwing orders at them.'

'I remember *you* doing that,' Kazharn said. He put down his glass, placed his hands briefly against his face. A spill of silver bangles slipped down his arms.

Meladriel was taken back in an instant to another memory. He dismissed it even before it could take form. 'We need to think about this rationally. In my opinion, we should form a team of those closely involved – and, much as it pains me to say it, this should include the wisp of fluff you're chesna with.'

Kazharn could not repress a short laugh at this. 'Who else?'

'Members of your staff you trust, perhaps?'

'They're all… *kids* really,' Kazharn said, clearly using the antiquated term deliberately. 'I'm not sure how they'd hold up if something really bad came at them. Modern Ferelithians are *not* equipped for trouble.'

There was a pause, then Meladriel said, 'Karn… who *is* there from the past who might help? Where did our leaders go, our original hienamas? I can't even remember them leaving Ferelithia.'

'That's because you distanced yourself from the community,' Kazharn said. 'Their departure was neither secret nor abrupt. If you'd been around more, you'd have known that. Ferelith was formally transferred into the hands of capable hara who wanted to build up the tribe, form a civilised settlement. Hara were drawn to this town in droves once it was ours – some of them perfect for the roles of leadership. You know that.'

'If you insist. But what puzzles me is why our former leaders didn't want to enjoy the fruits of their efforts. I didn't care at the time, nor since until now, but… What inspired them to leave?'

'It was when Thiede formed the Gelaming and started moving out into the world,' Kazharn said, 'when he initiated what he considered to be clearing up operations. Hara got spooked then. They saw what happened to the Uigenna and the Varrs in Megalithica.'

'*Did* they? I think it's more accurate to say they only *heard* what happened – allegedly.'

Kazharn made a flippant gesture. 'Well… whatever. They didn't want to risk the Gelaming investigating them and how they acquired the town. Jaddayoth offered freedom, so off they went.' He smiled rather condescendingly. 'You took yourself off for a while too, didn't you?'

Meladriel shrugged. 'So? I needed to sort myself out and I did. Then I came back. I didn't go through all that to walk away from the town we fought for and the tribe we made.'

'Yet you never really became part of it. I know that when the Municipallion was formed you were offered the role of high hienama at the Nayati Kelosanya. You refused. Why?'

Meladriel sighed, stared at Kazharn meaningfully. 'Please don't make me answer that.'

Kazharn sucked in his lips, nodded thoughtfully. He exhaled slowly. 'OK, maybe the moment is here. The one we both dread. We have to talk about *it*.'

Meladriel uttered a sound of disgust. 'No, we don't!'

'There was an "us" once, remember? We won't be in accord to deal with what's before us unless we face that demon head on.'

'There never was an *us*, Karn. You know that. You decided you preferred *him* to me, that's the end of it.'

'I admire your stamina to hold a grudge so faithfully. You take a long time to forgive, Mela.'

'Maybe it doesn't seem like a long time to me. Fuck!' Meladriel stood up and went to the window, his back turned to Kazharn. He hadn't meant to confess that.

'Mela, it's been... *decades*.' Kazharn said, an edge of exasperation in his voice. 'When I mention faith, it's not by chance. It's as if your distaste for me has become your religion. Can that be challenged? I don't know. If I say sorry now, will that appease you?'

'No, it'd simply be pathetic. Look...' Meladriel turned round. 'If you insist that we plunge our hands forensically into this mummified corpse, will you listen with your mouth shut for a minute?'

Kazharn gestured mutely.

Meladriel sat down again, drew in a deep breath. 'OK... In the early days, our leaders, who we trusted, taught us not to form deep emotional attachments. There was more than one reason for this, of course. The risk of death was high. We were told the old human concept of love was destructive. It really was – and is – and can be. But... it is also the light of life. Spiritual sustenance. Sublime, exciting, blissful, wondrous, mesmerising... all that. The lust of the chase. The sweet moment of consummation beneath the stars. We called it *kelos*, which means madness. Our local dehar is a deity of the irrational craziness of love. We can't deny it. So, there we were, so young, so *altered*, so full of fire and desire. We could not help but love – fiercely. But what we didn't account for is that, even among hara, the initial fire between two souls is sacred.' Meladriel used his hands to illustrate this concept, cupping them with fingers touching. 'Two hara come together, and for a while the blaze binds them exclusively. Nothing should touch that. Yes, once the flames have died down, the story might take a different path. Others may seek warmth at the hearth, and not be a threat. But that first flame… it was there to teach us what we *could* be. It was the beginnings of learning how to make new life. Karn, *that* is what you desecrated.' Meladriel dropped his hands to the table.

Almost immediately, Kazharn responded hotly, 'No! That is what *he* desecrated.'

'Oh, shut up!' Meladriel snarled. 'You weren't that helpless. Leupardra – let's just say his name, shall we? – thrived on causing trouble and hurt, on creating division. And you were weak and stupid. He bewitched you. You let it happen. *Slavered* for him. I had believed in us and yet our relationship was nothing but a flimsy lie, so easily torn apart. And that is why I went away and why I never wanted to be part of the Municipallion. I didn't want to be scalded by you, because believe me, what happened…' Meladriel closed his eyes, held his breath.

Kazharn said softly, 'Mela…'

Meladriel shook his head. 'No. Hush! I'm not done.' For a few moments there was silence, then he said, 'Chesna was supposed to be this adult, dignified condition. No possessiveness, no neediness, no dark shadow. But fuck that, Karn, however we wanted to kid ourselves it was still *love!*'

'I know,' Kazharn said, then raised his hands to indicate he'd say no more.

'Sometimes, back then, when hara were chesna, one of them died, was killed. It wasn't uncommon. You know that. Often, the grief felt by the survivor was terrible, life-changing – like a limb ripped away. As a healer, I was called on to help with it many times. And that's what your betrayal felt like to me. You were snatched from me, from right beside me. One moment you were there – my beloved – and the next…? You became, almost overnight, a stranger. Your eyes no longer saw me. Your hands no longer reached for me. Your breath was withheld from me. So part of me stopped breathing. It was as if you'd been killed, Karn, and I had no body to bury, no grave to mourn over. I was left alone, stunned, as if covered in your life blood. Does that explanation satisfy you?'

Kazharn was quiet for a while, eyes closed, his hands steepled against his face, hiding his mouth. Then, he lowered his hands and said, 'If it's any comfort, after it was all over, I knew how badly I'd treated you.'

'Which is why, of course, you rushed to make amends.'

'No. I couldn't. You can be *forbidding*, Mela. I did try, but you ignored my messages and hid when I sought you out. So… Now it's my turn to speak, so listen. I realised you hated me – *despised* me – and knew I deserved that. I fell for Leupardra's wiles, but I wasn't the only one. You know that, too. But still, when you went away, I hoped you'd come back. I hoped you'd become Ferelithia's High Hienama and that we could heal our friendship, at least. But no. You erected blockades of steel. You kept your distance, scorned the Municipallion and took up the life you chose, which clearly didn't include me. It also didn't include anyhar else who sought to make a functioning community from the aftermath of an atrocity. There was no opportunity for me to make amends. Can't *you* at least admit *that*?'

Meladriel made a sound, partly of frustration, partly of grief.

'We left it too long and then it was too late. We'd forged our lives, Mela. If I could have had you by my side, the one to raise a family with…'

'Just don't!' Meladriel snapped. 'That's unspeakable. We've each said what we needed to. For Aru's sake, don't take it any further.'

'I apologise. That was…'

'Yes, it was. So…' Meladriel inhaled slowly. 'Now that we've had that cathartic discussion, and both feel *so* much better for it…'

'I don't think it's finished…'

'It *is*,' Meladriel said. 'There's nothing more to say. We've revealed our truths and must trust that's enough for us to find common ground for the time being. Let's get back to the point of why we're even speaking again, shall we? Are you in accord with this?'

'Yes,' Kazharn said wearily.

'I think we must work with the painting of blue leopard and seek information. It's the only artefact we have at our disposal that's connected with Leupardra, so we should use it. So, speak to any hara you think appropriate to become part of our team. Tell them however much you think they should know.'

'Yes. I'll do that,' Kazharn said. 'I'll speak to the hara I mentioned earlier. Ulien's carer, Ihrec, should be part of the group. He's a strong har and has a calming effect upon others. I foresee this will be useful.'

Meladriel nodded. 'Makes sense. He is a guardian for Ulien, after all. We must build on that. But most importantly, we must look into the past, if we can, open the doors that were locked to us.'

'If that's possible.' Kazharn now appeared somewhat uneasy.

Meladriel smiled thinly. 'I'll make it so.' He was silent for a moment. 'And... your chesnari? Will he be able to work with us, do you think?'

'With *you*, you mean?' Kazharn shrugged. 'Thazri has made a career out of being my consort. He'll do what's necessary. He might look like fluff but he's pure iron inside. He hates secrets and being excluded. Once he's involved, I'm sure he'll be cooperative.'

'Good.'

There was a silence. Then Kazharn said, 'Do you have more wine? I appear to have finished this bottle.'

'Yes. I have more.'

'There's one more thing I want to say.'

'If you must.'

'The hearth I sit by in my home, it was never a roaring fire, Mela.'

'I never thought it was.' Meladriel went into the larder. 'Yet you still have Ulien.'

Chapter Twenty-Four

Out of respect for the Tigrina's position and to preserve his privacy, the suspect was brought to Phaonica for identification. This was to an office in the administration section of the palace where a swarm of minions worked, regulating the operations of the establishment.

The Tigrina entered a small room where two palace security agents were waiting for him. They asked if he was ready. He assented with a nod of his head and went to stand against the far wall, while the agents left the room. He felt nervous, almost sick.

The previous evening, Caeru had been accosted in his own garden, a series of tiered terraces reached from his apartment by a flight of wooden stairs. The garden was wild with tall grasses, tangled flowers, huddling fruit trees, hidden pools – the way Caeru liked it – but that made it easy for an assailant to hide within it. As to how anyhar could have reached the Tigrina's garden from the bottom of Phaonica Hill was – and would no doubt remain – a mystery. Had he flown in somehow? Manifested from the Otherlanes? Years ago, during the period now known as the Teraghast Troubles, Caeru had been attacked violently in his own home, but his attacker that time had been a har expert in Otherlanes travel. What he'd found in his garden yesterday evening in no way resembled an adept. But perhaps appearances could be deceptive.

He did not want to believe a har had come back from the dead. It was impossible that the very tangible creature in his garden could have been Leupardra.

Yesterday, Caeru had gone to his small patch of wilderness to think, to clear his head. He couldn't forget the strange har he'd seen on his way home from the theatre a few nights before.

At first, he'd thought it was an animal rustling surreptitiously through the grass. There was barely any sound, but at the edge of his vision he glimpsed the movement. This ceased when he turned his head to it. The birds in the garden fell silent. The air thickened and became difficult to breathe. Gradually, an urge to flee stole through him. This was no urgent inner command, but rather a plea to move slowly, as if casually. He knew then he was in extreme danger.

Pausing to caress the spike of a foxglove, as if entirely untroubled, Caeru began to make his way back to the steps. Again, he heard rustling behind him. He neither changed his pace nor looked round, even though the flesh on his back seemed to squeeze against his ribs and spine.

He reached the steps, felt the first spurt of relief as he put a foot upon them. Then the voice.

'Rue.'

Just his name, like a sigh on the night.

He didn't turn and took several steps upwards.

A hand grabbed his left arm, jerked him around. He looked down into the face of a young har, who he didn't recognise. He said, 'Let go of me!' in the most imperious tone he could summon.

The har did not let go. He smiled. It seemed such an innocent, genuine smile. 'You, of all of them, have achieved the most for yourself,' he said. 'Do you even remember your origins now?'

'Who are you?' Caeru demanded.

The har put his head to one side. 'Look at me,' he said.

His face was becoming more familiar by the moment, the features shifting subtly. Caeru refused to let them set in his mind. He looked slightly away, to the side of the one who held him. 'I don't know you. What do you want?'

'What has been given can be so easily taken away. You should think about that in your towers of ivory and silk.'

'Is that all you want? Simply to tell me that?'

The har laughed. 'No, of course not.'

'Then what?'

'Admit that you know me.'

'All right. Now what?'

'Say my name.'

Caeru couldn't speak. He knew in his blood and bones that to obey this directive would activate the worst kind of malign intention. Anger fizzed through him. Who was this har, daring to trespass in the gardens of Phaonica? Leupardra was dead. This wasn't him. This was little more than a harling, putting on an act. 'You can't intimidate me,' Caeru said. 'If you don't leave immediately, I'll summon the house guard. Allowing you to leave, incidentally, is a clemency I hope you appreciate.'

Again, the har laughed. 'I can still taste you, Rue,' he said, 'as if it were yesterday. You're my work of art.'

Caeru cleared his mind, shaped his thoughts into an arrow. This he cast out towards a specific target – the guards who were patrolling around the terrace.

The har before him seemed to shimmer. Then, he uttered an odd gulping cry. He spun round, his limbs flailing in panic, before hurtling off towards the tall grasses, the shadows of the trees.

Caeru bolted up the steps and by the time he reached the upper terrace the guards were there. 'In the garden!' Caeru commanded. 'An intruder. Find him!'

And find him they had. A young har who was nohar, who begged for his parents, who claimed not to know how he'd entered the Tigrina's garden.

Now Caeru stood at the back of the small office in the administration quarter of Phaonica and the intruder was led in for him to identify, cringing between those who escorted him.

Caeru stepped forward. 'Do you know me?' he said.

The har looked up at him, so young, terrified. Somehar's son. He shook his head miserably. 'Please, Tiahaar, I don't know how I got there. I really don't.'

Caeru looked into the har's face. 'Can you remember speaking to me?'

The har shook his head. 'I'm so sorry. I've told them. I don't know how...' He began to weep.

Caeru put a hand upon his shoulder. 'It's all right,' he said. 'You weren't yourself.'

He turned to the security agents. 'What will happen to him?'

'It's clear he has no recollection of events,' one of them said. 'We believe it's likely he's just an unfortunate individual who was chosen and then coerced, manipulated. He'll be kept under observation for a while.'

'Treat him well,' Caeru said, 'and bring his family to him.'

'There's a chance this might happen again.'

'I'm aware of that, thank you, Tiahaar. Do what you can to protect Phaonica and those within it.'

Back in his own apartment, Caeru sent a message to the Listeners' station: they must find Katarin har Roselane at once and have her brought to him as swiftly as possible.

Rue – as he was then – had known Katarin in Ferelithia. She'd still been human at that time, a young woman named Kate who'd believed there was no way she could become har. Many surviving humans had found refuge in Ferelithia. Kate had been Rue's best friend, in the days when the town had begun to make its mark upon the map of Wraeththu territories. His band had made a good living, everyhar had wanted to know them. Life for Rue, and all his satellites, had been one long party. Until Pellaz had come to change all that, an event that had led inexorably to Rue leaving his old self behind. But there'd been other changes too. Kate was now Katarin – of the Kamagrian; a type of har that women could become, who chose to be she rather than he. A word of difference between them, but that was all.

Katarin was still Caeru's best friend. She now worked for the Hegalion of Immanion as the kind of agent sent to gather information and occasionally take secretive action. At present, she was involved in work at an unknown location. But the Listeners were adept and managed to contact her and send a *sedu* for immediate transport. She arrived at Phaonica only two hours later and came to Caeru's apartment at once.

After they'd embraced and exchanged greetings, Caeru said, 'I hope this isn't inconvenient, Kate, but something's come up that I trust only you to deal with.'

'Oh?' Katarin threw herself untidily into a chair – a long, rangy creature with hazel-brown hair and deeply tanned skin. 'What's wrong?'

'It's to do with Ferelithia,' Caeru said. 'I need to fill you in on the history first.'

This he did, not that he knew much of what had happened all those decades ago. He'd had one task in the whole proceedings: to use his voice in some kind of invocation. He still didn't know precisely what this had been for and had been drunk when he'd done it. All he remembered was that the consequences had been catastrophic, and the entire human population of the town had perished. When he'd come to his full senses some days later, it was as if Ferelithia had always been harish. Nothing of the former occupants remained.

Katarin, slowly consuming a bowl of spiced nuts on the table by her chair, listened to this story without expression, although Caeru could tell she found it distressing. She'd lived a hedonistic life in that town, where now she was being told that thousands of her own kind had been slaughtered only a few years before her arrival. She had danced on ground where others had died so horribly: old, young, women, children, men. Clearly, the revelations didn't please her.

'I didn't want to have to tell you this,' Caeru said, 'but unfortunately you need to know.'

'OK,' Katarin said tonelessly. 'So, what do you want me to do?'

'My instincts tell me something is rising in Ferelithia, strong enough to reach out to Immanion. There was always a risk that what he did would...'

'He?'

Caeru sighed deeply. 'There was one har, in particular, who was responsible for our... victory... in Ferelithia. Now I have to tell you about him.'

But how to explain Leupardra? Caeru felt all the words he knew were inadequate, but he could only do his best. He ended his narrative with, 'If Leupardra, or somehar connected with him, is back, it can only mean something bad will happen. I need you to go to Ferelithia and investigate. Primarily, we must find out exactly what happened all those years ago and whether Leupardra lived or died. If the latter – *how* he died.'

'Perhaps a cult has arisen,' Katarin said. 'You know, young hara getting too far into the memory, trying to recreate... *something*.'

'Possibly, but I feel some aspect of Leupardra is directly responsible, if not the har himself.'

'A descendent perhaps?'

Caeru shook his head. 'I've no idea but... the har I've met on two occasions in Immanion feels very much like him. Except it wasn't.' He shook his head. 'It's bizarre.'

'Are you sure Leupardra died?'

'Well, that's what everyhar was told.'

Katarin raised her arms, gestured somewhat incredulously.

'OK,' Caeru conceded, 'it's a possibility he didn't, and is now influencing hara from afar. But we don't know what he wants. Is it only to cause discomfort and trouble?'

'Well, it's my job to find out,' Katarin said. 'Who's left in Ferelithia of our old crew. Do you know?'

'Karn is now a sort of phylarch, leader of the Ferelith,' Caeru said. 'The rest…?' He shrugged. 'As far as I know Amorel's lived in Megalithica for decades and Pharis went home to Alba Sulh.'

'Any others from *before* my time?'

Caeru looked away from Katarin's direct gaze. 'Well… our phylarchs and hienamas abandoned Almagabra in favour of Jaddayoth once the Gelaming became prominent. They changed their identities, left the past behind.'

'What about friends from the early days, those you were close to?'

Caeru frowned in thought for a moment. 'There was one who was quite involved… Meladriel. It was a mess really. Leupardra liked to manipulate others. He could sniff out chesna bonds like sharks smell blood. And he reacted pretty much the same way a shark would. Savagely. To say he caused rifts is an understatement. Meladriel suffered the most, I think. He lost somehar he cared for very much.'

'Did I ever meet him?'

'I don't think so. By the time you came to Ferelithia, Mela had distanced himself from old friends. He didn't want to be near Karn again – ever.'

Katarin nodded thoughtfully. 'So… your band. I assumed it got together in Ferelithia once it became a Wraeththu town. Is that not the case?'

'No, we formed a group years before that, moving around the Wraeththu territories of northern Almagabra under various names, playing for our food and a place to sleep. Those were good years – despite being unsettled. We eventually became affiliated to a small tribe – our income helped them, which was mostly bartering for supplies and so on. Then all the local phyle leaders got together and decided to take Ferelithia, combine forces to become the Ferelith. Maybe they had an idea to be something like what Thiede later became, but they lacked his muscle and ingenuity to create anything like the Gelaming. Let's just say that if Thiede was ever responsible for the killing of thousands, it never came to light.'

Katarin stared silently at Caeru for a few moments. 'I'm wondering now why I never asked these questions before.' She frowned, then smiled wryly. 'Seems I never really knew you, doesn't it?'

'We were all young,' Caeru said, 'with the attention span of butterflies. By the time I met you, I was enjoying myself too much and had no desire to dwell on the past.'

Katarin sighed. 'It was fun to be a butterfly,' she said wistfully, then hardened her expression and her voice. 'I'll leave at once.' She paused. 'Is this mission to be... *off-channel?*'

'I would prefer so,' Caeru answered. 'Keep etheric silence with your supervisors and your activities away from the Hegalion's sensors.'

'That's understood.' Katarin jumped up from her chair and hugged him. 'Let's get things moving and hope it can *all* be dealt with privately.'

'I trust you to do whatever's needed to resolve this problem,' Caeru said. 'And that means precisely what I said.'

Chapter Twenty-Five

Lunilsday, 29 Ardourmoon
Early evening

Ferelithia had changed so much, but then not at all. Katarin har Roselane stood at the harbour, this smaller version of the vast quays in Immanion, gazing at the plate of the sea, beyond the tangle of ships that lay motionless in the still evening. Behind her, the café society of the night was slinking out of doors.

Her heart was full of unshed tears; a physical weight in her chest. It seemed strange to her now that she'd not been back before. Here... she'd experienced the happiest moments of her life, a life she'd imagined would be short, and which she'd intended to live to the full. That girl she'd once been, feral with fear and anger and madness and joy, had had no idea how the future would change. She wouldn't have believed it. Rue had been happy then too, until Pellaz came and changed everything, altered both of their lives. It seemed petty to be angry about that, because look what they had become. The girl who'd been Kate would no doubt have been dead by now, but for the intervention of Pellaz har Aralis. Yet all that had come afterwards – the dramatic revelations and moments of amazement – seemed somehow dimmer than the years she'd lived in Ferelithia. It disappointed her that she saw no faces she recognised as she prowled the streets. Ferelithia had moved on without her.

She'd felt *the wrong*, of course, the moment she'd walked down from the hills into town. Rue's supposition had been correct. She sensed a nervousness, a lassitude. It was as if the town had a crushing hangover, could barely lift itself from bed, dehydrated and in self-inflicted pain. She noticed that shadows fell oddly, not quite at the angle they should. She saw a dog, sleeping on the doorstep of a house, wake up abruptly and growl at nothing. She saw dead *burned* flowers among the bright festoons that spilled from the baskets that hung from the buildings and over the gardens; living blooms struggling to conceal the rot within, perhaps aware that, despite their efforts, the sickness could only spread. Katarin could hear an echo of the hollow laughter of the dead, a sound without mirth. Hara here could not call upon their deity to protect them because Kelosanya was entirely useless for a situation like this. He could inspire only the shudders of desire within gasping hearts and the yearning to touch within aching fingertips. He would cower before whatever dank power now slunk through the streets of Ferelithia. And Ferelithia without its dehar was a town that had lost its point.

Still, despite the seeds of malignity whose roots had begun to burrow down into this once cursed land, Ferelithia yet drowsed in ignorance, still beautiful, its fair face unmarked by etheric pox, even if a malign rash had begun to bloom beneath its clothes.

Katarin turned away from the sea and walked to the centre of town, seeking its omphalos. This was, of course, the Municipallion and the Nayati of Kelosanya attached to it. Beautiful buildings, imbued with serenity and grace. The carefree, irresponsible children of Wraeththu's early years had somehow, amazingly, become architects and builders. They had *made this*.

Katarin was in two minds about whether to contact Karn. She could visualise how comfortably the har she'd once known had transformed into what Rue had described. A leader. In his quiet way, Karn had been the most powerful among them, even in the past. She had a feeling that if he already knew there was a problem – and how could he not? – he wouldn't welcome Gelaming interference. He would naturally be suspicious of it, because, outside of Immanion, it was almost every har's default calibration to be wary of Thiede's tribe. Leaders inevitably perceived threats to their leadership and their tribe's autonomy, perhaps justifiably. Should Karn feel any hint of this, every door in Ferelithia might slam in her face, making her task more difficult. Also, for Kamagrian, it was occasionally *challenging* to face old friends who'd known them only as human. There could initially be a kind of awkwardness, embarrassment even, in discovering a woman they'd once known – and most likely thought dead – had become like them. At such reunions, this was something hara tended to feel should be mentioned before anything else. 'Oh, so you became…?' She wished they'd just say, 'Thank the dehara you're alive. We both survived.' That was all that needed to be said.

Karn wouldn't say anything to make her cringe, she was sure, but his eyes might flicker with words unspoken. She realised with some surprise that she hadn't had such thoughts for a long time and was actually shocked to discover that, at some deep level, they still perturbed her. To everyhar she knew and met she was a parage of the Kamagrian, often mistaken for purely har, which she frequently didn't bother to contest. But here? It was different because, in some way, her old self lived on in this place.

So... Karn was out of the question, at least for the time being. That left only Meladriel from Rue's old contacts. She didn't know him, and as far as she was aware had never met him. Rue had been unable to provide any useful information other than the fact he believed Meladriel still lived in Ferelithia.

Katarin made her way to the bar she'd known as *The Red Cat* and was warmed to see it still existed – and with the same name. Now, there was a broader seating area outside, with trees and wooden tubs of purple and red flowers. The place seemed more affluent, but other than that it was recognisable – somehow reassuring. Katarin went inside, bought herself a beer and went to sit in the open air. For a while, she watched passersby, scanning them carefully. She also ran her inner sight over those seated around her – on the whole they appeared untouched, maybe just a twinge of discomfort here and there, the wisp of a bad dream, an inexplicable spasm of fear.

A young pothar came out, gathering up empty glasses, wiping down tables with a cloth. When he came close to her, Katarin said, 'Excuse me? Might I ask you something, Tiahaar?'

The pothar examined her for a moment, then nodded. 'Of course. How may I help, Tiahaar?'

'I'm here in Ferelithia for a few days and want to look up an old friend. Wondered if he still lives here. His name is Meladriel.'

The pothar smiled widely. 'You mean the crazy shaman Meladriel?'

'Well...'

'Sorry if he's a friend. Didn't mean it to sound that way. But yeah... there's a har of that name lives on the shore north of town. He's a hienama of sorts. Hara go to him for help with all kinds of stuff. Is that who you mean?'

'Well, it could be. I've not seen him for a long time.'

'His cottage is *Eko Melosa*. There's a sign... probably.'

'The house of the bee goddess.'

223

'Is it?'

Katarin smiled. 'Would you fetch me another beer, please?'

'Sure.'

Katarin knew five languages fluently and understood smatterings of others. Hara tended to mash up ancient words with more modern terms to create their own names for things – whether that be other hara, towns, houses or skills. Anything, really. Wraeththu had a strange affinity with ancient history – as if they believed they'd evolved from past ages rather than more recent human cultures. Wishful thinking perhaps, or maybe the rectification of a mistake. What evolution should have been. The thought made her smile.

'No, Kate, humans were *always* bad.'

The voice made her jump. She must've been daydreaming because a har had sat down opposite her, resting his chin in one hand, elbow on the table.

'Are you Meladriel?' she asked at once, imagining briefly the pothar had found him inside and passed on a message.

'Yes.'

Katarin narrowed her eyes. This har was young, didn't feel like first generation. Had she been sniffed out already? Her precautions had been thorough to present an *uninteresting* persona that nohar would look twice at, let alone think was an agent of the Hegalion. That meant what she saw before her was a lie, such as the one presented to Caeru in his garden. This lie knew her name, had pried into her thoughts.

'Nice to meet you,' she said. 'Would you like a drink?'

'That's very kind of you.'

She stood up to go inside, since there were no convenient pothara among the tables, but her new companion said, 'Please, there's no need for that. Sit down.'

She saw that a pothar was now hurrying towards them, pushing through clientele quite rudely. Muted outrage followed his passage. He appeared disorientated and carried two tankards of beer, the contents of which slopped over his hands.

'I'm impressed,' Katarin said.

Her companion grinned and gestured with both hands, implying modesty. He was good-looking in the way most hara are – not an outstanding specimen by some standards perhaps, but attractive. A simple costume of artfully mangled T-shirt and black leather

224

trousers that reminded her of the hara she'd once known here. His makeup was minimal but precise, his blond-streaked dark hair loose over his shoulders, devoid of decorations or braids.

'Thank you,' Katarin said to the flustered pothar. He placed the tankards upon the table and fled.

'So…' she said to her companion. 'Meladriel.'

'Mela, please.' The har lifted his drink, took a sip.

'The bees tell me there are strange things happening in Ferelithia.'

'Do they?' He rolled his eyes. 'Bees are such gossips.'

'Gossip isn't the same as lies though, is it?'

'Depends.'

'What's your opinion?'

The har grimaced. 'This whole place is a lie, Kate. If something bad happens, the hara here deserve it.'

'That's an interesting viewpoint,' Katarin said.

'What do you mean?'

'Well, most of the hara who live here now weren't around when this town was founded. I can't see why they deserve anything bad to happen to them.' She paused. 'Your sentiments are rather in conflict with your opening statement that humans were always bad. Why should you care what happened to them, in that case? Unless you know something I don't, of course.'

An expression without colour flowed over the har's face, weirdly giving the impression he blushed. 'Perhaps humans weren't the only victims in that scenario. How did you think the Ferelith accomplished what they did? They hadn't the means or the wit.' The har took another drink. 'Sometimes, there are prices to be paid.'

'By hara who aren't even aware something once happened to incur a price? That seems harsh.'

'Not if they are shown! Not if they *live* it!'

Katarin laughed a little, took a drink of her beer. 'That's a big grudge you hold, Mela. It *is* Mela, isn't it?'

The har's face hardened. 'Aren't you clever, *parage*.'

'Yes, I like to think so. Clever enough to see through a weak disguise, at least.'

'It doesn't matter,' said the har blithely. 'I respect you more than the idiot who sent you.' He paused. 'He can't hide there, you know, in his palace of dreams.'

Katarin leaned forward. 'I'm finding it difficult to feel sorry for you, even though I'm quite sure that pity is what you deserve. Rue isn't as weak as you assume. You think he's had an easy life?' She shook her head. 'Your information gathering lacks piquancy.' She leaned a little further across the table. 'And it's a well-known fact that suffering makes you stronger. I'd think twice, if I were you, before taking on Immanion, young friend.'

She found, perhaps inevitably, she was speaking to an empty space where once the har had sat.

For some minutes she sat drinking her beer. In Immanion, this *entity* had used the body of another to contact Rue, but what she'd just experienced was something else. He had a few tricks up his sleeve, this one.

Chapter Twenty-Six

By the time Seladris and Ulien reached *Eko Melosa*, Seladris was more or less carrying the harling. He was concerned Ulien had been poisoned, but perhaps he was simply in shock.

Suffused with relief, Seladris led the way down the short lane to the cottage. But once the trees and shrubs were passed and the cottage could be seen plainly, Ulien uttered a miserable groan. 'No! That horse, it's Gull. *He's* there.'

They had come to a halt upon the path, Ulien balking like a spooked horse himself.

'Who?' Meladriel asked. The horse in question, tied to a wooden rail at the side of the cottage, looked extremely well-bred, a tall, sleek bay, now regarding them with ears pointed forward.

'My father. What will he think? Will he be angry?' The harling appeared to be asking these questions of himself.

'The mighty Kazharn!' Seladris said, experiencing an unexpected frisson of joy. He was curious to meet this har. He urged Ulien forward. 'Come, we're nearly there. Don't worry about your father. Mela and I will be with you.'

Seladris didn't knock at the door – he considered the cottage his lodgings for now. He walked straight into the kitchen.

He'd expected to feel scorn and a sort of superiority, but when he saw the har sitting at the old worn table, the reactions that pulsed through him were very different. He felt apprehension, uncertainty, and also an inexplicable sense of defeat. But over what? He'd never met this har before. It was as if a star had plummeted from the sky, crashed into Meladriel's home, coalesced into a dehar. Kazharn shone with an invisible light that nevertheless illuminated everything. Every aspect of him was beautiful, but Seladris could perceive cruelty in him too, the possibility of harm, and the distance of deep, cold space – a strangely delicious concoction of facets that rarely failed to invoke the impulse to tame and conquer in harish hearts. It occurred to Seladris very briefly that he and Kazharn har Shadolis might have some things in common. He was also exactly the type of har Seladris had found attractive in the past.

'Seladris!' Meladriel exclaimed. He was standing at the table, pouring wine lavishly into large glasses. He seemed uneasy, somehow guilty.

'Ulien is hurt,' Seladris said, ushering the harling before him, now keeping his eyes fixed on Meladriel.

'How did...?' Kazharn began, getting to his feet.

Seladris interrupted without glancing aside. 'He came to me, my house, because he believed it was a safe place. The entity calling itself Tuli attacked him.'

Kazharn drew Ulien to him. 'What happened?' he asked.

'He got into our house again,' Ulien said in a slurred voice. 'Tuli... He was going to really hurt me. I had to shift, Kazzi. I didn't want to, but I had to...'

Seladris, noting with amusement the incongruity of referring to a har like Kazharn as "Kazzi", said, 'Mela, you need to look at the wounds.'

Meladriel took Ulien's arm, pulled him away from his father, and seated him at the table. Here, he began an examination.

'I bathed it, put salve on it, tried a little healing,' Seladris said, 'but he seems feverish, disorientated. Is that simply shock?' He turned to Kazharn now, risking the inevitable blast of power and crushing loveliness. 'I brought Ulien here so Mela could treat him. He didn't want to go home.'

'We have to do something!' Kazharn said abruptly to Meladriel, apparently dismissing Seladris as irrelevant. 'We can't just have leisurely discussions now. We must deal with this threat... banish it. We were capable of such things once. We must be so again.'

Meladriel went to look for materials on his shelf of jars glancing at Kazharn over his shoulder. 'Calm down, Karn. Panicking and getting angry achieves nothing. We have to identify what we're facing first.'

'Then we must do that – tonight,' Kazharn said, then, after a pause, '...and I'm not panicking.'

Ignoring this response, Meladriel arranged his equipment on the table and asked Seladris, 'Has the painting been taken?'

'Yes,' he replied. 'It was removed before we left *Inglefey*.'

'If we're to do something tonight, that must be the focus, Karn,' Meladriel said.

'Won't that be risky?' Seladris asked abruptly.

Meladriel nodded. 'Perhaps, but I think we have to use it as a tool of magic rather than simply fear it.'

Seladris grimaced. 'I'll try to adjust my feelings about it, then. I assume you'd like me to take part in whatever you do?'

'Yes,' Meladriel answered. 'Those closely involved must work together.'

Kazharn went to stand beside his son, rested a hand on his shoulder. 'How can we keep Ulien safe, Mela? Should he stay here, or at the Shadey Lane house? Where?'

'We keep him with us,' Meladriel said evenly. 'Try not to let your concern for Ulien consume you, Karn. It's what this *thing* would want. Where has the painting been taken?'

'A storeroom within Nayati Kelosanya. I've given instructions to the hienamas it must be warded... contained.'

'How much did you tell them?'

'What do you think?'

'I don't know. That's why I'm asking you.'

'Nothing other than it's been the cause of some apparently paranormal activity. I asked them to observe it, assuming its new location might deter unwanted *visitors*.'

Ulien was now leaning against his father, barely conscious. The wounds on his cheek gaped obscenely on so young a face.

Meladriel drew in a breath, shook his head. For some moments he didn't speak as he mixed creams, liquids and powders in a bowl, stirring them with a narrow silver rod. Then he spoke. 'When we took action in Ferelithia before, there were a lot of us. Karn.... I have to be straight with you: I'm not sure the small group we have is enough.'

'Then what do you suggest we do?'

Meladriel began to apply his mixture to Ulien's wounds. Ulien uttered small sounds of distress, writhed. 'Hold his head straight. This won't take long.'

Kazharn did so.

'I think,' said Meladriel, 'we need at least some of the nayati hienamas, no matter their inexperience with situations like this. I think we also need the guardhara employed at Olivian Grove, and others like them. The nearest you can find to the warriors of the early days. A robust measure of ouanic energy is essential.'

Kazharn appeared to think about this for a moment, then said, 'Very well.'

Meladriel hesitated before asking, 'What about the Municipallion, Karn? I don't know them, so can't make my own assessment, but do you think any of them should be involved?'

Kazharn pulled a mordant face. 'Let's keep them out of it for now. They must be informed if we can't deal with the situation ourselves, but I'd rather have more details and plans to present to them first. The Municipallion are... well they are simply well-meaning officials who keep the town facilities running smoothly and organise events. I promise you, they'll never have encountered anything like this before. I don't want to deal with a potentially outraged and frightened commotion until I have to.'

Meladriel laughed bleakly. 'I'll go with what you decide on that.'

'What about Veredis?' Seladris asked. 'He had an experience with the blue leopard too.'

'Who's that?' Kazharn asked Meladriel.

'Seladris's boss,' Meladriel replied. 'He owns *Inglefey* and was partly responsible for Seladris seeking my help. Veredis took the painting home for a night and was affected by it. The har he lives with is a friend of mine.' He turned to Seladris. 'I don't think we should involve Veredis in this. He's not suitable for what we have to do.'

Seladris nodded. 'I suppose so. He wouldn't keep quiet about it, probably. It was just a thought.'

'We might still need him later – and others,' Meladriel said. 'The thought wasn't a bad one, Dris. Thanks for the suggestion.' He had finished administering Ulien's treatment and beckoned to Seladris. 'Wash your hands,' he said. 'Then dry them on one of the cloths in the left drawer of the dresser. They've been sanitised.' He indicated with a jerk of his head across the kitchen.

Seladris nodded. 'OK.'

Meladriel gently pulled the gashes on Ulien's cheek closed. The harling uttered weak cries of pain, squirming in his father's hold.

'Uli,' Kazharn said almost in a whisper. 'Hold still for just a little longer.'

Seladris, drying his hands on a clean white cloth, said, 'What do you want me to do?'

'Hold the wounds closed for a few minutes,' Meladriel said. 'If you can direct healing into them, please do. Encourage the flesh to knit. Come, sit next to him.'

Seladris pulled a chair round the table, sat down.

'Here…' Meladriel placed a wad of fine cloth over Ulien's cheek, then guided Seladris's hands over the wounds, pressing his own on top of them. His hands were very hot; he withdrew them after only a few moments. 'Just stay like that for a while.'

Seladris couldn't help sending a mind touch to Meladriel, *You trust me to do this? Me, who usually brings only harm?*

And the reply. *There are many ways to heal.* Which of course could be interpreted in different ways.

'What shall I do?' Kazharn asked Meladriel.

'Go home,' Meladriel replied, but not harshly. 'There's nothing more you can do here. Send transport back for us. We have no choice but to move Ulien. I want to keep him near me but can't deal with Tuli here.'

Kazharn let go of his son, who then leaned towards Seladris. 'Do I take the painting into my house?' Kazharn asked, clearly uncomfortable with that prospect.

Meladriel appeared to consider this as he went to wash his hands at the sink. 'Not sure about that,' he said. 'Is there somewhere in the grounds we could use? Any sites that seem appropriate to you?'

'Perhaps the old shrine Ulien's so fond of,' Kazharn said. 'It was and is a sacred place.'

'The place where Tuli appeared to him?'

Kazharn nodded. 'Yes.'

Meladriel frowned. 'Maybe,' he said. 'I'll check it – make sure it's useable, and uncontaminated. But go… now. We should start as soon as possible.'

'I'll send transport the minute I get home.'

'And tell Ulien's hostling what to expect. I don't want scenes.'

Kazharn managed a wan smile, but didn't comment, said only, 'thank you, Mela.'

'Oh, before you go – and this is for all of us – we must guard our thoughts at all times. You must practice maintaining a caul of protective light around you that nothing can breach.'

'At all times?' Ulien murmured apprehensively.

Meladriel touched Ulien's shoulder reassuringly. 'I know it sounds hard, and you're worried you'll forget and let it slip, but just practice at it. You too, Dris.' He glanced at Kazharn. 'I assume you need no instruction from me.'

Kazharn smiled somewhat grimly. 'I'm sure I'll manage.'

'Everyhar must wear protective herb pouches, containing dill, fennel and salt, as well as a small piece of lapis lazuli and amethyst. Instruct your household in this, as well as the protective aura, and anyhar else who'll work with us. Get the herbs and gemstones from the market, Karn, or send a minion to do so.' He paused to let the sarcasm sink in, then added, 'We need to minimise risks.'

Kazharn ducked his head in agreement, smiling. 'Until later, Tiahaara.'

After Kazharn left the cottage there was silence for nearly a minute – a short measure of time that felt excruciatingly far longer. Meladriel cleared away his equipment and began searching his shelves and cupboards for the protective items he'd described to Kazharn. A sense of tension and awkwardness afflicted the air. Eventually Seladris said, 'Well, he's... *something*.'

'Yes, he is,' Meladriel said. He put jars upon the table, and some fragments of rough fabric. 'Will you help me make some pouches, Dris?'

'Of course....'

'Let's check our patient first.' Meladriel went to Seladris's side and pulled the har's hands from Ulien's wounds, removed the cloth beneath them. Now his fingers felt icy cold on Seladris's skin.

Ulien uttered a sound of discomfort.

'Will he have to be stitched?' Seladris asked.

Meladriel peered at the deep scratches. 'I don't think so. Harlings mend even more quickly than adults. The wounds are clean now. He should be all right.' He put his hands on the crown of Ulien's head for a few moments. 'I don't feel anything to be concerned about. What do you think, Ulien?'

'I think I should have told somehar about Tuli from the start.'

Meladriel laughed, patted Ulien's shoulders. 'The past is a quagmire of errors and we have to live on its boundary.' He returned to examining the items he'd placed on the table, opening jars, smelling the contents.

'So... Tiahaar Kazharn,' Seladris said tentatively, 'the phylarch of Ferelithia, no less.'

'More like archon, but yes,' Meladriel said. 'Cut up some of this cloth into squares, big enough to contain the herbs and stones.'

Seladris picked up the scissors Meladriel had put before him. 'An archon in your house...' He shook his head, raised his brows.

'I've told you about him.' Meladriel set down another jar, rattled it. 'These stones are lapis. I don't have many, but there's enough for us and a couple more pouches at least.'

'Words are inadequate.' Seladris paused. 'He's like a dehar of ouana – all that power – that stern beauty – it seems almost hostile.'

'Don't be ridiculous,' Meladriel said, pausing at his work. 'He's not like that. It's preposterous to think it.'

'He seems so to me, that's all.' Seladris cut out a square of cloth.

'Well, I can assure you he isn't. He has to project a certain manner so he can function in his role. It's armour, no more than that.'

'Really? He's like a glacier – slow-moving and full of destruction.'

Meladriel stared at Seladris for some moments. 'I'm sure his son is grateful for your opinions.'

Seladris realised he'd forgotten the young har beside him – or rather his relationship with Kazharn. There was a strange feeling inside him. Later he would identify it as jealousy, which he'd rarely felt in his life. 'I'm sorry, Ulien,' he said.

'It's all right,' Ulien mumbled. 'I know how my father is. Mela's right. He has to be that way.'

'He can be kind and gentle, can't he, Ulien?' Meladriel said.

'Yes... in his way. Can I help, Mela?'

'Please do. You can put the stones and herbs into the cloth. Just a generous pinch of each herb and some salt. I'll find twine to bind them closed.'

Seladris stared at Meladriel for some seconds. Why was he defending Kazharn now? All Seladris had picked up before was Meladriel's sense of resentment concerning the Municiphar. What had changed? However, he was aware that asking would be the worst thing he could do.

'How do you feel now?' Seladris asked the harling instead, aware he must utter no more remarks that might annoy Meladriel.

'Strange,' Ulien said, counting out small chunks of amethyst from one of the jars. 'But at least my face doesn't hurt as much.'

'That's good.'

There was silence for a moment, then Ulien said to Meladriel, 'My father behaves differently with you.'

'In what way?' Seladris couldn't help asking, even though he was aware it wasn't his place to do so.

'Without thinking,' Ulien answered.

Meladriel smiled in a strangely private kind of way that Seladris didn't like at all.

Any further discussion was cut short by a sharp rap upon the door. *Three visits to my house*, Meladriel thought, *yet this is the first visitor who has knocked.* He hadn't sensed, or even heard, anyhar approach. He glanced at Seladris who fastened an arm around Ulien protectively. All three were silent. Meladriel went to the window discreetly, looked out at an angle. He saw a tall, rangy har standing on his step, currently examining the articles hanging from the door. He perceived no sense of historical threats, but this one cloaked themselves well, nonetheless. He opened the door, said, 'Yes?'

The har appraised him with astonishingly pale hazel eyes. This allowed an extremely penetrating gaze, or the illusion of one. 'You are Meladriel... the shaman?'

'And you are?'

'A friend,' said the har. 'Please may I come in? I need to talk to you. I come in accord and offer no threat.' He displayed his palms, then touched his chest with one bunched fist.

Meladriel recognised the phrase and accompanying actions, and for a moment a wave of relief swam through him. *Somehar else with a history...* 'Yes. Come in.'

The har sauntered past him, then took stock of the kitchen and those within it, his eyes resting briefly on the items on the table. 'My name is Katarin,' he said. 'I can tell you know why I'm here.'

'Perhaps,' Meladriel replied. 'Do you live in Ferelithia? Or were you a resident in the past?'

'Very much past. I wasn't here at the start, but the har who sent me was. We're aware of recent and potentially damaging etheric activity connected with the history of this town. I've been directed to you.'

'Sit down,' Meladriel said. He indicated his companions, 'This is Seladris, and this is Ulien, the son of... Karn.'

'Really?' The har's raised eyebrows and brisk response told Meladriel all he needed to know about whether this har had known any of them in the past.

'You knew my father,' Ulien said.

'I did, yes. You have a look of him.' This could hardly be an honest observation as most of Ulien's face was covered in a dressing.

But Ulien was clearly incapable of preventing the glow of pride that shone from him at those words.

Meladriel could see that his visitor was now engaged in adding up numbers and arriving at all the wrong answers. 'I'm not Ulien's hostling – he's simply visiting to have his injury treated' he said hastily, then added, 'Tea or wine?'

Katarin sat the table. 'Wine, please.'

Meladriel paused before fetching the drink. 'Dris, you and Ulien finish off the pouches, please.'

'OK,' Ulien said.

'You were drawn here by the *activity*?' Seladris said to Katarin as he finished cutting up the cloth.

'Not exactly,' Katarin replied, gazing at Seladris's hands. 'My friend experienced some strange phenomena at home, so sent me to investigate.'

'And who is your friend?' Meladriel asked, having placed more glasses on the table, which now he began to fill.

'I think...' Katarin narrowed his eyes, sucked in his lips, then said rather theatrically, 'I think you'd have known him as Rue.'

'Aru's lim! Really?' Meladriel exclaimed.

'Rue as in Caeru?' Seladris asked. Meladriel had told him a little about the band he'd once worked with, and who their vocalist had become.

Katarin nodded. 'A surprise, yes, but it appears this strange influence hanging around carries far. I hope we can work together to resolve the matter.'

Meladriel experienced a series of unwelcome images involving Gelaming intervention, but then considered that Katarin did not appear to be Gelaming himself. There was something different about him. An agent, then, or perhaps simply an old friend of the Tigrina.

Katarin picked up the glass Meladriel had set before him, sipped. 'Mmm, very good. Did you make this yourself?'

'No, a friend did, but he employed the wealth of my honeybees in the recipe.'

'*Eko Melosa*,' Katarin said, and laughed.

Meladriel sat down opposite his visitor. 'Indeed!' He took a drink. 'Now, shall we begin? Will you tell me what Rue has experienced? Then you get our story. All of it. I give my word.'

'Accepted. It began at the theatre a few days ago.'

While Seladris and Ulien finished the protective pouches,

discreetly remaining silent, Meladriel listened to Katarin's story, which Katarin delivered succinctly, all the time trying to decipher Leupardra's purpose – if indeed Leupardra was behind any of it. Finally, Katarin revealed his most recent experience at *The Red Cat*.

'That was Tuli!' Ulien exclaimed, clearly having waited politely for Katarin to finish speaking. 'I know it!'

Katarin turned his laser gaze on the harling. 'You've also seen him?'

'Our turn,' Meladriel said, laying a hand upon Ulien's shoulder in a bid to silence him, 'but our story is longer. We don't have a great deal of time because we're about to embark upon… something. I'll be as concise as I can.' He glanced at his companions. 'Both of you keep quiet. You can tell Katarin more if we have time before we have to leave.'

Seladris sent him a mind touch. *Are you sure about this, Mela? We don't know this har.*

He's genuine, Meladriel returned. *He knows Rue. I can feel it.*

He began to speak.

At the end of it, Katarin widened his eyes and said, 'Well! Certainly a longer story. Might I ask what you propose to do tonight?'

'Draw the entity out if we can. We need to know who or what it is – a living har, a dead one, or something else entirely.'

'Would you object to me being present?'

'Not at all. I would prefer more hara than we have, to be honest. The original… *working*… involved dozens.'

'So, what bait do you have? It strikes me this Tuli is clever, not easy to fool.'

'Nothing can bait him. We can only count on his arrogance. I intend to call upon the egregore of the Cerulopard.'

'Do you?' Seladris snapped, eyes wide. 'Were you going to tell us?'

Meladriel slid a glance at him. 'Of course. The egregore might have dissipated, but I believe that if any shred of Leupardra is involved in our experiences, shreds of this magical entity will remain or have been awoken.'

'But what about those hideous *things*! Aren't they part of what Leupardra did? Can you really contemplate exposing Ulien to them?'

Meladriel sighed. 'Dris, if Tuli wanted to, he could have directed those *things*, as you call them, to do all kinds of mischief by now. Leupardra didn't have as much control over them as he thought, and I suspect whoever's meddling now doesn't either. If the Pale Ones are drawn to the painting, that seems their only interest. I'm not sure why, but I intend to find out.'

May I come with you to Karn's home?' Katarin asked. 'I would like to speak with him too.'

'Of course,' Meladriel said. He smiled mordantly. 'You might not recognise him, though.'

'I very much doubt he'll recognise me,' Katarin replied.

'You'll need one of these to help keep you safe,' Ulien said, gravely handing Katarin one of the spare protective pouches.

'Thank you,' he said, bowing to the harling. He put the pouch into his coat pocket.

Chapter Twenty-Seven

Once the carriage that came to collect Meladriel, and his companions passed through the gates of *Velvets*, Meladriel asked the driver to stop. Bidding the others to go up to the house without him, Meladriel went alone to visit the shrine in the grounds, following directions Ulien had given him. He wore one of the protective pouches around his neck on a leather thong. He'd told his companions he needed isolation to assess the place properly, but that wasn't the entire truth. He was also postponing having to meet the hated Thazri again, especially upon his own territory. The rank energy between them was something he could do without, but he also appreciated that the har must be included in whatever took place that night.

Meladriel walked across the lawns, past fountains that spattered him with cool droplets, and into the shadow of the groves, where the trees clustered together conspiratorially, seeming to watch him. He allowed himself to feel a needle of envy. To have all this... to wake up to it every day and walk in this ancient garden, which was tamed in some respects, but not too much. He could sense benign energy all around him, the spirits of nature – dryads in the trees, naiads in the bowls of fountains and the artificial streams that were like veins and arteries throughout the garden. The hesperides, nymphs of sunset, might wing down from the west in the lowering sunlight. The area felt wild even though it was not. He could imagine Ulien playing here; it must be a paradise for harlings drawn to nature.

At one time, Karn had explored this area and had decided: *this will be my home*. Meladriel felt sure the har had done this alone, before Thazri's time, perhaps when he'd first been elected by other hara to be among those who would lead them. What had he thought as he'd walked through these gardens, penetrated the abandoned house?

Don't! Meladriel told himself firmly and cleared his mind. Instead, he opened himself to whatever might hover unseen beyond his physical senses.

As he followed a path to the shrine, the trees folded over him, creating a tunnel, and he imagined them closing the way behind, an impenetrable shield of twigs and leaves. The air smelled strongly of earth and greenery crushed by the heat of evening, with the faintest hint of stagnant water. Bronze light found its way through the branches, turned the air to fire. The night rose in the eastern sky, just a hint of it now in the mellow encroaching gloam.

Meladriel crossed an ornamental bridge spanning a stream that was more like a long narrow pond. Then he came upon the hill with its crown of cedars, and the dark maw in its flank; his destination. Within the cave there might be an entrance to the underworld, leading down, down, down to a dark and dangerous realm.

As part of the trial, his inner voice raised itself to speak: *You defended Karn. You were angry Seladris dared to criticise him. Why?*

Because whatever happened between us, only I can speak ill of him. No har else has the right.

That makes no sense, Meladriel. Or, if it does, it raises disturbing potentials.

Be silent! Meladriel thought loudly to himself. *Cast it aside on the path. Concentrate on the moment, nothing more.*

He considered his journey was mythic – like that of a goddess descending into realm of the dead, discarding items of her power and her womanhood as she went. In some ways, his situation mirrored that. Soume had its own strengths but what was needed now was a rigid force to stand against a storm: ouana, unbending and – comparatively – unsubtle. He had once been able to call upon the aspect of the warrior as if calling to faithful dog – a dog trained to kill. Now, he must do so again.

The temperature dropped once he entered the cave of the shrine, but not in a supernatural way. Sunset rayed in narrowly through deep window-slits in the western wall. Otherwise, the running water, the thick rock, provided protection from the blaze of summer, even as the day went down. Kazharn's hara had brought the painting of the blue leopard here and had propped it against the eastern wall. Its deep jewel colours glowed in the ruddy light, the eyes especially seeming to shine. Meladriel inspected the picture again; it was strange and inspired discomfort, but it didn't feel *old*. *Who* had painted it and why had it fascinated the Pale Ones so much when it had hung in *Inglefey*? Perhaps the events to come would reveal that.

Meladriel went to the pool in the south of the shrine, knelt, and washed his face and arms there. He drank its water from his hand, found it good. Still kneeling, he held up his arms, elbows bent, palms outward, and said, 'I honour the ancient spirits of this sacred place. Come forth from your caves and deep pools! Come forth from the trees and the air! I ask for your protection against all ill. Astale, beings of the earth, the waters and the sky! Stand behind me!'

He put his hands together and raised them to his brow. 'I call upon Kelosanya, dehar of Ferelithia. Come forth in your beauty and stand at my shoulder! I ask you to bless my actions, to acknowledge that I work in your name to protect your hara. May your love be my armour. Astale, Kelosanya!'

He stood up, threw back his head and closed his eyes, arms outspread. 'I call now upon Agave, dehar of the flaming sword, warrior of the south, to stand at my side, to fill my body and my mind. Astale, Agave! Be with me now in all your fire! Help me smite the enemies of my tribe!'

There was silence then but for the trickle of water.

Meladriel lowered his arms, stood with his head bowed, his eyes closed. He'd called upon the essence of ouana to take precedence and now it resided within him like a coiled dragon. He felt like a colossus of physical power.

He'd half expected Tuli to appear, either to taunt him or to attack, but he sensed nothing malign was near. He did sense somehar else approach, however. Had he been fashioning invocations since the moment his feet touched the soil of the garden?

'I barely recognise you,' said Kazharn. 'You are the warrior now.'

Meladriel would not turn around. 'You know this is needed for the task.'

'Yes.'

'I must be here alone... to prepare.'

'I know. I'm here simply to ask for your... orders.'

'How many hara do you have?'

'Six of my houseguards, three hienamas of the nayati who I trust to keep this evening's events confidential, Ihrec, Seladris, Thazri, Ulien, and the Gelaming agent, which I assume is acceptable to you, since you brought him here.'

'Yes, it is'

'The guards and the hienamas have already felt etheric abnormalities around them over the past few days, so in this way are partly prepared for what's to come, but I'll explain fully when I go back to fetch them. I expect it will come as a shock.'

'I expect so too.'

'What will we do tonight exactly, Mela?' Kazharn asked.

'We'll call upon the egregore of the Cerulopard, hopefully make it speak to us.'

Kazharn uttered a choked laugh. 'Is that... wise?'

'We can't go into this like nervous harlings, Karn. We must establish our own power. Leupardra feeds on fear and uncertainty. You know that. We must be strong and direct.'

'We you certainly *appear* to be strong and direct enough.' Kazharn paused. 'What light shall I bring?'

'Two torches, naked flame.'

'Anything else?'

Meladriel turned then, saw Kazharn only as a dark silhouette in the entrance to the cave, a shape that could be a stranger. For a moment, uncertainty sliced through him. 'Tell me,' he said, 'When you cut my skin, when you pressed your bleeding flesh to mine, when you bonded to me, did it mean nothing?'

There was a silence, then Kazharn said, 'What? We didn't... I never would...'

Meladriel exhaled. 'Right, it's really you. Tuli would no doubt have said something else. Something... *nicer*. Fetch the others, would you?'

'If that had happened,' Kazharn said, taking a step forwards, 'perhaps Leupardra wouldn't have won. What I was going to say is, I never would have...' He struggled for a word.

'Abandoned me?' Meladriel sighed, shook his head. 'See? It's not that hard to say. Anyway, hurry up. We need to get started.'

'Mela,' Kazharn came forward. 'We *have* to be in accord. You know that. Must the past always stand between us?'

'You're right. I was wrong.'

'Not wrong... it simply can't interfere.'

'Please fetch the others.'

'Are we at peace?'

'Yes. We are at peace.'

Kazharn smiled rather bleakly. 'Don't let your ouanic armour slip, even for a moment.'

Ulien could tell that his hostling wanted desperately to be difficult. He didn't like the idea of Meladriel being on their property, never mind having to conduct some kind of ritual with him. He didn't want Ulien to be present but couldn't deny it was probably the safest option under the circumstances. Thazri couldn't help blaming Kazharn for what was occurring, because it was *his* past that had caused it. And now others were forced to help clean up the mess, risking their own safety. He felt, for these reasons, cornered, but also knew he shouldn't feel that way because it was necessary to be serene, confident and strong. Poor Thazri.

Before they went up to the shrine, where Meladriel was waiting, Kazharn asked everyhar to gather in a salon of *Velvets* and there revealed to them the history of the town, and how something evil connected with Ferelithia's inauspicious start had come back, intent on harm. To the hienamas of the nayati and the household guards, the information was surprising, perhaps shocking. They knew they were there for a reason, and that something peculiar had been going on in the town for quite some time. They'd heard rumours of Ferelithia's chequered past, which they'd believed had involved mere debauchery and decadence – a splash of local colour to enhance the town's reputation as a party location. They knew Kazharn wanted them to perform a ceremony with him, but they hadn't expected to learn all this... *darkness.* Ihrec regarded Kazharn with hooded eyes all the time he was speaking. Disapproval? Sympathy? It was difficult to tell, although Ulien was sure Ihrec had hidden histories of his own that might resonate with his father's secrets.

Under the direction of Ihrec, two of the household staff (who had been sworn to silence) had fashioned over two dozen protective pouches, which could be worn as an amulet on a length of twine. Ihrec had also performed a brief ritual over them. These were distributed to the gathering while Kazharn talked.

'Meladriel will summon the egregore of the Cerulopard, if it still exists,' Kazharn said. 'We must contain its energy in the net of our own. It must be interrogated in the hope we can discern what this Tuli wants or seeks to achieve. We must cut him off from his power source.'

'And if he comes himself?' Thazri said.

'Then we bind him,' Kazharn replied.

'Easy, then,' Thazri added sourly.

Kazharn addressed Katarin, the agent of the Gelaming. 'Tiahaar, I must state you're under no obligation to attend this operation.'

Ulien could tell Kazharn wasn't comfortable with the har being present, but protocol dictated he must remain polite.

Katarin displayed his palms. 'I must report back to the Tigrina, Tiahaar, so would appreciate being able to attend. It's possible that further *persuasion* might be needed to rid Ferelithia of this blight. Whatever your feelings on the Gelaming, you know they would help you in this regard. But first… let's see what can be done without them.'

Ulien detected in those words a shrouded empathy with the feelings of the Ferelith. *Keep Immanion out of it, if we can.* Strange, though. Katarin had said he knew Kazharn, yet there was no flicker of recognition in his father's eyes. For now, Ulien decided to keep quiet about that. Perhaps another embarrassing history was connected with the matter.

Kazharn inclined his head. He asked if anyhar had more questions, and some came from various members of the group, who were concerned about the potential hazards. Kazharn kept his voice steady and reassuring, as if what they must do was only a minor task, hardly more than an inconvenience, but he couldn't be feeling that, could he?

'And now, before we leave the house, I ask you to join with me to create a net of protective energy around all of our minds,' Kazharn said. 'For some of you, this procedure will be familiar. For those of you new to it, please feel free to ask questions about anything you don't understand. This is not a test, but a form of defence, so it must be created correctly.' He then gave instructions in a low, measured voice.

Ulien's injured cheek pulsed with a vague, stinging discomfort in time with the beat of his heart. Meladriel had given him some medicine to drink, which had numbed the pain but had also made him feel woozy, somewhat disconnected from his environment. He didn't feel afraid, but he did believe Tuli must know what they were doing. He was planning too, surely. Was he watching them as they shrouded their thoughts from him? Were they vanishing before his eyes, until he could see nothing but mist? He hoped this was the case.

The group made their way in silent procession through the garden, Ulien between Ihrec and Thazri who each held one of his hands. Then Ihrec began to sing in a low humming voice; a song that sounded like an invocation, perhaps to his own spirits of protection. Presently, Thazri hummed along with him, then further voices joined the swarm of sound. *Like Meladriel's bees,* Ulien thought.

The sun swooned down to the sea on the western horizon and the light was blood-red, the sky dusking into royal purple and indigo above the stain of sunset. The night crept westwards and the first stars glittered like sequins upon the gown of the heavens. Never had the world felt more alive to Ulien – the secret world of spirits and elemental beings. The garden seethed with them; eyes between the trees or peering directly from gnarled trunks; water speaking in a liquid, bubbling voice; shadows flickering all around. Flowers breathing. All beings of nature who belonged in this land had come back to it, now humankind had gone. They too would fight any threats to their territory. And then, filling the western sky, another presence, immense, glorious, its back to the sinking sun. A dehar, who hid his face behind a long veil of fine netting that wrapped his body as a layered robe, who smelled of honey, and was surrounded by a court of bees that wove spiralling patterns in the air around him. Ulien knew that nohar could see it but him. *Melosa*, he thought. *Melosanya... Kelosanya...*

His heart filled with a feeling so immense he couldn't describe it.

At the start of the path that led to the shrine, Kazharn lit the torches they had brought with them. He seemed so different to the har Ulien had lived with all his life. This was a softer, milder creature, the mask of the Municiphar set aside, and yet potent with a strength in contrast to that he usually possessed. He wore loose trousers and tunic of the finest linen, the colour of darkest red wine, embroidered at the hems with golden leaves. His feet were bare, his hair smoking loose around him; an archetypal symbol of soumic power. His only ornamentation was the thin bangles he wore upon his arms and which, Ulien realised for the first time, he never removed. This har, Ulien thought, without knowing how he could think it, was no longer merely his parent; this was a priestess of an ancient deity, who would speak with the gods and utter prophecies. Could Thazri see this too?

As he thought this, a voice asked him, *and what will* you *sacrifice upon this path?*

Ulien jumped, fearful it was Tuli who spoke to him, but then realised the voice had come from the sky, was all around him, was ultimately his own. *I sacrifice my fear*, he answered, *whatever is asked of me.*

Meladriel stood at the entrance to the shrine, also a different creature to the one Ulien had met before. This was a leader of hara, a warrior. He seemed to quiver like horses sometimes do when they are about to bolt. His eyes were wide and staring, the white showing all around the irises, slightly mad.

Kazharn went to this entity, bowed, and presented the lit torches. Meladriel took them and went into the darkness.

By passing the flame, my father has surrendered his leadership, Ulien thought, in awe. *And yet not his power.*

Kazharn stood tall and straight, waiting, and presently the order was uttered: 'Come.'

Kazharn went into the cave of the shrine, which was now lit by the shuddering flames. The group followed him.

By instinct they arranged themselves in a three-quarter circle, leaving a gap around the pool. Here, Meladriel stood alone, somewhat apart from the others. He gestured at two of the guards. 'Place the painting in the centre of our circle.'

This they did, so that the picture lay flat upon the ground. To Ulien, it seemed to be a portal. The colours writhed within it, when he glanced away, shiverings in his peripheral vision.

'Kazharn, stand in the north,' Meladriel said, his eyes staring at the roof of the shrine. 'Seladris in the west. Ulien in the east. The hostling and Ihrec should stand either side of Ulien. The rest of you, arrange yourselves between these quarter points.'

For a few moments, the group shifted as these positions were taken.

You should have spoken Thazri's name, Ulien thought keenly, almost as a mind touch but not quite, as he was nervous of this new ouanic Meladriel. He wasn't sure whether the har picked up the message.

Meladriel drew in his breath, closed his eyes and extended his arms. 'Honoured hara, we stand as one, in this fair evening of Ferelithia, but also beyond time. It is our task to understand the past, to penetrate it. For the duration of this rite we must be in accord, of single intention and purpose. Cast off all that lies beyond the walls of this shrine. Summon the strengths within you, the fruits of harakind. May our hearts beat together in the ceaseless rhythm of creation. Astale!'

A single voice that was all voices, repeated, 'Astale!'

There was utter silence – even the water seemed without sound.

Meladriel bowed his head, lowered his arms, sighed. He glanced pointedly at Ulien, then walked to the east and put his hands upon

Thazri's shoulders. 'Thazri, hostling of Ulien, in the sight of the dehara, and in the presence of the spirits of the land, the waters and the sky, I ask for amity between us.' He kissed Thazri on the right cheek. 'Astale.'

Ulien felt Thazri stiffen, but only in surprise. He muttered, 'Astale, Meladriel, there is amity between us.' And returned the kiss.

Ulien squeezed his hostling's hand. Thazri glanced down at him, smiled rather dazedly.

A conjuring of peace, yet now, surely, everyhar present must be wondering why Meladriel hadn't been able to say Thazri's name to start with, why he'd had to correct himself about it. Was the reason obvious to anyhar else like it was to Ulien?

In the north, Kazharn remained impassive, a being from the ancient past, ready to fulfil their purpose.

Meladriel resumed his place and beckoned to the group. 'Draw closer. Form a circle and join hands.'

Once this was done, he said, 'Focus upon the blue leopard in the centre. It acts as an entrance point to this sacred place. It is the symbol of the Cerulopard, who once walked this land, a tribe of the early times. I want you now to help summon the egregore of this tribe. We shall chant to call it forth. Maintain the chant, even when I break from it to speak, and no matter what happens.'

The chant Meladriel began was not comprised of words but sounds. It began as a low hum, similar to the song the group had uttered on their way to the shrine, but gradually this became vowels, meaningless, yet full of meaning. The voices evolved into a single plait of sound, spiralling round the chamber. As they chanted, so Meladriel directed them to raise their arms, slowly, still joined, containing the power within their circle.

Ulien could sense the energy rising, circling round them, a funnel of protective power, yet its apex remained open. Meladriel had not closed it into a cone. He glimpsed flashes of blue-white light at the edge of his vision. *Something* was coming. The air in the centre of the circle began to shimmer, *convulse*.

'I call upon the egregore of the Cerulopard,' Meladriel said. 'We summon you, Blue Leopard! We conjure you!'

He resumed the chant, his voice becoming louder, more strident. Those around him mimicked the sound. They uttered now a howl of command. They flung up their arms, broke the contact between them, released the energy they had raised.

And it came. *Something* came.

Ulien saw the colours of the painting become more vivid than seemed possible; bright, aching hues. The leopard appeared to writhe within its frame, as if seeking to pull itself free of the canvas, to stand real among them.

'All of you here present!' Meladriel commanded. 'Shape the power of our song into a cone of protection. Seal our circle from all beyond it. Seal it from beneath with a floor of light!'

The intention of the group was so strong and sure, Ulien could almost see this process with his physical eyes. They stood within a vibrating cone of light, invisible to the living eye, yet it could be felt. A tingle against the skin. A rushing breeze that smelled of ashes and dark, turned earth. Smoking blue light formed in the centre, twisting as if in agony. Then the blue leopard was among them: a transparent picture, like a memory, stalking around the circle – confused perhaps but still aware, alert. It was not contained exactly, but tranquillised. Long, lithe, peacock blue, turquoise, teal, with black spots that looked like patches of soot. Its eyes were a very pale blue, the pupils like coins of ink. It moved like smoke or oil, colours shifting, yet its long paws trod delicately upon the floor of the chamber. Ulien had never seen anything so beautiful; the idealised essence of a tribe.

'Karn,' Meladriel said, 'interrogate this entity. The rest of us will hold the seal intact.'

'Cerulopard,' Kazharn said at once. 'I command that you speak with me. Who of your tribe is in Ferelithia at this time?'

The leopard uttered a strange cough of a growl, then spoke. This was not a voice heard with a physical sense, but inside, an itch in the brain that made words. 'The Cerulopard never left,' it said, and the voice, surely, was Leupardra's: a sense of sarcasm in it, of humour. 'But you know that, Karn. Only one way to go, wasn't there?'

'Who are you?' Kazharn said.

'I am Leupardra,' said the vision. 'And I thank you, beloved, for reuniting me with the essence of my tribe.'

All at once, the vision and the cone of protection exploded into motes of light that were geometric shapes flying outwards like shards of physical matter. Hara uttered cries of shock and ducked down, shielding their faces. Only Kazharn and Meladriel remained upright, staring at one another in mute horror, the shards flying through them, but leaving them untouched. And Ulien, crouching down between Ihrec and Thazri, recognised in their expressionless masks the utter despair beneath.

Still staring at Kazharn, Meladriel raised his arms. 'I summon the light of Kelosanya,' he said. 'Come to us, dehar of beauty and peace. Fill this space with your divine power of healing and love. Banish all that is dark.'

But by this time, the entity was long gone.

Ferelithia

On this night, Ferelithia cracked down the centre, right along the main road that led through the town. There was no warning. Only a sudden sound like vast bones breaking and the land yawning apart. Some fell into it.

Stinking smoke rose from the sundered ground. Hara emerged from their dwellings, or out from the smoky chambers of night clubs and inns. The earth had shaken. It had broken.

Breathing the filthy smoke made hara ill – their eyes became red, their breathing laboured. They were frightened, not of what was happening to them now, but of things they couldn't possibly remember but did – things that had happened in the past.

Some reported seeing a har dressed in tatters sauntering through the streets. He would catch hara's eyes and say, 'This is just the beginning, dear friends. Breathe deep. Have a taste of what was.'

In the harbour, the sea was congested with strange flotsam, masses of tangled weed like bloated tumours that stank of rot. Dead fish rose to the surface.

Other hara told of seeing the tattered har, with his rags of hair dancing in the wind, standing on the harbour wall, singing to the sea. He was accompanied by a strange beast, some kind of big cat that appeared to be blue in colour. Yet it was hardly more than a shadow, slinking round his legs.

By morning, as hara tried to clean up the streets, which looked as if they'd been ravaged by a tsunami, the har had disappeared. Tourists left the town in droves. Some had been injured by falling masonry the night before. Citizens flocked to the Municipallion, demanding answers, demanding their leaders tell them what had happened and how they'd deal with it.

This was when the curfew began.

Remember who you are! cried the town, out across sea, high into the sky. *Become one. Become greater…*

But something was missing; an interface, a purpose.

Kelosanya wept.

Chapter Twenty-Eight

Amorel employed the most skilled hienamas that were recommended to him. After the dreams began, he'd wasted no time in contacting the one he trusted most. In two days' time, he would be on tour, an exhausting experience that would require him to be in peak condition. He'd managed to get through rehearsals, because the presence of other hara in the house tended to keep weird phenomena at bay. But once they went home for the day...

Now, healer and client sat in the dimness of Amorel's bedroom – Amorel on the bed, hienama on a chair nearby. The high walls of glass were shrouded in pale, softly shifting, linen drapes; the chamber faced north to avoid the sun.

Merphine har Froia was discreet and adept, dressed in the concealing robes of his tribe, his hood thrown back because he was indoors. His eyes were lined thickly with kohl. He had stood over Amorel for nearly half an hour, placing his hands upon various parts of the har's body, so lightly the touch could barely be felt. Now, as Amorel leaned upright against his pillows, the healer sat and listened to his client's account of dreams of the past and how those dreams were leaking into reality.

'I see him,' Amorel said, 'at the shoreline, the water running over his feet. At dawn and dusk – liminal times. He stares at me. And I see him in the shadows of my rooms at night, not too clearly, but I know he's there.'

'Does he speak?' Merphine asked gently.

'Only in the dreams,' Amorel said. 'He's calling for me.'

Amorel had spoken vaguely of a "dark history" with Leupardra, sure the hienama would intuit most of it without him needing to speak the hateful facts aloud.

Merphine nodded thoughtfully. 'I have sensed the presence of *coherent* energy. It is a programmed thoughtform that has been sent to you rather than a projection from a living being.'

'So it could simply be a *historical*... sort of message that has been... *unleashed?*'

Merphine pursed his lips. 'I think it must be rather more than that. Given the time it would have had to remain dormant, it seems unlikely it could remain so effective without a power source. It found you upon a different continent, after all, in a new life, and you have broken your connections to the past.'

'Perhaps it's always been with me,' Amorel said bitterly. 'I wouldn't put it past Leupardra to have infected us all with the magical equivalent of time bombs.'

'An elegant idea,' Merphine said, 'but I'm not convinced a har of that era would have possessed the training and focus to accomplish such a thing.'

'What must I do? I can't live... *haunted* like this. The dreams enervate me, as if I'm being sucked of vitality by some kind of arunic vampire. I've tried everything to rid myself of this, so please don't suggest meditation and cleansings.'

'No, I wouldn't suggest such procedures, in any case. It's clear what you must do.'

A pause.

Don't say it, Amorel thought wearily, then said it himself before Merphine had chance to. 'I must go back.'

Merphine nodded. 'That would be my advice. Seek help there, at the site itself. I assume there are at least a few hara remaining in Ferelithia who are known to you?'

'I've no idea. I haven't been in contact with any of them since I left and that was a very long time ago.'

'Well, perhaps somehar could go with you, then. I'll do what I can beforehand to discover what you might be facing. As you implied, if only facetiously, it *is* possible this phenomenon is affecting others – in my opinion highly likely, given what you've told me of that time – *and* what you haven't.' He risked a sympathetic smile.

Amorel pressed his fingers against his eyes briefly. 'Whatever you think is best. I'll have somehar organise a trip. But first I need to get through the tour. Before you do anything else, make sure I can do that – whether that's through hands-on treatment or mind-balms. I need to be purged of this *distraction* for at least six weeks. If I have to cover your fees to keep you with me the entire time, so be it. I can afford it.'

Merphine raised his eyebrows. 'Tiahaar, forgive my importunity, but you should go to Ferelithia right away.'

'That's impossible. Everything for the tour has been finalised. A lot of money is involved – never mind many hara's time and effort. My audience has been waiting for this.'

'I appreciate all of that,' Merphine said, his voice soft yet insistent, 'but I have to speak as my intuition advises. What you're experiencing is an acute event that will only get worse.'

'Are you sure of that?' Amorel shook his head. 'I don't wish to insult you, Tiahaar, but perhaps I should seek further opinion.'

'That's your prerogative, of course,' Merphine responded.

'The tour can't just be cancelled,' Amorel said. 'That's simply the reality of the situation.'

'It is for you to decide.' Merphine stood up. 'I'll leave a two-month supply of an appropriate mind-balm with you, which might help, but I can't stress enough how this is not a minor wound you can bind over. It runs deep, like an infection. I can only urge you to seek further opinions, as you suggested. I'm confident any other practitioner of merit will only repeat what I've told you. If you need me, you know where I am.'

'Thank you,' Amorel said. 'I'm not criticising your abilities or your diagnosis, but please appreciate what's at stake.'

'It's not my place to judge,' said Merphine. He withdrew a box of stiff card from the satchel he'd left beside his seat. This he placed on the low table by Amorel's bed. 'Take one of these powders before you sleep each night, in water and without food.'

'I will. Thank you.'

Merphine inclined his head. 'You needn't see me out. Good day, Tiahaar.'

'Goodbye, Merphine.'

Amorel lay back against the pillows, blinking at the ceiling. This was the last thing he needed, the worst inconvenience. He didn't want to confront the past, since he'd already buried it. He didn't want to see any of the others again. 'Just leave me the fuck alone!' he said aloud. 'It's done with! We were all kids! I can't be held accountable for what I did back then. I won't!'

The room remained silent, peaceful.

Amorel sighed, took out a small twist of paper containing a pinch of powder from the box Merphine had given him. There was a symbol inked on the wrap – a crude motif of deer antlers. He knew what it was. Garridan in origin, no doubt formulated primarily as a poison or a narcotic strong enough to affect a harish frame intensely. If not authentic Garridan, then a facsimile of one of that tribe's nostrums. Taking it might interfere with his ability to perform at his best, but what other option did he have?

Amorel got up and padded into his kitchen space. Here he poured himself wine and took Merphine's medicine along with it. The hienama had told him it should be taken with water, but so what? Amorel didn't care about the inevitable strengthened effect. The day was succumbing to the night; darkness would soon rise in the east as the sun lowered. He went out onto the deck, leaned against the white railings, staring at the sea, his glass held in both hands. His personal dark had begun in the east and still lived there. No wonder ancient humans had regarded the sun as a god, praying to it to return each morning. When the darkness came, claiming back the sky, it could seem as if it would last forever, unless you knew otherwise for certain. And in this life, all that had come after the Human Era and the madness of its decline, (which even after all this time still seemed so *recent* to him), there were no certainties, not really.

In the dream, he was waiting for Leupardra to come to him backstage before a gig, in a small shabby storeroom, which seemed separate from the reality of the venue beyond.

Why have I even come here?

Leupardra had flashed his eyes and that had been summons enough. *Meet me...*

Amorel could hear sounds beyond the door, his band calling to one another, laughing, the hollow, echoing whines and thuds of their crew preparing the instruments.

Then Leupardra folded out of the shadows, his hair tumbling down, his lips full, as if stung, full of venom. 'I want you now,' he murmured, pressing against Amorel's body.

'No,' Amorel snapped, trapped against a wall. 'There's no time. Anyhar could come in.'

'I don't care. I want you. Now.'

'What you *want* is Karn to find us, isn't it?'

Leupardra only laughed, but he stepped away, folded his arms. 'Oh poor, poor Amorel. How helpless you are.'

'I'm saying no, aren't I?'

'Not very convincingly, I'm afraid.'

'Just fuck off. You're a parasite, sucking everyhar's blood. I don't want you. You've done enough harm already.'

Leupardra flexed himself, became still, and in that moment transformed in Amorel's mind into something very dangerous. 'You have no idea how much harm I can do.'

'Wrong. I know absolutely how much.'

Leupardra laughed. 'Child,' he said. 'Stupid little boy-girl. You'll be doing my work soon enough.'

'Just fuck off!'

Amorel didn't want to show how scared he was. He thought Leupardra was deranged, but he did have power over hara. He knew how to subdue them, fool them, make them his creatures. Perhaps Amorel was the only har who saw through the glamour to the ugly truth.

'I'll leave for now, but you'll make amends later. You'd better make amends as hard as you can – and as deep.'

'Or else what?'

'Oh, I won't *tell* you. You'll just have to find out.'

Amorel knew he was dreaming a memory. It wasn't real, but even so, once Leupardra left that room, the door hanging open behind him, Amorel couldn't stop shaking. 'Aghama,' he said, trying to pray but not sure how. 'Aghama, help me.'

He woke up.

So much for the nostrum.

Amorel got out of bed, went to the kitchen. Here, he took from a cupboard a bottle of the murderously strong liquor that was distilled in the Gold Country. The drink itself was gold in colour; the fire of the sun in a bottle. He swigged from it. Beyond his window, the night ocean glowed softly.

Back then, the very next day after he'd rebuffed Leupardra in that storeroom, preparations for battle had begun. The band had been operating under the aegis of the local phyle leaders for a long time. They made magic from sound, from music; hienamas, in their way. During hidden rituals, they revealed faces their usual audiences never saw – so different to their everyday personae of swaggering vanity. All of them were proficient performers. It was no surprise their talents were in demand for occult operations, when dramatic voices and gestures held so much meaning. As they could incite audiences to intoxicated joy, so they could fill the hearts of warriors with fire, with recklessness, *belief*.

A har had come to them, given them orders. There was to be a war cluster near the town that would eventually become Ferelithia – the last human enclave in the area. Leupardra and his preening elite, of course, were already involved, had perhaps instigated everything, even though, for some reason, Leupardra allowed others to believe they outranked him and that he obeyed their orders. Amorel had never thought that. He'd always known who was in charge. So many beds carried the imprint of Leupardra's body, so many minds. And when he turned the sun of his attention upon you, you couldn't resist the light. It was divine sustenance, even as it burned you.

Forcing himself back to the present, Amorel shook his head fiercely to clear it, took another drink. 'I won't go back,' he said aloud. 'I deny you!'

'Oh, I don't want you back,' a voice murmured behind him.

Amorel froze.

'I just want you to know that soon Ferelithia will be ashes and so will you. All alone in your fragile pretty house by the sea, but the music is gone, all gone away. Your fingers will be dead sticks upon your instruments. I will take your tongue, your ears, your songs. *They* are your ashes.'

Amorel wheeled round. He saw a vague shape at the threshold to the room. He threw the bottle at it, which exploded against the door frame, glass and liquor flying everywhere.

Afterwards. Silence.

Too numb even to weep, Amorel felt his way to his studio, bumping off walls and even the minimal amount of furniture. His head was on fire. His skin.

He sat down at his piano. *Purge this sickness!* He placed his hands above the keys, summoning a tune within him, of light and progress and goodness: a passage from one of his best-known works. His fingers sank down, ready to conjure magic from the instrument, but no music followed. His hands broke damply upon the keys, splintering like old, rotten wood. He couldn't help but release a scream, holding up his ruined hands, which were no more than spiky rags of infested pulp. He was almost deafened by a vibrating shriek that raged within him like screeching feedback.

Amorel ran out madly into the night, down to the shore,

compelled instinctively to immerse himself in the sea. In his panic, he remembered his old friend Meladriel once telling him that sea water could always be relied upon as an emergency defence against etheric attack. Its protective properties were vast. But was it a memory? It was almost as if Meladriel was with him, murmuring instructions. After stumbling down the slope of dry sand, Amorel lurched gracelessly over the boundary between ocean and land. The tide was going out; he remembered also Meladriel telling him the outgoing tide had the power to draw sickness from a har, to bear it far, far away.

Amorel collapsed into the drowsy waves. He lay there on his back for a while, merely gasping for breath. Benevolent wrinkles of brine washed over his face occasionally, ran into his mouth, his eyes. Presently, he became aware his hands were stinging. Hardly daring to look, he raised them cautiously, saw they were whole again. *Illusion. Torment. But perhaps just a taste of worse to come.*

He staggered to his feet, swaying for a moment, the water swirling around his ankles, sucking at his pale linen robe. Then, summoning what remained of his strength, he made his way back to the house.

In a corner of his studio, buried beneath piles of musical manuscripts, was a psycaller he'd hardly used. This was a device owned only by the privileged few who had associates in Immanion, where such arcane apparati were fashioned. Amorel rarely had cause to communicate with anyhar urgently. Yet now, with shaking, clammy hands, he attached the contact claws to his temples, palmed the crystal in the power niche of the device, rubbed it alive, tuned in. Upon the network of stars that bloomed before his mind's eye, he floundered for a moment, unused to the sensations, then focused his mind to travel the paths that led to a trusted employee, a har he kept in service to deal with occasional *awkward* things. He poured his intention, his message, into the hollow in reality – the receptacle of another device – he felt form around his mind.

I need sedu transport to Almagabra. As soon as you can arrange it. Something has arisen that means the tour must be delayed. There is no other option. See to it. Contact me immediately once you've spoken to the appropriate hara.

Then he tore the claws from his head, retched, barely making it to the kitchen where he vomited into the sink.

Chapter Twenty-Nine

'Come back with me to *Inglefey*, Mela.'

'No, Seladris. I can't. I must go home... alone.'

Seladris wasn't even sure he'd experienced that exchange. Perhaps he'd only imagined it.

After the rite at the shrine, he went alone to his house. Was this a haven as everyhar thought? He wasn't sure. The rest of them had remained at *Velvets*.

In the chaos and confusion that had followed the rite at the shrine, Seladris had been barely noticed. He wasn't sure what he felt about that, aware only that everything had turned out how it usually did for him; failure, catastrophe, ruin. It could be no coincidence. At least there had been no deaths.

And yet now, as he stood at the window of his kitchen looking down over the town, he sensed that might change. He could smell the infection hanging over the buildings. There were loud discordant sounds coming in through the open panes, screeches as of huge metal plates grinding together, dull thuds as if the earth cracked. He saw gouts of flame, reports like gunshots – yet surely nohar in Ferelithia would still own a gun. Explosions, then, of some kind.

Shadey Lane was still and quiet, as if holding its breath, as if hiding.

They had left the painting of the blue leopard where it lay in the ancient shrine, but now it was empty, simply a mess of pigments fashioned into a particular shape. Its power had crept out of it.

Seladris looked down at his hands. They seemed to be covered in turquoise chalk. There were bruises on his arms that coiled like the leopard had once done within its frame; twisted, flung.

He saw his reflection in the window, and it was the har from Margenya, blackened and torn, eyes like glass marbles, blood upon his lips. This vision leered at him. Then he realised it wasn't a reflection at all. Something was outside. He turned his back on it and heard the echo of retreating laughter.

At *Velvets*, the participants of the rite were mostly in different rooms, as if placed in cells. Thazri and Ihrec remained with Ulien, not in his bedroom, but down in the main salon, where the windows were fastened tight, the drapes drawn across them. The air was too hot and smelled musty. Ulien had been given a calming nostrum; he was barely conscious, his mind empty. The soft voices of his hostling and carer hissed like a receding tide upon soft sand. He couldn't understand their words, although they must be discussing the events of the evening. He knew that they had lost a battle, yet it felt far from over. This was a lull between skirmishes, that was all.

Kazharn stood in the garden, like Seladris, looking down upon the town, beholding the same emblems of desolation, the brief towers of flame, the unearthly sounds. He felt powerless, in the same way he had so many years before.

There had been screams back then, and a terrible stink. The town hadn't burned, although there had been isolated blazes. The destruction had been worse than mere fire. *Unlife* had moved through the buildings, desiccating all that it touched. *They* had passed by, angels of death in their most literal form. The sea, pulsing with sick nodes of light, had surged unnaturally, as if wanting to hurl itself upon the land, but lacking the strength to do so. A human tide had attempted to flee but had found that roads turned around upon them, emptied them backwards to unavoidable extinction.

Kazharn had thought those most useless of words: *What have we done?*

But he knew, of course. He'd always known.

And on that night, Leupardra had come to him and said, 'See? See what I can do?'

And Karn had said, 'You didn't do it. We all did.'

Leupardra had laughed at that. 'I *made* you do it.'

All Karn could answer was, 'Yes.'

He'd felt tired then, wishing it was all over or had never begun. He'd known there was more to do: clearing up that, in some ways, was worse than battle. Leupardra had sown hate and distrust among Karn's friends, so they could find no strength or support in one another. They were barely even speaking now, couldn't discuss what had happened. Karn had known he was more alone than he'd ever thought possible. Tribe meant nothing. Love meant nothing. Not even friendship.

And then Leupardra's purring tones on the night air. 'Let me kiss you, my beautiful one. I'll kiss it all away.'

In the present, Kazharn uttered a sound of distress to dispel the memory. He'd given Leupardra what he'd wanted in the past, and had done so again, had been manipulated once more, as if no time had passed at all.

Leupardra believed he'd given Ferelithia to the tribe, so therefore it was his to take back.

And what can we do about it?

Meladriel had gone away, yet again, melting into the darkness, no doubt feeling beaten and humiliated.

Katarin had returned to Immanion. The har made Kazharn uneasy. He felt as if he knew Katarin, but how? Sometimes, in the way the har moved or smiled, a memory sprang out, but dim and cloudy. Once or twice, Kazharn thought Katarin had been on the brink of revealing something to him, but then withdrew, silent. Now, he'd gone back to deliver his findings to the Tigrina, taking his mysteries within him. Kazharn uttered a smothered sound of disgust. If careless, breezy Rue was all they had left to counter Leupardra's power, any plan must inevitably be meaningless. Therefore, it must be Gelaming who would come: full intervention. Kazharn had no doubt this is what would happen, despite what Katarin had said about respecting Ferelith autonomy. The fact was that the Ferelith had no teeth; they were feeble. To preserve life in the town – and the Pearl of Almagabra as an ideal – Katarin would have no choice but to report to the Hegalion. Left unchallenged, there was no telling what Leupardra might do, how far his ambitions stretched. And yet... how real was he? Was he merely a potent ghost? Did his power lie only in fermenting fear among the living, playing them off against one another? Or did he possess physical power, the ability to end life in reality? Or was he something else entirely, a living har who merely believed himself to be Leupardra? Where did the answers lie?

Before leaving Ferelithia, Katarin had said, 'I'll report back to you as soon as I can.' Already he must have contacted Rue, if only to order *sedu* transport.

Kazharn had felt the har's concern; despite his strangeness, the disturbing hint of familiarity, it was clear to see Katarin was an honest, principled creature, very different to the typical patronising Hegalion official. But he was still closely connected to the Gelaming, even if it didn't feel as if he was.

'I give you my word you'll be involved in all decisions,' Katarin had insisted, 'and also in whatever action is taken. Rue will back me on this, I promise.'

Kazharn sighed deeply. He'd really believed this night would have ended it all neatly. Now, he knew that in the morning he must face his peers in the Municipallion, tell them what had transpired. It was no longer possible to contain what Leupardra was doing. Everyhar had to know the truth, so they could try to protect themselves.

What was there to say? *This town was never ours, but we fought to take it. Now we have to fight again. This time without an army.*

Which meant no fight. Which meant Gelaming, who would seethe in and freeze everything, then pluck out the rot. Ferelithia would be sanitised and finally *theirs*, after everything, all those careful negotiations by the Municipallion over the years to retain control of their own tribe rather than simply becoming a phyle of the Gelaming. Perhaps this was no more than the Ferelith deserved. Kazharn shuddered, physically repulsed. Certain details of the past yet remained secret, even from his close allies, and must remain so. Did Thiede's hara still pursue justice concerning war crimes of the past?

Perhaps for the first time, he truly appreciated why the early Ferelith leaders had fled Almagabra. Karn had been too young and stupid to understand. All he'd seen was a victory, even if it had come at a high cost. Kazharn was denied that blissful ignorance.

Chapter Thirty

The forest steamed beneath the onslaught of an Alba Sulh heatwave. They came, sometimes, in the summers – these dog days of murderous, unrelenting heat, when the deer gasped amid the unshorn barley, and flowers and grass curled over into parched, dead crisps.

Every day, at dawn and dusk, Pharis reset the wards around the community, empowered by his own blood. If necessary, he would bleed himself dry to protect his home, until he was no more than a husk, folding up like a dying insect. He felt the heat was unnatural, a screen, a demonstration of power.

Aedisa said to him, quoting from a ritual text, 'the grass that browns in summer's inferno never dies. It returns with the crisp light of spring.'

Maybe true, but heat could be a weapon that might sap and enervate the strongest of hara.

Pharis had dismissed the initial surge of horror that had swamped him when he'd run to his injured chesnari in the sleep centre. Then, his first thought had been that Leupardra was back, vengeful and furious, and had tracked him down somehow. But now that fear seemed absurd. Pharis had been on the periphery of what had happened in Ferelithia. He'd deliberately kept himself somewhat distant, unsure whether his friends' actions were justified or even safe. They were surely effective, but still...

Leupardra had never targeted Pharis for seduction and manipulation as he had the others. There *appeared* to be a mutual respect and wariness between them, although Leupardra *had* said to him, on that fateful night, 'Pharis, you have more sense than the rest of your band put together, but don't think you'll come out of this with clean hands. You're not that clever.'

Pharis had simply laughed this off – *that* he'd found was the best way to deal with Leupardra.

'Yes, laugh,' Leupardra had said. 'I know why you do it.' He'd smiled, eyes so narrow. 'I like you. You'll be rewarded as much as any of the others.'

Pharis refused to give this memory credence, but still it rankled within him.

Since Aedisa's recovery, there had been no more dramatic paranormal events, but something – *something* – lurked at the boundary of Herne's Chase, an unseen predator in the heavy summer foliage. Pharis could smell aromas of those long-ago days in Ferelithia – the sea, the flowers, blood.

At night, brought to wakefulness by the fading echo of a nightmare, he would lie in bed, holding his breath, and presently a cry would break the heavy silence – like the mournful skreek of a bird of prey that devolved into the grunting cough of a big cat, becoming something of both. Then he would sleep again and be stalked through his dreams, by a lithe, invisible hunter. He would often wake exhausted.

Pharis was not frightened by these phenomena, because he had convinced himself they would pass as the summer aged. He refused to succumb to the belief that Leupardra – or any semblance of him – was responsible for them. To even *think* that was to give the notion power. Anyway, this time of year was prone to peculiar events and strange apparitions. Some of the entities who hid in the shadows at noon could read a har's mind with ease, pluck from it the phantoms of his undoing. This is what must be happening now. Alba Sulh was an ancient land but also compact in comparison with other countries. The cries and clamours of its history had sunk into the rocks and soil of its clan of isles. Sometimes a shred of this energy might wake up and cause a little mischief. Dark memories lurked in the ancient forests and the dreaming moorlands. It was feasible that a skittish or damaged client of the Chase had unwittingly awoken a fragment of latent energy, and it had fed thereafter on whatever source of sustenance it found to hand. Through Aedisa, it had sniffed out, deep in Pharis's memories, the choice morsel that was Leupardra. All manner of very deep thoughts could have transferred between Aedisa and Pharis as they'd created their pearls. It was entirely possible that all of Pharis's life experiences now existed somewhere within Aedisa's mind, and vice versa.

Pharis had discussed the matter at length with Fallami, Aedisa and other learned hara of his community, and all of them felt this must be the explanation. Pharis had nothing to hide; he told them everything – well, all that he knew. But as a precaution he kept up the wards. Just in case.

Two hara of a settlement some ten miles distant, had asked to be bonded in blood at Herne's Chase, beneath summer's canopy within the forest. A party would be held, attracting visitors from other settlements near and far. Herne's Chase was famous for its hospitality, and its ceremonies were satisfyingly elaborate, poetic and moving. The event would take place at noon. In return, the Chase would receive goods: carpets, blankets, boots of leather.

Pharis spent the morning checking the boundaries. The sky was clear, yet he felt the air was unsettled. He was sensitive to the weather but the heaviness in the atmosphere did not – to him – presage the kindling of a storm. Despite this, he performed banishings, at various points within the forest, to quell any questionable energy that might be employed to cause harm or disruption. In other places, he invoked elemental beings to act as savage guardians. He charged with protective power the springs, the groves and the rocks of sacred meaning. He called to the hidden hunters of the hills beyond the forests, and the fey people of the moors. Nothing could breach Pharis's defences. He lacked any shred of guilt, shame or uncertainty. His etheric armour was shining silver and his eyes were fire.

By 10.30, the site was ready, a wide clearing in the forest, around ten minutes' walk from Herne's Chase. A bower of summer blooms had been constructed and pavilions of painted canvas erected, in which the guests would later partake of the first feast of the day.

Pharis prowled the site, visualising the day to come. At the heart of Herne's Chase, the hara to be bonded would be undergoing, separately, a ritual bath and anointment, then would be dressed in costumes fashioned specifically for the rite. In an hour's time, the caterers would arrive at the pavilions and place food and drink within them, carefully covered to prevent insects contaminating the feast. Musicians and entertainers would arrive next and position themselves discreetly near the bower. After this, invited guests would walk in procession to the site. Once they were gathered in a circle around the bower, the hienama to conduct the ceremony would make his entrance, attended by a staff of four hara, who would carry the ritual implements and speak the calls to the elemental powers. All would be dressed in elaborate robes, their hair wound with ivy and oak leaves. Finally, the chesnari would join the gathering, again separately and each in company with their closest friends and relatives. The music would start up. Hara would sing. Petals would be flung into the shimmering air.

Pharis wished the bonding would begin. He found it impossible to dismiss the edginess he felt within, yet there was no reason for it. He made his round one more time, reinforcing everything.

And yet, despite his misgivings, the ceremony went smoothly and without interruption, exactly as he'd visualised it. Everyhar looked beautiful and radiated happiness. The sun shone kindly; its vicious edge blunted by the joy perspiring into the day. To augment the bonding, a stag and four does appeared at the edge of the trees. They watched the proceedings for a few moments, then glided away.

Pharis had to concede there was no evil here, no hint of bitterness or resentment. This was the new world in all its finery, celebrating its victory over the troubled past. Many of the hara present probably didn't even think about such things, because they were young and had known only this life. And that, Pharis thought, was how it should be. Angry ghosts cannot take root in the hearts of those who don't believe in them.

But, insisted a stern voice within, *just because a young har with no experience doesn't believe in a thing doesn't make it untrue. The har may be blinded by his own narrow tunnel of reality. Didn't our first hienamas teach us this of humans? Didn't that help us take this world from them?*

Be quiet, Pharis told this part of himself, *you're being ridiculous. This day is unblighted. And unless you stop thinking otherwise, I'll assume you're crippled by your past experiences, unable to see past them, which must therefore be purged by the most sanctimonious of Fallami's cleansings. You won't like that at all, will you? So shut up.*

And yet…

The day went on. Pharis joined Aedisa and their sons at the feast. When he looked upon his chesnari, his heart contracted almost painfully with an emotion that was beyond definition – perhaps the most primal form of joy and gratitude combined. Aedisa was perfect, as the ancient gods should have made humankind. That he existed at all seemed a miracle. *We are living myths,* Pharis thought. He drank some wine, but not to excess. The event, the day itself, was flawless. Everyhar was satisfied and intoxicated, not just with alcohol but with life. No doubt Herne's Chase would acquire a few bookings for similar events by the end of it.

Pharis was asked if he would lead the drumming once the bonfire was lit at sunset. He agreed to do so.

At one point, Aedisa said to him, 'What's wrong?'

'Nothing,' Pharis answered, 'why?'

'You seem… apprehensive,' Aedisa said. 'If you're worried about something, you must tell me.'

Pharis put a hand to Aedisa's face, leaned forward to kiss him. 'It's nothing,' he said, 'nothing real.'

'Are you sure about that?' Aedisa frowned a little. 'It's not that long since…'

'Yes, I'm sure.' Pharis forced a smile. It was the first time he'd lied to his chesnari.

As the sun sank, the second feast of the day was brought out to the site. A boar from the forest was roasted over a fire pit. Root vegetables were broiled in the fat, flavoured with herbs and summer berries.

Harlings, excited by the onset of night, ran around yelling, enacting their own incomprehensible childish rituals. A fat full moon held court in the sky, shining like a lesser sun.

The bonded chesnari, radiant in the smoulder-light of the fire, would lead the first dance. And Pharis was summoned to play the tall, deep hand drums, known as timbriels in Alba Sulh. Gradually, other percussionists joined the performance, playing upon different kinds of drums and instruments such as bells, chimes and rattles, which were presently joined by flutes and fiddles. This was the essential music of the tribes.

Once the spirit of the drumming took him, Pharis moved beyond reality. He *became* the primal rhythm, merely a channel for its timeless beat to manifest in the world. Hara undulated to the sound, adding their voices to the pulsing cadence. The archaic song of life circled and rose, sometimes falling, always in motion. Hara could not help but raise power in these circumstances. When the climax approached, they threw up their arms, uttering whooping sounds like animals and birds. They cast their love – of the world and each other – up into the sky along with the spiralling sparks of the fire. This was their offering to the land, energy of the most positive, innocent kind.

Pharis stood shuddering before his drums, barely able to breathe, never mind move. Energy coursed through his body like the waves of aruna. And in this moment, he saw them.

Long shadowy shapes at the edge of the forest to the east, their faces merely a pale blur some eight feet from the ground. They leaned forward, somehow unnaturally, as if twisted out of shape. Soon, they would move.

Pharis was shaken back to reality in an instant. Not even considering he should tackle this phenomenon alone, he sent out a mind call to Aedisa and Fallami, who were close to him. Pharis could communicate emotions and information at exceptional speed via mind touch. He conveyed a series of images, with the imperative to dispel. And they were interpreted by the recipients equally swiftly.

On one level of reality, the partygoers, embraced each other, laughing, still singing, still stamping the ground, while on another three adepts of Herne's Chase repelled an invasion before it could even manifest properly. They formed a barrier of shining light, which they flung outwards against the threat.

Whatever had begun to form at the edge of the gathering had not expected such an onslaught of opposition. To the surprise of those who were braced for a long and rigorous assault, it retreated without a fight.

Nohar suspected anything unusual had – or almost had – taken place.

By mind touch, Fallami requested Pharis and Aedisa to meet with him in person at a grove nearby within the forest, still close enough to the party so they could remain alert for threats.

Aedisa asked a friend to care for the harlings, then he and Pharis slipped away.

Once they were together, Fallami said, 'I'm not sure what I just witnessed, Pharis. Please enlighten me.'

'Those entities are not of Alba Sulh,' Pharis said. 'But I think they *are* connected with what happened to Aedisa.'

'They fled quickly,' Aedisa said, 'but they might only have been... scouting. What *were* they, Pharis?'

'I can't tell you that exactly, but I've seen them before – or something like them. In Ferelithia. It was vital they were dispelled immediately. They are...' He shrugged. 'They are *death*.'

Fallami stared at Pharis for some moments, eyes wide. 'Is it likely they'll return?'

'I've no idea, but I'm assuming their target is me, or those close to me.' He sighed deeply.

'You said it was just a sour manifestation,' Aedisa said, rather bitterly. 'Something mindless latching onto your memories.'

'Yes, I did. I didn't want to think otherwise, but now I can't deny the facts. I've seen such entities before. I've seen what they can do.'

'You said there was nothing to fear today,' Aedisa said.

'I'm sorry... I didn't want the opposite to be true, that's all.'

Aedisa shook his head. Later, Pharis knew he must deal with his chesnari's disappointment in him. He would have to explain why he'd lied, and that would be difficult, because he didn't know.

'The entities departed very quickly,' Aedisa said, breaking a silence. 'Perhaps they're not that strong.'

'They *are*,' Pharis said dismally. 'Trust me on that. But you're right. It didn't take as much effort as I thought it would to disperse them.'

'Which could mean they haven't gone at all,' Fallami said.

Pharis nodded. 'It could mean that, yes, or they've withdrawn because they didn't expect resistance.'

'Pharis,' Fallami said, 'this must be dealt with. We can't have hostile entities wandering about Herne's Chase at their own whim. If our clients are *affected*, well... I don't even want to contemplate that.'

'I know.'

'Then we'd better decide quickly what we intend to do about it.'

'I...' Pharis began, but then a movement at the edge of the trees caught his attention. Automatically, he began to raise a protective barrier while simultaneously sending the same suggestion to his companions.

But then, rather than grotesque hostile entities, a magnificent white horse stepped from the shadows into the moonlight. It trod delicately, its flawless pelt gleaming silver, as if made of lunar stuff. Upon its back sat a har, who said, 'Forgive me, Tiahaara, but I must speak with you urgently.'

Fallami began, 'Who are...?'

But Pharis broke in, 'Kate?!'

It didn't surprise Katarin that Pharis recognised her at once. He had always been the most spiritually inclined of the band, often appearing quiet and somewhat insular, while not really being that way at all. He *watched*. He saw beyond the superficial and always had. Also, she had been closer to Pharis than anyhar else, even Rue, the har she'd called her best friend. Pharis had confided in her too.

'Yes, Pharis, it's me,' Katarin said. 'I've come from Immanion. I think you know why.'

'Who is this individual?' a tall, regal black-skinned har demanded. His hair was fashioned into dreadlocks to his thighs and his air was that of authority, and a certain amount of disgruntlement.

'An old friend,' Pharis answered. 'From Ferelithia.' He turned to Katarin, gesturing at the frowning har. 'And this is Fallami, our High Hienama.'

Fallami exhaled through his nose. 'You are Gelaming, I take it?' He almost spat the words.

Katarin bowed her head. 'Not Gelaming, no. I represent the Tigrina in Immanion but am acting independent of the Hegalion. I'm here on vital business. As you can no doubt deduce from this, the phenomenon you experienced tonight isn't an isolated incident.'

Fallami shook his head with a brief stern glance towards Pharis. 'I think we'd better go to the centre house to talk.'

After Katarin had returned from Ferelithia and delivered her report to Caeru, they had discussed what action might be taken. The Tigrina had still wanted to keep the Hegalion out of it, at least until more information had been gathered. 'I *will* speak to Pell about it again, but not yet. I don't think there's any need at this point to interrupt his holiday. He knows I've asked you to investigate but won't mention this to anyhar else until I say so.'

'What about Cal? Does he know?'

'I'm sure Pell will have told him an amusing story about it,' Caeru replied, somewhat tartly. 'But whether he knows or not, I'm still inclined to keep this between us for now.' He smiled mordantly. 'The mere word Ferelithia makes Pell squirm. He hates to be reminded of when he was a little shit.'

Katarin had been unable to repress a burst of laughter. 'It's hard to feel sorry for him about that, but anyway… There aren't enough of them in Ferelithia to deal with this problem, Rue. They need support quickly – but the right kind.'

Caeru had grimaced. 'How many hara are we talking about? A great many or a few skilled adepts?'

'I don't think we need an army – we must simply find the motive for this attack, the perpetrator and then the weak spot. An event in the past inspired this. The answer lies there.'

Caeru had remained silent for some moments, then said, 'In order to heal or undo what's been done, I think…' He'd paused, wrinkled his nose. 'It might sound weird, but I feel some *re-enactment* must occur.'

'What?'

'I can't remember much of the original rite, because… well, you know very well what kind of har I was back then. Despite that, I think the procedure which started it all must somehow be repeated, but in reverse… or *something*.' He'd sighed. 'Truth is, much as I've argued with myself while you've been away, I'm sure of one thing. We need the others, Kate.'

'The others? Everyhar who was involved in that abominable *rite*? The majority of them have melted away into hiding.'

'Yes, the hienamas and the phylarchs have, but not the band.' Caeru had gestured emphatically. 'This isn't the ridiculous idea you think – and I *can* see you thinking it. We were *involved* in it, Kate. Our voices, our music, helped it happen. We were a team. You've already established contact with Karn and Meladriel. We know where Pharis and Amorel are, *roughly*…'

'If they still live…'

'They live.' Caeru had said simply.

Katarin had nodded. 'Very well. Let's see who we can find and what you all think once you're together. But I don't think there's much time before something irreparably bad happens.'

'Thank you. Act swiftly.' Caeru had smiled at her then. 'Does this mean you haven't remained in contact with Pharis *at all*?'

Katarin had looked away, faintly embarrassed. 'No… he left Ferelithia when you – *we* – did, as did Amorel. That was the end of it. You were in such a state over Pell, I didn't talk to you about it.'

'So, it was my fault?' This hadn't been an accusation; Caeru was still smiling.

'No... perhaps the excuse they needed to walk away. I never tried to persuade Pharis to stay. I think we all knew it was over.'

Caeru had reached out and squeezed Katarin's shoulder. 'I was and am your best friend, Kate. But Pharis was something else. Go and find him. He should be the first we recruit, since you know him so well.'

She hadn't answered.

'Don't you want to?'

She did, of course, but – similar to how she'd felt in Ferelithia when she'd considered contacting Karn – there was an annoying niggle within that Pharis would be scornful of her own transformation. Kamagrian had a mottled reputation among the tribes, not least because their leader Opalexian could be a difficult individual, and many parazha in Roselane held strange ideas even Katarin herself didn't agree with. But the "oddities", as Katarin and her Kamagrian friends referred to them, were the minority. Not every parage was the same. Kate knew doubting Pharis in this respect was absurd, because of all them he'd been the least judgmental, but even so.... She wouldn't be able to bear even a hint of aversion in his eyes. 'No, of course I'll find him,' she'd said brusquely. 'But... he might not be the same. He might not want to help.'

'We won't know until you find out,' Caeru had said. 'I'll request a *sedu* for you at once.'

She'd wondered whether it would be difficult to track Pharis down, but it had been remarkably easy. Herne's Chase Retreat was famous in Alba Sulh, as was the har who had once been in a band with the Tigrina. Pharis hadn't bothered to hide that. Perhaps all of them, in their way, still capitalised on their association with Rue.

Katarin had arrived at the Retreat near the end of the day's celebrations and had decided to keep her distance until the party broke up, not wishing to cause any kind of drama. The community of Herne's Chase appeared serene and untouched. As she observed them, she wondered whether she should even approach Pharis. It seemed clear to her that he and his hara were unaffected by what was happening in Ferelithia. He had a new life now; perhaps the past meant nothing to him. Physically, he'd hardly changed, his beauty merely enhanced by a sense of maturity. He was still the har she'd found the most attractive in the band – the object of a ruthless yet pointless longing. Yet he'd indulged her, *cared* for her. While she'd confided in Rue over most things, it'd been Pharis who'd listened to her angry rants about the unfairness of it all, how she could not be har. Aside from the fact he was lovely, his unattainability perhaps part of his allure, she had been drawn to his *stillness*, the way he'd never over-reacted to anything as Rue had always been prone to do, or been supercilious and patronising like Karn, or humourless and too serious like Amorel often was. Of them all, Pharis had been the mysterious witch – a real one, not simply a persona for the band. Unlikely, then, he'd be easy prey for Leupardra.

She'd watched him play, hiding among the trees, the *sedu* silent and motionless beside her, and had toyed with the idea of simply walking away once the performance was over. Leave Pharis to his life, what he'd earned. Tell Rue some story he'd believe. And then... the Pale Ones came.

Katarin was punched backwards – not by the presence of the entities, but by woven blades of energy hurled by Pharis and a couple of other hara. This etheric shield had brushed past her but was forceful enough to affect her physically. *Strong stuff!* she thought in awe. But not enough. Well-trained in etheric combat, Katarin wasn't sure the act of repulsion would remove the threat completely. For this reason, she felt it was right to assist. She sent a mind-touch to the *sedu*, which had naturally already picked up on the abnormal activity.

Please help them, she requested.

Nohar knew what *sedim* were really capable of, but Katarin reckoned that dispelling entities like those she'd just glimpsed must be no harder for them than swatting flies. Rather than becoming personally involved, the *sedu* allowed Katarin to borrow some of its energy, which it transferred to her immediately. This was like being handed a deadly weapon; it filled her being with a force too alien and painful to bear. She threw this out with her mind alone, desperate to be rid of it more than anything else; a rippling, pulsing mass of non-earthly power. Within moments, the things were gone, as if snuffed out. They'd only been projections, then, even if convincing ones.

Now, concealing the fact she still felt a little shaky, Katarin walked back to Herne's Chase with Pharis and his friends, skirting the party that was still lively around the bonfire.

Pharis put an arm around the dark-skinned har walking beside him. 'This is my chesnari, Aedisa. Aedi, this is...' He paused and glanced at Katarin. 'Would you like to introduce yourself?'

'Kat... now,' she answered, grateful for Pharis's sensitivity. 'but if you still want to call me Kate, please do. Rue always does.' Hara had generally changed their names after inception. Pharis was aware she might have done the same.

'Pleased to meet you,' Aedisa said, in a formal tone. Clearly, he wasn't that pleased, primarily, Katarin sensed, perhaps because her arrival presaged disruption to his life. And she was an agent of the Gelaming. The mere mention of that tribal name often tended to close more doors than it opened.

As they walked, Katarin explained briefly what had happened in Ferelithia, and that she'd been sent there to investigate. 'I don't need to ask if anything's happened to you,' she said dryly to Pharis. 'I saw what occurred earlier here. Was this the only incident?'

'No, the second *incident* but things haven't felt right for a while.' He explained what had happened to Aedisa, occasionally interrupted by Fallami, who appeared to think accuracy in every detail was essential.

When Pharis had finished the tale, Fallami said caustically, 'And now the Gelaming are involved. Delight!'

'Not exactly,' Katarin said. 'Rue is, of course, but that's because he was part of what happened in the past. I assure you, no har of Immanion but him knows I'm here.'

Fallami grunted, clearly still suspicious.

For a short while, there was a tense silence, then Pharis said, 'You're Kamagrian, then, obviously.'

Katarin nodded. 'I stayed friends with Rue...' She shrugged. 'That helped. He steered me in the right directions.'

'A strategic friendship,' Pharis said, which might have sounded disapproving if not for the smile that accompanied it.

Katarin grimaced humorously. 'Well, not deliberately, but...'

'I've never met a Kamagrian before,' Pharis said. 'Is it the same?'

Katarin shrugged. 'More or less, yes. We can do anything hara can.' She paused. 'Such as... I did rather more than observe what occurred here earlier. I helped you.'

Pharis rolled his eyes. 'Ah, I see. So, we're not the great adepts we thought we were. Your *Gelaming powers* saw off the enemy!'

'Not quite – the *sedu* assisted me.' She patted the neck of the beast ambling alongside her.

'Magic horses are always useful, clearly,' Pharis said.

'When they're in the mood. They can be like cats...'

Pharis pulled a face, then said, 'So, what *is* a *sedu* exactly?'

'Sssh!' she said. 'He *can* hear you, you know.'

'Will he answer the question?'

'No.'

So easy to fall back into the way they'd conversed in the past: it was almost painful.

They had reached the octagonal central building of Herne's Chase, a spreading single storey structure with a gently peaked thatched roof. Here, Fallami summoned one of his colleagues to take care of Katarin's *sedu*; not everyhar was still at the party. She didn't bother to inform him that *sedim* didn't need to be treated like horses, because it would be too complicated to explain. The creature allowed itself to be led away, patient, or merely uncaring.

Fallami ushered the group inside and towards a reception room. Here, bidding everyhar be seated, he said to Katarin, 'Now – may we hear your story in full?'

Katarin inclined her head. 'Of course. It's why I'm here.'

Fallami sniffed, then bowed his head too, perhaps a shade mockingly. 'Then tell us all you know.'

Katarin held nothing back – aware that the hara before her expected no less and would be able to tell if she omitted any facts. Also, she'd already established Fallami was particular about detail. She was often interrupted by his questions, which she dealt with patiently; it was her job to so do. After she'd concluded, she said, 'Rue believes that bringing some of the initial hara back to Ferelithia will help. He's spoken of some kind of re-enactment...'

'That would be insane,' Pharis broke in. 'We shouldn't have done anything in the first place. Trying to repeat the procedure is merely asking for trouble. Isn't there a risk it could make things worse? Also, none of us really knew the precise details of Leupardra's work, *how* he accomplished it. We'd be working blind.'

'Then what do you suggest?' Katarin asked reasonably. 'You've been *found*, Pharis, and not just by me. You must know this situation can't simply be *left*. It has to be faced for what it is and dealt with.'

'What about your *sedu*?' Fallami enquired. 'Immanion has a herd of them, doesn't it? Get them to deal with it.'

'Our relationship with *sedim* doesn't work like that,' Katarin said.

'They might aid us now and again, and in their own interests, but I'm pretty sure they would consider what's happening in Ferelithia a harish matter that must be dealt with by hara.'

'What's the point of them, then?' Pharis asked.

'Transport, mainly,' Katarin said, keeping her voice even. She was unsure why Pharis had become slightly hostile. Perhaps he really didn't want to be involved. She couldn't blame him. 'I can't force you to come with me to Ferelithia and take part in any action, but if you'd only attend the meeting there and offer your opinion, it would help, I'm sure. Take a reading of the place.'

'He'll go!' Fallami said. 'And so will I. I might not have been part of Ferelithia's history, but I've dealt with many strange and difficult circumstances over the years. This situation is affecting Herne's Chase, so I must be part of whatever action is taken. At the very least, I can assist with evaluating the facts and evidence, help form a strategy.'

'Thank you,' Katarin said. 'Ferelithia's hienamas are mostly second generation and have never had to deal with anything like this. If Karn agrees, you can share your experience with them. The way things are, I can't see he'd object.'

Fallami nodded. 'Are you in agreement with this, Pharis?'

Pharis sighed. 'Yes. If you're willing to help, then I must too.'

'You're all mad,' Aedisa said sadly. 'Mad but...' He shrugged. 'I can't argue with the decision. We can't risk anything else happening here at the Chase.'

Pharis leaned against him. 'Aedi, I'm really sorry...'

'Hush,' Aedisa said, putting the fingers of one hand to Pharis's lips. 'There's nothing we can do about it, except what seems the best course of action. If this force – this Leupardra – is so strong he can reach across countries and find you, he must be stopped. There's no choice. Merely dealing with any monsters that trickle out of his dark nest isn't enough; you must find the nest and destroy it.'

'We will,' Katarin said.

Aedisa smiled at her bleakly.

Chapter Thirty-One

Miyacalasday, 30 Ardourmoon

For the first time in decades, a barrier folded down in Meladriel's mind. While he was making breakfast, a tingle started in his head, followed by a familiar presence, that was also not familiar at all. A message. He opened himself to it warily and received a mind touch from Kazharn, to say that Katarin had reported back to him. The har would attempt to bring Pharis to Ferelithia, and perhaps, thereafter, Amorel. Through Katarin, Rue had sent his regards and had asked them to hang on for a day or two more. If things got desperate, they must contact him immediately. Katarin had then imparted a private etheric signature to Kazharn, which he hoped he'd never have to use.

There was a hesitation after the message – mental static – as if Kazharn didn't want to end the communication but was unsure what to send next. In sympathy, Meladriel asked: *how are things with the Municipallion?*

Difficult, Kazharn responded. *You can imagine. This is not a problem of their making. They resent having to cope with it. Some accusations have been thrown about. There's nohar else but me to throw them at.*

Will it affect your position?

I'm not sure.

What of the town? I've not left home today so I've not seen anything.

There's quite a lot of damage. Hara were injured. Hara are now furious or frightened. It's breaking down. What do you expect?

Meladriel balked at the sharp tone, poised to shut himself down, but Kazharn continued swiftly.

I'm sorry. Didn't mean to be snappy. This is all just... a lot to deal with. We don't know how bad it'll get. The nayati hienamas are working hard to heal the spirit of the town. The Municipallion have organised patrols to try and keep the population calm. I suppose you could say Ferelithia is under martial law. Hara are behaving...

Crazy, Meladriel finished, then asked quickly, *How's Ulien?*

Thazri and I decided that he, Ihrec and Ulien should go to Inglefey and stay with Seladris for the time being. As far as we know, it's the safest place for them.

I'll go see them later. I should check with a couple of friends also, make sure they're OK.

Mela…

Yes?

I'm at the Municipallion now but will be free shortly. May we talk? In person?

You must be really desperate.

No… You're the only one who truly understands what we're facing. We must talk about it.

What's to say? Presumably the Gelaming will arrive, arrange us in a line, tell us what to do and that will be that. Have a medal.

There was a pause. *I want to see you.*

All right. I won't go out until you've called in.

Kazharn arrived within an hour, just before noon.

Meladriel was visiting the nearest of his hives, next to his cottage, assessing the state of the bees. He had told them all that had happened. He'd intended to introduce Seladris to the bees today but knew now that wasn't possible. Perhaps another day. He sat on the grass before the hive, and the patterns his bees wove around him indicated he must prepare himself for further conflict. That was no surprise. He let them settle on him, closed his eyes. They fed him strength.

When he felt the presence of another har, he was not alarmed. The har wasn't hostile. He knew who it was.

'Mela,' said Kazharn.

Meladriel opened his eyes and the bees began to unwind from him like skeins of smoke. Kazharn stood some distance away, no doubt concerned the bees would sting.

'In some ways,' Meladriel said, getting to his feet, 'what's happening now is good for me. I'm finding parts of myself I've neglected for too long.'

'I can feel that.' Kazharn smiled wanly. 'You're yearning for a clean fight, to put things straight.'

'You could say that, or you could say I've waited long enough to put Leupardra in his place.'

'If it's him. I'm still not totally convinced.'

'Whatever it is, it's definitely *partly* him.' Meladriel got to his feet. 'Come with me. I must visit all the hives.'

Kazharn nodded, and for some minutes they headed towards the north-western woodland in silence. Then Meladriel said, 'I remember when I started my hives – the first one. It was by the woods back here, when I returned to Ferelithia. I found books in the cottage I took. Whoever lived there before me kept bees, but all their hives were derelict. I decided to build new ones, using ancient techniques. I experimented with different designs for a while until I found one the bees liked. I've stuck with that.'

'How many hives do you have now?'

'About two dozen.'

There was a short silence. Then Kazharn drew in a breath and said, 'Is... he *watching* us now, do you think?'

'Something will be. But it won't hear us, I'm sure of that. Nothing hostile can break through my protections now.'

'Yet you heard me call you.'

'I imagine that means I no longer regard you as hostile.'

'Tell me about your bees,' Kazharn said abruptly.

'I thought you'd want to discuss what happened last night.'

'Not yet. Tell me about the life of the hives.'

'All right.'

Kazharn listened in silence, but Meladriel was unsure how much information he was taking in. Kazharn, clearly, was breaking down as much as the town was. His authority had been punctured. He wasn't in control. His arrogance, his certainty, was crumbling. Meladriel was alarmed to see this. Kazharn was a figurehead for Ferelithia, as much a part of its heart – its omphalos – as the Nayati Kelosanya and the Municipallion. He must remain strong and focused for the good of everyhar. This, perhaps, was his moment of challenge, his dark night of the soul.

They had come to the pine woodland, where more of Meladriel's hives stood.

'I remember this place,' Kazharn murmured. 'When we first scouted the area.' He shook his head. 'We were so stupid; thought we'd just take the town for ourselves. We hated what we had been – human – and yet how were we any better than them?'

'Karn, don't,' Meladriel said. 'Look around you. I know many hara were vile after inception, hardly more than spiteful, unruly children, but as adults most of us are responsible custodians for this world, more so than humankind ever were. We know our place in it and our obligations. The conflict that granted freedom was a price that had to be paid. Maybe it was essential early hara were the way they were. Humanity would never have given up without a fight – what was left of them. They were wounded, cornered and vicious.'

'Mela…' Kazharn put his head to one side, sighed. 'Not all of them were guilty. You know that. That town… it was a refuge, a sanctuary. There were few fighters there, only exhausted refugees, the young, the old. We were greedy and brutal, just as bad as the worst of humankind.' He shook his head. 'How could we have shut ourselves down like that, done the things we did? It sickens me.'

'Karn… stop.'

'I can't. I've thought about it all night. It's like we've been living in a dream, a flimsy thing, looking in a mirror to admire our own virtues. But it's a lie. We don't deserve this place – or this world.'

'I think we do. Now.' Taking a deep breath, unsure whether he wanted to reach out in this way, Meladriel put his hands upon Kazharn's arms, shook him slightly. 'Come on, don't crumple like this. Ferelithia needs you. Don't flop about, wallowing in self-pity. The past is done. We can only move forward. Remember, hara *wanted* you in command here.'

'Maybe they don't, now they know the truth.'

Meladriel uttered a sound that was almost a growl. 'For Aru's sake, Karn, you sound like a whining harling. Listen to yourself. You can't break down into little wet bits after a single skirmish. Remember who you are. If younger members of the Municipallion judge you, it's because they weren't there at the beginning. They don't realise – or choose not to accept – what terrible sacrifices were made, so that they might come to be. You should inform them of that.'

Kazharn pulled away. 'Don't you understand? I don't want to be a har who was part of what Leupardra made us do.'

'Then he's manipulating you again, like he did before. Can't you see that?'

Kazharn put his hands to his face, silver bangles sliding down his arms – that sight to conjure a hundred memories.

'Karn, think. What we did here was *nothing* in comparison to what took place elsewhere, like in Megalithica. The Varrs butchered their own kind as much as they slaughtered humans. It was going on everywhere, a catharsis. But we *never* killed our own.'

Kazharn lowered his hands. 'Didn't we?'

Meladriel had never looked upon so deep an expression of despair. 'What do you mean?' he asked softly.

Kazharn shook his head. 'Not yet,' he said.

Meladriel took hold of him again. 'No. Absolutely *yet*. Now!'

Kazharn drew in a breath, as if the air pained him, then spoke quickly. 'Leupardra used his own – or rather *our* own. The weakest, the most damaged, the least useful, the least beautiful…'

Meladriel blinked, as if to clear his eyes would unscale them. 'What are you saying?'

'You heard me. He *fuelled* the Pale Ones with what he considered to be our… dross.'

Meladriel gasped. 'I found their remains!' He pressed his fingers against his mouth for a moment, then cried, 'Sweet dehara! The cellar by *Inglefey*. Had they lain there since the first invocation? I *burned* the evidence!'

Kazharn said, 'I didn't make you do that.'

'Perhaps I always suspected anyway. Just didn't want to remember or admit it. Shit!' Meladriel turned around, paced for a few moments. 'We have to tell them, Karn… the Gelaming.'

'Are you mad? They'd incarcerate us.'

'You think so? Like there aren't some bright minds in Immanion who have ancient blood on their hands. Tigron Calanthe, for example.'

'That's hardly a *good* example. He has rank in the Hegalion. We don't, and we can't take the risk.'

'Yes, we pelking well can, if it helps resolve this mess! Don't demonise the Gelaming, Karn. They might be meddling and over-bearing but they're not stupid, nor unjust. They didn't and can't punish every har who did a bad thing during the Devastation.'

Kazharn raised his hands in a placatory gesture. 'Let's wait until Katarin brings the others. Let's see how things go. You know the truth now. I'm sorry I kept this from you.'

'Really? I'm not surprised about it. Leupardra was a diseased creature. He was misplaced within our tribe. The early Kakkahaar would have welcomed him with prayers and song.'

Kazharn grimaced. 'Probably a good thing that meeting never happened, then. He would no doubt be sitting on the Council of Tribes by now, as the Kakkahaar leader Lianvis does.'

'Which just goes to prove what I said – the Gelaming are

prepared to forgive and forget. Can we agree on that?'

Kazharn nodded, his eyes downcast. 'Yes.'

Meladriel shook his head. 'This is bizarre. It's like we've swapped roles. I was the one moping about, crippled by the past, and you were the leader of our tribe who'd got over it. Now you're moping and I'm telling you what to do. How did that happen?'

'Isn't that simply part of our point as hara?' Kazharn said dryly. 'Fluidity of attributes?'

Meladriel huffed out a short laugh. 'If you insist. Anyway, I just have to check the moorland hives, then we can go back.'

'Take your time. It's fine.'

As they walked, Meladriel considered that relationships were tides, forever ebbing and flowing. Only a few weeks ago, he could never have imagined speaking to Kazharn again, never mind re-establishing some kind of tenuous frienship. He could feel that Kazharn needed reassurance, was – perhaps for the first time in decades – feeling shaky, as if the ground could give way beneath him at any moment. And who else could give him reassurance but Meladriel, the only har in Ferelithia who'd been there with him in the past?

If it wasn't for the bitterness that, even after all this time, still seethed within him, the crushing disappointment and bewilderment, Meladriel could reach out now and touch this har beside him. He knew this would be welcomed, be returned, become something more. Was it wrong to hold onto old hurt or simply a survival mechanism that should not be ignored? He could no longer tell.

On the dreaming moors, Meladriel asked his bees if he might take a comb from a hive. They fanned him with their wings, sang softly.

Kazharn stood back, said, 'won't they sting you?'

'No.' Meladriel reached inside, through a small trapdoor he could unlock. He took a small piece of the dripping comb, brought it out, slipped the wooden cover back into place. When he looked at Kazharn, he could see the har was remembering a time they had found wild bees in the forest, perhaps a swarm that had left abandoned hives near the town, set up home on their own. Then too Meladriel had been a honey thief, and Karn had protested, told him he was mad as he'd climbed the tree, a cloud of insects around him. He'd reached inside the hollow trunk.

They'd not stung him then, and they hadn't since. Bees knew Meladriel for what he was. He was accepted among them.

That time, so long ago, he and Karn had made a bed among the deep forest ferns. He had fed Karn honey, adored him, given him pleasure. They had felt inviolable, one har.

Now, Meladriel held out his hand to Kazharn, with the golden liquor stringing from it.

'The second gift,' Kazharn said. 'Will there be three?'

'Take it,' Meladriel said. 'You didn't taste the first.'

'How can you know that?'

'Take it.'

Kazharn took hold of Meladriel's wrist, lifted the dripping hand and fed from it. He did this in full awareness, never moving his gaze from Meladriel's eyes. 'Will I die now?' he asked.

'No more than you did back then,' Meladriel said.

Kazharn smiled, still holding onto Meladriel's hand. 'Oh, you killed me a little. I remember.' He ate the rest of the comb, licked the spilled gold, sucked it from Meladriel's fingers.

Inevitably, Meladriel felt the serpent stir within, a lifting of the head, the flicker of a tongue. 'Should we *consider*...?' he asked, aware he sounded faintly breathless.

'Consider we take back what was ours? What was stolen?' Kazharn shrugged. 'Why should we consider that? It seems reasonable we just take what's always been ours.' He grinned the kind of mischievous dark grin he'd used to have. 'Leupardra will not be pleased.'

'Hmm,' Meladriel said. 'I want to say that's not a good reason to do it, and that if there is something to take back, it's merely something we – or rather *you* – stupidly let go, but I would *really* like to infuriate that little snake.'

'Forget him,' Kazharn said. He put his hands upon Meladriel's arms. 'Forget the stupid me, too. I was his creature. I was weak. I threw you away – the most senseless thing I ever did.'

Images of faces flickered through Meladriel's mind: Thazri, Ulien... even Seladris. 'There's more than him to forget, though, isn't there?'

'Not here. Not now. We've stepped out of time, haven't we?'

Meladriel wasn't sure. His gesture with the honey had been deliberately provocative – now this. A few snatched hours? What, then?

'Don't think of it,' Kazharn said. 'It's not relevant. You've invoked this between us, Mela. It's a ritual we must complete.'

'Is it easier for you if we think of it in those terms?'

Kazharn sighed, shrugged again. 'Most likely. But I don't really care.'

'But is it right for us to indulge ourselves in the middle of all this... chaos and threat? Aren't we then becoming part of it? Where is Leupardra now?'

'In the lull between the storms, we gather our strengths,' Kazharn said. 'I find my strength in you.'

Chapter Thirty-Two

In the afternoon, Seladris had to escape *Inglefey* and go for a walk. His guests had arrived that morning, but he'd found already he didn't enjoy having them in the house. It wasn't just Ulien, Thazri and Ihrec, but also five of the *Velvets* staff and four of Thazri's closest companions. Apart from a skeleton staff to keep *Velvets* secure, its animals fed, the rest of the har Shadolis employees had been given leave. It was perhaps fortunate Thazri hadn't demanded that all of them camp out at *Inglefey*. As it was, hara were stuffed into the available bedrooms, some having to make their beds on sofas and floors.

Ulien just wanted to sleep, clearly still shaken by Tuli's attack on him. He wasn't any trouble, but Thazri and Ihrec clearly felt Seladris should sit with them and discuss the current situation endlessly, until it became almost meaningless. Thazri's staff wanted to prepare meals and clean, because that's what they were used to doing and they wanted their lives to feel normal in this most abnormal of times. The companions wanted to pretend nothing was happening, lounging around the sitting rooms, talking about trivial things.

Also, four of the *Velvets* houseguards were stationed outside to keep an eye open for anything threatening or unusual. Their mere presence was intimidating.

The place felt uncomfortably *busy*. Too many hara. Too much noise. And this was only the beginning. Seladris knew there'd be more to come: additional hara, endless meetings. *Inglefey* would grow smaller all the time while this happened. How long would it be before action could be taken, a counter-attack to end it all and restore normality? The spirit of the house had withdrawn into itself. It didn't feel like home.

Seladris wished Meladriel was with them, though. What was he doing, all alone at his cottage? Wasn't that dangerous? Shouldn't they all stick together? He wondered whether Veredis was all right? How was *Confitteri*? Had it been damaged? These questions had provided good excuses to go out.

The nearer he drew to town, so it became more obvious that

Ferelithia was a community under threat. Many buildings exhibited signs of damage – a few structurally, but the majority with broken windows and doors and vandalised gardens, like the aftermath of a riot. There were few townshara around, but Municipallion peace officers patrolled the streets in numbers. They did not stroll, as they usually did, since their work generally involved no more than finding lost harlings who'd wandered off in the crowds or giving directions to tourists. These were hara who now had a more serious purpose and they didn't particularly like it.

Curious, Seladris went up to a pair of them and asked what was going on. 'I've been away for a few days. Has something happened?' He wondered how the Municipallion would be handling the situation.

'There's been a series of earth tremors,' one of the officers said, clearly speaking from a script. 'These phenomena came to a head last night with the largest quake so far. It opened up an ancient, buried weapons facility from the Devastation. Miasmas have been released, which may cause hallucinations and/or mild illness. This is not life-threatening, and there is nothing to fear. Everything is under control, but the Municipallion asks that citizens keep indoors for now, until the all clear is given.'

'I see.'

'Go home, Tiahaar,' said the other officer.

'I will. I will. I'm on my way.'

Seladris walked to *Confitteri* – found its doors locked, the building empty. There had been minor damage to several windows. He wanted to check on Veredis but realised he didn't know where he lived, other than that it was somewhere on the northern high coast road, perhaps near to Meladriel's cottage. Meladriel would know, of course. Seladris could go to *Eko Melosa* and ask for Veredis's address. A perfect excuse for going there. It was important not to appear too eager. He was sure that Meladriel was skittish about potential relationships, as he was himself. Therefore, he would be cautious.

Away from the town, the day felt calmer, *healthier*, the sun shining benignly, the sea rolling languorously. The only unusual thing was that there were no hara upon the beaches, nor horses and vehicles upon the roads. In Seladris's opinion, this omission improved the landscape beautifully.

He mused drowsily as he walked. For the first time, he felt part of a community; whatever bad thing confronted the town was not of his doing. He was not afraid of inexplicable phenomena as the hara of *Velvets* clearly were. He'd lived through too many himself over the years. Now, he had a use, a purpose. This was somewhat disorientating, but not a situation from which he wished to run.

There was also Meladriel. The har had made him consider the possibility there was no separate vengeful entity stalking him, but that past unsettling events had either been coincidental, or had come from himself; from his own fear, guilt and shame. The dark shadow that had haunted him for so long was not to be feared, merely absorbed. Old hurts must fade, drift away, leaving only a bittersweet wisdom behind. Seladris had gradually accepted these ideas, simply because nothing bad had oozed out of him in Ferelithia. Instead, the bad thing had *come to him*, and not only him. If anything, his own peculiarities had been – and would be – a help in this situation. He was a har. He could make things happen. Now he had the chance to make things happen in a good way.

Late in the afternoon, Seladris turned onto the grass-fringed lane that wound down to *Eko Melosa*. He felt like a seething mass of anticipation. He knew the moment would arise when he could speak honestly to Meladriel about his feelings. Perhaps not yet, nor until this business in the town was settled, but soon. Seladris considered speaking to Veredis about it. The har could be acerbic but was clearly experienced in all aspects of life. Also, he was a friend. Friends offered advice in situations like this, didn't they?

As Seladris walked up the pebble and shell path to the side door, he noticed that a tall, well-bred bay horse was grazing in the paddock behind the cottage. He had seen one like it before, but then many hara in Ferelithia owned horses. Meladriel didn't have one, though. Had Kazharn perhaps given one to him today? That would make sense. Meladriel could get about quicker then.

The side door was closed firmly. Usually, Meladriel left it ajar, unless he was expecting visitors or wanted to shut the world out – he'd mentioned this humorously to Seladris, who had habitually shut the door fast whenever he'd passed through it. So, the closed door now meant Meladriel was either not at home or didn't want to see anyhar. Didn't it?

Alert to a small but insistent urge within him, Seladris approached the cottage quietly. He crept to the front window of the kitchen and looked in. The room was dark, empty, somewhat untidy. A chair lay on its side. Meladriel was normally a very tidy har. There was a slight smell of burning.

Seladris's breath had become shallow and fast. He felt a little light-headed. Something was wrong.

Cautiously, he edged past the never-used front door, and peered into the living room. This was orderly and unoccupied, looking as if nohar had entered it for weeks.

That left the back of the cottage, the small bathroom, the bedroom.

I don't want to see, Seladris thought. He didn't know why. Was it blood he feared? Death? Murder?

You must.

He thought he heard a sound. The feeble whimper of a har in distress?

The bathroom window had a blind over it but one of the bedroom windows was open. A ghost-veil of curtain shivered out of the pane. Seladris considered finding a weapon but there was no suitable object nearby. He paused for a moment, closed his eyes, then took a deep breath. He looked in at the edge of the window.

Quickly, he withdrew, held his breath once more. Meladriel was not dead, not hurt. He was with Kazharn in the bed. Was this possible?

Check again!

Seladris forced himself to make sure. Kazharn as soume was a goddess, his black hair spread about the pillows, across his face, in Meladriel's hands. He did not look like the Municiphar, but somehar much younger, much less severe. Seladris stared for some moments, unable now to look away, wondering why somehar else's simple pleasure could cause such pain to him. It was more than aruna, it was like worship, the slow sinuous movements, the open eyes, the caress of Meladriel's fingers upon that dreaming face, within that luxuriant hair. They were lost in one another. They would not notice him staring in.

Stop!

Seladris looked away, slid down the wall, crouched upon the moss-carpeted path. He should have foreseen this. The evidence had been there the day before. *My father behaves differently with you.*

Had this always been happening? How would he know? He was an outsider, really. One thing he knew for sure: The way Meladriel gazed upon Kazharn could only belong to one har at a time. Should

Meladriel take aruna with anyhar else, it would be less than this. He was, effectively, *taken*.

I need the address, Seladris thought, which seemed both ridiculous and the most important thing. But he waited. He sensed it wouldn't be long before he heard their cries of repletion. He didn't give them more than that. The moment Meladriel expelled a laugh, the most meaningful sound of delight the world had ever heard, Seladris went at once to the side door.

Meladriel eventually answered Seladris's repeated knocking. He opened the door, clad in a loosely belted bathrobe. He looked half asleep or drunk. He looked sultry and beautiful. The mere sight of him was like a knife in the gut to Seladris.

'What is it?' Meladriel said. 'Is something wrong?'

'Could you give me Veredis's address?'

Meladriel pantomimed quizzical surprise. 'What?'

'I need his full address. I want to see if he's OK.'

'The high coast road.'

'I know that – but where on it? Give me the address. It's a long road.'

'You want a *house number*?' Meladriel uttered a short laugh of incredulity. 'I don't know what that is. Doubt it has one anymore. It's the cream house on the high coast road. *One* of the cream houses. Really, Seladris? You've come all this way to ask me that? Why not just go up that road and ask somehar there?'

'Have I interrupted something?'

Meladriel's expression became dangerously calm. 'It's the cream house, two storeys, stables on the side. The garden is mainly granite and water features. You should be able to find it.'

'Thank you. May I borrow your new horse?'

'No. I'll see you later. Goodbye, Seladris.' Meladriel closed the door.

Seladris stared at the door for some moments. Without being aware of it, he snarled silently, his lips peeling back from his teeth unnaturally. He heard the murmur of voices within the cottage. Then he turned away.

Chapter Thirty-Three

Amorel arrived in Almagabra in the early evening, before Katarin had chance to begun tracking him down in Megalithica. He was transported by a *sedu* available only to those with the most exclusive connections. He hadn't travelled alone – a pilot on another *sedu* had navigated, because Amorel didn't have the ability to control such a creature himself. He was deposited on the outskirts of Ferelithia, discreetly, in a copse beside the northern coast road.

He'd been taking the nostrum Merphine had given him – more than once a day and not always at night – and this had deadened his mind to the extent he didn't have to consider why he was travelling halfway around the world to put himself in a position he'd never wanted to be in again. He didn't feel strong at all. He wasn't sure what good he could do, coming back to Ferelithia, but he knew he had no choice.

Appearing rather forlorn and lost at the dusty roadside, he carried a leather bag, with a change of clothes and basic toiletries, and had brought with him (in rather a cumbersome case) a bass guitar, the one he'd played in Ferelithia all those years ago. He'd never been able to part with it, even when he'd attempted to bury his past in a box beneath the sand of a distant shore. In a special room of his beach house, which was almost a shrine, he kept every instrument he'd ever owned since moving to Megalithica – they were part of his being. He claimed not to believe they contained memories – only music. Yet he was aware the battered bass that accompanied him now, the only instrument to have made the journey with him to Megalithica in the first place, knew this area. Perhaps it quivered, hidden in its case, recognising the smell of the air, the flex of the land. But perhaps not, because not everything felt the same as it had before.

A faint fug hung over the town to the south, like a dirty heat haze. Amorel remembered the air of the new, harish Ferelithia as always bright and sparkling, reflecting the presence of the entity they'd eventually named Kelosanya – a dehar fit for a party town. He remembered the band playing in the town, and in settlements up and down the coast – electric instruments when they were able to use them but, in more primitive conditions, instruments of earlier ages. Pharis, in particular, had loved that, but then the drums never lost their primal force; their fierce thudding roar could be heard under any circumstances. He recalled Karn stroking his guitar, making it cry and scream, watched over by that mysterious smile of his. Hara had loved him, the true front har of the band. He remembered Rue, slinky and screaming, tossing his golden nimbus of hair. Children. Pretty, irresponsible children, thinking they were dressing up, not realising the clothes were baked on, part of them. Blithe, careless, floating from one long party to another. The sky alight with fire.

But decades had passed. Maybe Ferelithia was different now, run down, grubby, no longer the Pearl of Almagabra, its lustre dimmed. Forgotten muck might seep through the ground, along with the smell of decay.

Amorel began to walk down the road. Old tunes skittered through his mind. What would he do when he reached the town? First a beer, of course. He'd find a bar where he could sit outside and assess the modern Ferelithia, perhaps discover something that would affirm it was right for him to be there.

Then… old contacts.

Before leaving Megalithica, he'd made enquiries and had learned what had become of Karn. Pharis was still a mystery. Rue was… Rue. Amorel couldn't imagine the Tigrina of Immanion becoming involved, or even interested, in any paranormal events connected with the past. Other old friends and acquaintances might remain, but he had no way of knowing.

He'd not attempted to contact Karn before leaving and had no inclination to do so now. He needed to reconnoitre first. Perhaps it would be possible to lay his ghosts to rest without involving anyhar else.

The sun leaned slowly into the sea to the west, and solar globes began to light up in the gardens of the dwellings along the shore below him. They looked like phosphorescent sea creatures. For a moment he wished, with an acute pang, he was at home, staring out over his own piece of ocean, wine glass in hand.

It seemed strange to him that there was no traffic upon the road, because when he'd last been in Ferelithia it had been a thriving social centre, hara drawn to its hedonistic ambience. The beaches to the north and south of the town had always been thronged with hara in the evenings, barbecues lit, bands playing, hara dancing to the earthy throb of drums. It all seemed so quiet now.

He was just passing a turnoff that led down to a shoreside cottage, when an enormous dark horse came thundering up the lane towards him. It happened so quickly that, at first, Amorel was not even sure what this pounding monster was. Instinctively, he half leapt, half rolled from its path before it could collide with him, falling onto his back in the seeding grasses beside the road. He lay like an upturned tortoise on the bulky guitar case; a most undignified position. He wondered if he could stand up; he was so shocked and dazed he could only move his limbs feebly.

A voice said, 'Forgive me, Tiahaar', followed by the sound of a har dismounting the horse. 'I didn't see you there.'

A strong hand took hold of one of his and hauled him to his feet. His first thought was: *I have changed more than he has. He looks so young, untouched.* His first words were, 'Karn, this is a... coincidence.'

The har peered at him for a moment – confirming what Amorel feared about his own appearance – then said, 'Amorel?'

'Yes.' He had no idea what to say, now he was faced with this old friend.

'I know why you're here,' Karn said, smiling. 'Please, come back down to the cottage. Let's make sure I haven't damaged you.'

'You haven't but... all right.'

Where have my words gone? Amorel wondered, as he allowed Karn to take his arm and lead him down the path, as if he was an invalid. He wanted to say more, ask questions, but words were stones in his throat. Karn had picked up Amorel's bag. The magnificent horse ambled behind. Was this a dream? It couldn't possibly be real.

'Are you back because things have been... *happening* to you?' Karn asked.

'In a way.'

'Did Katarin find you?'

'Who?'

'Rue's agent...'

'No. No.'

'He's been looking for you and Pharis. You can probably guess why.'

'I can't. Perhaps you'd better tell me.'

'It's a story.' Karn shook his head, sighed, glanced up at the road behind them. 'I was on my way somewhere, but... This is Mela's cottage. I can stay a while longer.'

'Mela's?' Amorel was surprised by that. He'd thought that rift would never be healed. In his eyes, Karn had been *amputated* from Meladriel, permanently.

'We can tell you what's happened,' Karn said, as if this was a casual conversation in a casual situation.

Amorel had to face he had been expected. They had talked about him.

'Immanion's involved now,' Karn continued. 'Inevitable because of Rue, of course. Leupardra has got to all of us, I expect.'

'This sounds worse than I dreaded.'

'It probably is,' Karn said dryly.

They had reached the cottage. Karn went in directly without knocking and Amorel followed. The wide low kitchen beyond smelled of herbs. And there was Meladriel, a ghost yet alive. It seemed both he and Karn had somehow become trapped in time. They looked no different to how they'd been so long ago. Hara didn't age in the way humans had, but even so maturity tended to look out from their eyes, experiences lingering in their smiles. They moved in a more graceful, precise way. These hara seemed young, not long past inception. It was uncanny.

'Look who I found,' Karn said.

Meladriel came at once to embrace Amorel. 'I wish I could be surprised, but I'm not. It's good to see you. You look... affluent.'

'You look freshly-minted,' Amorel said tartly, but returned the embrace. 'Karn just ran me over in the road.'

'Are you hurt?'

'No, not unless my back's broken.'

'It appears not. Did Katarin bring you here?'

'No, I don't know who that is.'

'OK. Can I get you wine? I assume your tastes haven't changed.'

'Yes, wine. Lots of it.'

Meladriel grinned. 'Sit down. I assume you want the story.'

'I do.' Amorel sat down at the table. He felt weary.

Meladriel poured drinks for Amorel and himself, then said to Karn, 'You'd better get back, hadn't you? You've been missing all day.'

Karn hesitated. 'I suppose I must. Both of you should come to *Inglefey* later, Mela. I'll send transport.' He inclined his head to

Amorel. 'I'm sorry I have to rush off, but we'll speak later on.' He paused. 'It's good to see you again.'

Amorel simply raised his hands in a compliant gesture, still dazed by what had happened in the past few minutes.

Karn and Meladriel stared at one another meaningfully for some moments, then Karn left the cottage. It was as if they'd taken aruna for the first time only minutes before. What was going on here? Amorel felt disorientated, as if he'd slipped into an alternate reality.

He drank in gulps the wine Meladriel had placed before him. 'Do you both live here?' he asked.

Meladriel shook his head. 'No. Karn's our archon, more or less. Did you not know?'

'Well… yes, but I thought, maybe…'

'He lives in a far grander place than this.'

Amorel nodded. 'Of course.' He paused, then fixed Meladriel with a stare. 'Tell me, then. Tell me why I'm here, because honestly I just don't know.'

Halfway through relating the tale, Meladriel produced a cold supper, talking as he prepared it. Amorel realised he was famished. He was glad to eat. Outside, the night had come, and through the kitchen window, he could glimpse the glowing sea. His head was aching, mainly – he decided – through attempting to take in everything Meladriel was telling him, while his mind was partially fuddled by a Garridan nostrum. As he thought that, Meladriel said sharply, 'You're taking something, aren't you? You should stop. It's not helping.'

Amorel expelled a huffing sound. 'My choice,' he said.

Meladriel smiled somewhat grimly. 'Always was. Anyway, the rest…' He took up his tale again.

Amorel listened as he ate. Some of the words drifted through his mind and out again, so that later he wouldn't be able to recall everything Meladriel told him. He would remember enough, however.

He realised at some point Meladriel had fallen silent and was staring at him. 'So now I know why I'm here,' he said, hoping that would suffice.

'And I need your story,' Meladriel said, arms folded in a businesslike manner, then adding, 'before anything else.' The words sounded slightly threatening.

'OK, it's not much in comparison to what's happened here, but...'

'Just tell me.'

Once he began, it was easy. This was so different to speaking with Merphine, who couldn't empathise in the same way Meladriel could. Meladriel asked questions Amorel didn't want to answer, deep questions like knives that drew blood. For the first time, since he'd moved to Megalithica, he told somehar else about his past. He spoke of his association with Leupardra, revealing how the har had played with them, setting them against one another. Karn had believed in the lies – perhaps more so than any of them. Meladriel's eyes had widened slightly during this part of the tale, but the information would hardly be a surprise to him. He had *never* been taken in.

Then came the difficult section – the hallucinations, the dreams, the threat of mutilation, of silencing his music. And there was a part of him – wasn't there? – who thought that maybe this was all he deserved.

At the end of his narrative, Amorel was weeping. He couldn't stop.

Meladriel, sitting opposite him at the table, reached out and took Amorel's hands in his own. He said nothing, let Amorel drain himself. After some minutes, he said, 'That's some poison out, then.'

'It's the nostrum,' Amorel said, wiping his eyes with the heels of his hands. 'It's shitting up my head.'

'Partly, perhaps, but sweet dehara, you're in a state, Rel. What happened to you?'

'I moved to a new country. I got rich. I got famous.' He shrugged, grimaced. 'Boring story.'

Meladriel did not react to these words. 'Do you have family, anyhar... special?'

'In a way. More of a business arrangement really. I do have a son. Hardly see him, though. His wants a different life to mine – ironically, he studies the past, restores old buildings.'

Meladriel shook his head. 'Wherever you lived, however successful you became, you never left here. It's affected your whole life. You do realise that, don't you? You made it easy for Leupardra to find you.'

'No, I buried it all...'

Meladriel put his head to one side. 'Amorel... please... This is me you're talking to.'

Amorel expelled a caustic laugh. 'They called you witch boy before you were even har... or so the legend goes.'

'I simply chose a path, as you did.'

At that moment, the sound of a horse-drawn vehicle drawing up outside ended the conversation. 'Well,' Meladriel said, getting to his feet. 'Now you have the delight of meeting Karn's family and some of his staff, and perhaps the enigmatic Seladris, who I think might've contributed to initiating all this mess. Brace yourself.'

'I just want to sleep. You've exhausted me, pulling that crap out of me.'

'Sorry. We're obliged at the moment to be part of a team.'

As the carriage, its roof folded back, rolled along the road towards town, Amorel said, 'It's so quiet, so dark...'

'Curfew,' Meladriel said. 'The Municipallion has told everyhar to keep to their houses or leave town for a while until... until the climax of our story, I guess. There'll be an ending one way or another.'

'And when will that be?'

'Not tonight. You're in no fit state and need to rest, and Katarin hasn't yet returned. Rue might be with him when he does.' Meladriel leaned forward to call to the driver. 'Can you take us along the high back roads, avoid the town?'

'Sure...' the driver began.

But Amorel snapped, 'No, I need to see it.'

Meladriel nodded once, settled back, called, 'Do as he says,' to the driver.

There were hardly any lights – some hara, it seemed, *must* have left town. Certainly, there were no tourists wandering around. There were no parties. Hardly any noise at all. A few bars were open, lit dimly, a couple of locals skulking about. The damage reminded Amorel of what a place could look like after a tidal wave had passed through – splintered, sludged, violated. Clearing up was clearly underway, but it seemed half-hearted. Flowers were dying in pots outside the shops, the clubs and bars. A sour smell of decay hung in the air.

In the centre of town, the Municipallion still stood, with its High Nayati attached to it. Structurally, they appeared undamaged, but their windows and walls were filthy and stinking, as if a sewer had burst over them.

Amorel forced himself to witness it all, didn't ask the driver to change route. He felt sick by the time the carriage turned onto the path snaking up into the hills, on the southern side of town.

Chapter Thirty-Four

By evening, Ulien began to feel more like himself. The previous day no longer felt *likely*, as if he'd only imagined it and had somehow got confused. But here he was in a different house, with refugees from his home alongside him. Something really bad was happening, and he still didn't know exactly what it was and what its consequences would be. Tuli had kept his distance since Ulien had fled to *Inglefey* the day before.

He couldn't help feeling partly responsible for the danger that faced Ferelithia now, even though Thazri had told him not to. His hostling had been emphatic that actions in the past had caused their problems now – Ulien was as much a victim of that as any other Ferelithian who was unaware of their town's dark history. Ulien wanted to believe this but he felt uneasy, apprehensive as if a doom was hanging over him, possibly one he deserved.

As the staff prepared dinner, Thazri began to worry that Kazharn hadn't turned up at the house. Could something have happened to him? Ihrec reassured him this was not the case, because he'd have been able to tell if that were so.

Ulien had a strange feeling inside him that he couldn't identify. It was both an itch and a pain. He was sure his father was at *Eko Melosa* with Meladriel, but he didn't say anything about it. Only a few weeks ago, even though it felt like months, one of Ulien's tutors had explained what the future held for his maturing body. He had learned about aruna in detail, its different purposes. The tutor had spoken unflinchingly of the sometimes insane, selfish demands of the body that could fixate on somehar until it got what it wanted. As a young har, Ulien could expect to feel this sensation at least once before maturity put a disdainful curb on it. Even in true adulthood, he would no doubt meet hara occasionally who could mysteriously invoke the madness. In the eyes of the afflicted, such hara could become divine beings, who must be pursued and worshipped. This was the condition known as *kelos* and the local dehar personified this state. 'Sometimes,' the tutor had said, 'you can smell it, upon yourself and around others. Possession by the spirit of mad desire.'

'What does it smell like?' Ulien had asked.

'Burning, sea pools and jasmine,' the tutor had answered, somewhat wistfully.

Ulien had caught a whiff of that scent yesterday, in *Eko Melosa*. Feybraiha might not yet be upon him, but Ulien could still sense the swirling emotions and urges in that cottage. Perhaps the "education" he'd received from Tuli had also contributed to a heightened sense of awareness around other hara. Ulien knew that Kazharn wanted Meladriel, had no doubt had him. But Seladris wanted Meladriel too. How bizarre and unwieldy was this business of desire.

Earlier today, Seladris had gone out and had not returned. Ulien wished he was there, because the hara from *Velvets* annoyed him. Apart from Thazri and Ihrec, they were trying to pretend nothing was wrong. They were stupid, like chickens clucking around pompously, while a hungry har with a sharp knife advanced upon them. Ulien was used to the vastness of *Velvets*; *Inglefey* felt too small and cramped with all those hara in it. It made him feel claustrophobic.

Ulien liked Seladris and hoped they could be friends. He would be pleased to have a friend like that. His parents had only ever funnelled him towards young hara who bored him. This was, he realised, partly why Tuli had fascinated him so much – a friend he found interesting.

Just as Thazri was on the verge of sending out one of the houseguards to search for Kazharn, Gull cantered up to the house along the empty road that yawned from east to west in the uneasy darkness. There was no stable building at *Inglefey*, but it had a walled, grass yard at the back, where a horse could graze safely. Kazharn came inside, and it was as if sparks and gouts of light were shooting out of him. He carried with him a cloud of scent: burning, sea water, jasmine. Ulien thought only he could see and smell these things. But then he saw that Ihrec was regarding Kazharn in a speculative fashion also; Ihrec had been quiet all day. To Ulien, Kazharn seemed to possess the life force of two hara; he was fizzing with it. The reason why was clear.

When Kazharn came into the living room, Thazri exclaimed,

'Kaz!' leaping out of the devouring sofa, so deep it was hard to escape from. 'Where have you been? I was about to send out somehar to look for you.'

'I had to calm down a lot of hara today,' Kazharn said, which Ulien could tell was not a lie.

'What's... the town like? I couldn't bear to go and look.'

'Messed up,' Kazharn replied shortly, 'like it's suffered a catastrophe. We've had to mobilise a protective force and explain to hara some of what's happening. A curfew has been initiated, because so far unusual activity in the town has only taken place at night. We've had to ask tourists to leave. Most will demand reimbursement.' He sighed. 'None of this is good, and no doubt part of Leupardra's plan. He's undermining my authority in the town.'

'Does that mean you could be removed from office?' Thazri asked in a voice of horrified alarm.

'The sacrificial head might have to be mine, yes,' Kazharn said.

'No! They can't be that unfair. How can they blame you? You're the only one capable of doing anything to help.'

'As far as they're concerned, I'm part of the cause.'

'But you're not!'

'I am, Thaz. Hara have good reason to be angry with me.'

Thazri clenched his fists at his sides. 'You can't take responsibility for it all. That's just stupid. What's done is done. You're a good har, the best leader...'

'Hush,' Kazharn said. 'We have to face the fact that our lives might change. But first we need to survive what's happening now.'

As his father spoke, Ulien saw the glorious light within him become dimmer. He was forgetting what had made him gleam so brightly. The aroma he'd carried drifted away, out into the night.

What has been given can be taken away so easily...

'Where's Seladris?' Kazharn asked. And now Ulien sensed the potential for a lie creep into his father's voice.

'He went out,' Thazri said, visibly shocked and disoriented by Kazharn's disclosures. 'He hasn't come back yet. Mentioned something about checking on friends. He's probably eating with them this evening.'

Kazharn nodded, somewhat distractedly. 'There is at least a little good news,' he said. 'Amorel has returned to Ferelithia.'

Thazri raised his brows. 'Oh? Katarin found him?'

'No, he's here of his own accord. Been suffering weird phenomena even in Megalithica and felt compelled to come back.'

'If that's the case,' Ihrec said coolly, having remained silent since Kazharn came into the room, 'might it not be part of Leupardra's plan to get you all here? You'll be so much easier to dispose of when you're all together.'

'Our unity is our defence,' Kazharn said, rather coldly. 'We simply have to be alert and take care, not believe everything we might see or hear.' He paused. 'I'm sure Leupardra will use trickery and deceit to divide us, as he always used to do. We mustn't let this happen.'

Ulien peered at his father thoughtfully. He could tell what Kazharn was worried about. *In the moment, it had felt so good, now those gilded moments could cause disruption, mistrust.*

The years settled back onto Kazharn like stifling dust. He became his modern self again – contained, aloof, controlling.

As the remains of dinner were being cleared away, Meladriel arrived at *Inglefey* with Amorel. Ulien was almost too afraid to see what would happen when his father was in the same room as Meladriel. Perhaps tendrils of light would shoot out of each of them and become entwined.

But in the event, they were impeccably distant with one another, making Amorel the centre of attention. What a sad, tired har he was!

While the adults talked, Meladriel caught Ulien's glance. They stared at one another, and then a mind touch came. *You see so much, don't you?*

Sometimes, things are too big not to see, Ulien responded. He said no more but sent some pointedly fleeting impressions.

Meladriel smiled, somewhat slyly.

After Amorel had told the gathering his story – which Ulien could tell lacked the most disturbing details – Thazri took charge of him. 'Our host isn't here – the har who leases this house – but I'll find you a room. One of my companions can share a room with somehar else.'

'Thank you. I'd like to bathe, if that's possible.'

'Of course. Are you hungry? I can get something prepared for you.'

Amorel shook his head. 'No, thank you. Meladriel fed me at his place.'

'Oh…' Thazri seemed surprised Amorel had been at Meladriel's home, perhaps thinking they'd met at the Municipallion.

But they're old friends, Ulien projected subtly, without words, towards his hostling, so that he'd believe the idea came from himself. *Isn't it natural Amorel would seek Meladriel out before coming here?* Ulien knew it was important no bad feeling entered this group. Thazri must not start wondering whether Kazharn had been at the cottage too.

'I'd simply like to bathe and then rest, gather myself,' Amorel said. 'I'll be fine tomorrow.'

There was the smallest of tense silences, then Meladriel said, 'I'll give you agmara, Rel.'

'No, really…' Amorel began.

'It wasn't an offer. I was just telling you,' Meladriel continued. 'Take your bath. I'll be up afterwards. I'll send you to sleep, so don't take anything for that.'

Amorel smiled grimly as he stood up. 'How I've missed your nagging about personal wellbeing.'

Meladriel laughed. 'That was part of my job, remember?' And there was the gleam again, flowing out of Meladriel like light-filled particles of honey. Some of it settled on Kazharn but he pretended not to notice.

Seladris had found Veredis's house on the high coast road. It appeared untouched, probably because it was far enough from town to have avoided damage. He stood in the road outside, looking in. He could see Veredis and Tika moving about like shadows beyond the enormous windows of the house. He couldn't tell what they were doing. What would they see if they glanced outside? A ragged ghost in the road?

Seladris felt numb, but perversely justified. His life was destined always to be unlucky, painful, humiliating. Meladriel had been wrong about him. Looking down at his arms, he saw they were bruised from wrist to elbow as if cruel hands had gripped him. He had *nothing*. Kazharn had everything: position, wealth, beauty, popularity, a family and now, it seemed, a lover. Why should one have so much and another so little? It wasn't as if Kazharn was a shiningly good har; he had darkness in his past, like Seladris did. Yet for some, the book of life closed discreetly upon horror and opened again upon a page of creamy vellum, where a new story could be written in golden ink.

There was no need to go up to Veredis's door and knock. Seladris could see from outside both he and Tika were unharmed. *Confitteri* was shut. There was no need to ask about work. Anyway, Veredis had made no move to seek him out, discover if *he* was safe. There were no obligations to honour here. But he didn't want to go home either. Not only was the place bulging with Thazri and his minions, but eventually Kazharn and Meladriel would be there. This was too much to bear. He had, then, nowhere to go.

He followed the high coast road aimlessly, getting further away from *Eko Melosa* with each step. Eventually, he took the turning that led into the hills where Olivian Grove lay. Few hara would be at *Velvets*. The majority had either fled to *Inglefey* or been given leave.

The houses of the prominent families of Ferelithia were mostly dark. They were taking no risks. They'd leave the town to its mess for a while. It was anyway senseless to put harlings in danger. So they would have told themselves. There were other party towns along the coast of Almagabra, even if not as celebrated as Ferelithia. The most affluent probably maintained villas in all of them. It wasn't as if they were difficult to claim and occupy.

The gates to *Velvets* were closed, and yet when Seladris put his hands upon the wrought iron bars, he found the lock hadn't been secured correctly. The gates gave a shiver and opened with a discreet creak. The padlock and its chain fell heavily to the ground.

Inglefey was the largest house Seladris had ever lived in but to him *Velvets* was a palace. Yesterday, when he'd been inside it briefly, he'd yearned to explore the place. Other hara could live hidden in this house and you'd never know about it. They could flit from room to room before you. He shuddered, but with pleasurable excitement rather than fear.

Yet now he had no yearning to explore the silent, empty rooms. He was drawn instead to the rising lawns, the watchful copses. He could hear the sound of running water. Was that a sly laugh? Spirits of the earth held their revels in this place.

Seladris strolled towards the old shrine deep in the gardens. He found it easily, following instinct rather than memory. The atmosphere felt different this night. Yesterday, he had walked with the others to the site, full of certainty and determination, sure their plan would work. But it hadn't. If anything, the enemy had been strengthened by their actions. Now, the night was tense; Seladris felt that anything could happen. The whole of Ferelithia might explode below him.

Inside, the shrine felt weirdly desolate. The walls emitted a faint glow, which he was sure they hadn't done before. Seladris could see clearly. The painting of the blue leopard still lay in the centre of the chamber. He felt outraged. This was *his* picture. How could they leave it here, where it could be damaged or destroyed? He dragged it to the wall by the entrance and leaned it upright against the rock. The colours seemed to glow in the dim light. Meladriel and the others… they'd thought the spirit of the blue leopard had left the painting. They were wrong. It had merely walked out of it for a while.

These hara he knew – what were they? Refusing to accept what they'd done, putting others at risk because of it? They had no shame. In the midst of a calamity, all Meladriel and Kazharn could think about, it seemed, was their own desires. They were like harlings just past feybraiha, caught up in arunic selfishness so that nothing else mattered, not even life and death. A blade of pure despising gouged through Seladris' body. It left a pool of foul poison in its wake, which he wanted to vomit up. But it had adhered to his guts and organs, become part of him.

'Talk,' Seladris murmured aloud. 'I'm here to listen. Were you wronged, Leupardra? Tell me your story. What is it you want? Nohar has asked you that, have they?'

Water trickled into the pool. Outside, the garden was silent.

'Why won't you come to *me*?' Seladris said sharply. 'Look at me. Am I not perfect for your purpose?'

Seladris sat down on the edge of the pool, trailed his hand in the water.

'I'm sorry I did what I did,' he murmured. 'I'm sorry I told them everything. Sorry I made them aware. I didn't understand.'

Still – silence.

He felt a pressure upon his shoulders. This was not the pressure of hands – something else. All at once, his whole body felt agonisingly squeezed. It was as if he was turning inside out. He squirmed but could barely move. He tried to make a sound, but all that came out was a gurgling croak.

Go with it, he told himself. *Prove yourself worthy.*

Another part tried to scream, *What are you doing? Don't! Don't!*

But then it was too late. He flexed his limbs and they were

supple. Turned his head upon his neck. He looked down into the pool and could see himself in it. Or was that another face below the surface looking up?

He knew what he had to do.

Ihrec went with Ulien to his bedroom. This was a very small chamber in the servants' quarters of *Inglefey*, tucked away beneath the eaves of the house. Ulien had chosen it himself earlier in the day while he and Ihrec had inspected all the available rooms. Ulien liked this one, because he felt safe in so confined a space. The rooms on the lower stories were too large, with too many corners where danger could conceal itself. Ulien had tested the narrow bed and had found it comfortable, even if it did smell old and musty. No one had slept there for a long, long time, Ihrec had said. But he was sure no one had died in it, human or har.

'Will we be safe tonight?' Ulien asked, as Ihrec brushed his hair. They were both sitting on the bed.

'I think so, honey bee.'

'Something will happen, though, won't it? The night won't be still.'

'It's possible, but don't think about it. We can't do anything tonight. We have to be patient and strong.'

'I think hara are behaving.... weirdly,' Ulien said cautiously, wanting to gauge Ihrec's reaction.

'Who?' he asked.

'My father,' Ulien replied. 'He's different.'

Ihrec didn't say anything, and the only sound was the brush hissing through Ulien's hair.

'Don't you think so?' Ulien said.

'He's under pressure. Hara behave differently then.'

There was a tone to Ihrec's voice that made Ulien realise, all too plainly, his carehar was aware of everything. It was why he had offered very little to conversations today.

'I know you know,' Ulien said gravely.

Ihrec put down the brush and kissed the top of Ulien's head. 'It's not our concern now, is it? Nothing good comes from gossip and spite, Ulien. Keep your tongue wrapped around a stone.'

Ulien laughed at this advice. 'OK.'

'I'll be next door,' Ihrec said, 'if you should need me.' He was sharing a room with two of the staff. He could have taken more luxurious accommodation within the house but had elected to remain near Ulien.

'Leave the door open,' Ulien said.

Ihrec paused. 'No, better not.' He smiled. 'Don't worry.' He stood up and was about to leave the room when the door was flung wide.

Ihrec stiffened, then partially relaxed. Seladris stood at the threshold. 'Tiahaar?' Ihrec said, faintly indignant.

Seladris stared at Ihrec.

For just a moment, Ulien had been glad to see the har, but then quickly realised there was something wrong. Seladris looked wild, the whites of his eyes showing all the way round the dark irises. He was grubby, as if he'd fallen over or had been clawing through dirt. His clothes were torn, and where his flesh was revealed it looked badly bruised. His hair was falling from confinement at the back of his head. There was blood on his face.

'Ihrec,' Ulien said, plaintively.

But Ihrec had already assessed the situation and reacted. He raised his arms, opened his mouth, yet before he could utter a word, or project the faintest mote of energy, Seladris lashed out, gesturing forcefully with both arms. He didn't make contact with Ihrec's body but threw him back so forcefully, the plaster cracked on the wall where Ihrec hit it. He slumped bonelessly to the floor, clearly incapacitated, if not something worse.

'Please...' Ulien began, as Seladris's head whipped round and fixed the harling in his feral gaze.

'You... are coming with me,' Seladris said, although it wasn't his voice at all. What Ulien had taken for bruises were tattoos, curling patterns that resembled both a leopard and a serpent. Turquoise blue tattoos. Ulien tried to scream, to call for anyhar who might hear him. But then he was caught fast in strong hands and the light of the world went out.

Chapter Thirty-Five

The mind touch was tentative, wavering, as if the har who sent it was unused to making contact over distance. It woke Caeru, who had gone to bed early that night, abruptly. The sender used a contact pattern Caeru revealed only to those close to him. The signal had not come from Katarin. Her messages always came to him firm and clear, like flowing water.

Who touches me? he enquired, making the thought strong and clear-shaped.

Rue... It's Karn...

Caeru sat up in the bed. *What's happened?*

There were no words, only a swirl of distress. From the half-formed thoughts and images Caeru perceived Karn's son had been targeted. He couldn't tell what had happened. *Be calm,* he sent. *Try to tell me in images if not in words.*

You must come here... Gelaming, was the only response, and then the connection broke up into a series of sizzles and strange, shrill echoes.

Caeru got out of bed and dressed himself. His head ached a little from the inept and scratchy intrusion, but this would quickly fade. He knew Katarin was still in Alba Sulh, observing Pharis. As far as he was aware, she had not yet made contact with him, but it would be very soon. However, some negotiation would no doubt have to take place thereafter, and it was doubtful, given the lateness of the hour in Alba Sulh, that she'd be able to return to Almagabra before tomorrow. Caeru felt that Karn needed help now, if only a token Gelaming presence to reassure him. Had the situation there already reached a peak? He needed more time, more information in order to assist most effectively. Generally, the Tigrina found others to solve problems for him, and had not yet decided who were the best hara to approach. He was sure it would be a bad move to alert the Hegalion to the situation, even if they could muster forces that would be the most effective against the problem. Relations between

Immanion and the Ferelith had always held a subtext of tension and distrust. The Gelaming administration would leap on this opportunity like famished bears. They would want to make a hard bargain. Even though he never visited Ferelithia, Caeru remained fond of it. He'd enjoyed many carefree years there. He sympathised with his former tribe's desire to remain autonomous.

I should have stayed in touch, he thought. *Would this have happened if I had?*

Yet all those years ago, held in the clawed hands of Kelosanya over Pellaz, the only thing Caeru had cared about was coming to Immanion, securing a place for himself here. He'd wanted Pell, of course, but he'd wanted the position of Tigrina just as much. This had suited him far more than being a vain, preening vocalist prancing around a stage. Ferelithia had meant nothing to him during those early years in Immanion. He couldn't fool himself otherwise.

Typically, there was nohar he could trust in residence at the moment. His consorts, Pellaz and Calanthe, were in Megalithica, visiting the Parasilian family in Galhea. Velaxis, Caeru's closest friend, was off somewhere in Thaine, undertaking tedious Hegalion business with a small tribe that wanted to be bigger. Pellaz's brother Terez and his chesnari Raven were in Jaddayoth visiting family.

Summer time. Holidays. Inconvenient. Normally, Caeru cherished these few weeks mid-year when he could be by himself doing not much at all. It was why he always declined to accompany others on their excursions to far lands. But this, clearly, was to be no ordinary summer.

Caeru couldn't confide in the younger generation of the family over this, because they knew nothing about Ferelithia's early history, and it would be far too tiring to explain it to them. He didn't want them to know, in any case. Bad things had happened during the Devastation that second generation and beyond had difficulty understanding and could get gnarly about.

Dressed to travel, Caeru went to the stables of Phaonica and requested the use of his *sedu*. The sleepy stable-har in charge seemed suspicious because this was an unusual request from the Tigrina; he never travelled alone and where would he want to travel by *sedu* at this hour?

'May I ask your destination?' said the har.

'No,' Caeru said, not rudely, but in a way that could not be queried. 'You may record the private nature of my requisition in your log.'

Next, riding along roads as if on an ordinary horse, he visited the night-station of the Listeners in a wing of the Hegalion. As in the stables, his appearance caused surprise and bafflement. Caeru asked to speak to the supervisor on duty and was taken to an office, where presently a senior Listener appeared. 'How may I help, Tiahaar?' he asked, bowing.

'I received a message from Ferelithia a short while ago,' Caeru said. 'It was facilitated by my personal signature. Can you ascertain exactly where it came from? The message was faint.'

The Listener hesitated, then said, 'Of course, Tiahaar. I'll do my best to help you. Please take a seat.'

He placed his cool fingers upon Caeru's temples and emitted a slightly uncomfortable ether-cloth of prickling energy, which encased Caeru's skull.

Having the electrical workings of your brain combed by strong yet invisible fingers is never a pleasant experience and leaves you vulnerable to prying. Caeru was aware the Listener would most likely pick up the content of the message as well as its provenance. Still, he had no desire to travel around Ferelithia trying to find Karn's residence. The har might not even be at home.

After a few excruciating minutes, the Listener withdrew from Caeru's mind. 'I have a location, Tiahaar.'

'Can you send it to my *sedu*? His name is Marqasit. He's in the northern yard.'

The Listener nodded, closed his eyes for a moment. Then said, 'This is done.' He looked worried, unsure of what to say. This was an irregular situation, but he could hardly interrogate the Tigrina.

Caeru was sympathetic and attempted to ease the har's distress. 'I appreciate you're obliged to report my visit and its purpose,' he said. 'You may record that an old friend of mine in Ferelithia has requested my help concerning a personal matter. I'll make my own report in full upon my return.'

The Listener ducked his head. 'Certainly, Tiahaar.'

Mere minutes later, Caeru's *sedu* dropped out of the Otherlanes outside the house named *Inglefey*. Not having passed through the town, Caeru was unaware of its condition, but it was clear something was very wrong in Ferelithia. The air smelled sour, somehow sooty, yet tinged with decay. There was a strong sensation of disturbance in the landscape. Caeru asked his *sedu* to conceal himself and wait.

How bizarre it was, simply walking up to the front door of the house and knocking upon it. Caeru couldn't remember the last time he'd done such a thing. Arrival at a har's house generally involved a retinue, and formally dressed hara waiting expectantly for him to arrive.

He didn't announce himself to the har wearing a dressing-gown who answered the door – clearly a member of household staff – but asked to be taken to Kazharn har Shadolis. It was telling his visit so late at night was not queried. It seemed few hara were in bed. A dank atmosphere of fear and extreme distress hung in the air. Caeru was led to a living room, where he met a dishevelled har introduced as Thazri har Shadolis, who must be Karn's chesnari. He could see nohar in the room he recognised. The three other hara present discreetly removed themselves.

'I'm… Rue,' he said, inclining his head to the panicked har standing rigidly before him. He felt slightly embarrassed revealing who he was, for reasons he couldn't work out. 'Karn contacted me a short while ago. I came as soon as I could.'

'Leupardra took our son!' Thazri exclaimed. 'The Gelaming must get him back before…' He peered past Rue into the empty hall. 'Are you alone? I know Kaz asked you to bring hara to help us. Where's Katarin? Didn't he find Pharis? Have you brought no hara at all to defend and help us?'

'May I speak to Karn?' Caeru said evenly.

'No… he's gone home… searching… He's called up the hienamas, every har we can find to help search…' He put his hands against his eyes for a moment. 'Sweet Aru, you came *alone*.'

'Tiahaar,' Caeru said, feeling it would serve no purpose to describe the garbled and incomplete nature of Kazharn's message, 'it wouldn't be in your tribe's best interest if I involved the Hegalion at this stage. We have to hope Katarin will bring Pharis here. If anyhar can persuade him, she can.'

Thazri was silent for a moment, then said, 'She?'

'Kamagrian,' Caeru answered. 'Didn't you realise?'

Thazri shook his head. 'No, everything's upside down at the moment… weird. When will… *she* get here?'

'I can't say. I'll attempt to contact her soon. My priority was to come to you at once.'

'How can you help get Ulien back?'

Caeru couldn't answer. The only help he could generally provide was the services of other hara. 'I'm here to assess the situation.'

'Well, I can tell you that now. This Leupardra is like smoke. He's possessed Seladris… well, we assume that's what happened. He's taken Ulien and I pray to the dehara my son is more use to this monster alive than dead. He slithers in and out of our houses, our dreams, even our bodies.' Thazri shook his head again. 'Meladriel… he's upstairs. You know him, don't you?'

'Yes.'

'Ulien's carehar was attacked during the abduction. Meladriel is giving him healing. Amorel is here too, but he's asleep. He came from Megalithica today.'

'Oh, that's good news. I didn't know Katarin had found him.'

'He… she didn't. Amorel came of his own accord.'

'Once everyhar's together, we'll devise a strategy,' Caeru said gently. 'Can you summon Karn home?'

Thazri stared at Caeru for a moment. 'I'm not from Immanion. I can't do messages over distance.'

Caeru didn't say, *don't be ridiculous, everyhar can, if they bother to practice and try.* He smiled. 'Never mind. Perhaps you can tell me everything that's happened here tonight.'

'Can't you call Kaz… Kazharn… Karn…?' Thazri shook his head. 'I don't even know who this bloody har is I'm consort to! You call him!'

'That's not how it works, Tiahaar. I have no signature to seek.'

Thazri shrugged. 'I've no idea how it works. I'm Gelaming, but not from Immanion, just ordinary.' He paused, narrowed his eyes. 'I thought you could do everything, you lot.'

'Only hara who are very adept, hara we call Listeners, can attempt to contact hara without signatures. It's a specialised job, even for those of us in Immanion.'

'What can you do, then, without them? What's the point of assessing the situation if you can't do anything?'

'We *can* help,' Caeru said, 'and we will, but for now it'll just be Katarin and me. We don't want any difficult political situations, do we?'

'I suppose not. I'm sorry.' Thazri slumped. 'I've been unforgivably rude, Tiahaar. Thank you for being here at all. It's just so…' He rubbed his face. 'I'm sick with worry for Ulien. We thought he'd be safe here. Clearly, *that* was stupid!'

'Don't apologise,' Caeru said gently. 'Believe me, I know how it feels when a harling is in danger. I've been in that situation myself – more than once.'

'Of course, Tiahaar, I know,' Thazri said. He shook his head. 'Forgive me. You once had a pearl taken from you by an attacker... it's part of our history. My situation must seem trivial in comparison.'

'Absolutely not,' Caeru said, 'terror and anguish are devastating when the fate of a harling is involved, no matter the circumstances. I was fortunate in that the outcomes were good for me and my family. Let's hope the same goes for you.'

'Please, sit down,' Thazri said. 'This isn't our home. We're here because... I'll explain. It's a long story. I'll just tell Meladriel you're here. Can I get you anything, something to eat or drink?'

'A hot drink will be fine, anything,' Caeru said. 'Then... I'd really like to hear in detail what's happened here tonight.'

Chapter Thirty-Six

Aloytsday, 31 Ardourmoon

The search for Ulien had been fruitless. Hienamas had scanned the town for Ulien's presence, while officers of the Municipallion had searched in a more physical sense. Kazharn wondered if he had to face the possibility his son was dead. He thought not. He hoped not. Leupardra wanted to torture and tease. It seemed unlikely he'd curtail the potential for further harm by killing Ulien outright.

Nor had there been any sign of Seladris. It was assumed he was as much a victim as Ulien was.

Kazharn returned to *Inglefey* at dawn, exhausted yet tense as a wire. He knew he wouldn't be able to sleep, and certainly not in that house. Thazri and Meladriel were still up, and Rue was with them. Kazharn was relieved his erratic message had made sense. He reported there had been no abnormal activity in the town that night. Leupardra must have concentrated his efforts on Ulien. It seemed likely he knew hara were gathering in Ferelithia to confront him. Privately, Kazharn feared that Ihrec might be right and this suited Leupardra perfectly. *The trouble is*, Kazharn thought, *not one of us is truly in control here. We're like a patchwork of minds. Maybe we're simply supposed to work together to prevail. But surely we should have somehar guiding us, who knows what we should do? I should know. Or Mela should. But we're blind...*

Caeru was very different to the har Kazharn had once known. He was calm, diplomatic, a soothing presence. Grown up – inevitably – and the product of decades of life in Immanion, the soumearch of a royal dynasty. The Municiphar could tell at once Thazri had warmed to the Tigrina, had found comfort in him. That was part of Caeru's job, of course. He was like a benevolent dehar to his hara. This was a mask he wore, but Kazharn could appreciate its benefits at present.

And, in the midst of the anxiety, confusion and fear, there was Meladriel. Kazharn could barely exchange glances with him for fear of revealing their renewed intimacy – mistrust and disappointment over that would not help the current situation. They'd had their hours alone – only the dehara knew if there would be any more to enjoy in the future. Meladriel didn't have Caeru's ability to project goddess-like benevolence, but even tired, he emanated an aura of strength and sureness. He simply lacked knowledge at the moment. Surely this would come?

Kazharn heard that a message had been received from Katarin, who'd informed the Tigrina he and his party should be in Ferelithia by mid-day. Caeru had queried the "party" aspect of the message. Who, exactly, did this comprise? Katarin was vague. An adept, he'd said. A friend of Pharis named Fallami.

As breakfast was winding down, during which everyhar had met in the dining room of *Inglefey*, Caeru asked to speak to Kazharn alone. They chose a room at the back of the house – rarely used, it seemed, since it felt dark, dank and uncared for. They did not sit but faced each other standing up.

'Gather your hara,' Caeru said to Kazharn. 'Once the pleasantries have been dealt with, we must get to work.'

'On what exactly, Rue?' Kazharn asked. 'How do you fight smoke?'

Caeru levelled his gaze on the Municiphar. 'We know his weaknesses, Karn. Leupardra was always vain, posturing, arrogant and reckless, but his most vulnerable spot was his susceptibility to flattery. That's our weapon, in my opinion.'

'We have no evidence the har behind this *is* Leupardra,' Kazharn said. 'He could simply be a confused and dedicated fan.'

Caeru laughed somewhat wistfully. 'And we had our fill of those, didn't we? But I'm afraid it's more than that. I know what I experienced, and it had Leupardra's mark all the way through it.'

'It would help if we knew his plan, if he'd offered specific threats. At the moment all we have to go on is the abduction of my son and some damage to the town. The rest is just speculation – fear of what *might* be rather than what *will* be.'

'He's having a wonderful time, isn't he?' Caeru said, shaking his head. 'Loving all this.'

'But is he still dead or...?' Kazharn raked one hand through his hair. '*What* are we dealing with?'

'I don't know yet, but we'll find out. We'll find strength in our unity.'

Kazharn pulled a sour face. 'Really? What about Amorel? He seems… fragile to me.'

Caeru expressed a sigh. 'He is. He won't be our strongest ally. I have more hope for Pharis. He was always quiet but forceful. From what little Kate sent me, I get the impression his time in Alba Sulh has honed his qualities.'

'Kate?'

'Our old friend, remember? The human girl.'

Kazharn frowned slightly. 'Yes, but… what has she to do with…?'

'Katarin,' Rue said shortly. 'Did you really not recognise her?'

'No, I thought that was a har, your agent.'

'She is, but a Kamagrian one. Never mind that. We can trust her. She's had both Roselane and Hegalion training. I rely on her when matters are… delicate.'

Kazharn nodded. 'I suppose I see it now but… not anything I'd expected.' He sighed, rubbed his hands over his face. 'I wish now we'd all kept in touch, considered, even in the vaguest terms, that this might happen. We could have been more prepared, stronger.'

'No use punishing ourselves about that,' Rue said. 'Let's see what Kate brings to us.' He paused, then said, 'There's another matter, Karn, that we should talk about.'

Kazharn raised his brows, said somewhat coldly. 'Aren't there many things we should talk about? Which topic do you have in mind?'

Caeru spoke carefully. 'What I mean is Ulien's… newfound travelling ability. You do realise the implications of this, don't you? In our experience, and by that I mean the *Gelaming* experience, hara who learn this ability beyond the guidance of *sedim* rarely do good with it.'

'What are you saying?'

'During the Teraghast Troubles, our enemies could travel in that way. We couldn't. Ponclast, the leader of the Teraghasts, was given certain powers by entities from beyond the Otherlanes. Ferelith had no part in that conflict, so you wouldn't know about this. The fact is, solo etheric travel isn't a skill that can simply be taught in our reality.'

'I thought some of the Gelaming could do it,' Kazharn said. 'Is that merely propaganda?'

Caeru shook his head. 'No… To help combat the Teraghasts,

Thiede gave Tigron Calanthe the ability, but Cal's never been able to pass that on. We wonder whether the *sedim* put curbs upon it, because… well, I can't go into the true purpose of *sedim* with you now – it would take too long to explain. Let's just say solo Otherlane travel is not part of our natural evolution at this moment in time.'

'I still don't get what you're trying to say about Ulien.'

Caeru took a deep breath. 'This is difficult. I'm asking you to consider that Ulien might have been… *corrupted*. We have no idea where Leupardra's power comes from. Since Thiede opened the Otherlanes and we've travelled within them, we've unwittingly provided a channel for things to leak out of them, in particular unhealthy things. Parasites, predators, unearthly opportunists. The fact is, we still know too little about them. But it's not beyond possibility that Leupardra has interacted with something like that – and anyhar who does is usually *infected*. Our Pard Witch also appears to have the ability to take control of hara, possess them. If that's the case with Ulien, there will no doubt be consequences. If Leupardra is infected, it's highly likely that will be passed on to those beneath his influence. If that's the case, you must prepare yourself for what must happen – and prepare your chesnari.'

'Prepare for what?' asked coldly.

'If and when we recover your son, I must take him back to Immanion with me. He might need special care to remove whatever might have been placed in him. It's possible the ability to travel won't remain with him once Leupardra is contained and his influence removed, but there could be other lingering effects.'

Kazharn's voice, when he responded, was tense and cold. 'Might… possibility… highly likely? I know my son, Rue. He won't be susceptible to corrupting influences.'

Caeru put a hand briefly upon Kazharn's shoulder. 'I'm sorry, Karn, but you *don't* know that. These influences are strong and alien. Ulien might not even realise…'

Kazharn shook his head, as if to rid it of these unwelcome ideas, then interrupted whatever Caeru was going to say next. 'Have you considered Ulien's simply bright enough to be able to learn something that will be of benefit to the world? Maybe he *is* our evolution.'

'I think that's unlikely,' Caeru said sorrowfully.

'What if I forbid you to take him away?'

Caeru sighed deeply. 'Don't be angry with me, Karn. I'm not saying these things to have power over you or to denigrate your son. I simply have to be honest with you. I've had experience of trouble like this – far more than any har should. Whatever's going on here in Ferelithia – we must expunge all of it.'

'I don't know you!' Kazharn spat. 'What happened to Rue, so spontaneous, so carefree, so… so innocent? I don't like this… this unctuous *politician*.'

'I'm sorry,' Caeru said. 'I'm still your friend, Karn, however things might appear. You had to know, that's all.'

Kazharn put his hands against his face. 'Why can't I help him?' he said, his voice breaking.

'You can,' Caeru replied softly. 'But you must do so with your eyes wide open.'

While Kazharn talked with Caeru, Meladriel borrowed a horse from one of the guards outside *Inglefey* and rode to the north coast road. Now, his mount stood before the cream, two story house, home of Veredis and Tika. He didn't want to be there but knew the time had come. Why did friends have to have annoying attachments? Thazri with Karn, and Veredis with Tika. The mere thought of Veredis looking at him with his usual distaste and impatience made him feel angry.

He led his horse through the front garden and tethered it to the rail erected near the porch. Then he knocked upon the door, hoping the occupants weren't still in bed; the hour was early.

Of course, it had to be Veredis who opened it, after less than a minute, dressed in a purple satin dressing-robe. He stared at Meladriel for several insulting seconds, then said, 'Yes?'

'Is Tika here?' Meladriel thought Veredis was going to say no, refuse him entrance. This was tiring so he simply pushed past the har. Veredis was immovable as stone, but Meladriel was larger and stronger. 'Things are happening,' Meladriel said. 'You know that, obviously. I'm here to tell you… both… about it.'

Veredis folded his arms belligerently. 'Is Seladris OK?'

'As it happens, no. Please fetch Tika. I don't have time to repeat myself.'

Grudgingly, Veredis bid Meladriel be seated and left the room. The front door of the house opened directly onto a huge open plan room, with a mezzanine above. The glass wall was off putting. Meladriel could never live with being on show all the time, no matter how far from the road.

Veredis returned swiftly, with Tika behind him, who was dressed only in the loose trousers he slept in. Meladriel stood up. His first instinct was to go to Tika and hug him, because the har looked so solid and dependable, but he could tell his friend was wary about what was to be said. Now was not the time for such comfort. Veredis, on the other hand, was simply incensed.

'I'll tell you everything I know,' Meladriel said. 'But the main reason I'm here is because the town needs your help.'

'No pressure, then,' Veredis said tartly. He and Tika sat on a sofa opposite Meladriel, who once again took his seat. He kept his story to the bare facts, omitting any personal detail.

'This is why you asked to borrow Rhea isn't it?' Tika asked, a little bitterly. 'You went to Kazharn's house. Why didn't you tell me then?'

'I didn't *know* enough then,' Meladriel said, 'but once events started escalating, I planned to come here and tell you everything. I just had to choose the right moment. That moment is now.'

'And we brought Seladris to you,' Veredis said in an uncharacteristically thoughtful tone. 'Almost... preordained.'

Meladriel nodded. 'You are involved, Veredis, by accident or design.' He paused. 'Did Seladris visit you at all over past two days?'

Veredis shook his head. 'No. The last time I saw him was at work, before everything went crazy. And now he's missing...'

'Yes.'

'Are *you* all right?' Tika asked.

Meladriel nodded. 'As you see... yes.'

'You don't seem...'

'I'm fine. Just concerned about the situation. I've not had much chance to sleep.'

'So how can we help?' Veredis asked in a determined voice.

'We need hara to assist with the ritual we're planning, hara of strength and courage, who aren't easily frightened. I know you fit that description even without knowing you very well. Tika...' He smiled at his friend. 'You have those qualities in abundance.'

'Not sure about the not easily frightened part,' Tika said laconically. 'Will it be dangerous?'

'It could be. We don't know.'

'Seladris...' Veredis began. 'Is he under this Leupardra's control now?'

'We have to assume so.'

Veredis uttered a snort. 'Couldn't you see this coming? You were, after all, helping him with his problems.'

'I'm not sure what you mean.'

Veredis rolled his eyes and made an exasperated gesture with both arms. 'We were all there, Meladriel, when Seladris's history came out. Is this perhaps the result of the darkness he carried within? Perhaps he isn't influenced at all. Perhaps he isn't a victim.'

'Ved!' Tika exclaimed. 'Is this the way to speak about a friend?'

Veredis shrugged. 'I'm merely being realistic. It seems to me, Meladriel, if you haven't thought of that, you're simply denying reality.'

'A potential reality,' Tika corrected. 'I'm sorry, Mela, Ved always thinks the worst of everyhar.'

Meladriel sighed. 'He may have a point. We simply don't know yet.'

'If I were you, I'd consider it safer to assume Seladris might now be part of the problem,' Veredis said.

'We'll certain consider it.' Meladriel stood up. 'Will you come to *Inglefey* later this morning, please? There'll be a meeting. We're gathering whoever we can at the moment.'

'You mean recruiting,' Veredis said. 'Very well. Give us an hour?'

'That's fine.'

Tika saw Meladriel to the door, where they embraced somewhat clumsily. 'Something's happened, hasn't it,' Tika murmured. 'To you, I mean. You don't feel the same.'

Meladriel nodded. 'Yes, something happened. Might be nothing.' He kissed Tika's cheek. 'I'll see you later.' He pulled a despairing face. 'Now to face the circus at *Inglefey*!'

Tika laughed. 'Dear Aru, how much is this mess dragging you out of your sweet little hidey hole? Poor Mela. Good luck!'

'Thank you.' Meladriel bowed stiffly, backing away.

Tika closed the door.

Chapter Thirty-Seven

Ulien woke up and didn't know where he was. The wounds on his face hurt – perhaps they'd opened again through the rough treatment he'd suffered. His head and body ached. He lay in a cramped, low ceilinged room that felt like a cellar, although there were small dirty windows at the top of one of the walls that let in faint predawn light. In this dimness, he could see hulking shapes, which were battered old barrels that might once have held wine or beer. He could see now that he was lying on a pile of disintegrating, gritty blankets that smelled musty. They were unpleasantly cold, and the damp had seeped through his clothes. His hands and feet were tied. After a few moments of absorbing his predicament, he realised he must gather his energies and take action, no matter how weak he felt. He must go home, spirit himself away, using the ability Tuli had given him. He closed his eyes and sought to focus his purpose. *Now!* But there was no magic within him, no vestige of that remarkable ability. It was if some part of his inner life had been cut away. He uttered a cry of anger and despair, then fell silent, staring at the cobwebbed ceiling.

He knew he should be frightened, because he was no doubt in extreme danger, but his mind was numb. Where was he? If it was somewhere in Ferelithia, his father and those who worked for him would have found him by now – wouldn't they?

He remembered then the details of his abduction. It wasn't Tuli who had snatched him but Seladris. Something bad had happened to him.

After a few minutes of lying still, listening to the rasp of his own breath, Ulien heard the creak of a door, followed by a stumbling step. He turned his head and peered into the shadows. He could make out the outline of wooden stairs, a shape coming down them. There was a mumble of irritation, then a figure loomed into view. At first, Ulien couldn't tell if this was Tuli or Seladris, until they spoke. 'Here's water.' The voice was Seladris's, which was slightly more refined than Tuli's.

Ulien realised these two hara looked very similar, especially now that Seladris appeared dishevelled and mad. The clean, contained surface of the Seladris he'd first met had masked the similarities.

'What are you doing?' Ulien said, turning his face away from the offered cup. 'Seladris, you have to let me go.'

'You must know I won't do that.' Seladris hunkered down beside him.

'Who are you, anyway? The Seladris I know is a good har. It's you, isn't it, Tuli? You've done something to him.'

Seladris put his head to one side. 'We are all many hara, Ulien. From day to day we shift and change, from moment to moment, even. You are gold to me. Currency that can buy things.'

'What can I buy? What do you want?'

Seladris grinned horribly. 'They have to pay for what they did.'

'And what did they do? Took a town from humans? Why do you even care after so long?'

Seladris stood up. 'I won't hurt you, Ulien. When it happens, you won't feel anything.'

'When what happens?'

Seladris smiled. 'There has to be a price,' he said. 'I have my reasons for wanting him to pay it.'

'Who?' Ulien asked. He was aware it was important to keep Seladris talking. He needed information.

'Your illustrious father, of course. He takes what he wants, where he wants. He's become drunk on the power he was given. He needs some sobering up. He thought he was strong and clever, could bury the past, but he misjudged.'

'What did he do to you?' Ulien asked.

Seladris emitted a long, soft sigh. 'He killed me,' he said. Swaying erratically from side to side, he headed back towards the stairs, left the cellar.

A short while before this, after Seladris had dumped Ulien, bound and unconscious, into a room underground, self-awareness had gradually crept back into his mind. He was horrified that he was part of Ulien's abduction, thereby turning hara he wanted to be his friends against him. At the time, it hadn't felt real, more like a nightmare from which he must inevitably awake. But no. There could be no going back from this. Why had he been so weak as to let Leupardra into him? So misguided. He'd seen Meladriel in bed with Kazharn – so what? It wasn't like he and Meladriel were that close. It was insane to be so affected by what was ultimately trivial.

And yet... He remembered sitting in the shrine at *Velvets* and feeling so strongly that, in some way, Leupardra had been wronged. His vicious lust for revenge was not without reason. He was a ganglion of pain, lashing out, desolate and alone. There *were* similarities between them.

Leupardra had given him the ability to travel through the ethers, like Ulien, but not on his own. Seladris had allowed himself to be led, hardly more than a senseless feather carried on a breeze he couldn't resist. Somehar else had been in control of his body; he'd been merely a passenger. He'd peered out with a numb sense of inevitability as his hijacked form had taken Ulien. At the time, he'd been incapable of feeling much at all, other than knowing this destiny had been waiting for him in Ferelithia all along.

After Ulien had been left in the cellar, Leupardra had dragged Seladris around for a while, using his body to inspect the environment. They were in an old building but not an ancient one. It was made of concrete, not stone. Humans of the last era had built it. Satisfied that no other hara were nearby, Leupardra had taken Seladris back to Ulien. The harling was awake by then, pathetic to see. Seladris wanted to garble an apology, explain, but his mouth could only speak Leupardra's words. He couldn't suppress them. Seeing the fear in Ulien's eyes had been hideous. He'd been shouting inside *This isn't me, Ulien. Really it isn't.* But Leupardra hadn't let those thoughts out.

Then those final words: 'He killed me.' Was that true?

After this, Leupardra had walked Seladris to the outside, and here had dumped him on the ground and abandoned him. For a while Seladris had slept, his dreams merely darkness, impenetrable darkness, through which he wandered blind.

After maybe half an hour or so, he awoke. He knew he hadn't been asleep long, because dawn was only just beginning to reclaim the sky in the east, where there was a faint line of saffron light. His body ached in every muscle, but otherwise he felt unharmed. Dazedly, he began to explore his environment, wondering if there was some way he could find Ulien and escape this place, redeem himself. Leupardra didn't seem to be around, but even so Seladris guarded his thoughts as Meladriel had taught him. Around him were several linked buildings, some of one story, others of two or three. There was also a large amphitheatre carved into the side of a mountain. Looking down towards the sea, Seladris realised he was a couple of miles south of Ferelithia. He could see dim lights in the town to the northwest. Did hara no longer sleep in Ferelithia? He sat down on a stone bench to gaze numbly at the town, and presently sensed somehar sit beside him. He turned quickly but nohar was there. 'Leupardra?' he said.

There were no words, not to begin with, but Seladris found memories surfacing in his mind, memories that weren't his own. And in this way he learned a history.

At one point, after Leupardra's time, this place had been one of the town's infamous night clubs, where the most hedonistic and questionable delights could be sampled. Intimidating nostrum dealers from Garridan had moved in, lithe and narrow-eyed, bringing down from Jaddayoth the most complex and devastating of their concoctions. They could make a har feel intense pleasure or pain. They could mimic death, make a har become somehar else, bewitch them to act unnaturally. They could also be hired to kill, should the need arise.

The club was named *Enervation*. It had flourished for a decade during the early years of Wraeththu settlement, until too many deaths and derangements (some of them embarrassingly inconvenient) had forced the newly formed Municipallion to step in and close the place down. The Garridan had withdrawn discreetly, taken their services elsewhere.

Seladris had the strong impression these memories weren't Leupardra's. They belonged to another har. It seemed most likely they were Tuli's.

'Who *were* you?' Seladris said aloud.

He felt a shift in the atmosphere, a stronger presence manifesting, yet there was still nothing to see. A voice spoke in his mind. 'Hear me, Seladris.' Leupardra.

This wasn't the har Seladris had hoped would answer him. Tuli, he felt, would be more malleable. 'I'm listening,' he replied aloud, trusting that if he cooperated Leupardra wouldn't feel the need to violate him again, take control of his body. Should he keep up the guard on his thoughts? Would Leupardra identify that and become angry? *Keep your mind empty,* he thought. *Focus only on him.* Warily, he lowered his defences, just a little.

'If I'd still been around in flesh,' Leupardra said, 'this place would have been mine. They remembered me here for as long as they could, you know. They worked in my name. They helped keep me alive in this world.'

The complex was a wreck, almost completely suffocated by vegetation. It looked like a tumble of ancient ruins, trees growing inside the buildings. Broken glass everywhere and rags of cloth. The graffiti still visible on the crumbling walls were like primitive cave paintings. And some of them depicted the Pard Witch, beautiful, enchanting, with the eyes of a demon. This place, in its way, was a temple.

'Come with me,' Leupardra said.

Seladris was unsure how he could follow an entity he could not see but became aware of pressure on the back of his neck. He moved forward to escape it and in this way was guided.

'Kelosanya is a toothless deity,' Leupardra said. 'An insult to the spirits of this area. The original gods were fierce and strong. They demanded blood sacrifice.'

He went on to describe some of the ancient gods, but Seladris could not take this information in. It had no bearing on his current situation, but at least Leupardra's meandering monologue gave him space to gather his strengths. He glanced to the side and found that Leupardra was visible to him now. It was as if his attention upon the Pard Witch had eventually enabled him to take on a visible form. Leupardra was both inside and outside, a murmur in the mind, yet also an emaciated yet winsome har walking beside him. A dark twin, only… perhaps they were both equally dark. For some reason, Seladris was compelled to reach out and touch Leupardra. He aimed for the arm, but his fingers passed through it.

'No Seladris,' Leupardra said. 'You cannot touch me yet. I'm not here, not really, just an image.' He smiled, rather sadly. 'You'll have to be patient.' He sighed, led the way into an alley between the buildings that was almost blocked with hanging vines. Seladris pushed them apart, while Leupardra glided through them.

'Hara have to be so careful,' Leupardra said. 'They can act as civilised as they like, but there's always the danger a greater power will come, and if they've sacrificed their strength and courage upon the altar of virtue, they will be vanquished.'

'Is there a greater danger?' Seladris asked.

'There might be, one day. It is best not to slaughter the warrior within in case he might be needed.'

Seladris thought then of Meladriel. *The warrior still lives in us*, he thought. *Sleep is not death.*

They came out of the alleyway and climbed concrete steps with an iron railing to halfway up a cliff. Here there was a lookout platform, and a lichened wooden bench, once painted white, most of which had flaked away. Leupardra indicated Seladris should sit upon it.

'Have you always remained in Ferelithia?' Seladris asked. 'Waiting…?'

Leupardra appeared to lean against the rail, staring down. His hair blew as if in the morning breeze. A convincing illusion. 'I don't know. I suppose so.'

'Did I wake you?'

Leupardra turned and looked into Seladris's eyes. 'I dreamed of you,' he said. 'You are part of me. I think it's more that I woke you. I needed you to come.'

'I'm here,' Seladris said gently, as you might to a frightened harling. 'You can tell me everything, now.

Leupardra beckoned for Seladris to join him at the rail. 'Let's watch what's left of the birth of the sun together,' he said.

Seladris did so.

'I took somehar from this club,' Leupardra said, 'when it was still a living place. I liked to come here, because I didn't know I was dead. And yet I did. It was strange. Anyway, I took him because he looked like me. I could step inside him and he could be my carriage through the world. I had a body again. His name was Tuli and he sought to poison himself to death, intending to enjoy to the limit every moment of that demise. I decided this was a waste, so one night, as he was dancing in a trance, I reached out of a painting of myself on the wall and took him. He doesn't mind. He sleeps a lot. I don't think there's much of Tuli left; to be honest, there wasn't much to start with. But anyway, you want to know the past, don't you? I'll tell it to you.'

The tribes who would become the Ferelith, Leupardra said, were immovable in their desire to take the town. Yet the humans who still occupied it were a special breed – strong in magic. They had aligned themselves with powers of the land. They had cast off all that they had been in order to become something else – a memory of earlier humankind who they felt had a right to survival.

The phyle leaders had looked up to Leupardra because they

believed him to be more powerful than the humans who were thwarting their plans. Leupardra did not disagree with their opinion. He knew that true power often comes from others believing you have it. He took aruna with all hara of influence, plus others who might be useful, and in this way controlled them.

Listening to all this, Seladris considered that while Leupardra might belittle Kelosanya, he certainly knew how to use that dehar's particular power for his own benefit. He had been adored, feared, trusted. The mascot of the tribes. Their witch.

He had developed a plan. It was precarious and perilous, but he felt confident he could carry it through. The spirits of the land were impartial clusters of energy. Prayers might sway them. Gifts might sway them. Whoever offered the most attractive sacrifices would undoubtedly gain their temporary complicity. Leupardra intended to offer a feast of a sacrifice, which could not be turned down.

Working with a few hienamas he considered just about worthy for the purpose, he discovered the power spot in Shadey Lane. He and his confederates could move unseen at night, on the outskirts of Ferelithia, and anyway the humans of the town tended to avoid Shadey Lane, believing it haunted and cursed. This underground chamber, Leupardra resolved, would be the Fane of Unmaking. He'd summon spirits here, shape them, give them a directive. And he would feed them.

Leupardra decided the entities he summoned wouldn't be concerned about the physical appearance or constitution of the sacrifices he'd offer them. The life force alone would interest them. Conferring with the tribe leaders, he selected fifteen of their weakest hara, the few who'd been damaged, either physically or mentally, during inception but had somehow survived it, and who now carried out menial work within the phyles, along with those whose injuries in battle had been so severe no amount of harish healing could mend them properly. The phyles, consisting of several hundred hara, had twenty-one impaired individuals between them.

Nearly half of the leaders were against the idea but were over-ruled, or rather persuaded. Leupardra argued that these broken hara could never lead the lives they'd been intended to experience. If anything, it was a kindness to release their spirits from the damaged husks of their bodies and allow their souls to be reborn, whole. Eventually, the reluctant phylarchs consented, many no doubt secretly concerned that this callous blood sacrifice would provide an unpropitious start to their new life. Still, they turned their backs on their doubts, unaware that their initial dissent would be remembered.

Leupardra selected the most badly damaged for the honour of sacrifice. He told them they would perform a secret, sacred duty for their tribe. They would be venerated as saviours and soon would be reborn as harlings, in perfect bodies. A few, of course, could barely understand what he said.

On the night chosen for the assault, Leupardra positioned key hara on the cliffs and hills around the town. Humans knew that Wraeththu could attack with sound, and would undoubtedly take precautions to protect themselves, but the howling songs that Leupardra would release upon the night were not intended to harm humankind. They were to empower the entities he summoned.

The sacrifices had been taken discreetly to the Fane of Unmaking, and here Leupardra began his invocation. His inner cabal stood with him beneath the ground; other hara were stationed outside as guards. Only those at Leupardra's side knew the true nature of the event. Those above ground knew nothing of the sacrifices. The Pale Ones came, manifesting as spindly, clicking shapes, mimicking only barely the human or harish form of torso, head, four limbs. The entities were weak at first, incoherent, until they were encouraged to feed. Leupardra ordered throats to be cut, so the Pale Ones would be drawn to the living power of blood. They knew then what to do. They drank and devoured lifeforce, until all that was left was a muddle of husks. Then, they clothed themselves in shadow and crawled out of the fane.

Hearing this, Seladris believed he must've found the remains of those poor creatures in the cellar next to *Inglefey*. He couldn't show emotion. He must remain impassive, interested in all Leupardra wanted to reveal.

The Pard Witch then described how the tide of unlife had moved through the town, taking every living person in its path. No one escaped. Not one. He told of how the hara he'd stationed upon the cliffs had uttered their cries and made their music, calling upon primal forces. They had fed the moving tide.

In the morning, Leupardra said, a wind came in from the sea and blew the town clean of the dust of death. Hara paraded in, singing, stamping. They danced in the town square and raised a flag.

With great ceremony, the tribe leaders brought forth the bodies of the sacrifices, and these were placed upon rafts piled with flowers. The phyle leaders declared that these unfortunates had died at the hands of humans – weakest of the tribe, they had been picked off heartlessly while everyhar else had been concentrating on the ritual that vanquished the town. The bodies of the sacrifices, in their shrouds of flowers, were set alight and sent out to sea. Songs of mourning were sung.

Seladris was shocked by this revelation. Then whose bodies had lain beneath the ground?

He'd lowered his defences too much, shocked by the information. Leupardra had heard him. Now, the Pard Witch laughed softly. 'You were wrong,' he said. 'So wrong. And now I will tell you why.'

Despite hara's efforts to cleanse the town, the air still held a taint of mustiness, of rotten wood and dead flowers, of attics and decomposing fabric. The Pale Ones remained, lurking nearby. Wouldn't they become hungry again? The tribe leaders were concerned and asked Leupardra to dismiss these monsters, unmake them.

Leupardra realised he hadn't considered the entities he'd summoned would be inclined to hang around. Perhaps they enjoyed the forms he'd conjured for them too much. He would never admit it to his leaders, but his control of the Pale Ones was limited. They had simple drives but were inexorable. He considered. He meditated. But it was clear he sought no counsel.

Two nights after the taking of Ferelithia, Leupardra called a meeting of all the tribe leaders. (Some of them, those most loyal to him, he spoke to in advance, privately.) He told the gathering that if the Pale Ones were not dispersed, they could render Ferelithia uninhabitable. He claimed the entities were cunning and had tricked him, when all he'd been concerned about was the triumph of the tribes. There was only one course of action available. The entities could not be unmade but must be bound and confined. Over time, their energy would dissipate naturally back into the environment.

The tribe leaders and their hienamas convened in the fane. Once they were inside, other hara were brought to the site and stationed above ground to aid with the conjuration from outside.

Meanwhile, at Leupardra's instruction, a few more hara faithful to him initiated happenings within the town. Fires were started.

Hara were attacked from the shadows, hara who suspected no danger. They had won their war, hadn't they?

Inside the fane, the Pale Ones were summoned with the promise of further sacrifice. 'Only a promise,' Leupardra said. 'We will trick them as they tricked us.' He placed strong wards around the chamber and symbols of binding.

The Pale Ones slithered in, unable to resist the call. They had cast off their robes of shadow and were creatures of thin twisted bones and bleached sticks. They came into the circle of hara and crouched expectantly.

At a signal from Leupardra, a proportion of the gathering turned upon their companions. The throats of any who had questioned Leupardra's actions were slit, as were quite a few more to make up the numbers, including those of several hienamas. The victims were hara Leupardra didn't particularly like or felt didn't respect him enough. Those loyal to him wielded the blades, and one of them, a young har who some felt had great potential for leadership, was Karn.

The Pale Ones fell upon the victims with glee.

While they were occupied, Leupardra and the others withdrew. The chamber was sealed, with a powerful ouanic symbol, resembling a spear, the weapon of the warrior, and a host of bindings. Leupardra daubed his own blood over the seals.

Those waiting outside, who had aided with the conjuration, were dismissed before the group fully emerged. There was trouble in the town, Leupardra said. Everyhar must go at once to see what was happening. They did – and discovered that hara had been attacked ferociously, their bodies ripped and mauled. Minor fires had broken out inexplicably, damaging supplies. Later, these events would be attributed to the etheric entities running amok before Leupardra had had time to bind them. Nearly two dozen hara had died in the mayhem, many more severely injured, while others had disappeared entirely – even several of the phyle leaders and their hienamas.

And so, with the power of Leupardra's will behind it, the lie was concealed. As far as everyhar else was concerned, he had done all that he could to contain the menace and he had succeeded. Now the town, and the tribe, were safe.

'Was Meladriel outside that chamber both times you conducted your rituals?' Seladris asked. By now, his defences were fully in place once more. There was a strange heat in his chest – a mixture of anger and grief.

Leupardra laughed in delight. 'Yes. Did he lie to you about that?'

'Did he know what you did?'

'Of course not. I've always respected Meladriel's abilities but have never trusted him. He was my tool. He did his job. Poor Meladriel. In those days he was always drunk or drugged, dealing with his tragically broken heart.' Again laughter, the cruellest Seladris had ever heard.

'Yet he obeyed you.'

'I can see that disappoints you, but yes. He's not the tower of strength and righteousness you believe him to be. Don't bother being in love with him. He's still in mourning, always will be.'

'You are right,' Seladris said. 'I shouldn't bother being in love with him. Not because he's still in mourning, but because he isn't.'

There was a silence. 'What do you mean?'

'Can't you see it in my mind?'

'Show it to me!'

Seladris decided that revealing this event to Leupardra was something he really wanted to do. He arranged his thoughts, allowing through his defences a strong image of when he had found Meladriel and Kazharn together. If anything, he intensified the scene, showed more than he could possibly have seen.'

'Show me!' Leupardra said, a blast of sound in his mind.

Seladris could sense Leupardra's confusion, almost panic. 'I *am* showing you!'

'I can't see it. What is it?'

'They are reconciled,' Seladris said. 'I saw it. Meladriel took Karn into his bed, not long ago.'

Leupardra's image had become shaken and blurred, his voice fretful. 'I don't believe you. I can't see it in you. You're lying.'

'It's the truth. I swear it. I tried to show you, but perhaps it's something neither of us want to see, so I can't reveal it properly.'

There was a deep silence then. Seladris cautiously re-established full defences in his mind. Why couldn't Leupardra see what he'd visualised so strongly, naked before the barrier of his protective measures? Was it simply that Meladriel and Karn reunited was something Leupardra had not accounted for? He'd thought his destruction of their relationship had been permanent. Perhaps he feared their united strength. Was it possible that together Meladriel and Kazharn could destroy this damaged, vicious creature?

Another thought came to Seladris then. *He is weak, not strong. All he has are illusions until the Pale Ones are empowered once more. He thinks he controls me totally, yet he does not. Is it the same with Tuli?*

Tuli, though, was no doubt a more willing receptacle for Leupardra's being. His life had been poor to begin with.

'What you told me can't be the end of the story, can it?' Seladris asked, hoping to steer Leupardra back to his narrative.

There was a pause, then Leupardra answered, distractedly to start with, although his image was steady once more. Clearly, Seladris's information had unsettled him greatly. 'No. You know it's not. Hara began to build our town, put away their feelings of grief, start anew. The Ferelith was born. I helped them. I inspired them. But I didn't know I held a scorpion to my heart. I didn't know he was weak and useless, full of unworthy feelings. I trusted him. He was the most beautiful. He was mine.' Leupardra became silent. He could not speak the words.

'Karn murdered you, didn't he,' Seladris said softly. 'That's what you said to Ulien.'

'My desire for him killed me,' Leupardra said, his voice cold. 'I allowed it to happen because I'd been weakened. I'd confided in him.'

'But why did he kill you?'

Leupardra was again quiet for some moments, then said, 'He would claim it was because I had... other plans.'

'Other plans?'

'I had a vision for the future. Our tribe would have rivalled the Gelaming. I would have been more powerful than Thiede, but no... Karn decided to have a moral spasm about it. Bullshit, of course. He merely wanted power for himself. Obvious when you look at what he's become. I should have realised, finished him myself, or I should never had confided in him in the first place. But... Kelosanya is a deceitful bitch. I was blinded. So he did it. He took me in the throes of delight, two weapons, one of flesh and one of steel. Both to my heart, of course, in one way or another.'

'And, by that time, he'd won influence among the other leaders?' Seladris asked tentatively.

'Of course. They had invented Kelosanya, bound themselves to him. They wanted to dance their lives away, living like children in a fantasy land of false happiness and the pretence of kindness. Fools.'

He brightened. 'Still, things will be different soon.'

'What happened to the rest of the Cerulopard?'

Leupardra uttered a snarl. 'What do you think? You won't find *their* bodies, Seladris. They were dismembered and burned; their ashes scattered into the sea.'

'I'm sorry…'

'What for? Nothing to do with you. All you need to think about is avenging them.'

'I will.'

'The Pales Ones will walk again, do what they are so good at. Nothing will remain.'

'I need to understand,' Seladris said carefully, 'how the Pale Ones manifested to me at *Inglefey*. You'd bound them, but we didn't open the chamber until after I saw them in my house.'

'Oh, they'd been leaking out over time. Powerless, though. Just memories. Ghosts. Hardly anyhar could even see them. You could, because we're so close in nature. Being in your presence allowed your friend to see them too. They could manifest more strongly once you opened the chamber.'

'You've influenced everything, haven't you?' Seladris said, injecting a note of respect into his voice. 'How did you… survive, discarnate, for so long?'

'Because I'm strong,' Leupardra said proudly. 'I put part of myself into various places, including the house you occupy. A mere wisp was trapped there. That wasn't intentional, by the way.'

'Yet Tuli couldn't enter *Inglefey*.'

'I was killed there,' Leupardra said abruptly. 'I couldn't go back inside, because my death exists there forever. I didn't want to live it again. But you helped with that, of course. I can enter the house when I'm inside you and not see or feel any horrible thing. I took back the wisp of myself when we went there together. Now I have no need to revisit.'

Seladris had to swallow hard; he felt sick. 'There was… evidence of your death,' he said with difficulty, trying to sound calm, but remembering the gruesome marks on the mattress.

'It took me a time to climb into your body,' Leupardra said, grinning. 'Listening to all that dog shit Meladriel told you. I'm the only one who can make you strong, Seladris. You mustn't feel guilty for the past at all. You should celebrate all you've done. Don't silence your ghosts. Use them.' He blinked at Seladris for several unsettling moments, as real as a har of flesh and blood beside him.

Seladris could think of nothing to say.

'We have suffered in similar ways, you know,' Leupardra said at last. 'I've watched you for a long time. I have particular requirements, you see. Tuli isn't effective enough, fragile little scrap. I need a strong body for what I want to do.'

'How did you find me?' Seladris asked, with difficulty.

'I travelled. I searched. I found. You were like a beacon to me, your spirit crying out into the ethers. I simply followed the call.'

Seladris found it almost impossible to speak now. This filthy *thing* had stalked him, violated him. Nausea threatened to overwhelm him, and he dared not vomit in front of Leupardra. That might be interpreted as weakness and change Leupardra's mind about him. '*When?*' Seladris whispered.

'In Margenya. It was beautiful. I saw your darkness and what it could do. I fed it, because you are like me. You needed to be reminded of your splendid difference, not become some tedious ordinary har. Your world had to explode around you.'

Seladris's heart contracted with shock. '*You* did that? The explosion?' For a moment, a fountain of relief spumed through him.

Leupardra laughed. 'No – *we* did it. You can't escape what you are, Seladris. Don't even try. You'll always be on the outside, shunned and despised. Only I see your qualities.'

You're lying, Seladris thought. Leupardra didn't hear it.

'I followed you around after that, keeping an eye on you. I know you felt me near sometimes, especially when you painted the picture of my leopard.'

'What? I didn't...'

'But you *did*. You sent it ahead of you to Ferelithia. We painted it together, when you were asleep.'

'I don't remember it.'

'You do. You dreamed of it quite recently.'

Seladris did remember then. Not just the dream, but the weird episode of plunging his hands into paint, creating the image. It had been like sleepwalking. How weak he must be, if Leupardra could repress the memory so thoroughly. He remembered a fleeting image of the canvas in his lodgings, facing the wall. And yet for so long he'd forgotten about it. When he'd sent his heavier belongings ahead of him to Ferelithia, he'd thrown the painting into the trunk without thinking. He could remember it clearly now, even if he couldn't recall hanging the picture on the wall in *Inglefey*.

'I can see you're confused and a little angry with yourself about the painting,' Leupardra said. 'Don't blame yourself. You couldn't remember because I hid memories of the painting from you for a while. This was because I needed you to be empty of anything to do with me when you came to Ferelithia, so you could find your way into the right circles convincingly. You did that so well. And I'm sorry it made you happy, because, well, those hara are not your future. The painting was a focus for you, so you could find yourself properly when the time came.'

'I see…' Seladris murmured. 'I understand now.' He fought to regulate his breath, his heart.

'I knew you would. Through the ritual you attended, you gave back to me the egregore of the Cerulopard. I couldn't have done that alone. But with you…'

'It wasn't just me, though, was it?' Meladriel couldn't help saying. 'Karn and the others called the egregore. Their call was stronger than mine.'

'Perhaps so. Elegant, wasn't it?' Leupardra smiled, and in that smile Seladris saw the bewitchment that had beguiled a har like Kazharn har Shadolis. 'But your presence was the catalyst, whether you felt that or not. Don't you understand? We are the same.'

We are not, Seladris thought. He remembered what Meladriel had told him about his own past. He must hang onto that, believe it. 'Yes, I too have killed,' he said evenly. 'In that we share a past.'

'I like you,' Leupardra said. 'We are brothers. I'll wake Tuli soon, then we can be lovers too.'

'I would like nothing more,' Seladris said. He conjured within his mind an image of Meladriel, but he was not alone. Kazharn stood by him. They were like etheric guardians. *Whatever you're going to do, Mela, you need to do it soon,* he thought. *If I can, I will help.*

One thing Seladris was now sure of, Leupardra had not been wronged. He'd been given immense gifts as a har and had misused them. He was a danger to life.

'Give more water to the harling,' Leupardra said. 'We need him alive for the time being. Comfort him.'

Now that Seladris knew he could keep Leupardra out of his thoughts, he considered that most of the har's assertion of power was a bluff. *Part of what gives you power is others believing you have it.* Leupardra had under-estimated him. Seladris was not as weak and malleable as he'd thought. He would play along for now.

Chapter Thirty-Eight

Having returned from Veredis's house, Meladriel stood in the kitchen of *Inglefey*, staring out of the window by the sink. He drank steadily from a glass of water. So little time had passed since he had experienced his first impressions of the troubles to come, and yet it felt like months. Pharis was due very soon, and then they'd have to decide what they were going to do. Theoretically, it was simple – draw Leupardra out into the open, find out exactly what they were dealing with, and then defeat it. But how to do that? Leupardra danced this way and that, slippery as oil, enjoying the mayhem and pain he was causing. And how did Seladris fit into all this? Had he simply been vulnerable and damaged enough for Leupardra to control him? Or was it something else? Meladriel had realised that Seladris must have seen him with Kazharn at *Eko Melosa*. He'd examined the outside of the cottage, once Seladris had departed, and had found psychic residue of the har's distress beside the bedroom window. That meant probably that Thazri would be told or would find out – eventually. Meladriel didn't want to think about the consequences of that. He and Kazharn had succumbed to Kelosanya, yet even now it didn't feel as if they'd done anything wrong. They had reached an understanding, healed the past, and would work better together because of it. The insect was a buzzing nuisance, but Meladriel knew he must feel compassion for this har; he was after all part of their team, and unity among them was essential.

His head began to ache above his right eye, and pressure gathered in his brain. Then came a soft yet explosive "pop" in the fabric of reality and three *sedim* manifested in the road outside. He recognised Katarin, of course, and the dark-haired, pale-skinned har was Pharis. His appearance was more striking than it had been in the past – he looked serenely competent too – prepared for battle. He'd clearly been working on himself. Their companion was a black-skinned, angular har with a Medusa-head of serpentine dreadlocks and a stern demeanour. This was the friend, the adept. Meladriel could see at once that this har could be both asset and impediment. He would need careful handling.

So engrossed was he in examining the new arrivals he wasn't aware of Kazharn creeping up behind him. Only when arms folded around him and a kiss brushed the back of his neck did he become aware. A bolt of energy sizzled down his spine. 'No,' he hissed. 'Don't.'

Kazharn released him. 'I couldn't resist.'

Meladriel turned round. 'We're not harlings, Karn. We must be discreet. Cause no bad feeling, remember?'

'We've released our imprisoned desire, Mela. It won't go back into its cage.'

'I know.' Meladriel leaned forward and kissed Kazharn briefly. 'But it's not our priority now. We have to find Ulien and Seladris – and disempower Leupardra before he does anything worse.' He stroked Kazharn's arm briefly. 'Where've you been, anyway? Thazri said you went out again.'

'Hara to talk to. I have to reassure them.'

'You can't be everywhere at once. Hara here need you too.'

Kazharn came to stand beside Meladriel at the window. 'Don't nag me.'

'But I enjoy it so much.'

Together, they watched Rue and Thazri come out of the house, trailed by minions, to greet the visitors. 'Pharis's friend looks like a handful,' Kazharn said dryly.

'Perhaps that's what we need,' Meladriel answered. 'We should join them.'

If anyhar had thought *Inglefey* had felt crowded and busy before, they mourned the comparative peace of the day before. Kazharn had summoned the members of the Municipallion and the hienamas of the Nayati who had not attended the ritual in the shrine. Now was the time for the whole story to be revealed to them. Members of the existing team were also present. *Velvets* staff rushed to provide refreshment – the western sitting room, which was the largest, had already been tidied thoroughly, sofas removed and replaced with functional chairs that took up less space. Guests were seated, orders taken, as if they were sitting in a high class Ferelithian restaurant, about to enjoy a leisurely lunch. Caeru moved among the company, oozing calm and goodwill, speaking in a low, beautiful voice. All eyes were upon him.

Veredis and Tika arrived in Tika's carriage. Veredis was clearly delighted to be in the company of hara like Caeru and Kazharn. Meladriel was amused to note the har was on his best behaviour – no sign of his usual snide short temper. From the moment he set foot in the house, he was networking furiously. Tika merely looked uncomfortable and intimidated. He gave Meladriel a mournful grimace. Meladriel winked at him.

Once everyhar was seated, the sitting room felt small and stuffy. The Municipallion sat stiff-backed and suspicious in their seats, eyeing everyhar else, clearly prepared to be scandalised by what they heard, despite Caeru's efforts to reassure them.

Meladriel stood by the door, leaning against the wall, arms folded. He had a feeling this meeting might be chaos, too many hara wanting to speak at once.

Kazharn stood before the gathering, below where the blue leopard painting had once hung, with Caeru at his side. He began to speak at length in a slow, measured tone. He described exactly what had happened during Ferelithia's early history – or what he'd told Meladriel about it, anyway, minus any mention of sacrifices. He paused to answer questions patiently. He did not rise to any cutting remarks. Eventually, despite the hard expressions on some of faces in the audience, Meladriel could see that Caeru's presence did much to support Kazharn's standing with those who might now be inclined to criticise his past. At appropriate moments, perhaps arranged beforehand between Kazharn and Caeru, the Tigrina took over the speaking. It was clear the Municipallion were both astonished and impressed that Caeru himself was involved in Ferelithia's problem. He had come willingly and privately – explaining that this business was personal to him. Clearly somewhat starstruck, the Municipallion expressed their gratitude. If such a high-ranking har was with them, surely the danger they faced was diminished?

Thazri was, of course, in his element. During any breaks, he fussed particularly over Amorel, who appeared disorientated by the whole experience. This was an Amorel Meladriel had never met. In the past, the har had always seemed so in control and contained, even if he'd always been rather too fond of his nostrums. Meladriel thought he must have time alone with Amorel soon to set about sealing any rifts in his energetic defences. He had come here seeking revelation and understanding on a personal level; he had not expected to find himself in the middle of a complicated and perilous situation like this. He wasn't yet fit for it. All the Garridan poison he'd been pumping into himself hadn't helped. After what had happened to Seladris, Meladriel was aware how vital it was to prevent the weakest of them being exploited.

The discussion went on for several hours, mainly to ensure everyhar present understood the cruel history that had led to this moment. Meladriel was relieved that, after their initial frostiness, the town officials didn't over-react or be awkward and demanding. The presence of Pharis's companion, Fallami, also helped with this. Once the room was open to questions and discussion between all guests, he took on a discreet yet commanding role. He radiated confidence and authority, if with a rather supercilious tone. He assured them that all would be dealt with once the facts had been examined. The Tigrina deferred to him politely. He seemed to be the expert they'd all hoped for. Too good to be true, surely?

When a full break was called, so that Thazri's staff could set out a buffet meal in the dining room, Meladriel signalled to Pharis he wished to speak with him alone. They went into the hall, where Meladriel indicated they should go outside.

'I know what you're going to ask,' Pharis said, once they were a short distance from the house and away from any windows through which they might be seen

'You do? Please enlighten me.'

'Fallami,' Pharis said. 'You're worried he's going to muscle in and try to take over.'

'Actually, no, I didn't think that, but I *did* want to ask you about him.'

'So...?'

'Is he as adept as he appears, or is that simply the public trappings of a har who runs a healing retreat?'

Pharis smiled. 'You can trust him, Mela. I'd trust him with my life, my soul and several lifetimes into the future.'

Meladriel nodded slowly. 'OK.'

'I mean it. He'll ask for time with you soon. Allow it. Don't let ego get in the way.'

Meladriel pulled a sour face. 'Is that likely with me?'

'Well... you've always been proud and stubborn, haven't you?'

'Lovely to see you again too,' Meladriel said dryly.

Pharis laughed. 'Don't pretend to be offended. Take what Fallami offers, Mela. Take it with both hands. You won't regret it.'

'To be honest, I'll take what help I can get at this point.'

'And ignore his manner. You and he are similar in some ways.'

'That's reassuring.'

Pharis sighed, tilted his head to one side. 'Try not to be sarcastic. I've already told Fallami not to be bossy.'

'I might've changed, you know. It has been a while.'

Pharis grinned. 'Yeah, course you have. Be nice.' He patted Meladriel's shoulder and returned to the house. Meladriel followed.

As Pharis had predicted, once the meeting began to relax into less formal conversations and hara were wandering between the rooms of the house, Fallami spoke discreetly to Meladriel. 'Tiahaar, I would like to examine the site outside. Would you accompany me?'

Meladriel stood up. 'Of course.' He was conscious of Kazharn's attention upon him as he left the house.

Fallami appeared to move smoothly and gracefully, yet Meladriel found he had to concentrate on keeping up with him. 'I'm not sure there's much left to examine,' he said.

'A pity,' said Fallami. 'Still, I want to see it.' His voice rang with mild censure.

Meladriel refused to justify his actions. 'Over here,' he said, gesturing.

The day was clean and crisp, clouds scudding across the sky, a wind blowing playfully. On a day such as this, Seladris had seen weird moving shadows cast on his washing. Meladriel told Fallami about it.

'Yes, most likely this was the first manifestation of the entities you call the Pale Ones,' Fallami said. 'It seems clear these were what manifested at Herne's Chase. Leupardra has wide influence.'

'Yet you dealt with them easily.'

Fallami nodded, somewhat thoughtfully. 'With the Kamagrian's assistance, yes. But they were far from home, from their source of power. Whoever sent them was short-sighted enough not to expect much resistance. It will be different here.'

Meladriel couldn't dispel the notion he was in the company of a wise teacher and must defer to him. This felt most unnatural, because Meladriel didn't defer to anyhar, but he couldn't deny the feeling was real. Oh well, this was a har Pharis said he'd trust with future lives. Best to go with it and see what happened. 'What do you feel?' he asked. He and Fallami were now standing in the crater left behind by the landslide.

Fallami turned round slowly in a circle. He was dressed in a dark crimson robe that left one shoulder bare. There was a pale tattoo on that shoulder, a stylised winged serpent entwined around a tree. Meladriel couldn't stop looking at it. 'Well I can see it's a tangle,' Fallami said. 'So many influences shaking around.'

'Can you pick up anything about Seladris's part in all this?' Meladriel asked. 'You've heard a little of his history, but it's a mess. He's a damaged har.'

Fallami nodded. 'That was taken advantage of, I think. But there may be more. Give me time and I'll try to find out.'

'There's something else you should know,' Meladriel said, now feeling reckless, and somewhat lightheaded because of it.

Fallami raised his brows.

'Leupardra animated the Pale Ones with the life force of hara. There were sacrifices.'

'Why didn't Kazharn reveal this at the meeting?' Fallami asked.

Meladriel resisted the urge to shrug like a harling being challenged by an adult. 'We don't believe it's something everyhar should know just yet, not until we're sure of what we're dealing with. We certainly don't want to spook the Municipallion. They're all second generation, but for Kazharn. I'm sure you understand.'

Fallami smiled mysteriously, nodded once.

'In your opinion,' Meladriel continued, 'is Leupardra the same har he was, who survived and has returned, or something else?'

Fallami twisted his mouth to the side. 'I can't yet say. He really *won't* want to reveal himself to me.'

'Understandably,' Meladriel said.

Fallami cocked an eyebrow.

'Well, you seem... formidable,' Meladriel said.

'Appearing that way is the best course when running a facility. It avoids distracting pettiness.'

'I'm sure.'

Fallami adopted a serious expression. 'Meladriel, I can't lie to you. I'm not here to fix everything, and it's not my job to do so.'

'I didn't think...'

'Yes, you did – at least after your preliminary period of thinking I might be a nuisance. Anyway, it's *your* responsibility. Don't be tempted to see me as a rope out of the abyss, which you want to grab on to and not let go of. I'm no older than you, and I doubt any wiser. I'm merely here to advise where I can, when my own experiences can be of use.'

'Anything you can—'

'The fact is, *you* are the high hienama here. Those officials and hienamas in the house are fit for no more than conducting naming ceremonies and blood-bonds. You've hidden yourself, and now need to claim your position – or reclaim it. You are no less than me, or you won't be when you've taken a grip of yourself. *You* must direct the others. And you have some remarkable allies in that house. They're not all helpless.'

Meladriel couldn't help smiling. 'Yes, I am grateful that. But it's difficult to feel confident when we're working in the dark.'

Fallami shook his head vigorously. 'No. Leupardra's fooling you. You're more than capable of penetrating any dark *he* can put out. It's just smoke.' Fallami took Meladriel's hands in his own. 'Leupardra is erratic and scattered. His assaults have no pattern. His main weapon is that hara fear him. And that is merely down to what he was capable of in the past, when he was strong and vital and had the support of many others.'

'So, you're sure it's him now? Not an etheric being, or some other har?'

Fallami pulled a sour face. 'I think it might be all of those, but he's at the heart of it – his anger, his grief, his loneliness.'

'You make him sound pitiable.'

'Because he is, but even so a spiteful little danger. Compassion has its place but so does discipline.'

Meladriel sighed. 'Some of us think his intention all along was to gather us here in Ferelithia, so he can dispose of us, no doubt with great melodrama.'

Fallami pursed his lips, gazing past Meladriel into the scrubland behind them. He had not let go of Meladriel's hands. 'He might think that's what he wants,' he said at last. 'But he seems a little stupid to me.' He directed his gaze back to Meladriel. '*Was* he like that, stupid?'

'I'm not sure I'd use that word. Psychotic, maybe. He had a scintillating side, of course. He needed that to control hara, and it worked. Few could see through the mask. But not stupid, no.'

Fallami nodded thoughtfully. 'Mmm… Where I was trained as

a young har, there is a term for such as he – the common language term is guisemakers. These hara were a phenomenon in the early days and a discrete type. Their psychic abilities were very powerful, while most hara were still struggling with simply understanding the gifts inception had bestowed. Guisemakers had an affinity with totem creatures, into which – it was said – they could shapeshift. They were mesmeric and could control others effortlessly. They were beautiful, charismatic. Not all were misguided. But some were. Some were very dangerous.' Fallami stared at Meladriel for a moment. 'Perhaps you are one too.'

Meladriel laughed. 'Me?'

Fallami narrowed his eyes. 'Which creature do you feel affinity with?'

'The bee,' Meladriel answered at once, even though a small part of him considered saying, 'none'.

Fallami nodded. 'I knew there'd be one. Yours is a very different path to that of the leopard, the wolf, the raven… popular types. Glamorous beasts. The bee…' He considered. 'So, you fight him one on one, simple.'

'Tiahaar!!'

Fallami shook Meladriel's hands briskly. 'Well, not entirely alone, but it is you who must match him. Show him who's really in control.'

'I can't call up swarms of bees, if you were thinking that. Nor can I shapeshift into one. The idea's… well, ludicrous. Can you imagine? "Here I am, Leupardra, prepare to fight!" And then – pouf! – I am a bee. A terrifying opponent. The leopard's paw swipes me out of the air.'

Fallami laughed heartily 'I didn't mean that. But the bee protects the hive, the queen, does it not?'

'And who is our queen?'

'That sultry, dusky beauty who worships at your feet. You know that.'

'You mean Kazharn,' Meladriel said flatly. 'Look, there's far more to—'

'Hush,' Fallami interrupted. 'It's not my business. Later, I would like to see your cottage, visit your bees. Shall we return to the others now?'

Meladriel realised Fallami hadn't really wanted to see the site, merely have this conversation. As they returned to *Inglefey*, he said,

'Would you advise me on something else?'

Fallami nodded. 'If I can.'

'*When*, in your opinion, should we begin to take action?'

'I would say a day or two. The Kamagrian and I have already discussed procedures to keep your group safe while you prepare yourselves. Part of that preparation should be a formal statement of intent to Leupardra.'

'Such as "we're coming for you"?' Meladriel couldn't help laughing at what seemed an absurd idea.

Fallami did not share his humour. 'More or less, yes. Intent and will are among your strongest weapons, as I really don't need to tell you. Or shouldn't have to.'

'Still, it's provocative. Might it not goad him to take pre-emptive action?'

Fallami shrugged, as if this concern was trivial. 'Be aware that might happen and prepare for it.'

Meladriel gave Fallami a hard stare. 'Were you some kind of military leader in the early days, Tiahaar?'

Fallami laughed heartily then. 'As a matter of fact, yes. I rarely use such skills nowadays.'

'I imagine there's little call for them as a healer.'

Fallami grinned mischievously. 'You'd be surprised. There can be competition between healing centres in Alba Sulh. Skirmishes might not end in bloodshed, but sometimes I need to employ a kind of military strategy to win.'

Meladriel grinned. 'I think Karn must feel the same with the Municipallion sometimes.'

'The trials of having responsibility,' Fallami said, sighing dramatically.

After a few moments' quiet, during which time they had almost reached the door of *Inglefey*, Meladriel stopped walking and asked, 'Do you think we'll be able to retrieve Ulien and Seladris before any confrontation with Leupardra?'

'I need to think on it,' Fallami said. 'As you will too, naturally. Ask your bees. Speak to your spirits. Send out etheric scouts to find them, if necessary.' Fallami pulled a quizzical face. 'Sweet Aru, you need to brush out the cobwebs, Tiahaar. You shouldn't need me to tell you that.'

Meladriel drew in his breath. 'You're right. I'll work on it.'

'You *could* work with the hostling,' Fallami suggested.

Meladriel uttered a scornful sound. 'For a job like this? You *saw* him, didn't you?'

'He's har,' Fallami said mildly. 'Never mind the packaging or superficial life choices. He's Ulien's hostling. There's a strong link between them. We can help him to perceive that link as a trail to follow.'

'I admire your optimism, but...' Meladriel shook his head, exhaled through his nose heavily. 'Ulien's and Seladris's safety is our main concern. We should try everything to attain it.'

Fallami made a small, querying sound. 'Have you considered that Leupardra might be more inclined to get the harling on side rather than destroy him?'

Meladriel grimaced. 'That's a disturbing possibility, but you might be right. It could give us more time.'

'As for this har, Seladris...' Fallami gestured languidly with both hands. 'Leupardra might already have him firmly under his control. Let's hope not irretrievably. We won't know until we liberate him.'

'There are... complications with Seladris too,' Meladriel said. 'I'll tell you if you'd find it useful. It's personal.'

'I think I can work out what that is. Please don't trouble yourself. This Seladris is vulnerable, that's all. You're not obliged to do anything you don't want to simply to appease him, or to stop doing anything you *do* want to do either. He's responsible for himself. Again, you know that really. What am I, a speaking mirror?'

'No,' Meladriel said, somewhat embarrassed. He paused. 'There's something else. One of our group, Amorel, he's... he's not that well. I'm concerned about him being involved in this. He too might be... vulnerable, a weak link.'

'Pharis will deal with that,' Fallami said. 'We've already discussed it.'

'I see.'

'Not your worry,' Fallami said.

'You're not a rope,' Meladriel said abruptly.

'What?'

'You said I might see you as a rope out of the abyss, it's not that. I was stuck on a cliffside, hanging on for my life, with a storm raging round me, unable to take stock of my situation in the chaos, confused by old emotions, with no chance of dragging myself to the top, because I thought all the hand and foot holds were unsafe. You were a hand that came out of the darkness and pulled me back up to a level place. For that I thank you.'

Fallami laughed, clearly flattered. 'That's a start,' he said. 'Although, if I did pull you up, it was only a short way. You'd made progress by yourself. Now start thinking about getting the others off the cliff.'

Chapter Thirty-Nine

That evening

Amorel sat on the bed in his room at *Inglefey*. The curtains were drawn, so the light was dim. Back home in Megalithica he had felt threatened, cornered, but here, in what was ostensibly Leupardra's home territory, he felt hidden. Perhaps this was due to the other hara around him, who only yesterday had been sucked away by time. Now he was among them again, but weaker than they were, far weaker.

Pharis was expected. When he came into the room, Amorel had to fight an urge to seek favour in some way. He'd been Pharis's boss once, not that Pharis took very much notice of irrelevancies like hierarchy. He simply did what he did. But now?

'How did I let this happen?' Amorel asked, indicating his own body with both hands.

Pharis had brought with him a leather satchel, which he placed on the dressing table. 'Don't bother trying to work it out. Just let me help you cast it off.'

Amorel was not inclined to argue. He thought somewhat mournfully of the nostrums he'd brought with him that Meladriel had sniffed out and thrown away.

Pharis withdrew several jars from the satchel, arranged them in a line. They would not be mind-altering, Amorel thought sadly.

Looking at Amorel, Pharis was reminded of some of the animals he'd healed – creatures who'd been injured badly and had curled in around their pain, bewildered and dazed. He had put his hands upon them, wanting at first only to soothe their minds. The fear in them distressed him more than any physical hurt.

Poor Amorel, wounded animal. He'd always had a tendency to be too hard on himself and find little joy in life. Yet he'd been a good leader. He'd been at adept at organisation and at making wise decisions. Even leaving Ferelithia and taking up a new life in Megalithica hadn't been a bad choice. The band, by then, was finished, a process that had started the moment Rue had laid eyes on Pellaz. Karn had clearly been losing interest for some time, drawn into the political life of Ferelithia. It was obvious he wouldn't remain a guitarist in a band for much longer. So the only thing to do was break up the group and start anew. But whatever Amorel had done to shed the past he hadn't succeeded. He had simply hidden from it. And it had found him.

'Take off your shirt,' Pharis said. 'Then lie down.'

Amorel did so, his fingers fumbling with buttons. His hands were shaking. 'Is Leupardra dead, do you think?' he asked, as if only to fill the silence. 'We always just assumed so.'

'Yes,' Pharis replied. 'He died. I'm sure of it. But the physical body means nothing to a creature like the Pard Witch. We just didn't realise that back then.'

'It's taken a long time for him... to come back.' Amorel lay down, put his arms by his sides.

'He's simply been waiting,' Pharis said. 'Hush now.' He put his hands on Amorel's chest, projected healing agmara into him.

For some minutes there was silence in the room. Beyond it, voices could be heard, the occasional sounds of hara moving through the house. Most of the meeting attendees had gone home now and the place felt quieter, less frantic. Thazri's staff were clearing up.

'I'm glad to see you again,' Amorel said, his voice now drowsy. 'I feel the same.'

'I was surprised to see Karn and Meladriel reconciled.'

Pharis laughed softly. 'I wasn't.'

'You always saw things others didn't.'

'Even at the worst of it, I knew Leupardra's victory was hollow. He wanted all of us, and sadly only I resisted, and Mela, of course.'

'I *did* resist, Pharis. I simply didn't succeed.'

Pharis smiled. 'Even Rue, to a degree although, to be fair, anyhar could have had Rue back then.'

They both laughed.

'I tried to mend things, you know,' Amorel said. 'After it was all over and we were remaking our lives. I knew where Mela was – in a settlement to the south. I went to him, pleaded with him to reconsider. It was obvious to me Karn was in bad shape and needed him. They should never have separated, but by all dehara, Mela can be stubborn when he's set his course. He wouldn't hear of it, even though it was obvious he was still grieving himself. He couldn't forgive.'

'Well, that was Mela all right,' Pharis said. 'You weren't the only one to try. I tried to stop him leaving, but if I'd persisted for any longer than I did, he'd have beaten me unconscious. Wisely, I withdrew.'

'Strange, isn't it.'

'Not really.'

'I wonder if it's just friendship between them now.'

'Don't be absurd! Even if they say that, and believe it, it isn't true.'

'Problematical, I suppose,' Amorel said. 'What with the consort and the social standing. Meladriel is hardly the kind of har to be the partner of a tribe leader. He despises others too easily. Can't say I blame him. I've never been that kind of har either.'

'Well, that's for them to resolve,' Pharis said. 'For now, it's important they're simply working together.' He slapped Amorel lightly on the stomach. 'Do stop talking, Rel. You're supposed to be floating off into realms of bliss beneath the touch of my amazing hands.'

'It's working, I can feel it. But I want to talk.' Amorel sighed deeply. 'I spend so much time alone, and I prefer that, but now I want to talk.'

'All right.' Pharis picked up one of his jars and unscrewed the top. A wondrous scent floated out, of roses and honey and carefree days.

'You've bottled the joys of youth,' Amorel said.

'The joys of restorative blooms actually. It might be cold.'

It was, but quickly warmed, spreading a delicious calm through Amorel's chest and stomach.

'Have we done what Leupardra wanted, coming here?' Amorel asked. 'I still wonder if it's the right thing to do.'

'I've thought about that too,' Pharis said. 'But more precisely, I wonder quite *what* drew us back together.'

'What do you mean?'

'I don't know, but... back home, when the Pale Ones came, or appeared to, it wasn't quite... real. I can't explain.'

'But who else would want us back together?'

'If it is anyone or anything, we'll find out very soon. I might be wrong. It was just a feeling.'

Amorel looked slightly scared now. 'We could be in terrible danger, about to do the most foolish thing we possibly could.'

'Indeed,' Pharis replied. 'We could. But then our universe has changed. Meladriel and Karn are at peace again, and they are... a force. We have Fallami, who is very strong and very wise. We have the Tigrina of Immanion on our side, and whatever Rue might have been in the past, Caeru is a far more potent creature. We have ourselves, remade, with all our experiences to draw upon. I think Leupardra underestimates us. That is our greatest weapon.'

'Yes... I see it,' Amorel breathed. 'He thinks we are still the hara he once knew, because for him time has not moved on.'

'Exactly. Now...' Pharis's hand slid down Amorel's belly, then lower.

'Is this part of the treatment?' Amorel asked.

'Very much so,' Pharis replied. 'And whatever unkind, and frankly unguarded, thoughts you had about my ointments, I promise you, this *will* be mind-altering.'

Chapter Forty

In the morning, Meladriel took Fallami to meet the bees. He'd gone home from *Inglefey* the night before to escape the complaints of Thazri, because Kazharn had absconded again. 'It's like he won't stay here for a minute longer than he has to,' the har had said bitterly.

Meladriel had half-expected to find Kazharn waiting for him at *Eko Melosa*, but he hadn't been there.

Today, a faint, sour smell of burning occasionally drifted on the breeze from the south, but otherwise the day was mellow.

Fallami did not speak of current problems as Meladriel led him round the hives nearest to his home. Instead, he asked Meladriel to tell him about bee husbandry.

'Don't you have bees at home?' Meladriel asked.

'Yes, of course,' Fallami said, rather scathingly, 'but I don't look after them myself. I want to hear about it from you.'

'As Karn did the other day,' Meladriel said. 'Only I don't think he actually wanted to know about the bees. He just didn't want to think about this shitty mess we're in.'

Fallami smiled. 'Don't punish him too much, Meladriel,' clearly meaning in more than one way.

'Bees, then,' Meladriel said firmly.

It relaxed him to talk of his profession – or rather one of his professions. He spoke of the knowledge that had been left behind by humans in books, how they'd been invaluable to him. He spoke of how tragic this was, reminding him painfully that a small proportion of the human civilisation had effectively destroyed the whole. The beekeepers, living alone to mind their hives, pottering about their daily tasks – had they deserved to die? And beekeepers *had* died in Ferelithia when the Wraeththu came, because they'd left their empty hives as evidence. Perhaps they'd been ageing men and women, trying to hide from the war that ravaged the earth, who'd wanted only to live out what remained of their lives in the old way, close to the earth. Meladriel didn't speak of the fact that Kazharn held similar feelings about the past and had tried to talk to him about it. One day they'd speak at length, but not yet. So he changed the subject, spoke to Fallami of the seasons, the different jobs he undertook around the year. He took Fallami into the shed beside the cottage where he bottled his honey, showed him the tumbler he used to separate it from the combs.

'What drew you to the bees?' Fallami asked.

Meladriel shrugged. 'I can't say exactly. I just knew. Perhaps it was the time in the forest when Karn and I found a hive in a tree. I felt I knew these creatures, and that they wouldn't mind sharing their honey with me.' He smiled wistfully in recollection. 'I was young, in love, with both Karn and my new state of being. Life seemed beautiful, exploding with potential. Perhaps they saw that in me.'

Fallami nodded thoughtfully, was quiet for a moment, then said, 'It's unfair, isn't it, those early days we had. We woke up to our new selves, eager to flex our limbs and make a new world, then faced the worst of goddesses, Akhlys, the deformed one who limps across the battle grounds, trailing blood and dust.'

'I've not heard of her,' Meladriel said, 'but I certainly *know* her. That name you gave her sounds local.'

'It is. She exemplifies exquisitely a specialised function. The ancients were so good at that. There are similar in my original country – the spirits of death. They have different names not pertinent to this landscape.'

'You know a lot, Fallami. It shames me. I've wasted so many years.'

Fallami shrugged, gestured elegantly. 'I studied mythology obsessively during my training, perhaps too much so. That is one of my weaknesses, becoming obsessed with detail. It fascinates me how different human cultures tended to revere the same deities, but under different names and guises. I wanted to get to know every single god and goddess that ever existed.' He laughed. 'I'm still working on that.' His face took on a pensive expression. 'We could have come to this part of the world as Aphrodite, a goddess of love, instead we chose Akhlys. We were a gift to the earth and it to us, yet...' Fallami shook his head. 'Maybe it takes a lifetime to get over it, and we have to be grateful our harlings are free to be what we so wanted to be.'

'There were many sacrifices, yes,' Meladriel said. He paused. 'Let's go outside. I'll take you to the next of my hives.'

'We must talk with the bees,' Fallami said. 'But I don't think this should be at the hives near your home. Bees carry memories down through the generations. There are other hive communities, I feel, who know more of your history.'

Meladriel wasn't sure how he felt about these pronouncements, but said, 'As you wish.'

They wandered from site to site, and at each of them, Fallami said, 'this is not the place to speak with your little friends.'

Meladriel followed this advice, because he agreed with Fallami's decisions. He knew exactly which hives they sought.

Eventually, they reached the spot at the edge of the forest and here Fallami said, 'This, I think, is the place.'

'I feel that too,' Meladriel said. 'It's a significant site, special to Karn and I. This time, I'll tell the bees everything. I'll visit the queen.'

'May I join you in your vision walk?' Fallami asked.

'Of course.'

'I mean, Meladriel, may we link minds for this? I don't know how much you're aware of my profession, but I'm a dream walker. I can connect with you easily.'

Meladriel stared at Fallami for a few moments, then nodded. 'I have nothing to hide from you.'

He composed himself upon the short prickly grass surrounding the hives, which was yellow from summer's heat. Nearby, a bird of prey emitted a high, short 'kree!' Fallami sat crossed-legged opposite him. They joined hands, and Meladriel closed his eyes, the afterimage of the tall black har like light against his closed lids, his hair like the tails of comets.

Fallami began by relaxing them with a humming chant, which lifted and sank like currents of air. The wordless song stole into Meladriel's mind like mist, lulling him, so his thoughts drifted on the brink of sleep. At this point, he became aware of Fallami's presence within his mind. It was not obtrusive, but encouraging, an opener of the ways.

Meladriel visualised himself outside of his body, both he and Fallami standing upon the platform before the door of one of the hives. He visualised the pair of them small enough to enter the city of bees before them. The guards at the entrance knew him, and accepted Fallami's presence because Meladriel vouched for him. The scene inside wasn't a faithful representation of a living hive, but rather a fantastical reimagining. It was a labyrinth of rich honeycombs, which were like towering golden stalactites and stalagmites, dripping with shining ichor: cathedrals of wax and nectar. He and Fallami, who walked beside him, were not bees, but smaller versions of themselves. They did not speak but followed a processional way to the centre of the hive. Worker bees, of similar size to themselves, went about their business around them. The air hummed.

Eventually they reached the throne room where an immense queen bee lay producing eggs, which the workers carried away. She reposed upon a bed of combs that leaked around her in a golden pool. Her head and limbs were small, but her lower body was monstrous. She could not move, had enjoyed only one flight in her life.

'Your majesty, may I speak with you?' Meladriel asked, bowing deeply.

'As always,' said the queen.

'This is my story,' Meladriel said.

When he spoke, it was as if his voice transformed into the humming of wings, became one with the sound that permeated the hive. The words murmured from him, without vowels or consonants, a new flight of language. It was pulled from him like smoke drifting from his body, weaving patterns on the air that occasionally flashed into a comprehensible image. The story took years, or perhaps no time at all.

'Great lady,' Meladriel said in his new tongue, 'give me your counsel on what I must do.'

'Look over the sea,' said the queen, 'as you always do. Into the whorls and patterns, the knowledge beyond the senses, the truth of all. They who speak in shadows. The one who hangs in the chaos of all light. There you will find your answers. Wrap your enemy in what is not and what cannot be. The drowned one will know.'

She raised her two uppermost limbs which Meladriel could see were tipped with perfect tiny hands. Her face had become that of a soumic har, soft and lovely. 'Take my blessings, children of nectar.'

From her mouth parts, she sprayed over her visitors a mist of sweet-smelling honey, the essence of all that promotes healthy life.

Meladriel opened his eyes and found himself staring into Fallami's heavy-lidded gaze. 'How well she knows you,' Fallami said. 'She is a goddess, who I'm sure is the modern form of an ancient deity named Melissa.'

Meladriel nodded. 'I know her as Melosa, but in this land, yes, her name was Melissa. Her priestesses shared the same name, all of them.'

Fallami planted his hands firmly upon his thighs, straightened his spine. 'The queen bee's words were like a code. Did you understand her meaning?'

'I think so, yes. She referred to a phenomenon I perceive sometimes – few hara can see it, although I believe it to be natural. I call it the unstorm. It's like a hurricane, but inside out. It has an eye, which is chaos, and its outer manifestation is a terrible calm, called the grume. Horrific things live in it that should not be seen. In its eye, I sometimes meet a being that appears as a drowned harling. I think she referred to this.'

'Do you know his name?'

Meladriel shook his head. 'I took him only for a symbol.'

'Which he is, of course, but I think it very likely this phenomenon would have been observed by ancient seers – human seers. They will have named it. This land is packed with gods, goddesses, spirits and elementals. All were named and known. Finding the name will be of use to us, I think.'

'You have a great respect for the ancients, don't you,' Meladriel said.

Fallami nodded. 'How could I not? The later humans who lost the world were another breed entirely. So many of them turned their backs on the past where so much learning lies. They forgot so many things. Their new foci of worship were not even deities – they were false and ephemeral ideas, like ugly abominations wearing butterfly wings. They had no substance beyond what is fleeting and meaningless. Those who were decent and good gradually became the minority.' Fallami stood up. 'Enough of that. I prefer not to dwell on such things, but it seems our current predicament tends to draw it to the surface.'

'Perhaps it's simply part of our lesson and also our solution,' Meladriel said.

'Very likely.' Fallami smiled widely. 'Now please show me your home. I'd very much like to see it.'

Fallami inspected Meladriel's cottage as if walking round a museum. He picked up objects and examined them, exclaimed softly in pleasure at certain things he found. Meladriel, somewhat bemused, made tea, realising with some amusement he spent a lot of time doing that, as if it was part of a ritual. And so it was – the preliminary when any hurt or confused soul came seeking his aid. It was also the magical act of gaining trust through the offering of hospitality. He found himself wishing he'd had a har like Fallami in his life, a wise teacher who he'd have been able to consult at any time. An eccentric and interesting type, who might drive him mad sometimes, but whose word could be trusted. Pharis was so lucky. But then, as Fallami had said, he was no older than Meladriel. If he was a teacher it was because he had applied himself to learning, something he could now share and use to help his community. Instead of taking this path, Meladriel had bitterly excluded himself from life. He had never undertaken caste training in the magical arts, beyond very basic, post-inception instruction from a har who didn't know much more about harish abilities than he did. He should have trained more, found a har to teach him. Even if he'd never taken up public life or a healing profession like Fallami had, he could have been of more use to other hara. He wouldn't feel so helpless now. As much as he might have wanted a Fallami, many others in Ferelithia might have wanted one too. He could have been that but for his proud, selfish wound-licking. A lifetime of it in human terms. *This has to change,* Meladriel told himself. He put down the tea things on the table and gestured for Fallami to sit.

'So,' Fallami said, 'tell me all you know about the unstorm. Every detail, no matter how small.'

Meladriel did so, aware that his guest was now focused entirely upon learning. Here was knowledge he lacked. He was hungry for it.

When Meladriel had finished speaking, Fallami said, 'For me, the best thing about our longevity is our capacity to absorb knowledge. How inconvenient it must have been, possessing such a weak body that expired before its time. So much never learned, never experienced. The life of a fly.'

Meladriel smiled. 'A sentiment that should be passed on.' He paused. 'You'd like to see it now, wouldn't you? The unstorm?'

Fallami threw up his hands theatrically. 'Of course! Do you need to ask? How often does it manifest?'

'It holds to no pattern. I can see three within a matter of months, then none for years.'

'Does anything prompt them?'

Meladriel grimaced. 'This time, I might say yes, but less so in the past, unless their purpose was to alert me to something I never bothered to investigate.'

'Mmm...' Fallami murmured thoughtfully. 'I wonder whether it would be worth you attempting to contact the spirit of the unstorm in trance. I suspect it's based on an ancient form, absorbed into the harish unconscious to become part of our belief system. You found it and named it, spiritual explorer that you are! That's what tends to happen. The unstorm and its denizens might feature in local mythology of earlier ages.'

'I did look into that when I first encountered it,' Meladriel said. 'My tribe did have the good sense not to burn the library in Ferelithia, and it's been added to over time by enthusiasts who foraged for old books. But I found nothing that really matched what I'd experienced. Plenty of mentions for storms, hurricanes and weather conditions at sea, but they were natural phenomena.'

'Things change over time, though. Interpretations may be revised or viewed differently. Look at how many deities and spirits were ascribed to the weather and the sea in this part of the world. It's the same the world over. I've a feeling your unstorm spirit has existed for a long time, but perhaps not in a form you'd immediately recognise. I suggest first another vision walk to gain more information. I'd be happy to do this with you.'

'Now?'

Fallami smiled widely. 'After our tea, of course. But yes, soon. We are on a quest, Meladriel, and need to pursue it!'

They went down to the shore, to Meladriel's sacred spot, where he built his ritual pyres. Together, they gathered driftwood and built a new fire. Meladriel had brought pine resin with him, which he crumbled into the nascent flames.

'May I lead this vision walk to begin with?' Fallami asked. 'I want to quest for information, and to do it my own way.'

'As you like,' Meladriel said.

'I'm not commandeering your work,' Fallami added, 'and will hand the lead to you later on.'

'I have no objection.'

They settled opposite each other across the fire, sidelong to the sea and closed their eyes. Meladriel allowed himself to fall back into the arms of trance. Fallami once again hummed a wordless chant that relaxed the mind. Meladriel felt he was unchaining himself from reality. He could see it in his vision, not a heavy chain of steel, but delicate, made from rare metals of far etheric realms. Perhaps this chain was the only thing that anchored him to the world. Fallami's voice rose and fell like waves, both in reality and inside his mind. And then he uttered words of command.

'Spirits of sea and land, we are awake to your presence,' Fallami said. 'Reveal yourselves to us. That which makes the sea grow wild. That which lurks in the clouds and rides the currents of air. We look back down the long road to the past. We walk this road. Speak to us, spirits. Show us what was, what is and what will be.'

Meladriel could see in his mind the road Fallami spoke of. To either side of it, the myths of old were enacted – heroes, deities, spirits – each playing their part in the tapestry of stories.

As he walked, he glimpsed those he recognised, even Akhlys as Fallami had described her, a frightening, misshapen thing, twisted out of shape by the atrocities of war, bearing the wounds of all upon her body. But she was not the unstorm, nor what dwelled in it.

He walked further back, into thick mist, and found he was walking upon the sea. Great, coiled beasts lifted their lithe, obsidian backs from the water, showing briefly through the thick air. He heard peculiar hooting and honking cries that echoed far. And then, in the distance, the feeling of the unstorm approaching, a feeling it was almost impossible to describe. The outer tendrils of the grume brushed against his skin, numbing him, yet filling him with a deep, dull ache.

He realised he was alone. Throughout, he'd been aware of Fallami's presence, even if he could not see the har, but now it had gone.

Before, when he'd met with the spirit of the unstorm, it had been within the liminal space between sea and land. His own territory. But now he was in the landscape of myth and dream; *he* was the visitor, the interloper.

He stopped walking.

All was silent but for brief, distant sounds that could have been the booming of waves or the cries of creatures that rode within them. The air was very cold, yet at the same time the heat of an invisible sun burned Meladriel's skin, its rays searing through the fog.

'Spirit of the unstorm, I summon you,' Meladriel murmured.

Even this soft sound carried far. 'I call upon your counsel. I call upon your aid.'

Stillness, silence.

'We know one another, spirit. You know my name. I would know yours.'

Then he saw a diminutive figure walking towards him. He stared for what seemed like a long time, and the figure grew no closer. Then all at once it was standing before him – like a freshly-drowned harling dressed in the flotsam of the sea and sunken ships. He was wound in torn fishing nets, and spars of sodden wood adorned his hair like a head-dress. His skin was green, pimpled with limpets and anemones of purple and black. His fingers and toes were webbed. His eyes were a dull greenish-white, yet not blind.

'Meladriel,' he said, the first time he'd addressed Meladriel personally.

'That is me,' Meladriel replied. 'Would you give me your name too?'

'I am the lone wolf,' said the spirit.

'Wolves cannot live in the sea, or in a storm,' Meladriel said. 'They are creatures of the land.'

'True, but that is my name. I am a daughter-son of Ekhidna, she who was born of sea scum and salt marshes. Her purpose was to breed monsters, or so humankind decided. They named me Oiolyka, the lone wolf, and I travel alone in the storm of unmaking. The older race believed in the wolves of the sea; those voices they heard howling in storms. Sometimes the *other* storm came to land. Their wise ones felt it. They could not know me, so made their own legends. They sought to tame me but could never see me. They heard me in the night, in their dreams.'

'*What* are you, Oiolyka?'

'The eye of inversion,' it replied. 'Through me, there can be change, a turning.'

'Can you help me?'

The spirit smiled, revealing the spiked teeth of a carnivorous fish. 'I have waited long for this imprecation.'

'Do you know Leupardra and does he know you?'

'I know what you show me.'

'Then I ask for your aid. Will you give it?'

'Yes. We know one another.'

'What must I do?'

Oiolyka held out his arms. 'Gather your company and place them upon the cliffs above the sea. Have them call to those that wear no flesh. The gathering must sing in the voices of earthly creatures, but it must also be music to the gods. Aphrodite is with you, but you must feed her.'

'The ancient goddess of love?' Meladriel asked. 'What part has she in this?'

Oiolyka lowered his arms. 'You know her, but only partly. You have reshaped her. Remember she is not only love and beauty, but also the power of the sea. She is a warrior. She is jealous concerning those she protects. You have let her sleep too long, and in her dreams she danced and kindled desire, but now she awakes to her true nature.'

'Kelosanya...' Meladriel said. 'He is the harish shape of Aphrodite.'

Oiolyka nodded. 'She has always been here,' he said. 'But you know her differently. She must relearn herself now too, become Kelosanya as he needs to be. Put your tribe upon the shore and in the hidden groves that lean back from the sea. Have them call there. Do you understand?'

'Yes, Oiolyka. What shall I do at this time?'

'You... You must go to the old temple up high.'

'The place they called the Sill of Shrines?'

'No, further south. A ruin in the side of a mountain. Do not visit this place until the appointed time. Take with you your most trusted allies. Your enemy's hubris will draw him forth. Call to me then and we shall see.'

'When, Oiolyka?'

'Not tonight, nor on the morrow. It must be as the sun sets on the third night from now. Gather them all, those who remain in Kelosanya's bower, the town you call Ferelithia. You must make no mistake, for those outside your cover will be taken. You must trust in yourself that I will come. You must trust in me that I will aid you. Ultimately, I will give to you the gift of inversion. It will be up to you how you use it.'

'I thank you, Oiolyka.'

'There is one other thing,' the spirit said. 'Do as your hidden self wills, Meladriel. Do not fight Fate. You must trust the future.'

'What does that mean?'

'You will know when the moment comes. Sacrifices must be

made for the greater good. You must make a worthy offering.'

Before Meladriel could even absorb these words, Oiolyka had gone. Meladriel felt he was sucked back through time to the present moment, becoming aware of his physical body as if it had been punched. For a few moments, he regulated his breath, grounded himself, before opening his eyes.

Fallami was staring at him. 'Do you know what to do?' he asked.

Meladriel answered. 'I think so. We have two days to prepare.' He paused. 'What did you see?'

Fallami closed his eyes briefly. 'A force that can alter reality, but it is unpredictable and volatile.'

'In your opinion, should I go with this?'

'You have no choice,' Fallami said. 'And you must tell Leupardra this.'

Meladriel got to his feet. Part of gaining power was believing you have it. Wasn't this Leupardra's armour. Well, let him see.

At the point where the gentle waves met the sand, Meladriel stood in the water. He imagined his ability to communicate taking shape inside him, the shape of an arrow. All of his intention he poured into this artefact, and then he wove his message into it. *Not tonight, nor tomorrow night, but the night after, we're coming for you, Leupardra. I'm not afraid to forewarn you of this. Be ready.*

Did he feel the confidence he bound into the message? Meladriel wasn't sure, but he knew it was vital Leupardra felt it.

That evening, another busy, chaotic meeting was held at *Inglefey*, during which Meladriel delivered his plan. There were objections, not least because Meladriel expected everyhar to act on his word without clear description of a desired result. 'What exactly is going to happen?' was upon the lips of everyhar from the Municipallion. The hienamas were more trusting, and perhaps looked forward to testing their skills. Thazri's friends were less confident, but Fallami sought to soothe them. Their role, he said, was vital, for they would emulate the maidens of the ancient temples, who interceded for humanity with the gods. These maidens were chosen because they were the essence of sacred femininity, and this trait was reflected in hara who could call upon the aspect of soume with great power. 'The essence of soume stands opposed to death,' Fallami said, 'because it represents the fount of life. This is the aspect you will bring to our work. You will be the hienamas of life itself.'

Thazri's friends appeared reassured, if also still somewhat dubious.

The hara of Ferelithia would be guided to positions around the edge of the town as Oiolyka had described. They would be taught simple chants they must maintain. Caeru would go to the Sill of Shrines and here sing as his intuition suggested. Katarin would go with him. Pharis and Amorel, and Thazri and Ihrec, would join with other groups of Ferelithians to lead them in ritual chants and the raising of power. Thazri, it appeared, was eager to learn and be involved. He did not seem to be afraid.

Meladriel, Fallami and Kazharn would go to the site Oiolyka had mentioned. Kazharn felt sure this was an abandoned building that had once been a party site early in Ferelithian history. 'There was talk of restoring it at one time,' he said, 'but plans never came to anything. Perhaps there was a reason for that.'

Meladriel explained the connection between the old gods and the new, and how Kelosanya was a harish reinterpretation of an ancient deity. He urged everyhar to connect with the dehar in their own way, to feed him with the power of their belief. The hienamas were surprised by this revelation and a few of them were uncomfortable with it. They didn't like the idea of a goddess revered by humankind being the template for the dehar of Ferelithia. The more open-minded among them swayed the argument by suggesting that gods were eternal, but to remain relevant they had to wear a shape that meant something to those who revered them. Aphrodite had evolved as the world had changed. She was Kelosanya now.

After the meeting, there was more work to do, but of a more personal nature.

In the attics of *Inglefey*, Fallami cleared a room of furniture. He had asked Ihrec to help him with this because they would work magic from the land of their human ancestors. Together, they had fashioned a circle of sand, salt and ochre on the bare boards, and had painted symbols within an outer ring of the circle using red and white pigment. The symbols were primarily protective in nature. Fallami's intention was to work in this room to find out where Ulien and Seladris were and what condition they were in.

As Fallami was gathering the materials for this task, some of them having to be fetched from elsewhere by hara willing to assist, Meladriel said to him, 'Remember Leupardra has eyes everywhere.

Is it safe for us to do this?'

Fallami had uttered a sound like a snarl. 'Leupardra will not see through *my* defences, trust me,' he said. Then, softening his voice, 'Don't misinterpret me. I meant that I'm not a resident of this town, nor a member of your tribe. I'm less visible to him. He knows the rest of you too well. Your moments will come, Meladriel, but allow me to assist you in this. It is a minor task.'

That evening, once everyhar not temporarily residing in *Inglefey* had left the building, Fallami asked for Meladriel, Kazharn and Thazri to join him and Ihrec in the empty attic room.

'Take us into the vision walk as bees,' Fallami said to Meladriel. 'We must be insignificant yet swift.'

'Lead us, and I will do so,' Meladriel responded.

It felt odd to be sitting in a magical circle with both Thazri and Kazharn, yet at the same time Meladriel felt weirdly disassociated with what had happened in the bedroom of *Eko Melosa* only the day before. It seemed like a dream now, a memory that was both sweet and wistful. In this present moment, Thazri was neither a rival nor an impediment; he was simply a har dedicated to a common goal.

Fallami's voice led them down into a dreamlike trance. This was not merely a visualisation but passage through the ethers into another layer of reality.

Meladriel felt the world he knew sifting away from him, falling gently like a faintly sparkling dust. All around, he could perceive the living essence of all things, the memories held in objects, in the echo of vanished voices. He could hear the sweet cold song of the stars and the slow stately music of a moon that was nearly full.

'See yourselves as agents of the hive,' he said to his companions. 'Your bodies are small but swift. Your senses are acute. Take wing!'

At once they flew up beside him, shimmering bees of gold and umber.

'There is a thread,' Fallami murmured, his voice vibrating in the hum of his own wings, 'that joins a harling to his hostling. You can see this, Thazri. You have merely to look for it.'

Thazri's voice was uncertain. 'I can't see it.'

'You can,' Fallami urged. 'Let your antennae guide you.'

Meladriel could see it – a faint golden thread extending from Thazri's etheric form. He had to concentrate hard to perceive it, but it was there. 'From your heart centre, Thazri,' he said. 'Like a shining hair.'

'Can you see it, Meladriel?' Thazri murmured.

'Yes, but not easily.'

'Tell me where it leads.'

'You need to observe it for yourself.'

Meladriel sensed Thazri's fury with himself because he was unable to see this link.

Why can't I see? I'm useless! Useless!

Meladriel considered for a moment, then opened a part of himself to Thazri. 'See what I see,' he said gently. *And hopefully see nothing more.*

After a tense moment, Thazri said, 'Yes! I *do* see it. Follow me.'

They flew beyond the town, towards the mountains that began to rise from the land to the south. Here, Meladriel began to perceive glittering motes of light, memories of earlier times, hara making their way up the mountains, singing and dancing, carrying torches.

Sometimes, Thazri panicked because the light of the thread grew dim to him. Meladriel and Fallami talked him through these moments, calmed him until he could see the way again.

'This place,' Kazharn said, 'it's the site the unstorm spirit spoke of. I'm sure of it.'

'The thread is stronger here,' Thazri added. 'Ulien's here. And the light is bright. That means he's unhurt, doesn't it?'

'Yes,' Meladriel answered, not sure if that was true. It meant at least Ulien wasn't dead. 'We'll find him. Lead us, Thazri.'

'But how will we get him out? We're... we're not really here, are we? He must be guarded, surely?'

'Perhaps we can communicate with him, guide him,' Meladriel said. 'Let's find him first and see.'

'He's inside!' Thazri said excitedly. 'He shines so clearly I can see him through the walls.'

They flew down to a small window, which apparently let onto a basement. Inside, the light of a young soul burned strong.

Thazri was impatient, impulsive. He sent a shout through the ethers. 'Ulien!'

Meladriel sensed movement inside the building. He became aware of Ulien's presence; the harling seemed unhurt but weak.

'Hush!' he said to Thazri. 'Don't shout. You might...'

But Thazri had found a way through a hole in the glass. His entire being cried Ulien's name.

Meladriel heard Ulien say, 'Thazri?'

And then a vile cold feeling poured through him. Thazri's frantic cries had alerted other beings to their presence. Meladriel saw the Pale Ones rise up from what he'd taken to be ancient, rotted sacks.

'Out!' Fallami boomed. 'Out now!'

With a searing physical wrench, Fallami ended the vision walk. Meladriel found himself back in his body, but it didn't seem to fit him properly. He retched, aware his companions were uttering sounds of distress, writhing upon the floor around him.

'Breathe!' Fallami commanded. 'Long, deep breaths. This will pass. Don't panic. Breathe!'

After what seemed a long time, but was perhaps less than a minute, Meladriel felt he belonged in his body once more. Thazri was leaning against Ihrec, held in the har's arms. Kazharn appeared dazed.

'I'm sorry for that abrupt and uncomfortable departure,' Fallami said, 'but it was essential those entities didn't become fully aware of us.'

'We know where Ulien is,' Meladriel said. 'And that's where we'll be heading the night after tomorrow.'

'He might not be safe until then!' Kazharn snapped. 'Perhaps I should go up there tomorrow with a troop of the Ferelithian guard.'

'No,' Fallami said. 'That's the worst thing you could do. For now, Leupardra doesn't know we've found Ulien. Let it stay like that.'

'I didn't see Seladris,' Meladriel said. 'Did anyhar else?'

'There's another har there, perhaps more than one,' Fallami said tightly. 'I got the impression their wills were not their own. Their lights were weak.'

'Can we release them?' Kazharn asked. 'I mean… when we go there in reality?'

Fallami shrugged. 'We can only assess that when we find them.'

Chapter Forty-One

The following day involved further meetings and preparation. The hienamas were holding ceremonies in the Nayati Kelosanya throughout the day, urging all Ferelithians to attend at least one of them.

Kazharn was missing again, apparently having stayed out all night. Meladriel assumed he was returning to *Velvets* to sleep, since he didn't enjoy the crowded conditions at *Inglefey*. Strange he hadn't mentioned it, though.

Meladriel was sure his message to Leupardra had been received, so he must be aware the town was readying itself to fight back. And yet he made no move. Meladriel mentioned this to Fallami, who suggested this could indicate Leupardra wasn't as ready to take on the elite of the Ferelith as he liked to make out. 'I suspect he's gathering his strength,' Fallami said. 'As well as observing, of course.'

'Shouldn't we strike before he's ready, then?' Meladriel asked.

Fallami shook his head. 'Oiolyka gave you a time. We must stick to that.'

Meladriel wasn't convinced. What form would attack take? The Pale Ones converging, sucking the life from every har they passed? They'd done that before. Would any protective measures they took be enough?

Thazri took Meladriel aside before dinner to thank him for all he'd done the previous night. Meladriel hadn't expected that, nor did he want thanks. 'I'm concerned about Ulien's safety as much as you are,' he said. 'But remember Leupardra could be watching us. We mustn't speak of it.'

At least Pharis seemed to have helped Amorel find balance. 'Is he well enough to stand with us tomorrow?' Meladriel asked Pharis.

'He will be,' Pharis answered, somewhat fiercely.

Tonight would be the last dinner the company would share before the ritual, because Fallami had told them they must fast after a frugal breakfast tomorrow. He and Pharis would mix a brew that everyhar could imbibe throughout the day, but nothing else must pass their lips.

Kazharn had been absent all day, speaking personally to inhabitants of the town. Meladriel wished he could speak with him alone before the following night but realised this probably wouldn't be possible. Anything beyond conversation was unimaginable. Hara wanted to talk to both of them continually. Kazharn was summoned this way and that, and representatives from the Municipallion and the Nayati Kelosanya, plus their staff, were in and out of *Inglefey* all the time.

Kazharn returned to *Inglefey* in time for dinner. He looked exhausted. Meladriel had to watch as Thazri made a show of fussing round him. *Was* there any love in their relationship? Perhaps in the new life that seemed ordained for him, Meladriel would have to face nearly every day the one thing he'd avoided for decades – being close to Kazharn, yet a light year distant. He'd have to watch him with another har who had claim to him, with whom he'd created a harling. Would the sting of that ever be drawn? If he became more like Fallami, maybe it would.

But tonight, Meladriel couldn't face it. He took a plate of food from the immense buffet Thazri's staff had prepared and went outside. He sat on the ground at the edge of the empty plot, staring at the raw earth. He could barely taste the food he put into his mouth. The night stole down.

When he heard footsteps approaching, he realised his departure from the gathering had been merely a ploy to achieve a desired outcome. And here it came. Kazharn.

'Seeking some peace?' he asked, sitting down beside Meladriel.

'Along with quiet, yes. I live alone. I can't cope with the noise in there.'

'I used to have a house to escape to as well,' Kazharn said.

Meladriel uttered a disgruntled sound. 'You still do. Don't think I haven't noticed! I don't know why this whole sideshow hasn't been moved to *Velvets*. It's bigger and far more suitable. I thought the reason we stayed was for Ulien's sake. What point is there in remaining here now?'

Kazharn paused before answering, then said, 'I think Thazri feels safer here.'

'OK.' Meladriel forced his tongue to remain still, not voice the sarcastic remark that fought to escape his mouth.

Kazharn stroked Meladriel's hair, briefly, barely touching him. 'You've won him over, you know.'

'Great. I'm very happy about that.'

'Mela…'

'It'll take time. Don't worry. I won't bolt again.'

'I wasn't thinking about that.'

'What, then?'

There was a pause, then Kazharn said, 'I thought maybe we could sneak off to an empty house and find some peace together.'

'My place?' Meladriel answered at once, wishing he could've left a dignified pause also.

'No, *Velvets*. Don't you want to see it?'

'Not really, no. Do you *want* me to see it?'

'I think so. I have rooms of my own there. We could drink ourselves mindless before this fast we have to endure.'

'We'll be missed. Hara will notice.'

'We can say we have work to do.'

Meladriel's instinct was to leap to his feet, grab hold of Kazharn so the two of them could flee to *Velvets* with the speed of hunted gazelles. But a disapproving, prim aspect shouldered this fond image aside. 'Karn, really? Thazri might be won over, as you sweetly think, but he's not stupid. Well, not that kind of stupid.'

'I don't care.'

'Yes, you do. It's simply that you're afraid there's a chance we might actually die tomorrow, and you want one last moment of bliss in case we do.'

Kazharn expelled a somewhat hollow laugh. 'I won't deny I have fears about the future. Even if we emerge victorious and unscathed, circumstances might keep us apart. Some kind of death anyway. That's what you're thinking too, isn't it?'

Meladriel sighed deeply. 'Yes, perhaps… but I don't have a chesnari to offend or a position in the town to hang onto.' He took hold of one of Kazharn's hands, long and cool in his own, darker than his olive skin. He had once thought their skins next to each other reminded him weirdly of some kind of delicious food. He'd been high on a mind-altering nostrum at the time, but it made him smile, remembering that.

'What is it? You're grinning. I hope it's because you're considering my proposal.'

Meladriel squeezed Kazharn's hand. 'Karn, I want to be with you now more than anything, but we have to be of one mind tomorrow. We can't have Thazri being resentful. He has his part to play. Perhaps afterwards we can think of a way to…'

'No, now,' Kazharn interrupted. There was a plea in his tone rather than command. 'I feel it's important we have some time together. Tell Fallami you want to go back to the shrine in my garden.'

'Absolutely not. He'd want to come as well.'

'Well, you could try telling him the truth. It's clear he likes and respects you. I'm sure he could provide a convincing excuse for us.'

'I'm not going to ask a har I barely know – a high hienama at that – to lie for me so I can sneak off with you.'

Kazharn gestured exasperatedly. 'Then just tell them all you want time alone to prepare for what's to come. I'll deal with my side of it. Trust me.'

Meladriel shook his head, but he didn't feel angry or coerced. He wasn't sure what he felt, but said, 'This is insane.'

'I know,' Kazharn replied. 'I'm being impulsive. I'm never that nowadays. Please, Mela.'

'This is Kelosanya in all his mad glory.' Meladriel shook his head, blinked fiercely at the stars. 'If we do this, there might be risks other than the obvious. We'd be away from our allies at a crucial time. It'd be outrageously rash and irresponsible.'

'Isn't that the spirit of this town?'

Meladriel stared for a moment at Kazharn. 'All right. We might have to conduct an excruciatingly painful rite of accord tomorrow, but all right. Going against common sense, and praying to all dehara we won't regret it, I agree to this ill-considered indulgence.'

Kazharn stroked Meladriel's hair again, this time less tentatively. 'I believe… *know* we have a right to this, so don't feel guilty about it.'

Meladriel knew, on one level, what they were thinking of doing was wrong, but on another so right. It wasn't merely being reckless, it was like being young again, the glorious freedom of it. There was power – and hope – in that. And surely, if it wasn't meant to be, there'd be obstacles before them, and that would be the warning to stop.

They went separately into *Inglefey*.

Meladriel spoke of his desire to meditate alone upon the event to come and everyhar accepted his words, didn't question them. Fallami, Meladriel wasn't so sure about, but if the har had suspicions, he didn't voice them. He went so far as to say, all the while gazing at Meladriel through slitted eyes. 'Perhaps more of you feel this way. If so, seek a quiet spot and find your peace. Think objectively about what is to come. Summon your inner strength. Be with your dehar. Remember what it is to be har.'

A hand in the darkness.

The front door of *Velvets* stood ajar, a spill of mellow light falling onto the wide front steps. Meladriel stood at the threshold for a moment. He felt this was a nexus point. To step across that line into the light beyond would mean something; he didn't yet know what.

Kazharn was waiting skittishly in the hall. He looked absurdly young, almost coltish in his discomfort. He hurried forward when he saw Meladriel come through the door. 'Part of me feared you'd back out,' he said.

'Yes, well, you know what I'm like,' Meladriel said. He smiled, shut the door behind him.

It was a beautiful house – spacious, elegant, understated. Thazri, it appeared, had good taste. Meladriel was inclined to linger now, to explore, but Kazharn wanted to flee the main house, take Meladriel upstairs to his private rooms. Perhaps he felt eyes upon him in the empty hallways and salons.

Kazharn occupied a large sitting room, beyond which was a cavernous bedroom. Both were decorated in shades of bronze and gold. The floor tiles were a mosaic, their design mostly hidden by thick rugs. Clawed feet stuck out from beneath fringes, occasionally a snarling dragon face. A bathroom led off from the bedroom. Meladriel used it to give himself some time to slow his heartbeat. This room too was huge, low lit, and filled with greenery. The bath within it was more like a swimming pool. It was filled with scented, steaming water the colour of seaweed, clearly recently prepared. Ferns dipped into it. He went back to the sitting room.

'Do you spend a lot of time here?' he asked, taking a seat on one of several brocade sofas.

Kazharn put a vast goblet of wine into his hands. 'Some. I sleep here, mostly.'

'It feels like an expensive hotel.'

Kazharn shrugged. 'Perhaps because that's about all it is.'

'Yet you wanted me to see it.'

'Yes. That was partly the reason. I wanted you to see my reality.'

'I feel very sorry for you.'

'Put away your weapons, Tiahaar. Don't be mean.'

Meladriel leaned back, stared at the painted ceiling. Strange creatures peered back at him. 'This is more difficult than I thought it would be. This is your other life. I don't fit here.'

'I have something to help with that, if you want to go further back in time.'

Meladriel straightened on his seat, took a gulp of wine. 'Oh? How so?'

Kazharn went to an ornate gilded cupboard against one of the walls and took from it a wooden box that was intricately carved with birds and vines.

Meladriel recognised the container. He had once held it – many times. 'Please tell me that whatever you have in that box hasn't been there since... forever.'

Kazharn grinned. 'No, it's new, I promise. When I do get time alone, sometimes I like to forget everything, walk a vision path that's purely for pleasure.'

Meladriel laughed. 'How do you get it? Do you send a minion to find some furtive dealer for you?'

'No, I still have one or two old acquaintances who visit the town. We catch up, occasionally.'

'Friends from Garridan, or who *know* hara from Garridan?'

'I would never acquire anything less.'

Meladriel shook his head. 'You... *Amorel*, you!'

Kazharn opened the box. Within were neat compartments, mostly empty. In one were a few rough lozenges, dark magenta in colour.

'Desiraa,' Meladriel breathed, as if looking upon a sacred object. 'I never thought to see that again.' It was a nostrum designed to enhance aruna, its visions.

'So, shall we?'

Meladriel pursed his lips. 'Hmm... I'm tempted, but not sure it's wise. The effects might linger beyond the morning.'

'We don't have to take the lot, Mela! Let's accept *those* days are long gone.'

'I'm not sure we ever took sensible amounts of this stuff, so have no idea of sensible outcomes.'

'Not much about Desiraa is sensible, whatever the quantity. But take one. We'll be fine by morning.'

Meladriel picked up one of the lozenges, which felt gritty between his fingers. He swallowed it with wine. There was a taste, bittersweet... It took him back in time even before the nostrum began to work its magic. His chest felt heavy, as if with grief.

Kazharn sat down beside him, swallowed a lozenge also. 'Do you remember,' he said, 'the first time we took this, when we wanted to walk with gods?'

'I remember you wanting to write a song about that, yes,' Meladriel replied. 'It sounded like the words of the Aghama in the moment, but the next day was nothing more than some odd noises and words that made no sense.'

'I think we had to be high to understand the song. We might've discovered the secrets of the universe.'

'Oh, we certainly did that.'

Kazharn's face took on an earnest expression. 'Hold onto that thought, Mela. Don't think of anything that happened after. For now, we must believe it never happened at all.' He put down his wine, took Meladriel in his arms. 'Let's just think... we've been away from one another on a long journey and many things have happened to us. But we knew, always, there'd be a return, however hopeless it might've seemed at times. So here we are, alone in the night, together again.'

Meladriel silenced him with a kiss. Sweet fantasy.

Inevitably, shedding clothes like an outer skin, they moved into the bedroom, fell upon the enormous bed that smelled only of clean linen. There was a lonely, wistful feeling to the room, Meladriel thought, but perhaps the Desiraa was already influencing his mind. He felt as if waves of seawater were flowing over his skin, making him shiver and tingle. There was no tomorrow. There was only now. It would last forever.

Sea creatures. Floating in an endless sea filled with narrow beams of light that came from a white sun. Meladriel felt boneless, like a jellyfish trailing elaborate tentacles. Kazharn bloomed within him, pulses of light and clear water. Nothing was hidden any more. Nothing. There was no division between them. How stupid to have thought there ever had been.

There came a moment of utter stillness, not unlike the grume in some ways, but this was a motionless state of pure ecstasy rather than the hideous creep of unlife. It was the *meaning* of life. It was Kelosanya, a towering dehar in which no shadow could hide. 'Take my gift,' said the dehar. Everything felt strange, frozen, not entirely pleasant yet also desired. A pure needle of pain went through Meladriel's body, like a stitch in thread. Something was wrong.

'Karn,' he tried to say, but no words came out of his mouth, only a series of clicking 'K... K... K...' He couldn't move. Kazharn lay heavy upon him as reality surged in: he seemed unconscious.

Meladriel shouted in his mind into the ethers. *Kelosanya, if you are with us, keep him out! Oiolyka, protect us!*

A serpent was poised to strike, to kill. But perhaps that was simply a dehar, poisoning the enemy. Meladriel lay gasping beneath an immovable weight. He closed his eyes.

He was unsure for how long he slept, if it could be called sleep. When he opened his eyes, the sky was still dark. Kazharn was a lump beneath a mound of quilt beside him, into which he'd apparently cocooned himself. Meladriel was naked and cold; the predawn air that came in through the open windows was chill. There was a sour taste in his mouth. His body ached. Echoes of Desiraa swept through him like wavelets. Sea water came out of his soume-lam. *Was* it sea water? Against his fingers the substance was viscous, somehow sparkling, odd. Was there blood in it? He'd not seen anything like it before. What had happened?

He got to his feet and stood there wobbling for some moments. He felt he was about to vomit. He must get to the bathroom but was unsure he could walk without falling over. So much for his tolerance of the mind-candy substances of his youth. One lozenge, though? Should it make him feel this bad, this strange? Whenever he'd experienced it before, everything had seemed sublime. He'd always woken up from it smiling, sure that life was good, his body zinging with energy, his mind still somewhere off in the clouds. An unreal feeling, of course, but never unpleasant or painful.

Carefully, he felt his way around the bed. He had a yearning to immerse himself in water. Kazharn's bath was waiting. Before he reached the bathroom, his legs gave way and he fell heavily to the floor. The impact was agonising, searing along one whole side of him. He'd have to crawl now, but it was so hard to do so…

Then Kazharn was beside him. 'Hold onto me, Mela.'

Meladriel couldn't operate his arms, so Kazharn was forced to half drag, half carry him.

'What's happened?' he asked. 'Karn, I'm poisoned.'

'Hush. Get into the water.'

Meladriel clawed his way inelegantly into the bath. At first, he sank beneath the surface and a had a dim desire to stay there, but Kazharn hauled him up.

'What's wrong with me?'

'Nothing. Nothing's wrong with you. It's just… a reaction. The Desiraa… I think.'

'What do you mean?'

'I might be wrong. I don't know. It all got… very strange.'

'Was the nostrum bad?'

'No. I'm sure it wasn't.'

'Was it… was it *him*? I daren't say the name. You know who I mean. I felt there was something with us. At first, I thought it was Kelosanya, part of our shared dream, but could it have been… hostile?'

Kazharn shook his head. He looked stricken. 'I'm so sorry,' he said. 'I had no intention… It shouldn't happen like this.'

'What?' Meladriel felt his body go cold in the blood-heat water. His stomach churned.

'I can't be certain. We'll have to find out, but I think…'

'Look, just say it.' Meladriel didn't want to hear, but he already knew. Kazharn had experienced this before, or something similar. Something less… weird. It couldn't possibly have happened, but it had.

'You are with pearl.'

Before Kazharn could say another word, Meladriel could think of only one thing: sacrifice. A cost in life. He would be Akhlys, limping torn across a battlefield, dressed in bloody, dusty rags, with blood pouring out of him: the life within him – taken.

'Mela,' Kazharn said, 'you mustn't think I planned this. You don't think that, do you?'

Meladriel turned his face away. 'No. But it *was* planned by something. I'm sure of it. It's why I let you persuade me to come here. It's why I was stupid enough to take that poison you fed me. It's why you thought it was all such a good idea – Kazharn,

371

Municiphar of Ferelithia, acting like a newly-incepted har with no thought of consequences.' He turned back to look into Kazharn's eyes.

'What do you mean exactly?' Kazharn asked, a faint autocratic tone coming into his voice.

'Don't think about it,' Meladriel said. He felt the strength returning to his limbs, along with resolve. 'Forget what happened.'

'But... why? I don't understand...'

'It won't be with us for long, so just...' Meladriel shook his head. 'I can't explain. I just know. This pearl isn't a harling, Karn, it's... something else. That's all.'

'You're wrong. It's meant.'

Meladriel pulled himself from Kazharn's hold and climbed out of the bath. Water splashed over Kazharn's bare skin. 'Oh, it's meant, all right. I just wish I knew the meaning, and whether it's good or bad for us.'

'You're making no sense. It's happened, and we must accept it. We must see this as a blessing.'

'Oh, shut up!' Meladriel snapped. 'Blessing? If it's anything remotely positive, it's a sacrifice. I know this because the spirit Oiolyka intimated as much to me, even if it *was* in riddles.'

'Then you're simply choosing the cruellest interpretation.'

'Or it could be worse than that... some hideous abomination put inside me by our enemy. We have no way of knowing.'

Kazharn shook his head. 'No. This is *our* creation, nohar else's, made in Kelosanya's light. Surely you felt that? Nothing from that warped monster was in the room when...'

'Don't be such a child!' Meladriel interrupted, unable to bear any intimate description Kazharn might utter. He snatched a towel from the floor.

Kazharn held out his hands. 'You're angry, confused... Please, just think about this. Come back to me.'

Meladriel towelled himself dry as he went back into the bedroom. His whole body ached, but he no longer felt weak. He put on his clothes, following a trail of them back into the sitting-room.

'Where are you going?' Kazharn asked.

'Home,' Meladriel said. 'You should go to *Inglefey*. Thank you for the interesting evening.'

Chapter Forty-Two

Pelfazzarsday, 3 Fruitingmoon

Seladris had spent the night outside, sitting on the upper steps of the amphitheatre, gazing out to sea. In nearby Ferelithia, his friends must be preparing to get Ulien back, perhaps even himself. What did they think of him? Had they intuited the truth, or did they now simply believe the worst about him – that he was a betrayer. But no, he couldn't believe Meladriel would think that badly of him. Meladriel *knew* him, had healed him.

As the sky began to lighten, Tuli brought food and water, unpacking it from a cloth bag onto the stone steps. Handing a bottle to Seladris, he said, 'Take some of this breakfast to the harling also. He probably won't accept it from me.'

Seladris nodded. He knew he had to remain tractable, play along, but for how long? How could this possibly end in a good way?

'We could be brothers,' Tuli said, almost simpering.

Seladris smiled thinly. 'I need to know,' he said. 'Please tell me. What will happen?'

'You don't need to worry.'

'I want to know. How can I work with you if I don't?'

Tuli narrowed his eyes. Would he be so easily taken in?

'You can have Meladriel. Kill him if you want. I haven't yet decided what I'll do with Karn.'

Seladris forced himself to bite into the bread Tuli had given him. He was starving, but how could he possibly eat? His throat was dry, closed up, his stomach clenched. 'What about their allies, the town... all of them?'

Tuli laughed. 'It's no different to when the humans tried to stop me before. They tried to protect themselves against attack, but it was pointless and ineffective. The Pale Ones will do as I ask, as they did the last time. We have very little to do ourselves.'

'You... *empowered* them before. What empowers them now?'

'Oh, I took a few souls randomly for them,' Tuli said casually. 'Karn's cringing dogs are trying to protect themselves now, but it doesn't matter. I got what I needed before they knew to do that. Tonight, it will end.'

'And afterwards?'

'We'll go somewhere else,' Tuli said. 'The Pale Ones can just stay here. Nohar will come to Ferelithia again. It will remain derelict for ever. Haunted.'

'Where will we go?'

'Somewhere we can start a new tribe.' Tuli stood up. 'They're planning to attack me tonight, as if they can simply call my name and I'll go to them.' He laughed harshly. 'Still, there are preparations I need to make. I'll take a look around, see what they're up to. It's hilarious. They think they have power. They don't.'

'Do you see everything?'

Tuli paused. 'Of course. They can't hide anything from me.'

You don't see everything, Seladris thought. *You can't see all of me, can you?*

'You're very clever,' he said.

Tuli preened. He got to his feet, raised a hand and bounded off into the shadows below.

Seladris drew in his breath, closed his eyes. He had a firm, clear idea of what he must do, something that, at one time, he'd have been too terrified even to think about. *Thank you, Meladriel...* He drew in his breath, exhaled slowly. 'I am a har of many parts,' he said softly. 'I call on that which has been with me always. My shadow. You are my bane and my strength. But I know you now. We will work together.'

He sat in silence, imagining this part of himself, a part that had formed in the days following the death of his parents, his tribe. The shadow self that had guarded him, a shell of iron and resolve.

'I know you...' Seladris said. 'I have no wish to banish you or unmake you. We are one. Come to me. We must work together again to save ourselves.'

He became aware of a strange, fizzing prickle in the atmosphere, a feeling he recalled well now. He remembered the shadow that had stood over him in the dank places, had placed long fingers over his mind and closed it, when being open would have driven him insane. *Thank you,* he said in his mind. *I thank you for caring for me when I had nohar to help me. I thank you for clearing my mind of horror. I thank you for avenging my innocence and that of those who were taken with me.*

A voice came back to him, no more than the faintest whisper. *My duty, beloved.*

He opened his eyes and a figure of smoke stood before him with eyes of red mist. He hadn't imagined this conjuration would be so easy, but then this being was simply part of him, a part he'd feared and despised, misunderstanding its meaning and source. He looked upon the Seladris of Margenya, the Seladris of harlinghood, the part of himself that had stepped outside the body to do things his essential self could not bear to do.

I am with you, it said. *I always have been, my love. Your protection, your shield.*

'Things are different now,' Seladris said. 'You must act as I tell you. No more random destruction. You must become a guided arrow, rather than an explosion. Do you understand?'

Whatever I did was always to protect you, said the shadow. *Safety lay only in constantly moving. I had to ensure that.*

'I know,' Seladris murmured. 'We were wrong. But now we are new. We have open eyes.'

As long as you love me, I will do as you ask, said the shadow.

'I do love you,' Seladris said. 'But now you must hide. Don't let Leupardra or any of his minions become aware of you. Come when I ask.'

They will not see me, my love. The smoke dissipated.

Seladris breathed deeply and slowly for a few more minutes. Then he got to his feet.

Ulien had tried to sleep, but his mind was too active. He couldn't move. He was uncomfortable and was desperate to urinate. Must he soil himself where he lay? He had screamed into the ethers, visualising it so strongly even his physical throat had become sore, despite the fact he hadn't uttered a sound. But there had been no reply, no sense of help nearby. In the night, he'd thought rescue had come, but it had been so muddled in his head. Perhaps a waking dream. His face throbbed. He wept, and tears ran into the wounds. He was sure they'd opened wide again.

He heard somehar come down the cellar stairs and braced himself for the presence of Leupardra. *I hate you!* He thought.

'Ulien.' The voice was Seladris's, but he sounded different.

Ulien wriggled, trying to turn over. Hands were upon him, undoing his bonds.

'Ssh, don't make any loud noises,' murmured Seladris. 'I've brought you food and water. He's away for now.'

'Is it really *you*?'

'Yes, Ulien.' Seladris struggled with the tightest of the knots. 'I'm sorry I brought you here. I was weak. I let him in, but I'm going to help you now, I promise.' He cast away the cords. They landed like dying snakes, writhing a little before falling still.

Ulien threw himself upon the har crouching beside him. 'I thought he'd taken you for good,' he cried. 'I was alone. It was like you were dead.'

'I *was* taken,' Seladris said. 'but now I'm me again. We've got to be very careful and let Leupardra think we're under his control. Do you understand?'

'Yes,' Ulien said. 'How can we escape?'

'We need to be patient. Leupardra told me our friends will act tonight. We must make him think we're on his side.'

Ulien nodded against Seladris's chest. 'My face hurts. I need to pee.'

'OK, see to your needs and then we'll clean your face with some of this water. I'll give you healing too.'

Ulien got to his feet unsteadily and then went to a corner to relieve himself. It felt like he'd never stop.

When he returned to Seladris he said, 'Can't we just try to get away now?'

Seladris shook his head. 'We can't risk it. Leupardra isn't here now and he's using Tuli's body to sneak around in Ferelithia. But he could return at any moment. He might have set guards we can't see. We just have to wait and trust.'

'When he comes back… will he get inside you again?'

Seladris looked away briefly, sighed. 'I might have to allow it, but Ulien, I absolutely promise he's not in control of me. I only have to let him think he is.' He smiled. 'Drink. We need to take care of ourselves. We need to be ready.'

Chapter Forty-Three

Meladriel emerged from a kind of trance-dream, sitting upon the shore, the incoming tide swirling around his seated body. He was soaked from the waist down. At least he'd had the sense to take off his boots. They lay in the encroaching water further up the beach, their laces beginning to swim. Meladriel got to his feet, retrieved his boots. Glancing at the sky, he saw it was nearly noon. He'd been out of himself since returning home just before dawn, drawn as always to the sea, its healing embrace. Now, he felt numb, inside and out. He felt in no condition to take on the task appointed to him that night.

'Damn you! Damn you! Damn you!' he yelled at the sky. He wasn't sure who or what he was damning, maybe everything, including himself.

Compelled to perform his usual comfort ritual in the cottage, he began to make tea. There was no point being angry at Kazharn, he thought, unless of course he *had* planned it all. Meladriel was sure Kazharn wouldn't have done so out of malice, quite the opposite, but the making of a pearl bound hara together. There was no escape from it. Distance made no difference, nor feelings, nor other hara. The bond was forever, or until the fruit of their union died. Even then... perhaps the bond survived, a shivering, wailing ghost. One thing he knew for certain, because so much had been revealed within the influence of Desiraa – Kazharn was unhappy and had always been so. He was an accomplished actor, and found respite in his work, but knew he was a poor consort to Thazri and not much better as a father to Ulien. His chesna-bond was a sham, a social convenience. He had many acquaintances but no friends. He was alone in the Municipallion, with much younger hara around him who couldn't possibly understand what it was like to be first generation. He was cut off from the world, as if his senses were partially impaired. And he was like this because, once, he had done something terrible. Meladriel wasn't sure what, because Kazharn had constructed the staunchest defences around his dark memories.

But it was there, poisoning him deep within.

The creation of a harling – a pure and restorative balm under normal circumstances – could not heal that. Their reunion could not heal that. It went far deeper.

Anyway, it was most likely they'd lose the pearl as Oiolyka had appeared to predict. Wasn't it better that happened rather than to lose Ulien or somehar else they cared for, somehar whose life was already in full bloom?

Perhaps he could talk to Fallami... but no. Fallami had made it quite clear Meladriel shouldn't lean on him for everything. This was personal. He had to deal with it himself. And really it was very simple. He'd come out of this situation as a potential hostling or not. He mustn't feel or think anything about it until the outcome was known. *Be the warrior again,* he told himself.

But he'd never intended to have harlings in either role of pearl creation. It had never been his path. This pearl might survive. What then?

Stop it, he told himself. *Think only of what you must do tonight.*

But this proved almost impossible. A memory sprang into his mind of the very moment he'd begun to lose Karn, and he also remembered why. It had happened shortly before the plans to take Ferelithia had been made – maybe a month at most. He and Karn had been with a group of tribe mates, sitting around a fire, smoking and drinking into the night. Pharis had been playing hand drums, Rue had been singing. But then somehar had started talking about the prospect of hara breeding, and how the thought made him sick. Karn had said, 'Why feel that way. We have to continue somehow, don't we? Isn't to deny that to reject what we are? You might as well die tomorrow.'

'You mean *you'd* do it?' somehar else had asked, laughing.

Karn had turned to Meladriel then, his smile the reflection of their mutual feelings. 'With the right har, yes. In fact, I know I will. One day.'

This had prompted sarcastic hilarity. And Meladriel had laughed too, punched Karn amiably in the arm, hard enough to bruise. Karn's smile had faltered. He'd appeared wounded, confused. Seladris wished he could have said, 'I want that too', but he'd felt embarrassed in front of their friends. Even so, Karn's implication for their lasting relationship had touched him profoundly. He just couldn't show it. He could make up for it later, though, tell Karn that their future was forever, and whatever Karn wanted from it would come.

But Leupardra, skulking around the campfires, had been drawn to this exchange. He'd seen a precious thing, so beautiful and fragile, and had decided then to break it. He'd sat down among them, his aura in flames. He'd begun his careful, balletic assault. By the end of the night, the first of Leupardra's poisonous tentacles had sunk into Karn's brain, unnoticeable at first, of course, but by the end of a week had possessed him. Who knows what promises he had made?

If Meladriel hadn't laughed, would those tentacles have had any power? Maybe they'd have shrivelled and burned the moment they touched Karn's skin. At that point, Karn and Meladriel been together for nearly six years.

Don't think.

Meladriel changed his clothes. He must go now to *Inglefey.*

The house appeared quiet, almost deserted – perhaps hara were keeping to their rooms or had gone out – but Meladriel was glad to avoid noise and invasive presences. Thazri was in the kitchen with Fallami, seated at the table. They appeared to have been sitting in silence. Thazri got to his feet when he saw Meladriel in the doorway. 'Where's Kaz? Have you seen him?'

'Not today,' Meladriel said. 'Why?'

'He went out last night and hasn't come back,' Thazri said. 'I've sent hara to look for him, but...'

Meladriel met Fallami's glance. Fallami raised his brows.

'Have you tried looking around *Velvets?*' Meladriel said.

'They probably did look there... I don't know,' Thazri replied

'Perhaps *you'd* better find him,' Fallami said.

'OK.' Meladriel sat down, conscious of Fallami's gaze upon him. 'What preparations are left to do?'

'I believe everyhar in Ferelithia is aware of where they must go this evening and what they must do,' Fallami said. 'Caeru, Pharis, Amorel and Katarin have gone into the town. The Tigrina will raise morale, that's his job.'

'Please find Kaz,' Thazri said. '*Please*, Meladriel. I'm worried.'

'If Fallami isn't worried, there's nothing to worry about,' Meladriel said.

'Did I say I wasn't worried?' Fallami asked archly.

'No, but if you were, you'd be out looking for him yourself,' Meladriel replied in the kind of sarcastic tone he usually reserved for his dealings with Kazharn.

Fallami smiled, catlike. His eyes flicked briefly to Meladriel's belly, but the smile didn't waver.

Meladriel paused, then said, 'I'll go and look for Karn, then. Until later, Tiahaara.'

Outside, he asked one of the houseguards for the loan of a horse. A crisp wind blew in off the sea. The day was bright, yet the sky surged with clouds. Meladriel headed for Olivian Grove. Of course, Kazharn would still be at *Velvets*. If hara had looked for him there, he simply hadn't wanted to be found.

Meladriel sent out a message. *I'm coming. Don't waste my time. Just be there.*

There was no response.

To himself he thought, *we're more alike than it seems. He's alone in a family, but I have no family, not even animals apart from the bees, and they hardly share my home. Why have I never owned a horse, or lived with cats and dogs? I don't even have chickens or a goat or cow for milk. I call myself self-sufficient yet barter for everything that involves living creatures. I've lived like a hermit. I'm just as ridiculous as Karn is. I should at least have owned a horse. Punishing myself by dragging a cart everywhere, like somehar out of a dour, moralising fable. Pathetic.*

These thoughts, surprisingly, cheered him.

He urged the horse to gallop up the drive to the house, hoping Kazharn was looking out of a window. There was no tethering rail at the front, though, so his dramatic arrival had to be deflated somewhat by having to go into the stable yard and put the horse into a stall. He gave it a net of hay to nibble, stood for a moment stroking its glossy neck.

The stable was long, dark and silent. No other horses were in residence; they must be out in the paddocks on the hillside.

Somehar came into the building, blocking the light at the entrance. He must have raced out of the house. A voice said lightly, 'Are you armed?'

Meladriel laughed. 'No. They sent me to look for you.'

Kazharn came up beside him. 'I've considered whether it's feasible to run away.'

'It is,' Meladriel said, 'although you won't be remembered in

380

history very fondly.'

There was a silence. Then Kazharn said, 'I don't know what to say, how to make it right. I wish we'd never come here last night. It's ruined everything.'

'No, it hasn't,' Meladriel said. 'Well, only if we let it. I'm sorry I ran off. I didn't cope too well with the idea of impending pearl bearing.'

'I didn't make it happen.'

'I know. But maybe we don't have to deal with it, like I said.'

'Leupardra didn't make it happen either.'

'I know that too. It might not be what we think. Let's just do our job tonight and see what happens afterward.' He paused. 'Thazri is worried about you. You should go to *Inglefey*, reassure him and your staff there. He's still your chesnari.'

'He was never that!'

Meladriel rolled his eyes. 'Well, whatever he was and is, he shares your life and no doubt thinks your bond is chesna. This only goes to show how stupid he is, in my opinion, but never mind that. Do your duty, Municiphar. You've managed to do so for a long time.'

'I think you're wrong,' Kazharn said.

'No, I'm not. You have a family. You have a duty.'

'I didn't mean that. I think you're wrong about the pearl.'

Meladriel stared at Kazharn for some moments. 'Don't *hope*, Karn. Please. It's avoidable hurt. Don't think. Just *do*.'

Kazharn nodded, said nothing.

'Now I've stabled this horse, we might as well spend time together,' Meladriel said, with a brightness that sounded false, even to himself. 'Let's go for a walk. You can show me the clifftop path to the Shrine of Sills, where Rue will be tonight.'

'OK,' Kazharn said, without much enthusiasm. 'I wish we could go and get Ulien, but I know you'll say no to that.'

'We wouldn't get him, I'm sure. It would be dangerous. We need to choose our moment when we're a united front, when we become part of the Army of the Ferelith. Ulien's safe for now.'

'You don't know that. I can't *feel* it. It seems wrong, just doing nothing.'

Meladriel took Kazharn's face in his hands, kissed him. 'Today, we concentrate upon simple pleasures, merely being alive. There is nothing beyond the sun, the sea, the living wind. We'll walk barefoot upon grass and listen to the gulls cry. I'll hold your hand

and you'll feel nothing but contentment, I promise.'

'Impossible,' Kazharn said.

Meladriel embraced him, made him share breath, showering him with the images he described.

When it was over, Kazharn leaned against him. 'I want to tell you something,' he said. 'Something about the past.'

'Not yet,' Meladriel said.

'It's important.'

'Hush. Keep it safe. Save it for tomorrow. We can talk about everything then.' He believed it to be about the pearl, about the memory of that discussion around a campfire – merely because he'd been thinking about it too. He walked out into the sunlight and Kazharn followed.

Chapter Forty-Four

Aghamasday, 4 Fruitingmoon

Before the sun set, hara took up their appointed positions along the cliff tops and beaches surrounding Ferelithia. The town itself was deserted. Hara walked in procession to the ritual sites, carrying torches, as yet unlit.

Meladriel, Kazharn and Fallami would go to the ruins of *Enervation*. Leupardra would feel them approaching. He would know the occupants of the town were working together, in full knowledge of what threatened them. They were not the original human population, frightened and in ignorance. Did he really have so much faith in the Pale Ones that he believed it would be easy?

Caeru would go to the Sill of Shrines with Katarin and a dozen others.

Pharis and Amorel would remain at *Inglefey*, in the copse above the site of the landslide.

Thazri and Ihrec would go to Olivian Grove, to the shrine in the gardens of *Velvets*.

Other high-ranking members of the Municipallion and the Nayati Kelosanya would station themselves at sites that had been chosen beforehand by scrying and by throwing seeds upon a map to identify random locations. Some had experienced visions that had told them where to go. Citizens of Ferelithia would be divided among the sites, Veredis and Tika among them.

Everyhar sang softly as the procession advanced, with different groups peeling off from it to take up their appointed places.

The town looked horrible, defeated and crumbling, but the song assured everyhar present that the damage could be undone, rebuilding would create a Ferelithia more magnificent than before. Kelosanya was a dehar of beauty and love and wild desire. He was a dehar of life and its celebration. Darkness had no part in him, but the ferocity of a protector did.

How still the night was, how breathless.

Caeru took the high path to the Sill of Shrines, Katarin beside him. They were accompanied by hienamas of Kelosanya and three Municipallion peacekeepers. If it wasn't for Katarin, Caeru thought he could so easily fall back through time, to the event when he'd first come to this place. But the Kamagrian was there, solid and real. She would add her voice to his.

The company was silent as they came down the final, narrow track to the Sill. The path was treacherous with loose stones. Somehar slipped, uttered a small sound of surprise, and hands reached to steady him.

Caeru led the way to the centre of the platform, the darkened shrines above and below. The others stood in two lines behind him, Katarin directly at his back. He raised his arms, closed his eyes for a moment, spoke privately to his patron dehara, who were Lunil and Aruhani. Then, he opened his eyes once more, looked down from the high cliff. He saw the soul-lights within the hara of Ferelithia, winding their way to their designated sites, most in position now, for his destination had taken one of the longest times to reach.

He waited for the first call.

Pharis and Amorel walked to the wound in the earth beside *Inglefey*. Amorel felt a tension inside him, faint wisps of terrible memories. Some of the hara from *Velvets* would work with them this night, along with all nearby residents of Shadey Lane.

'Will those *things* come from here?' a har asked nervously, eyeing the turned earth before them.

'No, they are gone,' Pharis said.

'Will they come back?'

'We shouldn't aim for that,' Pharis said dryly. 'Containment didn't work. Dissipation will.'

Amorel's face was pale in the dimming light. He reached out to take the har's arm. 'Don't fear,' he said. 'Stand with me.' Presently, he began to sing, a song so wistful and lovely that it made the hara around him hold their breath. He sang of strength and courage, of the righting of wrongs, of learning and growth. He came to a chorus, and here the song changed, so that others could learn the refrain and join in with it, repeat it into the night, where it became light and sparks and rose upwards.

Within the gardens at *Velvets*, Thazri and Ihrec led a group of hara to the shrine. The group comprised most of Thazri's staff and friends, plus a dozen or so hara from the town. He and Ihrec had decided they shouldn't gather within the shrine itself, but on the top of the hill above it, so they'd be able to see all the torches once they were lit. At this time, they would light their own torches and connect with everyhar else, becoming a web of light and minds.

Thazri knew his life beyond this night was inevitably going to be completely different to how it had been only a week or so before. He wanted to be resigned to this, but part of him… yes, there was still hope. He wanted to believe that at the end of conflict, Kazharn would return to *Velvets* and would hold him and praise him for his part in the defence of Ferelithia. He would see that Thazri was different, a bigger har than before and that more important things mattered to him. *If this is possible, Kelosanya,* Thazri prayed privately, *then I beg you to make it happen.*

Ihrec then began a chant, his voice mournful yet beautiful. Gradually other voices joined in. Ihrec took hold of Thazri's right hand, squeezed it. Thazri opened his mouth to sing, opened his heart to hope.

In Ferelithia, the Pale Ones crawled unseen, quivering, alert, waiting, hungry. The town was utterly motionless, as if feigning death, hoping the threat within it wouldn't notice its shallow breath. Kelosanya, as yet, was unfelt.

Meladriel, Kazharn and Fallami rode to *Enervation*. Before setting off, they'd armed themselves. Kazharn carried a selection of blades, beautiful artefacts that looked as if they should be wielded only in ritual, rather than as weapons that could maim and kill. Meladriel wanted to take his bow, which he used for hunting rabbits and birds, but Kazharn said, 'Don't bother. I doubt we'll have the luxury of distance between us and what we'll face. Take one of my blades.'

Meladriel had agreed, although he still took the bow, and the quiver of arrows he'd made, tipped by iron, fletched by feathers he'd gathered from the forests and moorland.

The roads were dark, and the site itself abandoned, dead. Could anyhar be alive in that place? Meladriel dared not think the worst.

They dismounted some distance from the main entrance, tethering their horses to the trees. Although the gate was unchained, it was locked effectively with tangled vegetation. Kazharn took a knife from his belt, hacked away the vines. A tart, green scent came from their severed fronds. Beyond the gate, steps and terraces led upwards.

Meladriel knew that Leupardra was watching, but there was no sense of how the Pard Witch felt. Was he angry, full of self-confidence? Was he even slightly worried now, seeing the preparations that had been made to thwart him? His attacks had been clandestine, minor. He hadn't gone for any of the major players. This must tell them something, surely?

Meladriel did not feel that he was on his way to a battle. Everything was too quiet and empty. Kazharn was closed off and silent, no doubt wrestling with demons of the past.

We are coming for you together, Meladriel thought, making his words soar to whoever might hear it. *Karn and me. You achieved nothing.*

Fallami gave Meladriel a stern glance.

Kazharn smiled bitterly. His hand clenched upon the handle of the knife. He held it up before him, as if to show it to any unseen eyes that might see.

Timing would be crucial. If Leupardra was allowed even a few seconds to empower his entities, and if the unstorm was conjured too late, they would fail.

'Are you ready?' Meladriel asked.

Kazharn and Fallami gave their assent.

They began to climb.

'Seladris, you must help me now,' Tuli said. He had come into a room that had once been a café, where Seladris and Ulien had chosen to wait. They sat amid rubble at a cracked table, upon a broken bench that just about supported their weight. The cellar had been too dank and dark. Here at least they could see light outside.

'What must I do?' Seladris asked.

Tuli leapt onto the table, crouched there. 'Well... I need to do two things at once. The Pale Ones must be sent out to crush those who think they stand a chance of survival. They've spread themselves out, in an attempt to obstruct me, but are too stupid to see that won't help at all. Nothing can stop the Pales once they're on the move. But... I need also to deal with Karn and Meladriel. They know we're here, which is a good thing, really. Saves time having to seek them out. Now remember, we don't want them dead, Seladris, not at all, but they have a powerful har with them. They must be disabled, and you must use your darkness to do that.'

'Will you not be here to help me?' Seladris asked.

'Part of me will, because I never stop watching, as you know. But I need to concentrate upon the Pales.'

'I see. Very well. That shouldn't be difficult.'

Tuli raised an admonishing finger. 'Don't let any ridiculous feelings of compassion undermine your resolve,' he said. 'I did that once and it was the death of me. Stay cold.'

'I will. Very cold.'

Ulien had been sitting quietly, partly behind Seladris, during this conversation. Now he said, 'What about me?'

Tuli turned his head slowly to gaze at the harling.

'You,' Seladris said with unconvincing levity, 'will help me. Remember what we talked about? We must undo the wrongs of the past.'

Ulien nodded, then jerked his head towards Tuli. 'But he still wants to hurt me.'

'No, he doesn't,' Seladris said. 'He knows how useful and important you are. Isn't that right, Tuli?'

Tuli was silent for a moment, then said, 'Those who help me are rewarded. Those who oppose me are not.'

'There, you see?' Seladris said brightly.

Before he left, Tuli gestured for Seladris to come to him. 'Keep an eye on the harling,' he said. 'I'm still not convinced you were right to release him.'

'He trusts me,' Seladris said. 'I want to keep him. That's OK, isn't it?'

'All right but be alert for tricks. Remember whose blood runs in his veins.'

'He won't trick me. His parents virtually ignore him. He's eager for somehar to care for him. I will do that.'

Tuli nodded. 'Make sure Kazharn knows that when the time comes. I'll be back as soon as I can. Keep your mind open for me.'

Tuli ran away, quickly absorbed by the shadows of the ruins.

Seladris returned to Ulien and slumped back onto the bench. 'It's really difficult saying things that aren't true, but which also aren't lies.'

'Should you say that aloud?' Ulien asked in alarm, eyes wide. 'He could still be watching us.'

'No, he's preoccupied. I can tell. He thinks I'm like him, that I want to be part of him.'

'That sounds dangerous,' Ulien said fearfully.

'They're coming for us, Ulien. Just concentrate on that. We might have to fight but it won't be against those we love.'

When the sun was merely a sliver above the horizon, Caeru's group lit the first of the torches. They held them high, so others stationed at the high places would see them. Gradually, the flames began to spread, like a river of orange and yellow light.

From a vantage point came the first call, sounding like the half-animal cries that Wraeththu had once screamed as they surged into battle. A cry that could still a heart.

Answers came from around the bay. Torches blazed. Caeru lifted his arms, threw back his head. From his body emerged a primal hymn, no words, merely sounds. This sound became amplified, flowed outwards. Others took up the song. Drums sounded and horns were blown. Caeru's skin prickled as if tiny beads of sweat broke out all over him. The Pale Ones had heard the call. It drew them.

The ruins of *Enervation* were eerie and still. Nohar spoke as they climbed what seemed to be endless steps to the buildings themselves. Meladriel could perceive older ruins beneath the cracked concrete, their roots going down into the earth. The air became heavy, requiring more effort to breathe.

But they did not pause.

Eventually, Meladriel stepped onto a wide paved terrace, in the centre of which reared a stilled fountain. At one time, water had gushed from the mouths and loins of attenuated marble *kelosi* – coloured water by the look of it, because the pale stone bodies were streaked with turquoise and saffron, as if with diaphanous scarves that had dried onto them. The scalloped bowl at the base was filled with dead leaves.

Fallami and Kazharn stood motionless behind him.

'What can you sense?' Meladriel asked Fallami.

'What can *you* sense?' he asked in return.

'Not much... strange. I thought the air here would be thick with presences, a thousand versions of Leupardra intent on murder.'

'I certainly don't feel that,' Fallami said. 'The air here is forlorn.'

'Does anything live here?' Kazharn asked. 'Dare I call for my son?'

'Not yet,' Meladriel replied. 'There are more terraces above us before we even reach the main building.'

They began to climb once more. Meladriel extended his senses, probing the environment. He perceived furtive movement in the thick vegetation that shrouded the walls and steps but saw nothing with his physical sight.

They crossed two more terraces, each with their statues and fountains, which were broken and looked thousands of years old but were not.

As they mounted the last flight of steps, Meladriel felt a feathery touch skitter across his mind. His name. *Meladriel.*

He froze and gestured for his companions to do likewise. *Who?* He sent back.

'Me,' said a voice aloud. And there was Seladris, a battered and tattered Seladris, coming down the steps above them.

'Stop!' Meladriel commanded.

Seladris did so. 'It's all right,' he said. 'It's me. *He's* not here.'

'Where's Ulien?' Kazharn demanded. 'Bring him to us. Now.'

Seladris smiled, a little crazily, as if drunk. 'He's safe, don't worry. We've both used our wits and have waited for you.'

Fallami stepped up beside Meladriel, gestured at Seladris. 'Come here.'

Seladris did so. He trod carefully upon the steps, his feet bare and dirty. His arms were badly bruised.

Fallami took Seladris's face in one hand, stared into his eyes. Seladris did not flinch or try to look away. 'He's clean,' said Fallami.

'We're going to get Ulien and leave this place,' Meladriel said evenly. 'Will you help us do that, Dris?'

'Yes. I've been waiting for you.'

'Mela, don't trust this,' Kazharn hissed. 'It's too convenient.'

'He's *unoccupied,*' Fallami said. 'For the moment, anyway.'

Kazharn made an impatient gesture. 'What else is here, though?'

'Nothing's here,' Seladris said. 'Leupardra has gone to Ferelithia to command his creatures. He left me here to disable you. He doesn't know I'm free. I fooled him.'

'Leupardra could come back at any time,' Kazharn said. 'I vote we bind this har before we do anything else.'

'With what?' Meladriel said somewhat tartly. 'Don't be ridiculous, Karn.' He directed his attention to Seladris. 'Take us to Ulien but be aware we're looking into you. If you're genuine, I apologise, but we can't take the risk you're not.'

'I know. Follow me.'

Fallami held out his hand to Seladris. 'Take hold of me,' he said. 'Don't let go.'

'Hurry,' Seladris said. He began to sprint up the steps, almost pulling Fallami behind him. The others followed.

They came to a building and here Ulien ran out to them. His face, which had begun to heal so well, looked swollen again, the wounds leaking. He threw himself against Kazharn, almost toppling him. But before any words could be exchanged, there came a deafening, high-pitched screech, like that of a gigantic bird of prey.

A whirling mass of smoke and rags manifested among them. It enveloped Seladris, dragged him from Fallami's hold.

Meladriel leapt back and, without thinking, snatched an arrow from his quiver, nocked and released it. The pulsating mass exploded outwards – briefly – then coalesced again. Seladris cowered on the ground, his arms over his face. Fallami began to drag him away. Kazharn had retreated down the steps a little, clearly wanting to get Ulien away but knowing also that he should help. He didn't know how. What use could a knife be in this situation?

Grey tendrils thrust out from the roiling mass. They grew hard, like clawed hands, and clicked out to grab hold of Seladris. Again, Meladriel fired an arrow. The entity flinched away as before but didn't appear harmed.

'Leupardra!' Meladriel screamed. 'I call you. Show yourself! Are you brave enough?'

A sound that was part laughter and part screech issued from the shape before them. A part of it broke away and began to twist and writhe. It formed into the egregore of the Cerulopard, a hideous misshapen creature that was hardly leopard at all. Its blue was that of an infected wound. Its jaws dripped poison. It slunk towards Meladriel, uttering a sound that was like bones breaking in a vice.

This was the moment.

Remembering what Fallami had told him about his totem creature, Meladriel visualised an immense swarm of bees flying around him in a shimmering net. He would sting this misshapen beast slinking towards him. With a furious cry, firing in quick succession, he filled the blue leopard with arrows, the bees spiralling around them. The leopard cringed and yowled, shook its head with pain, yet still it came, inexorable, its jaws snapping upon the image of the swarm. Its eyes burned.

What now? Bees were not enough to deter this concentrated sickness of intention. Must he try to fight it with his bare hands and the power of his will?

Then, behind him, he heard Kazharn cry raggedly, 'Here I am, Pard Witch! As before… But you have no power now. You are an illusion! Stay dead!'

Then, a flash of silver, flying past Meladriel's head. He flinched away from it and saw one of Kazharn's knives hit the leopard in the flank. At once, it leapt into the air, twisted and writhed, slithered back into the vile mass from which it had come. Kazharn's blade clattered to the ground. The undulating entity contracted and retreated a little, as if drawing up its limbs defensively. Somewhere within that viscous smoke was Tuli, but he could not be seen.

'Remember me now?' Kazharn spat harshly.

'Hush,' Meladriel said, 'listen.'

Eerie calls resounded from along the coast, those primal sounds that Meladriel had heard so often in the past before battle, when the night air was still, and hara crouched ready to attack.

'Hear that!' he yelled. 'Your monsters can't withstand it. What called them once will undo them. Surrender to us, Leupardra. You have no substance in this world. We do not fear you. Show your true self to us.'

The entity convulsed for a few moments, like hands squeezing some thick viscous material. Then it folded into a recognisable shape. A har stood before them. He looked a lot like Seladris, but this was not the Leupardra Meladriel remembered. Tuli, then.

'Summon your abominations here,' Meladriel said. 'My power against yours. Do you dare to?'

Tuli flared his nostrils, sighed impatiently. Meladriel noticed that his filthy shirt was dark and wet with blood down his left side. So, an etheric injury wounded enough to cause physical hurt.

Tuli glanced at Seladris, who had got to his feet. 'One last chance to redeem yourself,' he said, apparently ignoring Meladriel's challenge. 'I'll overlook your disobedience. Send out your darkness and bind them all. *Unmake* them all!'

Meladriel laughed. 'You have no power to do it yourself?'

'Do it now, Seladris,' Tuli said, 'or I must end you.'

'All right!' Seladris said. He shuddered into a hunched position, his hair hanging over his face in matted tendrils. His skin became mottled, like the charred crust of lava that had crept down the side of a volcano.

Ulien uttered a dismal cry. 'No, Dris. Don't!' He struggled to escape his father's hold, but Kazharn held him firm.

A shape coiled from Seladris, similar in some ways to the entity Leupardra had conjured, smoky, insubstantial, yet somehow hideous to look upon.

This, Meladriel realised, was the expression of Seladris's inner demon, which was also his power. He wondered whether he and his companions could take that on as well as Leupardra.

A guarded mind touch came from Fallami. *Call Oiolyka. Now!*

Meladriel was unsure he'd have the time to do so. What if the unstorm didn't come? Somehar heard his unguarded thoughts. Words misted through his mind.

You do have time.

The mind touch hadn't come from Fallami, nor from Kazharn. Meladriel recognised it at once. Seladris.

You are with us?

Yes. Be prepared. This will be uncomfortable.

Meladriel heard a scream that was both inside his head and in reality. Everything went black. This was not the darkness of night, nor even of being in a room without windows, or a cave far underground. This was an utter absence of light or its possibility. He sensed confusion, movement, his companions in pain. Furious howling. And then Seladris's touch in his mind.

I will give you time. Call it now.

Beyond the confusion, Meladriel could hear the strong, sure voices of the hara of Ferelithia. He could sense the Pale Ones staggering through the streets, drawn this way and that, confused but still hungry. He sensed, as if at some far distance over the horizon, the presence of Oiolyka waiting to manifest. Now, his own voice rang out, and the voices of Ferelithia rose to meet it. He called to the unstorm with wordless invocations drawn from the core of his being. A star of light awoke within him, growing brighter and stronger, a beacon.

He experienced a wrench in his guts, a sharp tug of pain.

This is it, he thought, quite without feeling. It seemed hardly anything to give, after all. Was this even a sacrifice? No, it was simply a dream, an expression of sentimental love, no more than a perfect rose offered from one hand to another, only to be left to fade and die, cut from the stem, withering upon the dry ground. He could almost see it. *Take everything.*

Then there was Kelosanya, filling the sky, visible even in the unlight of Seladris's darkness. *Do you not understand, Meladriel?* said the dehar. *What is the essence of sacrifice? To give of oneself, yes. To give something precious. Lay down your armour.*

Meladriel wasn't sure what this meant but had no intention of lowering his defences. He could sense that Seladris was weakening. Leupardra's power pulsed and writhed in rage within the fragile caul that bound it. This wouldn't last for long. Leupardra was wounded, maddened, so intent upon destruction he might annihilate himself at the same time as he destroyed his enemies. It was clear to Meladriel that Leupardra no longer cared about that. That cloud of diseased darkness, the expression of a mutilated soul, would explode with the power of as much hate and rage that the Pard Witch could muster.

The unstorm was coming, moving too slowly over the sea, expanding as it travelled.

Meladriel felt a surge of energy wash over him. Fallami, clearly in great pain, sought to share his strength, to help Meladriel shore up his defences, give him more time. Not enough, surely.

You must surrender the offering… Now… Meladriel wasn't even sure where that command came from – Kelosanya, himself?

The light within him had become warm. Whatever discomfort Leupardra threw at him was diminished by this. Kelosanya, filling the sky before him, this dehar of love and celebration, had taken on an unfamiliar form. He seemed now to be a dehar of stronger substance. His voice was no floating ethereal star-song but a call to arms.

What do you love, Meladriel, beyond the fire of aruna and the allure of beauty? Is it not your freedom, your isolation, your life upon the fringes of Ferelithia? True sacrifice for you isn't to offer up a new life that you see as a future impediment. No, true sacrifice would be to take responsibility for that life. It is also to immerse yourself in the lives of hara around you, to use the gifts you've been given for the good of all. It is to surrender your precious loneliness at the altar of another's love. I see all, Meladriel. I see how you punished Karn by refusing to hear his apology, his regrets. You knew they were there, even though you have conveniently forgotten. Remember now: others told you. Amorel, before he went away. Pharis, in a sorrowful glance. You knew Karn grieved, but in your pride you drew pleasure from turning your back and keeping it turned, wanting him so badly your yearning became twisted inside you. If you would win your battle, you must learn to give, to forgive and to nurture. Give these things as sacrifice and you will be invincible.

So, these are your terms, Kelosanya, Meladriel thought bitterly. *How you hide your true light.*

Be it so. Do you agree?

You ask me to sacrifice myself. But what choice do I have?

Then say it.

Meladriel wanted no more communication – whether it was with a dehar or with his inner self. He had to give something with meaning. That much was obvious. A harling he didn't want wasn't that. And if he was to take up a life with Kazharn, it couldn't be to inflict death by a thousand small cuts upon him, with coldness and cruel words. And he knew how capable he was of doing that. As the years passed, and the initial fire of desire settled into a more enduring flame, the blade of his tongue would strike. Recriminations, reminders, accusations. He could almost hear it.

I am waiting, Meladriel. Don't think too long about this.

I don't want to be a hostling, nor be responsible for anyhar else in this world, but so be it. Yes. I sacrifice willingly all you ask.

For a moment the dehar felt like a living, ordinary har in Meladriel's mind. *If it's any comfort, and you will not believe it now, you need not feel you've just signed your life away into servitude. What you see as hell might well be joy.*

Just bring it on, Kelosanya. Do your lovely worst.

The grume flowed around him in a sudden rush, like a tidal wave, deadening the world. Meladriel could feel the agony of the others around him as Leupardra's twisted pain crawled through them.

The Eye was nearly upon them.

'Oiolyka,' Meladriel said. 'I call upon you to dismantle all that is evil, all that opposes life and light! Take into your Eye all that is hateful and unwell. Cleanse this place and those within it. I ask this in the name of Kelosanya, dehar of Ferelithia and the life of this land.'

The Eye burst upon them, dispelling all darkness in a brutal, spiralling light, in which spears of solid radiance shot out in all directions. Meladriel felt these shards pass through him, drawing out all that diminished him. He would take up the banner that had once been offered to him.

'I am High Hienama of the Nayati Kelosanya,' Meladriel yelled in a ringing voice. 'Leupardra, I order you to surrender your hold over these bodies you have violated! I order you to submit to me or suffer the consequences, which is unmaking! I will end you!'

'Just try!'

'Oh, I will.' Meladriel imagined his mind was a sun and its rays reached out to everyhar in Ferelithia. *Join with me,* he told them. *I am the High Hienama of Kelosanya and I call for you to add your voice to mine.*

It came as a roar, like the cracking of the earth or the splintering of the sky. Thousands of screaming voices that surged against the Pale Ones and cast them down to dust. This avatar of sound swept through the town, along the coast and up the terraces and steps of *Enervation.* And here, the wave crested, plunged down.

The unstorm vanished as suddenly as it had come. Seladris's caul of darkness withdrew. There was only a fair Ferelithian evening around them, Fallami gasping upon the steps, Seladris sitting dazedly nearby, Kazharn shielding Ulien with his body.

And there was Tuli, hunched down before Meladriel, an emaciated har, battered by life and even more so by the presence of Leupardra, his consuming hate and pain. He raised his head and held up his hands. 'Please, Tiahaar, if he leaves me, I will die. He hurts now. Very small. Tiahaar, do not take my life.'

Fallami got to his feet, brushed down his robe fastidiously, adjusted it around his shoulders. He looked at Meladriel. 'Well, what is your verdict?'

'Is Leupardra still in this har?'

Fallami nodded. 'I see a part of him is. But he's... disarmed. How clear now to see that he was always weak, deluded.'

Meladriel nodded. 'You wore masks, didn't you, Pard Witch, to disguise that fact. Tuli was your strength, your life force. And, I think, there was always far more of Tuli in this world than of you. You offered hope to a life that had none. It was taken. But now is broken.'

Tuli snarled, but weakly. The voice that came from his body was harsher than it had been before, but still it shook. 'I took Karn from you, didn't I? I did that. He was mine.'

'Oh, for a very short time,' Meladriel said. 'I bear no grudge. I pity you. Stand up. We're leaving.'

The snarl fell from Tuli's face, his eyes became unfocused. He appeared dazed, unaware of his surroundings once more.

'Is it safe to take him with us?' Kazharn asked.

'I believe so,' Fallami said.

'And I do too,' Meladriel said. He reached out and took hold of one of Tuli's arms, hauled him to his feet. 'You can't remain in Ferelithia, Tuli. I shall ask the Tigrina to take you to Immanion. You'll find mercy there, I'm sure, and – I hope – healing. Are you agreeable to this?'

Tuli put filthy fingers against his face. 'Don't take my life.'

'I'll assume that was yes,' Meladriel said.

For some reason, he couldn't face looking at Kazharn. He felt awkward, as if the dialogue he'd had with the dehar – perhaps ultimately with himself – had been heard by all. He went to help Seladris stand, began to support him down the steps.

'Mela,' Kazharn said, some feet away. He had lifted Ulien in his arms and the harling's head drooped over his shoulder. But this was not the body of a child, easily carried. Ulien would not be a harling for much longer, that was clear.

'Yes?'

'Are you... well?' Kazharn asked carefully.

'Yes, all of me is well. Nothing is lost.'

All that feeling held within Kazharn – was it intimidating? And would it feel like submission, should Meladriel discard his armour for it? Meladriel didn't like to submit, because it always felt like defeat to him, never compromise. And yet, Kazharn was prepared to accept all of him, had done so in the past until Leupardra had poisoned his young mind, fed his fears and seduced his body.

Remember the days of honey, before Leupardra blighted everything.

It wouldn't happen overnight, but Meladriel could see now there might be a future for them. Somehow. There would have to be changes for both of them, some painful. He smiled at Kazharn; all he could manage for now.

A mind touch came to him. *I wanted you to know, yet now it seems pointless, like I missed my moment. You wouldn't listen to me. But now you must. It was me who killed Leupardra, so long ago. I had to.*

Yes, that's pointless, Meladriel sent back, as a reflex. The information was a kick to the stomach, but also, weirdly a relief. He passed a gentler message. *But it's gone now, Karn. Let it go.*

There's more...

Karn, just leave it, for Aru's sake. We're not finished here yet.

396

I'm going to tell you later. All of it. Whether you want to hear it or not.

Yes, yes… if it makes you feel better. But whatever you did back then doesn't matter to me now. He paused. *I'm sorry. Of course, I'll hear whatever you want to tell me. But mostly I want us to look ahead, not back. We started to reclaim what was ours. We're not done with that yet.*

'Tiahaara?' Fallami said, somewhat sternly. 'Perhaps they still need our assistance below.'

Love me?

Yes. Love me too?

Always.

Together, they descended the steps, left the ruins behind.

Ferelithia

Hara came down to the shore, just to the north of the town, beyond the harbour, where the long white sands began. Ferelithia felt exhausted, beaten, yet now there was peace. It could sleep, drift down and down beneath the sea, never wake again. So tired...

But hara were building fires upon the beach. They weren't tired. They were awake and strong. They uttered cries of victory spontaneously, yet they weren't finished with their work this night.

There was Rue, a long-lost son, hardly recognisable, dressed in leather, a warrior with the heart of soume's greatest secrets. He led more hara to the shore, and they cheered at his arrival. Ferelithia remembered Rue – dancing in the moonlight, a carefree child, the ultimate expression of youth – hedonistic, sensual, but also innocent. Grown now, but still with those qualities within him. He was accompanied by Pharis and Amorel, and many other friends. This was how it should be. They had all done well this night. They should celebrate together.

Should I sink down into the darkness? thought Ferelithia. *Or should I party until dawn?*

Instruments were brought out, as in the days before the recent blight. Musicians and dancers ran over the beach towards the massing group. Drums began to pulse into the darkness over the sea.

Finally, Meladriel walked upon the sand, that troubled son. Ferelithia had always watched out for him, as he sidled round the outskirts of town life. Had always known, perhaps, his isolation wouldn't last. With him were Kazharn, Ferelithia's living avatar, and the visitor from afar, Fallami. Seladris was there too, wounded but joyous. He had found himself in this town. He had beaten the horrors of history. Kazharn's son, Ulien, walked beside him, holding onto his father's arm. Weakened and hurt, but determined to be at this meeting, to walk there on his own feet. A bright and beautiful child who knew more than he could possibly have learned so far in life.

Ferelithia knew the names of all hara that lived within its

boundary. It knew their lights. There was a different light within Meladriel now – a promise for the future. He carried a pearl from which would come a harling who would become a har of importance. More stories for the future.

Ferelithia sighed. If only its heart hadn't been stilled, it could fill with emotion for the bravery of its hara, their hope and radiance.

Hara arranged themselves in an immense circle, in the centre of which burned a fire. Some began to dance, and the drums grew louder. Ferelithia heard the inner voice of Pharis swirling in the air, talking to it directly. *Live! Get up! Live!*

Ferelithia twitched. Could it rise? So tired…

Now Caeru threw up his arms and uttered a wordless song, joined by many others. It was insistent, impossible to ignore. Feet stamped the ground. Hands clapped loudly. Harlings shrieked. Dogs ran about the hara, barking. Cacophony, yet such sweet music.

The egregore of Ferelithia raised itself slowly and at once the pain began to drain away.

Within the beat of hearts and drums, another beat was heard. Hara felt it beneath their feet, all around them in the air. The beat of Ferelithia's heart. They yelled louder, howling into the night their desire to raise and heal.

There was a mighty crack within the town, followed by a strange groaning sound. The ground shook. Hara looked back but did not need to run and see what this meant. They knew because they had ordered it. The main road through Ferelithia, which had been ripped apart some nights ago, became whole again. The rift was sealed. A wind came in off the sea, filled with a mist of brine. It fell as salty rain, sluicing the buildings, washing away the filth of Ferelithia's violation, the dust of its assailants.

Hara were soaked to their skins yet did not cease their ritual of celebration. They laughed and screeched, their hair and clothes plastered to their bodies. And yet the fire at their centre was not extinguished, even when lesser fires went out.

But not every har of the town was there. One had crept away by himself. Ferelithia knew who this was, felt his pain. Poor Thazri.

As the first flush of day appeared in the east, the rain ceased, and all fell silent. Hara were waiting. Some dropped to their knees. And then, before them, a dehar rose from the sea, more beautiful than the dawn. Kelosanya. Aphrodite. Eternal. The sun rose behind the dehar, became one with him. Everyhar saw this vision, and would talk of it often, a tale that would be carried forward through the generations, linking incepted to pure born. The tale of the night they saved Ferelithia, took back what was theirs. And the morning when a dehar appeared before them, seen by their living eyes.

The vision faded slowly, until only a scented breeze remained. Kazharn ordered hara to go back to the town, to bring flowers, as many as they could carry. When this was done, the Municiphar ordered the blooms to be thrown into the sea. The hara of the town walked to the tideline in silence. Once they reached it, the blooms were cast upon the waters.

'We honour all those who ever fought and lived in this town,' Kazharn said in a ringing voice. 'Human, hara, those who lived in fear at the end of days, and those who created a community here. None are forgotten. Kelosanya, we ask you to grant your blessing upon these souls. Henceforth, this day will be a holiday in this place, a time of celebration and remembrance. A time of happiness and song. But we will remember also in silence, at the brink of the sea, the price that was paid before. Astale, Kelosanya. May you burn forever bright.'

A cry went up. 'Astale, Kelosanya.'

Meladriel went to stand by Kazharn's side at the water's edge. Ferelithia could see they held one another, even though their physical bodies did not touch. All was as it should be.

Ferelithia exhaled a breath of flowers and brine, and sang, softly, a song of joy and renewal.

Chapter Forty-Five

In his kitchen, Meladriel looked out upon the morning. He had stayed at the celebration as long as seemed appropriate, but inside he'd felt exhausted and drained. Eventually, he'd had to slip away. Just a swift mind touch to Kazharn. *I need space. I'll see you later.*

The sky was clear, the sea like a plate of rippled glass beneath it. Meladriel was making himself sandwiches of sharp cheese and tart pickle and decided that after eating them he'd go out to sit upon the shore. He felt so overtired he doubted he'd be able to sleep, although that was all he longed for. Also, his mind was so full of thoughts it had jammed into frenzied loops, but he *could* sit in peace, breathing out the frenzy, staring at the water. Better to be numb, soothed by the voice of the depths.

It was all over now, wasn't it? Pharis had dealt with Tuli, sent him into a deep sleep. Kazharn had arranged for the har to be confined within the Nayati Kelosanya, guarded by hienamas, although it was doubtful he would wake for at least twelve hours.

Meladriel sat down at the table, picked at his food. The cheese and pickle tasted too strong and the tastes didn't complement each other as they should. His senses were off kilter. He noticed his plate was chipped.

What would happen to him next? There could be no easy extraction from all that had happened. Emotional mess, the reconstruction of Ferelithia's damaged buildings, new relationships, the fact he'd stupidly appointed himself High Hienama, (which wouldn't be forgotten, and might not even be welcomed by everyhar), not to mention the forthcoming, inevitable thorny dealings with Immanion. He'd stood at Kazharn's side before the entire population of Ferelithia, at a moment some might think should have belonged to Thazri. He could foresee only future unpleasantness. Would it be possible to slip away from it all, back into his old life, and let other hara deal with everything? Until he had one more life to deal with, of course. How, in all the dehara's names, was he ever going to cope with having a harling? The thought of caring for another life all day every day was horrifying. *No need to think of that yet*, he thought. And what of his renewed closeness to Kazharn? They couldn't walk away from this. Their defences lay in tatters around their feet. They faced each other raw.

Meladriel heard a horse's hooves outside. *So, he can't sleep either, or has been driven out from home. Or something.*

Kazharn knocked but came right in, said somewhat tentatively, 'Is this all right with you? I need to lie down in peace, that's all.' He too looked worn to a thread.

Meladriel went to him, embraced him briefly. 'I'll give you breakfast. Sit down.'

Kazharn did so, and for some moments rested his arms on the table, his head upon them. He looked so young, vulnerable.

What masks we create, Meladriel thought. 'They're all still at *Inglefey*, the whole circus?' he asked, slicing bread.

Kazharn raised his head. 'Yes, the place is packed. They're all so relieved and happy. It was driving me insane. It took me an age to get away. Why the hell won't they sleep?'

Meladriel laughed. 'Well, let them have their fun. You're welcome to stay here.' There was quiet for a few minutes as Meladriel finished making another batch of sandwiches. These he placed on a plate and set it before Kazharn.

'Give me something alcoholic as well,' Kazharn said. 'I need it.'

Meladriel provided a full glass of yenayva, undiluted, and poured a glass of mild beer for himself. He sat opposite Kazharn at the table, arms folded on the wood. 'So? What are you going to do?'

Kazharn drank from the glass, winced. 'I can't live a lie any longer. Today I'll speak to Thazri.'

'I don't envy you that.'

'But are you happy about it?' Kazharn took a bite of sandwich.

Meladriel said nothing, reached out to take hold of Kazharn's free hand. His skin felt cold to the touch.

'I'll have to leave *Velvets*, obviously,' Kazharn said. 'I was thinking of finding another property, smaller... somewhere on the coast. Near here, perhaps?' He hesitated, as if preparing to weather an attack.

'Sounds like a good plan,' Meladriel said carefully.

'I thought maybe... we could spend time together in a place like that. Not that I expect you to abandon your home. Nothing like that.'

'Karn, stop it. You don't have to tread on eggshells around me. We've gone past that, haven't we? We were both to blame for losing one another, yet equally *not* to blame. We're grown up now... mostly. Anyway, I'm going to make an effort to curb my inner bitch, if you could curb your inner school teacher.'

'*School teacher?*'

'That whole, "I know best" thing you have. You know what I mean. Anyway – deal?'

'All right,' Kazharn said, then shook his head. 'I can't believe you think I'm like that.'

'Well, you are. Anyway, I really don't think I can live with somehar else full time...' He grimaced. 'Of course, I'll have to eventually...'

'You won't have to cope with that alone, Mela. What do you think I am? We'll share that responsibility.'

'Or you could find me an Ihrec, I suppose. My principles might go sailing out to sea at the prospect of a carehar.'

'Consider it done.'

Meladriel grinned. 'No, it feels like cheating. But maybe somehar to give me space now and again when you're busy. I don't want to be a Thazri, with staff doing everything for me. It's disgusting. If I'm to be a hostling, I might as well attempt to do it properly.' He released Kazharn's hand and dragged his fingers through his hair. 'The problem is, I've lived alone since... *then*. I don't know how to spend all that time with other hara, even ones I care for. I'm sure you'll irritate me like crazy, and probably our harling will too, so yes, I'll need to keep this house. It can be my workplace and my retreat, but I'm willing to try living with you, as a family, as much as that makes me curl up inside like a spider threatened by imminent death. If it doesn't work out, we can think again. The fact is...' He groaned. 'Even now I hate to say it, but we're in love, so have to put up with each other.'

'I've never heard anything so romantic.'

'Thank you. Does Thazri know where you are?'

'I told him I was coming here, to you.'

'And he of course gave you his blessing.'

'Not quite. Let's just say he's not as relieved and happy as the rest at *Inglefey*.' Kazharn pulled a sour face, then softened. 'I've been thinking about him too. There *is* a balm I can apply to the wound. He fears losing his status in the town more than losing me. If we're no longer a couple, most of those shallow idiots he spends his time with will disappear, because it won't be so prestigious to know him. Being the *ex* of the Municiphar is nowhere near as impressive as being his consort. However, in the light of an inevitable closer relationship with Immanion, I'll suggest Thazri's given a position in the Municipallion, as a liaison representative with the Gelaming. He gets on with Rue, and admires him greatly, of course, so that might mollify him.'

'Might. He does care for you, unfortunately.'

Kazharn frowned. 'I can't see that.'

'I can, but you're right in one respect. Giving him status of his own will help.'

'There are aspects of life we'll still share. He's still the hostling of my son.'

Meladriel pulled a mordant face. 'Yes. And what will Ulien think about all this?'

Kazharn smiled. 'He likes you a lot. I can't see a problem there. Sadly, we've never been a close family, so it's not as if he has to witness loving parents breaking up. He has an old head on young shoulders, and very soon he'll be going through feybraiha, becoming adult. I'd like you teach him about the things his current tutors cannot – the magic of our world, its creatures, its histories, both hidden and recorded. He must become truly har, using his natural abilities fully. I don't want him to neglect all that, as I did.'

Meladriel smiled, refilled Kazharn's glass. '*When* exactly were you having all these ideas?'

'After you stormed out on me last night.'

'I see. Do you think you'll still be Municiphar, once the dust has settled?'

Kazharn shrugged. 'If I'm honest, last night part of me hoped not. But from what my colleagues have said to me this morning, it seems I've been redeemed to some extent.'

'Well, nohar does it better than you, so they'd be stupid to get rid of you really. Only an idiot would want your job… if they weren't you, of course.'

Kazharn made no response to this remark. He looked apprehensive. 'Mela, I have to tell you the truth about the past. We can't attempt a life together if that lie is between us.'

'You killed Leupardra. So what? I'd have done the same given the chance.'

'It isn't just that. I lied to you about other things. I didn't want you to know because… well, I thought we'd never be with one another again. It's a bad story, and a part of my life I'll regret for ever. I'm risking what we have by telling you, but will you listen?'

'OK,' Meladriel said, a little worried about what Kazharn might say.

The full story was difficult to sit through. What Meladriel had believed had happened was bad enough, but the second wave of killings was something he'd never suspected. He couldn't help interrupting at that point.

'How could you do that? These were your friends, hara of your tribe. They'd done nothing except offend Leupardra. Were you really so in thrall to him?'

Kazharn stared at him steadily. 'I did what we all did to get through difficult times – I altered reality in my head. That's no excuse, I know. But I was obsessed with Leupardra. He wasn't just a megalomaniac psychopath, but charming, funny, beautiful and full of promises. He made us think what we did was essential. I did terrible wrong. I know that. I'll never be able to forget.'

'Was this why you threw yourself so fully into making Ferelithia what it is? Your atonement?'

'You don't need to ask. I'm not saying it's atonement enough, however.'

Meladriel found it hard to remain calm about how much Kazharn had withheld at the initial stage of their investigation. There had been no trust at all. How had they got past that? Accord had come upon them quietly, sneaking beneath the sniping and snarls, almost barely noticed. He knew then he had to sit and listen without flinching. This was the har he had lost and found, the har he loved.

'We gradually realised that Leupardra and his Cerulopard followers would have to go,' Kazharn said. 'Our leaders were worried about their own futures. The whole situation had got far too nasty, even for them. Leupardra had greater plans. He wanted to take Thiede on.'

'Perhaps you should have let him,' Meladriel said dryly.

Kazharn shook his head. 'We did think of that, but decided it was too dangerous, too much of a gamble. Leupardra would have gone to any lengths for power, which I don't think Thiede did, or would. He *might* have become as great as Thiede, or at the very least carved out some kind of cruel empire for himself that could have made even the Varrs and Kakkahaar look tame. You must agree that the idea of Leupardra being a figurehead of our kind is an extremely dark one.'

'Wholeheartedly!' Meladriel said, horrified by the thought.

'So... He *did* have to go, and the leadership asked me to deal with it, because Leupardra trusted me. By that time, the enchantment that held me in stone to him was beginning to crack and those around me could see it. We knew how powerful Leupardra was and, because of that, how difficult to remove. We couldn't just vote him out, tell him to go. There was, to everyhar's eyes, only one way to rid ourselves of him. I agreed to do it, because I was afraid of him. I wanted to be free of him. He had ruined my life, made a murderer of me. I had lost the har I loved. And what other option did we have? He was crazy. I think working with the Pale Ones made him far worse.'

'How did you...?' Meladriel couldn't complete the question. He felt nauseous.

'A blade. It happened at *Inglefey*.'

Meladriel put his hands against his face. 'That explains so much.'

'I know. Imagine how I felt when you came to me with that story about the place. And I couldn't tell you.'

'How could you *sleep* in that house over the past few days?'

'I didn't. I avoided *Inglefey* as much as possible. Didn't you notice?'

'Meetings in town... of course. The watertight excuse. And the mysterious absconsions at night.'

'I'd have had to be chained to the bed to stay there, and even then would have gnawed through a limb to escape.'

Meladriel smiled thinly. 'So... Leupardra vanished...'

Kazharn nodded. 'As did his followers, although I had no hand in that. The hara who'd been responsible began to creep away to other lands. Those of us who remained let hara think Leupardra and his phyle went with them, although some suspected the truth. Rumours of Leupardra's death arose. We didn't stop them. But I was left alone to cope with the results of my decisions, my actions. And you... had gone.'

Meladriel sighed. 'I wish you'd come to find me back then, knocked some sense into me,' he said. 'I wish I'd been there for you. I wish I'd not left Ferelithia, because I'd have taken that burden from you in a heartbeat. I wish I'd been the one to stick that little snake with a knife. I wish you didn't have to live with it, because I can see, deep down, despite your words, you feel what you did was wrong. I wouldn't have killed *for* the Pard Witch but would never have considered it wrong to end *his* life. He was poison, *evil.*'

Kazharn sighed sadly. 'I won't lie... I never will to you again... but quite honestly, I wish all that too.'

'You'd let me kill for you. How sweet!' Meladriel took Kazharn's hands in his own. 'How strange it is that Seladris came to this town, trailing ghosts so similar to our own and to Leupardra's, to the town itself. I think he was a catalyst, but an essential one. He swung events in our favour last night. We owe him a great debt.'

'Fallami made sure everyhar knows what he did,' Kazharn said. 'He's not well, and they put him to bed before I left, surrounded by grateful hienamas to aid his sleep and recovery. I could tell he was happy with their gratitude. To hear it from you, though... I think that would mean a lot more to him.'

Meladriel nodded. 'He's an exceptional har, and if I've contributed to helping him heal in any way, I'm glad to have done so. I'll speak to him tomorrow.'

'The first day of your new career. Congratulations!'

'Don't push it, Karn,' Meladriel said. 'Bed?'

'That would be welcome.'

To Ulien, *Velvets* felt different. There was an emptiness at its heart. This must, of course, be because his father had gone. It hadn't been a shock to discover Kazharn had left the house to go to Meladriel. There had been a rather uncomfortable meeting between father and son in the afternoon, when Kazharn had come back to the house, braced to deal with difficult meetings. At first, they'd spoken of the night before, with Kazharn reassuring Ulien he was now safe. 'Leupardra is truly contained now,' he'd said. 'Tuli will be taken to Immanion. It's no longer our problem.' He'd stroked Ulien's face. 'Your scratches are so much better already. How do you feel?'

'Tired, and a bit dazed, but otherwise fine. I *am* fine inside, if you were worried about that.' Ulien had sighed. 'But I suppose that has to be checked and tested.'

'Well, wouldn't it be safer, just in case?'

Ulien had shrugged glumly. 'I suppose I'll have to endure it.'

'I'll make sure it's as brief as possible, and not at all uncomfortable.'

There'd been a pause, then Ulien had said, 'I have no right to complain. I *should* be examined because I was stupid. So stupid I could've damaged myself forever.' He'd swallowed hard, determined not to succumb to tears. 'I'm sorry for the mistakes I made. Meladriel said I mustn't be angry with myself, but I am.'

'As the days pass, so the anger will fade, and so will the bad feelings inside,' Kazharn had said. 'I'll help you, I promise. None of it was your fault, Uli. A cruel clever har took advantage of your youth, that's all.'

After that had come the more uncomfortable conversation. Kazharn had tried to explain to Ulien why he must move out of *Velvets*. Ulien had felt like he was the parent, reassuring a troubled harling. 'I understand,' he'd said. 'I could tell from the start there was something between you and Mela. Only an idiot wouldn't have seen it.'

For a moment, they'd smiled at one another, not daring to laugh because they'd both thought the same thing, which was too cruel to voice aloud. Then Kazharn had said, 'Hara had their suspicions, though.'

'Yes, Ihrec did. Hara talk.'

Kazharn had nodded thoughtfully, then brightened. 'I'm going to find a house, smaller than this one, near to the sea and to Mela's cottage. I want you to think of it as your second home. You'll have your own room and can come and go as you please. I feel confident there are no dangers to harlings in Ferelithia now! You'll need a pony of your own, of course, to come to me.'

'Will Mela live there too?'

Kazharn had laughed, a little awkwardly. 'Well, he'll be there a lot, I'm sure.'

'Will he teach me?'

Kazharn had reached out and stroked his son's face. 'Yes, of course he will. He should probably teach us both, although he claims he still has much to learn himself.'

'I'm happy for you, Kazzi. It's right this should happen.'

Ulien had felt there was more Kazharn had wanted to say, but that had not been the right moment. He'd had Thazri to talk to next, after all. They'd embraced and said farewell and had arranged to meet the following afternoon, when Kazharn would take Ulien with him to begin the search for a house. Ulien felt excited about that. He loved exploring and what strange old places might still stand on the coastal road? He'd felt compelled to get out of the house for a while after that, not wanting to be anywhere near his parents while their fateful discussion took place.

Now the rest of the afternoon stretched out before him and Ulien wandered the gardens, thinking. He did feel good about the future. He liked the idea of having a second home, where he might have more freedom (because his father was certainly a changed har) and he also longed to have Meladriel as his teacher. He fantasised about what this might be like, the amazing things he'd learn. He imagined also having his own private space in a wonderful old house that spooked him as much as he loved it. There would be no evil hauntings, though. Only adventures to experience.

Hunger led him back to *Velvets* in the early evening. The moment he stepped in through the window doors to the main sitting room, an air of oppression fell over him. The house was too quiet.

I have to find him, Ulien thought. *He'll need me.*

It took a while. Ulien searched all the downstairs rooms, found Ihrec in the kitchen, talking in a lowered voice with a few of the staff. They went quiet as he came in.

'Where's Thazri?' Ulien asked.

'He wants time alone,' Ihrec replied. 'Dinner will be in an half an hour, Uli. We'll eat in here today, OK?'

'Yes,' Ulien said. 'I'll be back soon.' He raced upstairs.

Thazri wasn't in his own room, nor in Ulien's. Ulien opened every door, but there was no sign of his hostling. But then, of course... those other rooms. He went to Kazharn's apartment. And here, sure enough, his search was over.

Thazri was sitting on the end of the immense bed. He wasn't weeping, nor were his eyes red. He was completely still, his hands clutching each other in his lap. One of Kazharn's old guitars lay on the bed beside him. Clearly, Kazharn hadn't yet removed all of his belongings.

'Thaz?' Ulien said at the door.

Thazri looked up. He was like a stranger, diminished, shrunken. He didn't say anything.

Ulien went to the bed and sat beside his hostling. He reached out and put a hand over Thazri's own. He was freezing. 'Ihrec said we'll have dinner in the kitchen.'

'I'm not hungry,' Thazri said. 'Don't worry. Go ahead, Uli. You must eat. You've been through a lot.'

'We both have. But we have to go on now.'

Thazri shuddered then. 'I'm not sure how I can…' He couldn't continue.

Ulien put his arms around Thazri, kissed his hair. He didn't know what to say.

'He's offered me things, Uli,' Thazri said.

'What things?'

'A place in the Municipallion. A title. An income. He wants me to represent Ferelithia with Immanion.'

'That's all good… isn't it?' Ulien said.

'He thinks it'll make me feel better. He thinks all I care about is prestige and position.' Thazri looked up at Ulien. 'Is that why I've lost him, Uli? Is it? He thinks I'm a shallow empty excuse for a har.'

'No…' Ulien took a deep breath. He shouldn't have to talk to a parent like this, yet the words were inside him and he knew they were important. 'It's got nothing to do with how you are. He was always Meladriel's. You know that. He was just… on loan for a while.'

Thazri uttered a wavering laugh. 'You sound twenty years older than you are.'

'I think it's true, though. Don't be too sad. Well, not for long. There'll be good things for us soon, I know.'

Thazri enclosed Ulien's hand in his own. 'Your feybraiha for one. It won't be long, Uli. I expect all that's happened will bring it on sooner.'

Ulien didn't want to think about that. 'Mmm. I meant more… in the town, with friends. Aren't you curious about working with the Municipallion? You might even go to Immanion sometimes, be part of Caeru's circle. Won't that be exciting?'

Thazri examined Ulien shrewdly. 'I'm not an imbecile, Uli. At this moment in time, those are the last things I care about.' He sighed, glanced around the room, which felt as if it had been abandoned for years. 'I mostly slept alone, across an expanse of house, and yet… to know these rooms will never be used again… It's… weird. I miss him so much, even though he was hardly here. Maybe I *am* mad, after all.'

'You're grieving,' Ulien said. 'That's allowed. Please don't stay here, though. Will you come downstairs, just to be with me? We can have our dinner in the sitting room.'

Thazri sighed. 'All right. Let me have a few more moments, though. I'll be down in a while.'

Walking downstairs, Ulien experienced a pang of guilt that his life had suddenly got so much more thrilling while Thazri's had – to him – diminished. Thazri wouldn't have his own room at Kazharn's new house. He wouldn't be taught by Meladriel. The thought of his own son having those things would no doubt cause him pain. Ulien wondered how he could stop feeling bad about his good fortune. He wanted to show everyhar his happiness, to tell them about it, but he couldn't because Thazri was so upset, and unbounded joy and excitement in the house would be inappropriate. These thoughts, perhaps, were the first symptoms of feybraiha.

He went into the kitchen and asked Ihrec if he could speak alone with him. Ihrec came into the hallway and shut the kitchen door. 'What is it Uli?'

'I've been with Thazri,' he said. 'I'm not sure how to deal with him. He's so sad.'

'He's had a shock,' Ihrec said. 'He never thought Kazharn would end their arrangement, that's all. It means big changes for all of us. You know that. We need to let Thazri work through it and be there for him if he wants company, but we mustn't smother him.'

'He's coming down for dinner, but we'll eat in the sitting room.'

'It's good he's doing that. Well done for persuading him.' Ihrec smiled. 'Don't worry, Uli. Thazri is a strong har. He's just… disorientated at the moment. I know him very well. He'll be all right.'

'Will you join us later?'

'If he asks for me.'

'No. Just join us later. Please? I think he'll want to see you.'

Ihrec appeared unsure. 'If it wasn't you asking, I'd say no. I've suffered the consequences of crossing Thazri's boundaries before.'

'It'll be different now.'

Ihrec nodded. 'Perhaps you're right. I'll join you after dinner. Bring coffee in.'

'Perfect.' Ulien hugged Ihrec. 'Thank you.'

He went out into the garden for a while as the preparations for the meal were completed. Bronze evening light slanted across the lawns and flower beds. Ulien extended his senses, just a little. Could he still travel in the way Tuli had taught him? He was afraid to try. It might bring something awful down upon him. But he could feel *something* – a tremor in his body, an urge to fly. Soon he would have a teacher who might help him explore and control this ability – if it was truly still there.

Chapter Forty-Three

Aloytsday, 7 Fruitingmoon

Seladris had allowed himself to be looked after for two days. He'd once had parents who'd cared for him like this. Even if he couldn't remember much of that time, to bask in nurturing attention was more healing than the healing itself. Eventually, though, he'd had to face he no longer felt weak but restored. He must shake himself, get out of bed and see what could be done with his life. It would help when his house was his own again. The *Velvets* hara had returned home, but Pharis, Fallami, Amorel, Rue and Katarin were still at *Inglefey*. It hadn't been made clear to him for how long. Still so much to talk about, apparently. Meladriel did not come to the house. Perhaps he was avoiding everyhar because of the rumours that had broken out, which had already been confirmed as news rather than speculation. Meladriel's life, clearly, had changed dramatically. Seladris told himself not to break over this. The news was hardly a surprise, merely inevitable. Life must move on.

After breakfast, Seladris walked to *Confitteri*, unsure of what he'd find. But the doors were open, and hara were busy at work inside. There'd been breakages and some equipment would need to be replaced, but the damage could have been far worse. The air no longer smelled of delicious baking ingredients but of damp and mould. By the end of this day, he supposed, that would be remedied. Heading to his workroom, Seladris managed to avoid any large groups of colleagues. Those he passed greeted him cordially, if a little awkwardly. Once in his own room, he closed the door and began to assess the damage. Water had got in and ruined all of his notes, including some he'd had for years. The bases of cakes that had been prepared to fulfil orders had of course gone rotten. There was a large crack in one wall. Two windows were broken.

As he was depositing items for disposal into an empty flour sack, the door burst open and Seladris was grabbed from behind. At first, he thought he was under attack, until he was turned around and saw that Veredis had him. 'They said you were here!' Veredis exclaimed.

'Why didn't you come to me at once?'

Seladris pulled himself free. 'I was clearing up.'

Veredis shook his head. 'I'm not sure you should even be back here yet.'

'I'm fine. Please don't fuss. I just want to take up where I left off – if that's all right with you.'

'Of course. Don't be ridiculous.' Veredis paused. 'Are you angry with me, Dris?'

'Angry? Why should I be?'

Veredis sighed. 'Because I doubted you. If you don't know that already, I want you to hear it from me now, because I'm sure it'll get back to you, one way or another.'

Seladris continued to tidy up. 'Doubted me? You mean you think I was a willing participant in Ulien's kidnap? Or worse?'

Veredis shrugged awkwardly. 'Not think – *thought*. I'm sorry. It just seemed like a possibility, after all you'd told us about yourself. I'm so glad I was wrong.'

Seladris didn't say anything.

'You'll be staying on here, then?' Veredis asked.

'I didn't have any other plans. There are orders waiting, which I suppose hara will still need after all the fuss has died down.'

'I thought *our leaders* might have other plans for you.'

Seladris shook his head. 'Not that I know of.'

There was a silence, then Veredis said, 'Please tell me everything's OK between us. I can't bear thinking it's not.'

Seladris smiled wanly. 'Everything's OK. Don't fret. I'm still rather dazed, that's all.'

'I hope you'll tell me about it, when you feel ready. Will you come to dinner tonight? I mean... not to tell Tika and me things, just to eat.'

'Thanks. I will.'

'Excellent. I'll send somehar to help you clear this mess up. See you at lunch maybe.'

'Yes. See you later.'

Once Veredis had left, Seladris laughed to himself. That har would never win awards for tact or diplomacy. Still, his manner was endearing in a strange sort of way. And who could blame him for thinking the worst? For a while it could have been true. And Veredis at least valued their friendship. That could not be said for others, it seemed.

Resolving to put such thoughts aside, Seladris continued to

work. A young har came to help him and at lunchtime they were called to the garden, where a buffet meal had been set out for all the staff. The moment Seladris appeared in the garden, Veredis swooped down and embraced him, making it clear to everyhar what Seladris's position was in the pecking order at *Confitteri*. 'I think we need a cheer for our hero!' he yelled.

Seladris cringed in embarrassment. 'Ved, please don't.' Too late, hara were cheering him.

Veredis kissed his cheek. 'Lap it up,' he said, grinning. 'You deserve it.'

Seladris pulled a pained face. 'That kind of thing… It's not really me.'

Veredis laughed heartily. 'Don't we know it!' He paused, gazing across the garden. 'Oh…'

'What?'

'I assume that har over there isn't here to see me.'

Seladris saw Meladriel standing at the gate to the garden, clearly looking for somehar. Without saying a word to Veredis, he hurried at once across the lawn, wriggling as discreetly as possible through the crowd of hara. Once at Meladriel's side, he pushed the har through the gate and closed it behind them. 'Come,' he hissed, dragging Meladriel by the arm into the bakery.

'Hello, good to see you,' Meladriel said, laughing.

'Shut up. Don't let them see you. I can't bear more talk, even though Veredis is no doubt announcing it to everyhar at this very moment.'

'What talk?'

'Just making a meal out of things. I don't want them talking about anything.'

Seladris took Meladriel to his workroom. He not only closed the door but locked it.'

Meladriel raised his brows. 'Can you enlighten me as to my fate? Death by eggbeater?'

Seladris shook his head. 'Maybe I *wasn't* ready to return here. Anyway, how can I help you?'

'I'd like three cakes please.'

'Seriously?'

'No. I'm here to see how you are.'

'Oh… fine, fine. Considering.' Seladris paused. 'I hear you're to be congratulated.'

Meladriel pantomimed puzzlement. 'On what?'

'Landing a Municiphar. Is it true?'

Meladriel shrugged. 'I think you know the answer. Let's just say we had an argument that lasted decades but have matured enough to make up. I'm sorry if I made you think... well I'm not going to say what, because we both hate that sort of thing.'

'No need to apologise. It's been a strange time. Strange things happen. Strange notions.'

'Timing, really.'

'Yes. Timing.' Seladris smiled tightly.

'What are your plans now?'

'Just to carry on. I like it here,' Seladris said, hoping his voice sounded airy. In fact, there appeared to be a stone in his throat. 'I have my house now, free of hauntings.'

'That's good to know. I hope we'll see each other. We've been through too much not to remain friends.'

'There's no reason we can't be.' Seladris paused. 'You *saved* me, Mela. You exorcised my demons. You united my being. There aren't enough expressions of thanks in the world that could cover my gratitude.'

'We worked together,' Meladriel said. 'I believe you were meant to come here and help sort out the messes of the past. Neither of us are in each other's debt. It was simply a task we had to do.'

'You're so gracious!'

Meladriel laughed. 'Well... I suppose I have to learn to be now. At least we'll have each other to complain to about public life.'

'Yes, shells are broken it seems. We can't crawl back into them.'

'Well... You never know what might be found upon the shore.'

Seladris smiled, didn't comment. 'I would like to make an order for honey in the near future.'

'A special cake?'

'Maybe.'

'Let me know.' Meladriel paused. 'Well, I'd better go. I just wanted to drop in on you before anyhar else, even though I did have to go to *Inglefey* first to track you down. I'll see you soon.'

'I'll look forward to it.'

Meladriel nodded, walked to the door, then stopped. 'Fuck it,' he said, walked back to Seladris and took him in his arms. Seladris didn't resist. Why should he? He shared breath with Meladriel until his inner sight was prickling with motes of light, and there was no more breath to give.

'Sorry, I just had to.'

'It's fine,' Seladris said.

'I wanted you to know that you mean something to me. I love Karn with every mote of my being and want our lives to be one for ever, but you and I have shared too much not to be close. The best of friends.'

Seladris slapped Meladriel on the chest with both hands, pushed him away gently. 'Shut up. Just go now before it gets awkward.'

'See you soon.'

'Yes.'

Seladris had to lean against the wall for five minutes before he felt steady enough to walk outside.

Veredis was lurking at the garden gate, a quivering mass of enquiry. Seladris smiled at him.

'Well!' Veredis said. 'Will you be bringing a guest with you tonight?'

Seladris laughed, rolled his eyes. 'No.'

Veredis laughed also. 'I meant Caeru, actually. Could you manage that? Bring the Tigrina to my house?'

'Are you serious?'

'Well, I wasn't, but looking at your face now, I'm not so sure.'

'I'll see what I can do.'

Veredis put his hands against his mouth, his eyes wide.

'Don't explode,' Seladris said. 'He might say no.'

At *Inglefey*, Katarin har Roselane was preparing to leave. Caeru was disappointed. He had big plans for a more formal celebration in the near future and wanted Katarin to stay for it. He stood with her outside the house as they awaited a *sedu* that was coming to collect her. There were some minutes before one could arrive.

'Do you really have to go?' Caeru asked, for perhaps the fifth time.

'Yes. I took time out from work to come here but need to get back. There are other delicate situations in the world, you know.'

'Is it just that, though?'

Katarin sighed. 'Really, Rue. I'm not that much of a party type and as far as I'm concerned, the real celebration took place on the shore at the climax of our rite. There's nothing more to add, other than hara congratulating each other again and having an excuse to get drunk.'

'Why do you always feel so excluded, Kate?' Caeru demanded abruptly. 'Don't deny it. I know what you think. You make it happen, though.'

Katarin put a hand on Caeru's arm. 'It's just what is,' she said gently. 'Don't say any more. It's just what is.'

'But…'

'I did the job you asked me to do. Now it's done.'

At that moment, a portal opened and a *sedu* came through, shaking its mane, scattering ice crystals. Katarin spoke to it softly, then vaulted onto its back. She glanced at the house, as if expecting somehar to come out. Then turned away.

'When will I see you?' Caeru asked. 'Will you be with us for Shadetide this year?'

'Probably,' Katarin said. 'Have fun, Rue.' She blew a kiss to him, was gone.

Caeru sighed. Some things he couldn't fix, nohar could.

In the house, Amorel and Pharis were lying in Amorel's bed. They had taken aruna together, which Pharis continued to insist was therapeutic. Amorel could think of no good reason to argue about it. They had spent most of the time since the ritual in that room. But now Pharis was talking about his family, his life in Alba Sulh. He painted an idyllic picture. 'I have all that to go back to,' he said, 'and much as this trip has been *interesting* and educational, I'm looking forward to going home. What about you?'

Amorel was silent for a moment. 'I *have* been thinking about it. What you describe… I've never had that. All I've got is a chesnari who feels like I merely hire him a couple of times a year, and a son I barely know. A lonely life in a lonely spot. The only positive aspect is my music.'

'You can have that anywhere, can't you?'

Amorel sighed. 'I suppose so.'

'I'll let you in on a secret,' Pharis said, grinning. 'I'm going to abduct you.'

'What?'

'After Rue's big party – which as we both know is really a cementing of more intimate relations between Ferelithia and Immanion – I'm going to take you home with me.'

'Won't that be… a bit, well… awkward?'

Pharis pulled a quizzical face. 'Are you mad? Did you think Aedi would be jealous because I roon with you?'

'Well, don't chesnari feel that way about that sort of thing? Proper ones, I mean.'

'Don't be absurd. He knows all about you and what healing methods I've used. I've kept in touch with him since I got here.'

Amorel sighed. 'You have great talents, Pharis. I can barely send a mind touch across a room.'

'I trained. But anyway, I've already asked Aedi how he feels about it, and he wants you to come to us too. I think he's planning on grilling you about my past.'

'I don't know...'

'It won't be forever, just a couple of months. You'd become bored of Herne's Chase eventually. You're not a naturally rustic type. But we'll get you completely sorted out and then you can plan for the future. Maybe you should come back to Ferelithia then. You have hara here who care about you as much as I do. I think a sound base, with real friends around you, would help keep you on the right path in life. You still have so much music in you, Rel, but you must write it in contentment. Believe it or not, and despite what tortured artists of all types have claimed since the dawn of time, that is actually possible.'

'Ferelithia...' Amorel turned onto his back, stared at the ceiling. 'I should be worried about my tour now, thinking about how I can repair things and get it moving when I go home. But then...' He glanced at Pharis. 'Now I'm away from it, it doesn't seem so important.'

'You don't have to make decisions yet, Rel. Just tell your hara you're in retreat and will be in touch once you're well.'

'I think I *am* well... mostly.'

'Don't tell them that.'

There was a pause, then Amorel said, 'Thank you, Pharis. For all you've done.'

'No need. I like mending broken things.'

'I was as broken as it's possible to get and remain alive, I think,' Amorel said, smiling wanly. 'Maybe a lot us who saved this town were the same. We saved ourselves in the process.'

'Write a song about it,' Pharis said.

'Song? It's worth an opera!'

Their laughter could be heard downstairs.

Chapter Forty-Four

Rue summoned them the next morning to yet another meeting at *Inglefey*. This one, though, was different. First, it comprised only members of Rue's old band, plus Meladriel and Seladris (the latter invited only because he was the householder), and second, it had nothing to do with paranormal events or serious plans for the future. Rue had gathered them to plan his party.

He ushered them into the sitting room where once the blue leopard painting had hung. There was no chance of it returning. One of the *Velvets* staff had gone to the shrine the previous day and had found the painting had decayed completely. He'd burned the remains.

Kazharn sat defensively on the sofa, arms crossed. 'I know what you're going to suggest, Rue, and I'd rather you didn't.'

Caeru laughed. 'Are you afraid, Tiahaar?'

'No, but it'll be... undignified.'

Meladriel snorted with laughter and said, 'Un-*what?*'

'What's the problem?' Seladris asked.

'He wants the band to play at the party,' Pharis said. 'I assume it's that. Rue's desire is hanging rather heavily on the air.'

'I think it would be a perfect event,' Caeru said, apparently taking no offence at any scepticism. 'For one, it'll demonstrate to the hara of Ferelithia there isn't as much division as they think between hara like them and hara like us. Secondly, it's a tribute to the town...'

'I've made enough sacrifices, thank you,' Kazharn interrupted.

'How do the rest of you feel?' Caeru asked patiently.

'I'd like to do it,' Amorel said, simply.

'Same here. It'd be fun,' Pharis said.

'Karn...' Caeru peered darkly at Kazharn. 'You can be just as sultry and mysterious as you ever were – or are. I assume you still know how to play.'

'He has guitars in his rooms at *Velvets*,' Meladriel offered sweetly, earning a glare. 'You did play them, didn't you?'

'We have no time to rehearse, get ready...' Kazharn said, but it was easy to tell he knew he was losing.

'I remember all our old songs,' Caeru said. 'I could never forget them.'

Amorel and Pharis uttered sounds of agreement.

'Don't worry that you'll be the one to fuck up,' Meladriel said cheerfully to Kazharn. 'We can ask Tika to join you on second guitar. That might cover any...'

'There will *not* be any fuck ups!' Kazharn snapped. 'That isn't the problem. I just... Well, let Tika join anyway. He's second generation. It'd be a meaningful gesture.' Then he added coldly, 'Why not get a choir of harlings too, while you're at it? Make it as humiliating as possible.'

'Your suggestions are appreciated,' Caeru said dryly. He smiled at the rest of them. 'I'll plan it for two weeks' time. Are you visitors able to stay on here that long?'

Pharis and Amorel assented that they were.

'I don't want anyhar from Immanion there,' Kazharn said. 'That's a condition.'

Caeru hesitated, then said, 'As you wish.'

'Do you really think the Tigrina should be prancing round a stage, though?' Kazharn said. 'Won't the Hegalion have something to say about it?'

'No, because they're aware my prime function is to generate good feeling and positive publicity,' Rue replied. 'This is a new era for Ferelithia. I'm quite sure younger hara will be intrigued to see you in your previous... occupation, Karn.'

'No doubt they'll get a good laugh out of it, yes.'

Caeru ignored this remark. 'We can start rehearsals today. I've already drawn up a provisional set list. It'll be easy, trust me.'

'I have to go out with my son,' Kazharn said. 'He's going to help me look for a house.'

'After that, then. Perhaps you could visit Tika while you're out...'

'No!' Meladriel said quickly. 'I'll do that while Karn's with Ulien. You'd intimidate him, Karn. You can come with me, if you like, Rue. Spread a little sparkle.'

Caeru laughed heartily. 'With pleasure.'

'I'll inform Veredis,' Seladris said. 'I'm going into work when we're done here.' He pulled an agonised face. 'Veredis wanted you to go to dinner at his place last night, Rue, so will no doubt gallop home from work to see you this afternoon.'

'Why didn't you say? I could've gone.'

Seladris rolled his eyes. 'Let's just say it would have been excruciating to sit through the grovelling devotion.'

Rue laughed. 'But your friends are my friends. I wouldn't have minded.'

Kazharn expelled a wordless scornful sound. 'You really want to be that little peacock of a har again, don't you, Rue.'

'Do stop being a bitch, beloved,' Meladriel said lightly. 'That's my job.'

'Maybe I do,' Caeru replied mildly. 'Like Pharis said, it'll be fun. Try to get into the spirit of it, Karn. You might enjoy yourself too.'

What Caeru had counted upon, correctly as it turned out, was that once Kazharn had an instrument in his hands and the music started up, his instincts took over. He remained sour-faced and distant, which Caeru didn't care about because that had always been Kazharn's stage persona anyway.

Posters were put up around the town, announcing that the Municiphar's former band, including the Tigrina, would be appearing under the name Eos, to celebrate the new dawn of Ferelithia. The gig was free; anyhar was invited to attend. There was no great concert hall in the town – its entertainments traditionally took place in night clubs and bars, or else on the beach. So the event would take place on the shore north of town.

Tika was intrigued enough to agree to joining the band for this occasion. At the news, Veredis was driven into a froth of excitement. While Seladris might've failed to produce the Tigrina for dinner the other night, Veredis could now be close to this august har on his own terms. Caeru had suggested *Confitteri* could help provide refreshments at the site, along with the proprietor of one of the local bars. Caeru involved as many local business hara as possible – creating decorations, providing the stage and its lighting, and so on. He wanted the entire town to feel that this was their event.

Amorel asked if he could perform the song he'd begun to write about all that had happened. Nohar withheld permission for this.

Fallami was staying in Ferelithia until Pharis was ready to return. He was familiar with the procedure of planning events and asked if he might introduce the band before they played. 'If I'm here I want to have a part,' he said. 'Plus there are a few words I want to say.'

Pharis had whispered to Meladriel. 'Let's hope it's only a few.'

Agavesday, 22 Fruitingmoon

On the evening of the concert, as Caeru prepared himself with Pharis and Amorel, he said, 'If only Kate had stayed. I'm sure she'd have loved this, revisiting a joyous time from our early days.'

'Why did she go so quickly?' Amorel asked.

'Work to do,' Caeru said briskly. 'Do my eye makeup, Pharis. Like you always did.'

'I'll make you look like a woodland creature now,' Pharis said, laughing. 'My tastes have moved on.'

Caeru sighed. 'No, just like you used to.'

Inside, Caeru felt tearful, but he wouldn't embarrass anyhar by showing it. He couldn't help but be reminded of his past in the town, the breathless excitement he'd felt as Pharis had painted him up for the gig where Pellaz would be in the audience. He hadn't known the outcome, of course, but inside there'd been an inkling his life was about to change. He'd felt the enormity of it, hanging in the air. And now he could remember it, decades later. Ultimate bliss, followed by ultimate horror, culminating, eventually, in a life that was contented.

'Stop remembering,' Pharis said, taking Caeru's chin in one hand. 'I don't want any leakage to ruin my work.'

'I was thinking of Thazri,' Caeru said, who had in fact come into his mind at that moment. 'We're alike in many ways. I too know how it feels to love somehar who is forever obsessed with somehar else. I've spent so much time acting on a stage, smiling, performing my role faultlessly, while bleeding to death inside. I want to help him, Pharis.'

'The mere shine of your smile will do that,' Pharis said, grinning.

'I'll speak to Karn, but I think it'd be good to take Thazri with me to Immanion for a few weeks. As long as that doesn't interfere with any plans Karn's made for him.'

'Good idea,' Pharis said. 'Stop wriggling.'

'I want Ulien to come back with me too for a time, so it's a perfect excuse if I ask Thazri to accompany him.' Caeru sighed. 'I've no doubt Karn will fight me over Ulien, but I do think it's important he's checked by our greatest hienamas.'

'Well, it's a trip to Immanion so I doubt Ulien will object.' Pharis pulled Caeru's hair. 'Now shut up. Let me finish.'

'We mustn't lose touch again,' Caeru said.

'We won't.'

'We must meet at least once a year at one of the seasonal festivals,' Caeru said, 'whether in Immanion, here, or in Alba Sulh. I won't let you forget.'

Later, a carriage came to take them to the site. Already, a crowd was gathering, although the band was secreted into a temporary backstage area.

Meladriel was in charge of organising the stage. It felt like no time had passed at all as he issued orders to young hara, telling them where to place the instruments and the lights, making sure the guitars were in tune. Makeshift in comparison to the past, of course, but nonetheless evocative. He told himself this was the band before Leupardra had contaminated them, when they'd been as one, with few arguments and lots of laughter and stupidity. The songs had come back so easily, as if the last gig had only been a week ago. Strange, really. Snatched embraces between rehearsals, feeling as if he was still sharing breath with Karn when there was a whole room between them. The hunger to join with him, disorientated and mystified by the depth of his need. *Enjoy it*, Meladriel told himself, *these raging fires last only so long*. But gentler fires were just as warming.

And then the moment was upon them. The sun had sunk beneath the horizon, and the moon rode high. The stage was in darkness but the crowd before it held tiny lights. Fallami walked onto the stage. He stood there in silence for some moments, staring at the crowd. Then he shook his head. 'There are no words,' he said, 'that can't be expressed better in music. Hara of Ferelithia, I give you Eos.'

Pharis came on first, sat behind his drums, then Amorel and Karn, followed by Tika. A rumble of drums, a clash of cymbals, then the first plangent chords.

Finally, in a burst of light, there was Rue, with his halo of tangled hair, clad in leather from the waist down and very little else. He looked mischievous, scrawny, beautiful, divine. 'Are you ready?' he yelled.

The crowd roared.

Epilogue

The next morning, Meladriel went to visit Tuli at the Nayati Kelosanya. He was curious to see what the har was like beyond the bizarre circumstances they'd found themselves in a couple of weeks or so ago. He'd been informed that Tuli was now fully conscious but often confused. The hienamas controlled his behaviour with nostrums, because nohar really knew how much of Leupardra might remain within him. He would go to Immanion tomorrow, at the same time Caeru left Ferelithia. Gelaming healers would come for Tuli, transport him by *sedu* back to the city. It had been decided this two-week wait was acceptable, because Tuli always seemed least troubled when Caeru visited him. Let him have this short time of quiet before Immanion's hienamas started probing his mind.

When Meladriel went into the small yet comfortable room where Tuli was confined, he was faced not with a snarling antagonist but an ailing, fragile creature, who seemed little more than a starved harling. He sat on his bed, hugging his knees, wearing a soft woollen robe. The parts of him that could be seen - his face, wrists, hands and feet – were pitifully thin. His eyes were too large, framed by rags of hair.

Meladriel said, 'Tuli, is it possible I could speak to Leupardra?' He had questions that had been eating at him, particularly after certain things Pharis had mentioned about the times Leupardra had apparently invaded Herne's Chase.

'He doesn't want to come out and talk to you,' Tuli answered.

'OK, can I ask him questions and you answer for him?'

Tuli nodded. 'You can ask.'

'Good. I want to know how he managed to contact Pharis and Amorel and affect them so strongly. I ask this because you were his main source of vitality and strength. I can see how you might have gone to Immanion, because that's not so far away, but I don't think you went with him to Megalithica and Alba Sulh. But perhaps I'm wrong. Will he tell me?' If there was another accomplice hiding somewhere, Meladriel wanted to know.

Tuli closed his eyes for a few moments, then opened them and said, 'He doesn't know what you're talking about.'

'I think he does. He tried to hurt Pharis and Amorel.'

'He didn't. He says you called them here.'

'OK.' Meladriel was baffled. Was this the truth as Leupardra saw it? Neither he nor Kazharn had attempted to call Amorel and Pharis. They'd talked of the band, but certainly hadn't tried to contact them. 'Did Leupardra make Rue come here?'

There was a pause. 'He can't remember doing that.'

'He does understand there's no point lying to me, doesn't he?'

'He's not lying.'

Meladriel stared at this creature before him. Was this really all that was left of Leupardra? Had he been an illusion all along? Had any power he'd appeared to have been handed to him by the fear and guilt of others? But... he'd still called up the Pale Ones. Perhaps that had been easy. They'd never truly gone away.

'Tuli,' Meladriel said. 'Do you understand what will happen to you now?'

Tuli nodded. 'Yes. They told me I'm going somewhere else, where they'll take care of me.' He paused. 'They won't hurt me, will they?'

'No, there's nothing to fear,' Meladriel said. 'I wish you well.' He paused. 'If Leupardra should want to talk to me in the future, tell your carers and I'll come.'

Tuli didn't say anything. He turned his face to the wall.

Meladriel left the room and wandered into the main chamber of the temple, where a vast granite statue of the dehar dominated one end of the room. Meladriel stood in the centre of the wide space, upon the gleaming wooden floor, his arms folded. Beautiful coloured light came streaming in from the high windows, which were stained green, gold and scarlet. He stared at the statue for some moments, then said aloud, 'Did you contact them, Kelosanya? Did you stir up the past to heal the present? Or was it something else?'

The dehar stared back impassively. Incense smoked wafted around him like transparent veils. There was only silence.

The Calendar of Wraeththu

January - Snowmoon
February – Frostmoon
March - Windmoon
April - Rainmoon
May - Flowermoon
June - Meadowmoon
July – Ardourmoon
August - Fruitingmoon
September - Harvestmoon
October - Vintagemoon
November - Mistmoon
December – Adkayamoon

Monday – Lunilsday (Nil'sday)
Tuesday – Miyacalasday (Cala'sday)
Wednesday – Aloytsday (Loyt'sday)
Thursday – Agavesday (Gave'sday)
Friday – Aruhanisday (Aru'sday)
Saturday – Pelfazzarsday (Pelf'sday)
Sunday – Aghamasday (Ag'sday)

Glossary of Terms, Places and Key Characters

Aedisa: Pharis's chesnari.

Aghama (AG-am-ar): Allegedly, the first Wraeththu, worshipped as a god by some.

Agmara (ag-MAR-uh): the life force of the universe, used for healing.

Almagabra: Country of the Gelaming.

Althaia (al-THAY-uh): The period of changing, usually around three days, during which as human mutates into a har following inception.

Amorel: a musician and former resident of Ferelithia, who moved to Megalithica.

Archon: The leader of a tribe and its phyles.

Aruhani: (Aroo-HAR-nee) A dehar of aruna, life and death.

Aruna: (ah-roo-nah) Sexual communion between hara.

Blue Leopard, the: another name for the Cerulopard, (which see).

Calanthe (Cal) har Aralis: One of the Tigrons of Immanion.

Caeru har Aralis (KY-roo): Tigrina of Immanion, consort of Pellaz and Calanthe har Aralis.

Cerulopard, the: an early tribe, led by Leupardra.

Carehar: a har employed to care for an individual, such as a harling or an invalid.

Chesna: (CHEZ-nah) A close relationship between hara. A chesna-bond is a formal recognition of this state.

Chesnari: (chez-NAH-ree) a har who is in a chesna-bond with another.

Confitteri: a bakery in Ferelithia

Dehar: (DAY-har) A Wraeththu god, (pl. dehara).

Enervation: an abandoned night club in Ferelithia.

Fallami: the High Hienama of Herne's Chase Retreat in Alba Sulh, where Pharis works.

Fenice: a guardhar at *Velvets*.

Ferelithia: Wraeththu settlement in Almagabra, home of the tribe of Ferelith.

Feybraiha: (fay-BRAY-uh) The coming of age ceremony, when a harling reaches sexual maturity.

First Generation: the original Wraeththu hara who were incepted from humans, as opposed to second (or beyond) generations who were born to hara. (See also pureborn.)

Garridan: A province and tribe of Jaddayoth, whose hara are famous for their intoxicating nostrums and deadly poisons.

Guardhar: Somehar employed to provide security.

Har: Wraeththu individual (plural: hara).

Harling: Young har until Feybraiha, the coming of age.

Hegalion: Another term for the Hegemony, and the governmental building complex in Immanion where they meet.

Hegemony: The ruling body of Gelaming in Immanion.

Hienama: (Hy-en-AH-muh) A har who is both teacher and priest, responsible for hara's caste training and well as officiating for communities in a spiritual capacity.

High Hienama: A hienama of high rank who is usually in charge of a Nayati or healing centre.

Hostling: A har who carries a pearl (Wraeththu foetus), who hosts the seed of another.

Househar: a har employed in a domestic capacity.

Ihrec: Ulien har Shadolis's carehar.

Immanion: Capital city of Almagabra.

Inception: The process by which a human is transformed into a har; the transfusion of blood and the attendant ceremonies.

Inglefey: a house in Ferelithia, leased by Seladris.

Jaddayoth: A collection of lands in what was once Northern Europe/Asia, some of which is wild and ungoverned territory, where hara are able to lose themselves, should they need to.

Kakkahaar: (KAKK-uh-har) Desert tribe of Southern Megalithica, famous for their dark magical practices.

Kamagrian: (Ka-MAG-ree-an) A branch of Wraeththu that favours the feminine aspect of their being.

Kate (later Katarin): Human woman, friend of Caeru, Tigrina of Immanion, who is an occasional agent for the Hegalion.

Kazharn har Shadolis: the Municiphar of Ferelithia, leader of the Muncipallion.

Kelosanya: the dehar of Ferelithia.

Leupardra: (Loo-PARD-rah) known also as The Pard Witch, a har who was instrumental in taking Ferelithia from its human population.

Listeners, the: A group, employed by the Hegemony in

Immanion, dedicated to psychic communication over long distance.

Lunil: (LOO-nil) A dehar of magic, emotion and the moon.

Lurei: (loo-RYE) a guardhar at *Velvets*.

Megalithica: Western continent, where Wraeththu allegedly began. Its leading tribe is the Parasiel, formerly the Varrs.

Meladriel: A shaman of Ferelithia.

Miyacala: (My-uh-KAR-la) A dehar of initiation and knowledge.

Municipallion: the ruling body of the Ferelith.

Nayati: (Ny-AH-tee) A building or sacred space given over to spiritual practices.

Otherlanes: Etheric pathways beyond this reality that can be travelled through the use of a *sedu* (which see).

Ouana (Oo-AR-na): Masculine principle of hara.

Ouana-Lim: Masculine generative organ of Wraeththu.

Parage: A Kamagrian individual (pl. parazha).

Pard Witch, the: a title of Leupardra.

Pearl: Wraeththu embryo, the shell that contains it.

Pelki: Rape (hence *pelker*, a profanity, meaning rapist).

Pellaz har Aralis: Tigron of Immanion, a leader of the Gelaming.

Phaonica (Fay-ON-icka): The palace of the Tigrons and Tigrina in Immanion.

Pharis: a musician and former resident of Ferelithia, who moved to Alba Sulh.

Phylarch: The leader of a tribal phyle.

Phyle: A community within a tribe, with its own land and leaders.

Pureborn: A second-generation har born of hara rather than incepted from humans.

Red Cat, The: a bar in Ferelithia

Roon (Slang): A verb for taking aruna, a noun for aruna, from which derives 'roony', or desiring aruna, and roonfriends, pertaining to hara who are not chesnari but have a physical relationship.

Roselane: A country of Jaddayoth, and also the tribe who inhabit it, who comprise Kamagrian, hara and human.

Sedu: An otherworldly entity, which appears in this reality as a horse, that can travel the 'otherlanes'. Plural: *sedim*. These creatures are used mainly by the Gelaming.

Seladris: a har who moved to Ferelithia to work at the bakery *Confitteri*

Sharing of Breath: A kiss of mutual visualisation.
Soume (SOO-mee): Feminine principle of hara.
Soume-Lam: Feminine generative organ of Wraeththu.
Thazri har Shadolis: Kazharn's chesnari/consort.
Thiede (THEE-dee): Leader of the Gelaming, he was the first
Wraeththu, and the most powerful.
Tiahaar: Respectful form of address (plural: Tiahaara).
Tigrina (Tee-GREE-na): The Tigrons' consort in Immanion.
Tigron (TEE-gron): The Archons of the Gelaming, Thiede's
protégé Pellaz and Calanthe.
Tika: a friend of Meladriel, who lives with Veredis har Mith.
Tuli: a har of Ferelithia.
Uigenna (EW-i-GEN-a): Warlike proto-tribe of Megalithica.
Ulien: (OO-lee-en) Kazharn's son, hosted by Thazri.
Varrs: Originally the most powerful and organised tribe in
Megalithica, eventually defeated by the Gelaming, and thereafter
became known as Parasiel.
Velvets: Kazharn's palatial residence in Ferelithia.
Veredis har Mith: the proprietor of Confitteri and Seladris's
employer.
Wraeththu (RAY-thoo): The race of androgynes who came to
replace humanity on earth as the ruling species.

About the Author

Storm is the creator of the Wraeththu Mythos, the first trilogy of which was published in the 1980s. However, the influences and inspirations for the Wraeththu world go much further back than that and continue into the future as she plans more stories for it.

Her other full length works cross genres from science fiction, to dark fantasy, to epic fantasy, to slipstream. She has written over thirty books, including full length novels, novellas, short story collections and non-fiction titles on magic and esoteric subjects. Her short stories, which she continues to write prolifically, appear in diverse magazines and anthologies.

Storm is the founder of Immanion Press, created initially to publish her out-of-print back catalogue, but which evolved into the thriving venture it is today. Her interests include magic and spirituality, movies, music and MMOs. She lives in the Midlands of the UK with her husband and four cats.

Books by Storm Constantine

The Wraeththu Chronicles
The Enchantments of Flesh and Spirit
The Bewitchments of Love and Hate
The Fulfilments of Fate and Desire

The Wraeththu Histories
The Wraiths of Will and Pleasure
The Shades of Time and Memory
The Ghosts of Blood and Innocence

The Alba Sulh Sequence
The Hienama
Student of Kyme
The Moonshawl

Wraeththu Mythos
Blood, the Phoenix and a Rose
A Raven Bound with Lilies (short stories)

The Artemis Cycle
The Monstrous Regiment
Aleph

The Grigori Books
Stalking Tender Prey
Scenting Hallowed Blood
Stealing Sacred Fire

The Magravandias Chronicles:
Sea Dragon Heir
Crown of Silence
The Way of Light

Standalone Novels
Hermetech
Burying the Shadow
Sign for the Sacred
Calenture
Thin Air
*Silverheart (with Michael Moorcock)

Short Story Collections:
The Thorn Boy and Other Dreams of Dark Desire
Mythangelus
Mythophidia

Mytholumina
Mythanimus
Mythumbra
*Splinters of Truth (NewCon Press)

Wraeththu Mythos Collections
(co-edited with Wendy Darling, including stories by the editors & other writers)
Paragenesis
Para Imminence
Para Kindred
Para Animalia
Para Spectral

Songs to Earth & Sky, *edited & with 3 stories by Storm Constantine*

Non-Fiction
Sekhem Heka
Grimoire Dehara: Kaimana
Grimoire Dehara: Ulani (with Taylor Ellwood)
Grimoire Dehara: Nahir Nuri (with Taylor Ellwood)
SHE: Primal Meetings with the Dark Goddess (with Andrew Collins)
Whatnots and Curios
Zodiac of the Gods (with Graham Phillips)
Coming Forth by Day: A System of Khemetic Magic
*The Inward Revolution (with Deborah Benstead)
*Bast and Sekhmet: Eyes of Ra (with Eloise Coquio)

Available as Immanion Press editions unless marked with *

IMMANION PRESS

Purveyors of Speculative Fiction

A Wolf at the Door by Tanith Lee

Includes 13 tales, most of which appeared only in magazines or rare anthologies. 'A wolf at the door' implies hidden threat – until the door is open, we don't really know what's out there. And now the beast is upon you, scratching at the wood, its hot breath steaming on the step. Will you survive the encounter? Perhaps, once the door is opened, what you might have thought to be a threat turns out to be something else entirely. But of course, it can also be a werewolf...
ISBN 978-1-912815-04-3, £11.99, $15.99 pbk

The Lord of the Looking Glass by Fiona McGavin

The author has an extraordinary talent for taking genre tropes and turning them around into something completely new, playing deftly with topsy-turvy relationships between supernatural creatures and people of the real world. 'Post Garden Centre Blues' reveals an unusual relationship between taker and taken in a twist of the changeling myth. 'A Tale from the End of the World' takes the reader into her developing mythos of a post-apocalyptic world, which is bizarre, Gothic and steampunk all at once. Following in the tradition of exemplary short story writers like Tanith Lee and Liz Williams, Fiona has a vivid style of writing that brings intriguing new visions to fantasy, horror and science fiction. ISBN: 978-1-907737-99-2, £11.99, $17.50 pbk

The Heart of the Moon by Tanith Lee

Clirando, a celebrated warrior, believes herself to be cursed. Betrayed by people she trusted, she unleashes a vicious retaliation upon them and then lives in fear of fateful retribution for her act of cold-blooded vengeance. Set in a land resembling Ancient Greece, in this novella Tanith Lee explores the dark corners of the heart and soul within a vivid mythical adventure. The book also includes 'The Dry Season' another of her tales set in an imaginary ancient world of the Classical era.
ISBN: 978-1-912815-05-0 £10.99, $14.99 pbk

www.immanion-press.com
info@immanion-press.com

The Wraeththu Chronicles

The trilogy that launched the Wraeththu Mythos in the 1980s. In 2003, Storm Constantine revised and expanded the original novels, inserting new scenes, reinstating material that was cut from the initial drafts and correcting mistakes in the text. The stories were also updated to accurately reflect current Wraeththu canon.

For this latest edition, the author has made further small adjustments to the text to present a more polished, definitive version. With covers by Ruby to match the new editions of *The Wraeththu Histories*.

The Enchantments of Flesh and Spirit – Pellaz Cevarro relates the tale of his inception to Wraeththu, his doomed love for the damaged Cal and his eventual rise to Tigron.

The Bewitchments of Love and Hate – Swift, the Varr leader Terzian's son, reveals the history of his tribe's ill-fated conflict with the Gelaming, and the lingering, devastating effect Cal had on his father that changed the Varrs' future.

The Fulfilments of Fate and Desire – Cal tells his own story, revealing the deceptions, betrayals and cruelty he inflicted on others in order to survive. Angel and demon, Cal has a life-changing effect on all hara he meets.

Details can be found on our web site
www.immanion-press.com

Wraeththu Story Anthologies

The 'Para' series of Wraeththu short story anthologies began with *Paragenesis* in 2010. Four more have followed, and others are planned.

These collections explore different aspects of Wraeththu: their origins, their future, their anomalies, their spiritual affinity with animals, and the ghosts that haunt them. *Para Spectral* includes the short story that inspired the novel *Breathe, My Shadow*. All titles include stories by Storm Constantine & Wendy Darling, as well as contributions from other Mythos writers. Full details on our web site.

www.immanion-press.com